After distinguished naval service during the Second World War, Alexander Fullerton learnt Russian at Cambridge, on a Services course, then worked in Germany with Red Army units. He predicted the lowering of the Iron Curtain, a forecast that was rejected by the SIS, whose Russian desk was at that time manned by Kim Philby. After passing the interpretership exam (CS) he was at once returned to sea in submarines. He resigned and was released in 1949, and worked in South Africa as an insurance clerk, in a Swedish shipping agency and as a publishers' representative. His first novel was published in 1953. In 1959 he returned to Britain to pursue a publishing career, but abandoned it in 1967 to write full-time. He is now the author of over thirty novels.

'The action passages are superb. He is in a bowel-gripping class of his own.' *Observer*

Special Deliverance

ALEXANDER FULLERTON

SPHERE BOOKS LIMITED

Sphere Books Limited,
27 Wrights Lane, London W8 5TZ.

First published in Great Britain in 1986 by
Macmillan London Limited
Copyright © Alexander Fullerton 1986
Published by Sphere Books in 1987

TRADE
MARK

Printed and bound in Great Britain by
Cox & Wyman Ltd, Reading

1

The aircraft shuddered, lurching as it lowered its bulk through the last shreds of the clouds' underlay, and the five men shifted their feet, reaching to the wire jackstay to steady themselves. But they were in level flight again now; and the hydraulic door at the tail end of the cavernous, thunderously noisy hold was swinging open. A light came on above it, glowing red. The process at this point took on a quality of inexorability that was terrifying: it was *happening* now, unstoppable, and Andy MacEwan found it impossible to accept that in about one minute he was going to walk out through the doorway, drop into wind-torn space four hundred metres above the near freezing South Atlantic. Harry Cloudsley, glancing round and down at him, allowed him a brief, sympathetic grin, but said nothing – partly because anything worth saying had been said, maybe also because the lung power that would have been needed to make it audible would be better saved for use when he hit the water. Cloudsley would be jumping first, then Andy, then Tony Beale, Geoff Hosegood, and Jake West. Finally, the three containers. Men and containers were already linked to the jackstay by static lines that would jerk their 'chutes open as they fell. At Harry Cloudsley's shoulder, dwarfed by

Cloudsley's towering frame, the stocky Marine sergeant who would *not* be jumping with them was standing with his feet apart, fists on his hips, eyes fixed on the red light which any second now would turn green. Despite the sense of unreality and the slight sickness induced by fear Andy knew there wasn't a damn thing he could do except go through with it. He could throw a fit, but the stick of men would still move forward, carrying him with them – out. . . .

A voice – it was Colour Sergeant Beale's – yelled into his ear, high-pitched to cut through the din but only saying what had been said, in so many words, a dozen times in the last hour: 'Be OK when we move, Andy, you're going to love it, right?' Before he could even nod the light turned green, the stocky sergeant swung to face Cloudsley with his mouth open, shouting, but Harry was already on his way, striding out through the gaping doorway with Andy close behind him, actually in the frame, the wind's suction, brain screaming protest but limbs ignoring it so that he was conscious of his own movements but as if he himself had no control over them; he'd felt a blow on his left shoulder and then the world was a grey-white seascape swinging, turning on its side as he fell into space.

The first parachute opened – khaki, a dun-coloured mushroom abruptly taking shape under the ceiling of grey, fast-moving cloud. John Saddler was in the wing of his ship's bridge with binoculars trained upwards; he'd seen the first man tumble from the aircraft and the stream of the 'chute before it flowered, but it was a white one he was watching for particularly. Everything around him meanwhile highly mobile and very noisy. *Shropshire* down to a few knots, plunging to the sea and to a northerly blow of force five to six, rolling hard. Clouds heavy, and under them the stout-bodied Hercules spewing its load like a fat fish shedding spawn. The white 'chute came second, and now more khaki blossomings – a

2

stick of eight in all, five men and three containers all out and swinging down towards an icy sea.

Saddler thought, *Sooner them than me*, and called without turning his head, 'Away Gemini.' *Shropshire* rolling and plunging, with just enough revs on to hold her to this course. He'd heard his order being passed into the bridge, from where it would by now have been transmitted aft by telephone, and the Gemini inflatable would be pushing off from the destroyer's side where it had been waiting. Its coxswain had been told he was to get to the white parachute first, if possible within seconds of its human load hitting the water.

Before the load – lad – froze, or suffered damage of a kind that might not be in the best long-term interests of John Saddler's daughter Lisa. Not that the parachutist would be getting this preferential treatment because he did happen to be Lisa Saddler's boyfriend; it was because he was a civilian and straight from a City desk, an outsider whom the Special Boat Squadron had recruited and were now referring to as their 'guest artist'. Captain John Saddler, father of Lisa, shivered inside his padded nylon jacket. Descent from cloud level into that turbulent ice-water might be no problem for the case-hardened SBS men swinging down under their khaki canopies, but in the few weeks they'd had Andy MacEwan with them in England they could hardly have raised him to their own incredibly Spartan standards. Lowering his binoculars he saw the Gemini just about standing on end as it climbed a morass of foam, white sea sheeting back, powerful outboard screaming, the coxswain crouching low over his controls and the other crewman hanging on tight, both men's faces upturned to the white parachute – which wasn't far above the khaki leader, the first of the SBS team splashing in – *now*. . . .

Above them, the Hercules was circling and climbing, thrusting up into the overhang of cloud for its return flight to Wideawake.

Saddler saw all five men picked up before he went back inside. An hour or so later he was welcoming Andy MacEwan to his day-cabin, one level below the bridge. MacEwan in Royal Marine uniform now instead of a wetsuit under

3

parachute overalls: not exactly spick and span, since he evidently hadn't shaved for a day or two and could have done with a haircut, but with one pip on each shoulder representing the ultra-short Short Service Commission they'd fixed up for him – or rather for themselves, so they could see him and expect him to do as he was told. He saw Lisa's father glance at the rank insignia, and admitted, 'I'm an impostor, I know. Wasn't *my* idea.'

Twenty-six, rising twenty-seven. An inch or so below average height but ruggedly built, blunt-featured, with intelligent grey eyes. He might not have belonged in the uniform but he looked the part, he filled it. Except for the long hair. . . . Saddler said, 'All my fault, and I'm glad to have the chance to apologise. I only thought they might pick your brains, never dreamt they'd go so far as to co-opt you.' He pointed at a chair. 'Make yourself at home. Like some coffee?'

This was early afternoon. Sunrise in these remote Atlantic wastes came at about 11.30 a.m., by Greenwich Mean Time which was what the Task Force was keeping. The SBS section had dropped out of the sky just in time for lunch, and they'd be on board for only a few more hours; *Shropshire* was hurrying them west now.

MacEwan admitted, 'It's still a bit – surprising.'

'I'd have thought the word might be "terrifying".'

'Well.' A shrug. . . . 'Dare say it'll have its moments.'

He was no gas-bag, this MacEwan. His reticence, in fact, was a characteristic with which Lisa found fault – according to her mother. . . .

He added, 'I'm only along as guide, you know. And interpreter.' *Shropshire* pitched heavily, dipping her shoulder deep, trembling all through her 520 foot length as she recovered and her forepart lifted. She was in transit to the fly-off position, and the Sea King helicopter which would be taking the SBS party into mainland Argentina would be landing-on before sunset. Saddler said, 'I have a broad idea of the objective, Andy, and it's as worthy a cause as I ever heard of. All I can say is bloody good luck to you, and the sooner it's done, the better. If it *can* be done.'

4

There was a scene in his mind's eye as he said it, a memory two weeks old but still vivid. Men dead, bodies smashed, oily black smoke pouring from a ship's split side, helos flying in extra pumps and medical aid, lifting out the casualties. Then the long fight to keep the ship afloat. The fight had been lost, and there'd be other losses yet, more deaths, you knew it and you had that image stamped in your mind, the reality of disaster and recognition that defence systems now being tested in battle for the first time were not infallible, were nothing *like* infallible – especially against sea-skimming missiles, the AM39s.

He pulled his thoughts back. . . .

'I'd like to explain how I came to let you in for this, Andy. Even though I didn't guess quite how *far* in. . . . We were in Devonport – under sailing orders, tearing round like mad apes, half the ship's company still not back from leave, blind rush to get to sea. Right in the middle of it a Royal Marine detachment rolled up with a truckload of stuff they wanted us to bring along. Which we did, naturally – I suppose that may be part of the reason that we were picked for this job now. But a visiting Admiral, also the Bootnecks' officer, was having a coffee with me, and I was asked what I thought our prospects might be down here. I mentioned a couple of problems, one being our lack of any real defence against sea-skimming missiles, and the Admiral suggested it might be worth trying to nobble those – either the Exocet missiles or the Super-Etendard aircraft that carry them – before the shooting started. He looked at the Marine and added, "Right up *your* street." He knew him, apparently, and from what was said then I caught on to the fact this lot were SBS. And of course they must have taken the idea a lot farther, from there on. But what I want you to know, Andy, is that when I told them about you – the fact I knew this chap who had intimate knowledge of the country and so on – I never dreamt they'd shanghai you. My only thought was they might usefully pick your brains.'

'About all it was, to start with.' MacEwan nodded. 'I had a call at the office – from some guy in the PR department, Navy, Ministry of Defence – would I come along and answer questions on a subject of which he'd been given to understand I had

5

special knowledge? He mentioned your name. Casual but guarded, was the tone of it – you know? Naturally I guessed – only one area where I've any "special knowledge", and the Task Force was being mounted – you'd already sailed, Lisa told me – and it was all anyone was thinking about just at that time. So there I was – and at one stage I heard someone suggest, "Ought to take him along. Couple of weeks' hard training, tone him up a bit." They asked me what sort of swimmer I was, and that *is* something I'm not bad at.' MacEwan added, 'The idea seemed nutty, at first.'

'Does Lisa know what you're doing?'

'God, no!' His glance seemed to question Saddler's intelligence. He explained, 'She thinks I'm in the States. Business trip resulting from the temporary severance of our trading links. As far as the office is concerned, since we're hamstrung as long as this lasts it's a good time for me to be away, too. Nobody'll be expecting to hear from me for a while.'

'You really think *she* won't?' Saddler smiled. 'My daughter won't be expecting you to write?'

'Well, I – I explained I'd be on the move a lot.' He shook his head. 'It was left sort of vague, you know?'

Saddler could imagine. Andy MacEwan's natural obduracy, reinforced by a need for blackout on this business; and Lisa's frustration, which had been fairly evident even before this. . . . He'd seen it, heard it, more than once, and been careful to keep his head down, leave it to the women. The relationship between Andy and Lisa wasn't as clear-cut as either she or – more outspokenly – her mother would have liked it to be. They'd been going around together for more than a year, and in recent months they'd been sharing a flat; Anne Saddler didn't like this, wanted the relationship legitimised. If she'd been on board and could have met the dripping parachutist when he'd come up the Jacob's ladder she'd as likely as not have asked him there and then what his intentions were in regard to her daughter; and she'd have expected her husband to be working round to some such question now, he guessed. He could almost hear the outraged tone: *You didn't even ask him?*

6

As if it mattered. Even back home, in its context. Except he did like what he'd seen of Andy, wouldn't at all mind having him for a son-in-law.

'Have you seen her lately?'

'About – twelve days ago. Just for a few minutes. I haven't been given much time off, you see. And of course she hasn't been too ecstatic about that.'

It wasn't difficult to imagine. He acknowledged, accepting blame again as the telephone buzzed, 'I have a lot to answer for.' He got up, went to the desk. MacEwan meanwhile glanced round the cabin. It had been designed for occupation by an Admiral, but with none on board – thank God – Saddler had its spacious luxury for himself, while his executive officer had what would have been the CO's accommodation.

'Yes?'

Ian Prince, operations officer, was on the line, telling him about a signal just in from *Hermes* concerning the change-over of helicopters. The Wessex was to be sent away to make room for the Sea King to land-on, and this was now to be brought forward by one hour because *Shropshire* and the carrier group would be passing within convenient range of each other at that time.

'All right, Ian. Warn the Flight Commander.'

Hanging up, he checked the time, pausing to glance out for a moment at the wilderness of sea through which his ship was ploughing, plunging, with nothing in sight except salt water and a low roofing of cloud. The Wessex was on its pad now, chained down – sonar useless in this turbulence and also at this speed. But the wind might have dropped by a few knots, he guessed. This suite, on 01 Deck, one level below the bridge, occupied the whole width of the superstructure, so the day-cabin had this wide curve of windows – all of them now salt-streaked, running wet. Below him was the gleaming rectangular bulk of the quadruple Exocet mounting – the surface-to-surface type, MM38, each missile enclosed in its own steel container filled with an inert gas. No maintenance or pre-flight checks, you couldn't get at the missiles themselves even if you wanted to; when the firing button was pressed, in

7

the Exocet console down in the Ops Room, the front of the container would be blasted away, its securing bolts exploding a fraction of a second before the missile streaked out. Unlike the AM39, the airborne type, which was not enclosed, therefore *could* be got at – by men with the nerve and skills to attempt it.

He came back to his chair. 'I really should congratulate you, Andy – on being able to measure up to SBS requirements.'

'Oh, well.' A shrug. 'All I had to do was sharpen up physically. And one or two things like parachuting. My value to them, as you just said, is that the area they're interested in happens to've been more or less my back yard. I have contacts there – one in particular who's important to us now – and of course I talk the lingo. It's not plain Spanish, you know, the stuff they talk. So I can pass myself off as a local if I need to – which a *real* Spanish speaker couldn't.'

'Fantastic.'

'Not really. Except for schooling – and recent years, of course – it's where I'm from, what I *am*.'

'And –' Saddler remembered this suddenly, thinking of that family background – 'where your brother still is?'

He saw the wary look. Andy had never talked much about it, but one of the few things the Saddlers did know was there was an older brother who ran the family sheep station. Both parents being dead, and Andy having opted to join the wool-trading company in London which had his family name in it. But he owned half the property in Patagonia, Lisa had told her mother.

He'd nodded. 'Far as I know, yes.'

'So how would this war affect him?'

A slow nod. 'Good question.'

Saddler frowned. Aware of the kind of irritation his daughter might sometimes feel. 'Is there a good answer?'

'There isn't an easy one. And it's a subject I've been required to go into lately in what journalists tend to call "in depth".'

The SBS, of course, would have needed to know enough to be sure of his loyalties. Saddler said, 'We'll leave it, then. Forgive my idle curiosity.'

8

'The short answer might be – if this tells you anything – my brother won't be talking about the Falklands, he'll be calling them the Malvinas.'

'I see.'

But anyone born and raised out there, Saddler thought, surely would do. The loyalty factor might be more complicated, in fact, than he'd hitherto appreciated. Relevant to this thought was another fact passed on by Lisa – that Andy and his brother were the fourth generation of MacEwans to have lived and farmed there; and wouldn't roots that long make them more Argentine than British? But the young man facing him neither looked nor sounded in any way South American. He'd been to school and university in the UK, of course – and then chosen to make his home in London. He asked him, 'Any chance you might see your brother, on this trip?'

'No.' The headshake was quick, decisive. 'No chance at all.'

A double rap on the cabin door interrupted them. Saddler still watched the younger man, curious. Then he called 'Yes?' and Nettlefold, his secretary, pushed a prematurely balding head around the door. 'Will you see Lieutenant Cloudsley, sir?'

He didn't have to answer that question. Cloudsley came in at a rush – a big man travelling fast and ahead of his feet, the ship having caught him wrong-footed as she performed one of her more spectacular lunges. Cloudsley fetched up hard against the bulkhead – apologising to Nettlefold, whose feet he'd trampled on in passing. Turning to Saddler: 'Very sorry, sir. Believe me, I have *not* been at your wardroom's liquor. Hello, Andy.'

'Better sit down.' Saddler pointed at an armchair. 'Before you break a leg.'

About 220 pounds of Royal Marine transferred itself to safety. Cloudsley was about the same age as MacEwan – but six-five, Saddler guessed, and broad in proportion. Black-haired, – incongruously long black hair, for God's sake – and unshaven over sunburn.

A double-take on that; they were both tanned. Fresh out of

England, in the month of May? He guessed at sun lamp treatment, for Argentine-type complexions, and recalled that the Special Boat Squadron's motto was *By Stealth, By Guile*.

Cloudsley asked him, 'How's it going generally, sir?'

'If you mean this war, the answer is it isn't.'

'Because – one's gathered – they won't oblige by coming out where you can clobber them.'

'Exactly. We're supposed to win the air and sea battle before your fellow Bootnecks land, but all we're doing so far is shadow boxing. They're saving their strength, of course. You'll have heard about *Sheffield*?'

A nod. 'Were you close, when she was hit?'

'Close enough.'

'If we could have gone in weeks ago, right off the bat, that thing might've been a damp squib.' The big man shook his head. 'Couldn't have, of course. We needed the time we've had – to get the show organised on the ground, put Andy here through his paces, and last but most important of all for the boffins to work out a technical *modus operandi* for us.' He paused, and then changed the subject: 'What's your role in the Task Force, sir? You have Seaslug, don't you. . . ?'

'Seaslug and Seacat. Both outdated. We're also twenty years old, and frankly not a hell of a lot of use. All right for jobs like this one, of course, but otherwise you could say our role is almost entirely NGS.' He interpreted for Andy MacEwan's benefit, 'Naval gunfire support. Hitting shore targets, very often in support of Special Forces teams, SAS and SBS.' He looked back at Cloudsley. 'You said – a "technical *modus operandi*"?'

'Right.' The SBS man nodded. 'How to screw up an AM39 missile so it won't fly. Or won't fly straight, or explode, or whatever. They had an open brief – misdirection, malfunction, anything that would effectively castrate the thing. By no means an easy problem to solve. Certainly *wasn't*, in fact after a couple of days they came back and told us it was impossible. At that stage they were concentrating on buggering up the radar guidance, the homing head. As you can imagine, there was a lot of gloom around, for a while.'

'But' – Saddler was puzzled – 'what's wrong with the old 1940s SBS tradition, a lump of plastic and a pencil fuse?'

'Ah. If only . . . ' Cloudsley sighed. 'Unfortunately' – he jerked a thumb vaguely towards Whitehall, eight thousand miles away – 'orders from on high, policy decision.' He cocked an eyebrow. 'She who must be obeyed? Well, God bless her. But we're not to do anything that might be seen as spreading the war to the mainland, thereby upsetting people and losing world support. Nothing noisy or violent – no bangs, and no avoidable harm to Argie personnel on their own ground. Bit tricky, really.'

'I'd imagine *very* tricky.' Saddler added, 'And what puzzles me in particular is how you can hope to cover all the ground – three of you, or four' – he glanced at Andy, back at Cloudsley – 'with Río Gallegos, Río Grande and Comodoro Rivadavia – they could all have Exocets deployed on them by now – such huge distances apart. Gallegos is more than just one airfield anyway, isn't it?'

'Well, sir.' Cloudsley frowned. 'The answer's probably not entirely to your liking – or ours, for that matter. The fact is, missiles already deployed to the operational bases are out of our reach. Our target's just one place which the Argies don't know we know about. A new airbase and missile store, not *all* that far from the MacEwan mutton factory. Not next door, exactly – and unfortunately we can't use his place anyway—'

'By Patagonian standards of distance,' Andy interrupted, 'it's almost next door.'

'Right,' Cloudsley said. 'Enormous distances – as you said, sir. They have farms the size of English counties, I gather. But anyway, American satellite intelligence watched this place being built. An airfield of sorts – pilot-training in Pucarás, it seems – but the interesting bit is one large hangar with its own perimeter fence and guardhouse. It was being thrown up in a hurry, the Yanks were keeping an eye on it, and just recently some AM39s have been arriving. In ones and twos, flown in by helos – heaven knows where from originally. We knew they were shopping around, and there've been hints of potential suppliers – Libya for one, and Israel, South Africa's been

11

mentioned – and a Peruvian naval transport tried to collect a consignment from Le Havre a week ago, but the French turned it away. . . . Anyway, they've now found a supplier, the things are arriving and that's where they're putting them, presumably until the missiles already deployed have been expended. They *may* believe they're safer there than on the operational bases. The location's well insulated, you see, by wide-open spaces, mile upon mile of damn-all in every direction, and some distance from either the coast or the Chilean border.' Saddler crossed two fingers, to keep a question in mind while the SBS man added, 'It's also conveniently placed as a distribution centre for those three main bases. So it makes sense, from the Argies' point of view. It's also possible – not certain, but we're told it's on the cards – they may have some tame Frogs there, for maintenance or pre-flight checks, whatever. There's an accommodation block beside the airstrip. It wouldn't mean the French would necessarily know about the new deliveries, they could have been diverted from some other consignee, and it's thought the technicians were there already, you see?'

Saddler nodded. 'And you do have some way to – er – screw them up?'

'Yes, sir.' A smile. 'Missiles, or Frogs. Missiles will be a *little* difficult, but—'

'Hang on.' The telephone buzzed. Joking apart, he thought, how the hell you'd do it, sabotage an AM39 without blowing it up – even if you could get that close to it in the first place. He was on his feet, at the telephone, dealing with a query from the officer of the watch; then, while he was at the desk, putting a call through to Hank Vaughan the commander (WE), which stood for Weapons Electrical, about a defect his people were working on, a breakdown on the port Seacat director. Vaughan reported progress to the extent that they'd identified the trouble. The incidence of defects – in Vaughan's own language, of equipment 'throwing wobblies' – was increasing daily. Hardly surprising, admittedly, in a twenty-year-old ship that had been at sea now for a solid month, most of that time in lousy weather. Saddler told him, 'Let me know as soon as it's operational,' and put the phone down. Seacat was obsolescent, but for close-range anti-missile defence it was all this ship had, apart from a pair of Oerlikons, WW2 weapons, up on top. He came back to his visitors, remembering he'd crossed his fingers as an *aide mémoire* to a question he wanted to ask – he put it to Cloudsley now.

'Couldn't you have gone in by parachute? With the MacEwan place so handy, and time rather vital?'

'Yes.' Cloudsley drew a breath like a sigh. 'We need to be in there *now*, you're right, sir. We did aim to go in by HALO drop, too. But – well, several factors, here. One, when the scientists worked out how we might nobble the missiles, we saw we were going to need a certain weight of extra gear. The weight's mostly batteries, actually. Two, the new base has a radar installation, and maybe ground and air patrols. We have to be *bloody* secretive about it, not only because we don't want to be caught but because if they knew we knew anything at all about this place they'd deploy all the missiles right away. Which wouldn't help *you* much, sir. Then again, we can't drop close to the target without the overflying aircraft being detected, and if we landed far enough away to avoid it it'd be next to impossible to do a yomp there, with that weight of equipment and over ground which provides no cover whatsoever – so we'd only be able to move at night, and short hauls, too. . . . Tell you the truth, we just about gave up, at one stage. Someone suggested bombing the place instead. Of course *that* wasn't to be allowed. Then' – he pointed at Andy MacEwan – 'genius here came up with some answers.'

'Some quite ordinary things I told them turned out to be useful, that's all.'

'Still leaving the time factor as a major worry, I admit.' Cloudsley added, 'But even if we get there in time to nobble two or three of them – when you think of the lives and damage just *one* can—'

'Right. Absolutely.' Saddler nodded. He'd seen it, *still* saw it, in his mind's eye. He said, 'I have another question for you. If you're allowed to answer it. You're Special Boat Squadron, and there must be a hell of a lot of Patagonian coast you could land on, so why not go in by sea? Alternatively, why the SBS

13

and not the SAS?'

'Ah, well,' Cloudsley began, with a straight face, 'they wanted men with brains, you see—'

'Come on, now. . . .'

'Sir. Well, the answer to the last bit is that the idea was so to speak born – here in your ship, I was told – with one of our chaps present, and so it became the squadron's baby because it was ours from birth, sort of thing. Then when the planning got under way, the idea was certainly to have gone in by sea – by submarine, of course. But the fact is – as was then pointed out – there's no SSK down here yet.'

Saddler took the point. An SSK being a patrol submarine, conventionally powered, small enough to be able to operate in coastal waters, whereas the nukes, SSNs which were on station now, were too big to get in close enough – on that coast – for beach landings. Nukes didn't much like to surface, anyway, in close proximity to their enemies. Cloudsley added, 'If all goes according to plan, we'll be taken *out* by submarine, when the job's done.' He reached sideways to the table, to touch wood.

At 1620 the carrier group was thirty miles to the south, still on what had become known as its 'racetrack' daylight patrol on this east side of the islands, but steering southwestward, beginning to close in for whatever night operations had been ordered. Bombardments, anti-shipping sweeps, or insertions or extractions of Special Forces teams. It had been a quiet day for the Task Force so far: Harriers had splashed one Mirage, and that had been the sum of the day's action. Boredom was the enemy, at such times, and John Saddler could see it in many of the young faces around him. He was in the Ops Room, on his chair and wearing the communications headset which gave him the Command Open Line in one ear and, in the other, occasional laconic exchanges between the CAP – combat air patrol, Harriers from the flagship *Hermes* – and their fighter control ship, which this afternoon was the Type 42 destroyer *Glasgow*.

Now his own ship's broadcast: 'Hands to flying stations!'

It was the slow way to get the helo into the air. If you wanted to do it in a hurry, the order would have been 'Action helo!' His eyes moved around the weirdly lit cavern of the Ops Room, thinking that to a newcomer it might have resembled a scene from some sci-fi drama. Hum of machinery and fans: light bleeding orange from radar monitors, filtering silver over the big plot where everything that moved on, under or over the sea and in range of the ship's electronic sensors was plotted and its movements constantly updated by the radarmen clustered round it. So young looking, some of them, they might still have been at school: boys with men's jobs, while his own was not only to direct and control their joint efforts but also, please God, to keep them alive, eventually get them home to mothers, fathers, wives, girls. . . .

Saddler pulled off the headset, replaced it with his gold-peaked cap. He told Joe Nicholson, a lieutenant-commander and Anti Air Warfare Officer, 'I'll be on the bridge.'

Leaving the Ops Room, passing the little hole that was his sea cabin, he stepped into the one-man lift, jerked its gates shut and thumbed the button. It leapt upwards – a *whooshing* noise and a rocket-like ascent – and jerked to a slamming halt three decks higher. It provided a very fast means of transference from one command point to the other, its only snag being that in really bad weather the flexing of the ship's hull could jam the cage in its shaft, which for the commanding officer of a ship in action might be something of a nightmare. It had never happened to Saddler yet, but in rough seas he was always glad to get out of it. He turned right – for'ard – then right again into a passage that ran athwartships behind the bridge, and thence into the bridge itself, to his high chair in the front of it. Holt, the Australian lieutenant who was officer of the watch, asked him, 'Permission to fly, sir?' and he nodded as he reached for binoculars, thinking for the thousandth time that the routine question almost demanded a silly answer. *Shropshire* was altering course through whitened sea, changing to a new leg of the anti-submarine zigzag. Alpe, a sub-lieutenant who was second officer of the watch, pressed a switch in the helo-operating console: lights would glow green now, back aft on the flight deck, authorising take-off. It was simpler to send the Wessex away for a few hours, making room here for the visiting Sea King, than to manhandle it into its hangar, which this much movement on the sea made tricky.

The Sea King from *Hermes* would be refuelling during its stay on board *Shropshire;* it had been fitted with extra tanks, apparently, and would be landing-on with them empty. And Cloudsley and his team – which consisted of Colour Sergeant Beale and Marines Hosegood and West, and of course Andy MacEwan – would have their heads down now in the cabins temporarily allocated to them. They'd had some work to do first, sorting and re-packing gear, but by this time if they had any sense they'd be enjoying the last comfortable sleep they'd be likely to get for quite a while.

Holt had pulled down the mike on its hinged deckhead bracket and was admonishing the quartermaster, for using too much wheel – or not enough – in making the last zigzag alteration. *Shropshire* smashing through the waves, sea exploding back in sheets and streamers across the wet, shiny-green fo'c'sl. Only some horizontal surfaces were green now, everything else having become dull grey; white paintwork and black had been over-painted before they'd left Ascension Island. Saddler pulled on his jacket and moved out into the bridge wing, opening the side door easily but then needing all his weight to force it shut again, squinting up against wind and spray to see the Wessex claw its way up above the ship and then swing away on course to join the carrier group. Its cruising speed of ninety knots, boosted by a tail wind, would see it down on the flagship's deck in less than twenty minutes.

2

A Sea King's standard load was twenty men, and on this trip
there were only five plus its crew of three. It left a lot of empty
cabin space. Andy MacEwan, in a rear seat with Geoff
Hosegood on his left, was strapped in now – feeling fairly
rotten – with the others' broad backs in front darkening the
space between him and the faint radiance leaking from the
cockpit. Outside, *Shropshire's* highly unstable flight deck rose
and fell and tilted, the white of wave-crests visible in nauseat-
ing close up when she rolled this side downward; then as she
swung back, stern rearing, you saw only the spill of light from
the flight-deck officer's caboosh.

If it went on much longer, he'd be sick. Motion violent,
noise ear-bruising, vibration bone-rattling. How in hell they'd
even get the heavy machine off the gyrating deck in these
conditions he couldn't imagine. But outside, they'd removed
the rotor cuffs and were crouching ready to knock off the
securing chains.

The Sea King had landed-on at 1700. Andy, who hadn't felt
inclined to sleep, had been up there in the bridge wing to watch
it clatter down out of the sky; and later, after the ship had been
called to dusk action stations and eventually relaxed again into

17

two watches, John Saddler had invited Cloudsley to bring the SBS team up to the chartroom for a rundown on the navigational angles; he'd shown them the ship's position, track and rate of advance to the fly-off point, which she'd been due to reach at 0430.

Had reached, now. He checked the time: his watch showed 0428. Geoff Hosegood saw him doing it, shouted, 'OK, Andy?' White teeth gleamed under the black, droopy moustache which he'd cultivated in the past fortnight. Hosegood came from Chatham in Kent, but with that moustache he'd easily pass for a Latin – for an Argentine. Brown eyes to match: the eyes of a quiet and thoughtful man. Andy raised a thumb – in somewhat less than truthful answer – and shouted, 'Fine.' He wasn't feeling anything like fine at this moment, and Hosegood had seen it, had intended the question as an encouragement and wasn't fooled now either. Geoff was married, with a baby daughter and a pretty wife; he had snapshots of them and never took much persuading to bring them out and show them round, although he wouldn't be carrying any such things as photos now. Sitting back, grasping the arms of the metal-framed webbing seat, feeling the upward lurch as noise expanded and its quality changed, his gut perversely trying to stay down there as the helo lifted. The whites of Harry Cloudsley's eyes showed through semi-darkness as he swung round, glancing back; Tony Beale too, Colour Sergeant Beale's large-nosed, long-chinned face with a similar enquiry in it; and Andy raising the same thumb – with some degree of honesty this time, relief already noticeable. But in any case he didn't want them nursemaiding him, treating him as a softie who might be in need of support and might therefore be a liability to them; and Geoff Hosegood reading this, too, turning away, deliberately leaving him to himself as the big helo hoisted itself thunderously into the dark night sky, the five-thousand-ton destroyer already a small and diminishing disturbance in black, white-streaked sea. *Shropshire* would be turning now, not quite reversing her course but making a hairpin turn to head back south of the islands, having passed north of them to reach this position on the western edge of the Exclusion Zone.

Cape Virgin bearing 250 degrees, 180 miles; visualising John Saddler's chart, *Cabo Vírgenes* being the headland at the entrance to the Magellan Strait. The Sea King's course-made-good (course adjusted for drift, effect of wind) would actually be 246 degrees, to leave that cape to starboard and pass inland up the middle of the strait, entering not Argentine territory but Chilean and then after a while edging round on to a northerly course up the Chilean side of the Andes mountains.

Back door entrance, and a long flight ahead now. Andy settled back, shut his eyes and began to think about old Tom Strobie, whom he'd dragged into this tightrope-walk as ruthlessly as John Saddler had let *him* in for it. In fact more so – Saddler hadn't *knowingly* put a man's life in danger.

The SBS had asked him at that first meeting, in Whitehall, 'Can you think of any family or individual within striking distance of this location who'd be likely to give us a hand?'

'Oh, certainly.' He hadn't needed any time to ponder the question. 'Man by the name of Strobie. His land's to the west and southwest of ours.'

Before this there'd been questions about his own family – which meant, in effect, about his brother, and he'd told them enough to put a stopper on that line of thought, their original idea which, understandably, had been to use the MacEwan *estancia* as their base. There was to be a longer session of probing into his personal background and connections later – by different people, not the SBS themselves – but at this stage the quest was for practicalities, for any way – if a way existed at all – they could make use of his local knowledge or associations. And Strobie's name was the one and only answer to that question. Maybe very few of the sheep-farming families of Chubut, Comodoro Rivadavia and Santa Cruz would truly give a damn for the Falklands/Malvinas, no matter how many thousands of citizens screamed their heads off in the Plaza de Mayo in BA; but they'd toe the line, certainly wouldn't stick

19

their necks out now the thing had started. In any case, why should they? Patagonia had been their home for generations, the Argentine had provided them with their livelihoods and in good times made them rich, and their parents and their own children had been born there. Some were of kelper stock, Falklanders themselves or descendants of Falklanders who'd moved of their own volition to live under Argentine rule, so pragmatically they'd have no reason to regard the same rule as necessarily abhorrent to present Falklanders.

Andy had explained, 'The truth is, you see, *I'm* the maverick.'

And Tom Strobie was maverick to a high degree. He was also a more recent immigrant, his loyalty to the British Crown clear-cut and unequivocal, just as it had been all his life. The only doubt in Andy's mind had been – still was, but the proof of that pudding would be seen pretty soon now – whether he'd be in shape to be of any practical help. Tom would be well into his later seventies by now, could even be touching eighty, and in a scrawled Christmas message eighteen months ago the words 'bloody arthritis' has been decipherable amongst others that were not.

(Then some lines, a whole paragraph, that was entirely legible. Strobie had written – and Andy had re-read it so often that he still had it clearly in mind – *You should never have given up so easy, lad. She wouldn't have, if it had been you turning her down! You walked away like a bloody prima donna and my guess is you could have put up a fight and won. What's more I'd guess she's wishing you had, by now.*)

But the so-called 'arthritis': he'd known that the ailment might be arthritis or might be anything else that caused pain. The only thing unusual had been the fact of Tom mentioning such a thing in his letter: that seemed ominous. He'd suffered from aches and cramps as long as Andy had known him, which was all his life – he'd always had 'bad days' and 'less bad days', but he hadn't been near a doctor since he'd removed himself from their hands in about 1949 or '50. He'd been a Merchant Navy skipper, having run away to sea as a youngster before the first world war, and in the second he'd been awarded the

George Medal for his conduct when the freighter he'd commanded – in a convoy to Malta, carrying ammunition in her holds and cased petrol on deck – had been bombed, set on fire and sunk in a series of explosions. Strobie had saved several lives, and come close to losing his own; in a sense it might be said he *had* lost it. He'd finally been dragged corpse-like – a mutilated corpse at that – from the burning sea, aviation spirit alight and flaming on its surface like brandy on a Christmas pudding; he'd been in it, under it and surfacing into it more than once to get others away. He'd had no hair or skin left on his head, hands, arms or torso, and in some areas he'd lost more than skin. Like one eyelid, and his lips. He'd survived, thanks partly to his own powerful constitution but also initially to the skill and determination of a destroyer's young doctor, but with only one eye that worked properly and with the appearance of something Dr Frankenstein might have created. After the war he'd gone to live and farm in Patagonia because distant relatives – to whom he'd once referred, Andy remembered, as 'those fucking old lesbians' – who were well-off and lived in Buenos Aires, had inherited a sheep-station and offered their war-hero fourth cousin thrice removed the job of running it, and because he'd reckoned, rightly, that in that vast, thinly populated territory there'd be fewer strangers' eyes to widen in shock at the sight of him – the start of horror, the quick turn away. . . .

Tom's grating voice, in memory: *'Used to get my bloody goat. Not as I'd blame 'em, mind.'*

The SBS had asked him at that meeting, 'Are you sure of this fellow? We wouldn't want to be going out on a limb; and you see, there's no way to check up on him, without risk. No time, either. Can you be certain?'

He'd told them yes, he could. If Tom Strobie was still himself, hadn't gone to pot – from old age, the effects of his injuries, and the state of isolation in which he'd lived for the past thirty years.

'And if you convince him you're on the level. A letter from me might be the best way to set about it. If there's some way to get it to him.'

21

There'd been a tentative suggestion then of sending in Andy himself to see Strobie and set it up, since he'd be accepted by Strobie without question. 'A natural for him, isn't it?'

They'd been talking across him, as if he wasn't there. And as if he'd already volunteered.

'God's sake, man – teach him all he'd need to know, in – what, a couple of weeks?'

He'd seen the negative reactions to that and happily gone along with them, having no great desire to risk his neck. He knew next to nothing then about the SBS, but he'd gathered they were all Royal Marine volunteers – the pick of the volunteers – and that all Marines were fully fledged commandos even before any 'higher education'. The one who'd put that rhetorical question – he was a major – added, 'The only way in there reasonably quickly would be by HALO drop. Teach him that, for starters, by next week?'

Then he'd softened it: 'No offence, MacEwan. Point of fact I'd say you look like suitable material. But with the time factor we're up against it's really not on.'

At a later stage it had been mooted that he might be taken in with them as a guide and interpreter only, and this seemed more realistic. Preparation for it hadn't been quite as near child's play as he'd intimated to John Saddler; there'd been plenty to learn, as well as the toughening-up. And during that time it was all still very much in the air, because their first two plans had to be scrapped. First when they were told there'd be no submarine available for a beach landing – because no SSK could get out there in the time available – and the second time when British Aerospace scientists came up with a solution to the problem of emasculating Exocet missiles – which earlier they'd said might be impossible – and the solution entailed taking in exceptionally heavy equipment. A third scheme therefore had to be devised, in lieu of the really desperate expedient of bombing from the air, which was rejected out of hand at a high level. And the new plan was based on facts Andy gave them, and his own suggestion – advanced very diffidently and with every expectation of having it laughed out of court – concerning, prosaically enough, the movement of sheep in

22

Patagonia at this season of the year.

The truth was, nobody was in any mood to laugh, most of them quite ready to clutch at straws. There'd been one explosive objection: 'But Christ, what about the time angle! You're talking about *crawling* in!'

'Remember the tortoise and the hare, Joe?'

The major who'd shot down the idea of sending Andy in alone to set things up with Strobie had pointed out that a lot of time had been wasted already, and it could be as long again before they could have this business on the move; time was a gamble now in any case, but at least you'd be in there finally, with a fighting chance.

Connecting with the new scheme, it was decided that one SBS officer would go in by parachute well ahead of the main party, by HALO drop – the technique of high altitude, low opening – carrying a letter from Andy to Tom Strobie and asking for his cooperation. Which in fact was a basic essential, you couldn't move far without it.

'Drop on Strobie's land?'

'Too close, surely? Even for one guy on his own. We don't know what kind of radar it is on the new base, but hell, they must have long-range radar at Comodoro Rivadavia – and even at Deseado, maybe – that'd pick up an over-flying Hercules. And that'd be enough to give us away, or could be.' It was the same major talking. 'If Strobie's land adjoins the target area?'

Andy told him no, it didn't. That really would have been too much to hope for. But the distance would be only about thirty miles.

'A lot too close. I'd say make the drop at least a hundred miles south, then yomp it. One man alone with nothing to carry except his rations – moving only by night – well, what the hell? Otherwise, we'd risk showing interest in the target area, and they'd deploy all those bloody things *prontissimo*.'

He'd phrased his letter to the old man cautiously, only introducing the bearer and asking Tom to help him on his way. So no outsider getting hold of it – from a dead parachutist's pocket, for instance – would learn anything of value.

23

'Tom Strobie,' he'd told Harry Cloudsley, who at about this stage had been named as leader of whatever team went in, 'is a rock of a man. If he's alive, free, and in his right mind, he's exactly the guy you need.'

Ugly as sin. Allowing no mirror in his house. He'd growled, 'Scared meself a few times, before I chucked 'em out. Beard don't cover enough, worst luck!'

But Francisca had faced him, without even blinking; Francisca of all people, who was so exceptionally easy to look at. Beauty facing the beast. . . . Strobie having offered, a few days earlier, 'All right. Bring her along. If you really want to put her through it, poor kid.'

Andy had warned her, and she'd shrugged it off; then when the time came she didn't only face old Tom without showing even a hint of revulsion, she walked over to the chair from which he'd begun to hoist himself up, put her hands on his shoulders and pressed him back into it; then stooped, kissed his cheek. Straightening then, speaking quietly in her softly American-accented voice – her mother was American – 'Sorry if I seem forward. But I heard so much about you' – moving her dark head towards Andy – 'from this guy MacEwan. . . .' Andy seeing the gleam in the old man's eye, hearing his growl, 'My word, boy. My bloody oath. I'd say you struck pure gold!'

Francisca: seeing her in his memory as she'd been then – light-blue eyes, charcoal-black hair, skin with a sheen of that same gold on it. Wide, full-lipped mouth: when she smiled straight at you, he remembered, you felt weightless, gone. And since it had all folded – well, the memories didn't fold, the image of her was indelible, coming between your eyes or your brain and any other—

Lisa, for instance.

He pulled his thoughts back into the present. Noise, lurching, buffeting wind as the helo thundered westward. Wondering what they'd do if when they got in there they found Strobie

24

hadn't reacted as they were counting on him to react, or if the HALO dropper hadn't got to him. Strobie could be dead, or in hospital, or prison; or the parachutist – an SBS lieutenant by the name of 'Monkey' Start – could have been caught. Andy had asked Cloudsley what he'd do in a fix like that, and the big man had only stared at him as if he'd asked a question in some foreign language; then shrugged, muttered, 'God knows. . . .'

The snag was, you couldn't know until you did get in there – *right* in, in two days' time. Use of radio had been ruled out, because the Argies weren't to be allowed any hint of activity or interest in the area of their missile dump, not even within a hundred miles of it. So you'd only find out when you met up with the man who'd been dropped in from a high-flying Hercules C.130 on a dark night about a week ago. Or, as the case might be, when you did *not* meet up with him.

'Captain, sir. Surface contact. . . .'

Waking into the rush of emergency as the ship went to action stations. Middle of the night, part of a dream to start with, then reality – in the Ops Room, pulling on his headset over the white anti-flash hood, simultaneously scanning the big plot then moving to peer over a PO's shoulder at a radar monitor, hearing semi-suppressed excitement in the control team's voices – a target, a live one, some Argie ship trying to run the blockade.

'White system closed up, cleared away.'

White system being the gun, the twin-barrelled semi-automatic 4.5″ on the foc's'l, and that voice had come over the wires from the MRS 3 TS, a gunnery nerve-centre on 04 Deck, two levels down from this one. They had an item of wizardry in there called a Box 11 or Fire Control Box, from which the master gunner, Sub-Lieutenant Derek Cadell, would be getting target course, speed, inclination, range, and presently on the bright strip of a radar scan he'd see the splashes of his fall of shot. Saddler meanwhile assessed the position in more general terms, satisfying himself there could be no friendly ships in this sector, that it could only be an enemy heading either for Falkland Sound or to carry on around East Falkland and up to Port Stanley before daybreak. He told his officer of the watch over the Open Line, 'Come to port to zero-five-zero.' *Shropshire* was off Cape Meredith, the southernmost point of West Falkland. From the position where she'd flown-off the Sea King she'd come down on course 130 degrees, southeastward, then altered to 110 an hour ago, having established a safe clearance of the coastline – safe *enough*, a margin of safety compatible with the need for a fairly rapid eastward transit. Closer inshore there were several potential dangers that had to be borne in mind. One, navigational, was kelp, the masses of floating weed in which you could all too easily immobilise a ship's propellers. Then shore guns: in some places the Argies had set up howitzers. Third, there'd been talk of shore-mounted Exocets, a rumour of MM38s, the ship-borne variety, having been taken out of dockyard storage or even out of Argentine warships and set up for coast defence. The rumour might not have much truth in it but you couldn't discount it, or ignore *any* such threat when you were eight thousand nautical miles from home with no dockyard facilities and precious few reserves; but here and now he was satisfied that he could safely turn and close the range because (a) there was no kelp off that headland: tidal streams of up to three knots and a heavy race that came with southerly winds guaranteed it would be kept clear; (b) even if they had an Exocet installation on that point it couldn't be fired at *Shropshire* while the blockade-runner was still closer to it and would claim the missile's attention; and (c) he had no intention of taking her in as close as fourteen thousand yards, which was the range of Argie howitzers.

'Course zero-five-zero, sir.'

He'd seen it, on the course indicator on the bulkhead. Wind and sea were on the beam, but the stabilisers were holding her reasonably steady.

'Load the hoists with SAP.'

'White – salvoes!'

'Salvoes' was the order to load. There was a two-man crew with a supervising PO in the gunhouse, thirty men in the White system as a whole, many of them in the deep below-decks extension of the turret where shells and cartridges would now be lying in the hoists ready to start flowing upward when fire was opened.

'Radar confirms surface target.'

Dozens of factors went into the calculations, comprised the flow of data the computer-controlled system needed to digest. In the TS the master gunner reporting 'Radar locked on target', watching a dot of blue light held on the centreline of a ship-shaped image of the target, while the patter of war cries linked compartment to compartment, circuit to circuit. The gun director, a chief PO at his own console a few yards from Saddler, presiding over radar monitors, banks of switches and panels of indicator lights, had passed the order 'Surface – blind – joyball!', using a forefinger on the 'joyball' control to mark the target's radar image on his tote screen and thus keep it in the forefront of the ADAWS computer's mind; with all the calculations made, White system lined up and primed for its first ever action against a real-life surface target, the final requirement now was Saddler's authority to proceed.

He said evenly into his microphone, 'Command approved.'

Fifty seconds ago he'd been fast asleep. In some dream that had had Anne in it.

'Engage!'

Cadell, master gunner, ordered 'Shoot!'

Distantly – thud . . . thud. . . .

Left gun. Right gun. Blue flashes in a control circuit as each fired. On the radar scan in the TS one splash showed up as short; a petty officer reported, 'One hit, one short.'

Seconds ago, there'd have been men asleep in the blockade-runner. Now there'd be none sleeping, might be some dead. With the guns in timed-alternate firing, a seaman's toe depressing a pedal at the Tallboy to maintain the rhythmic flow of electronic pulses, twenty rounds per gun per minute and hitting steadily – by now there surely would be. The knowledge brought no satisfaction, none at all. Destruction of the

27

target was essential, but the shedding of blood, the blasting apart of bodies, was as unappealing as it was unavoidable. Inside the gunhouse the two-man crew, in anti-flash gear and anti-static boots, worked like parts of the one machine, synchronising the servicing of the smoking breeches with the time-alternate pulses, and never missing one. Loader crashing a green-painted shell into the loading tray, gun captain dropping the cartridge in behind it and his right arm continuing in one smooth movement so that the back of his fist hit the pad to activate the loading ram, the ram whipping over to throw shell and cartridge into the breech, breech shutting as the ram withdrew, right gun catching the pulse, firing, running back as the left gun crashed, recoiled, motion fast and smooth, continuous, cordite reek thickening, the turret's jerking quick and sudden as aim was kept constantly adjusted against the rolling of the ship; if you'd had the time to let yourself think about it, you could get sick in here.

Saddler heard his OOW's report over the Open Line: 'Big explosion, sir, on Red zero-five!'

'Radar lost target!'

Saddler said, 'Cease fire.'

Derek Cadell ordered from the TS, 'Stop loading, stop loading, stop loading!'

Seventy seconds had passed since he'd said 'Command approved.' Now he told the officer of the watch, 'Bring her back to one one zero,' and pulled off his headset, just catching the report 'All guns empty'. He headed for the lift.

Anne had written in her last letter – which, come to think of it had been some while ago – 'The whole country's praying for you. Me twice as hard as the rest. But apart from the obvious, horrible anxieties I do realise how important it is just at this time for you personally, professionally. . . .'

It had annoyed him when he'd read it, and it still irritated. What she'd been saying in that passage was that she hadn't forgotten he was in the promotion zone, a stage in his career when he'd either go on up to flag rank or go *out*. You didn't hang around, in today's Navy, you either progressed to higher levels or you made way for a younger man. But as far as he,

John Saddler, was concerned, the Navy could make up its own mind and either way he'd be happy to go along with the decision. This was the point. Anne thought he cared about it, but he genuinely didn't give a damn. He'd had quite a different attitude seven and a half years ago when he'd made captain's rank at thirty-nine; he'd seen the ladder reaching to the heights, himself racing up it. Now, it didn't matter. If they wanted him to be an Admiral, he'd be one, but if they didn't there'd be plenty of challenge and satisfaction, even excitement, in trying something new – and, incidentally, getting to spend more time with Anne than he ever had so far.

Her preference, he knew, would be for him to leave the Service. But she was sure he had his heart set on getting to the top: no matter what he said, she believed his denials were only insurance against disappointment – and, as always so unselfish that at times it quite annoyed him, she'd decided to want for him what she believed *he* wanted.

The lift banged to a stop on 02 Deck. He wrenched the gates open, dragged them shut behind him, went quickly round the corner and then into the darkened bridge. As well as the first and second officers of the watch, Jay Kingsmill, *Shropshire*'s second in command, was there; and David Vigne, navigating officer, heron-like with his long legs, sharp nose and slight forward stoop. They were all wearing anti-flash gear, and had binoculars trained out on the bow as the ship swung back to her easterly course. Kingsmill told him, 'Blew up, sir. Carrying ammo, I'd say. Or those mines we heard were coming. After the bang there was a bit of a burn low on the water, but nothing there now.'

Except dark night, black white-veined sea. There was an eight-hundred-foot hill to the north of the headland, he knew, and a disused metal light structure; radar could find both, but the eye could not. . . . The inclination to move in closer and look for survivors had quickly to be rejected: the target had been close inshore, hugging the coast for cover and for safety, and what had been its comfort would be *Shropshire*'s danger. There were five hundred lives *here* to think about. Saddler ordered, lowering his glasses, 'Secure from action stations.'

*

The Sea King had flown westward up the middle of the Magellan Strait, no more than twenty feet above the water. The Strait belonged to Chile, as did the land bordering it, Punta Dungeness about seven miles to starboard and Punta Catalina on Tierra del Fuego the same distance to port, both of course invisible. But fifty miles inside, when the helo left the water and had land under it, Chilean land, the Argentine airbase at Río Gallegos – their nearest operational fields to the Falklands – was only another fifty miles due north. There was a long haul ahead of them, in darkness all the way and flying low to stay under the reach of radar; this made no problems for the pilots because the Sea King was equipped with Passive Night Goggles, an American device that was proving immensely valuable. PNG, apparently, had made it possible for Special Forces teams to be put into the Falklands by helo at night as easily as in daylight; Cloudsley and John Saddler had been talking about it a few hours ago in *Shropshire*'s chartroom.

Andy liked Saddler. He'd met him before, of course, but only briefly and with Lisa or her mother present, everyone making polite conversation. He felt grateful to him now for not having brought up the subject of his relationship with Lisa; and he'd admired what seemed to be a quiet, un-pompous style of command.

'Hey, Andy! Company!'

Geoff Hosegood had reached over, poked his shoulder; 'company' was the Sea King's navigator, leaning over to show them a plastic-covered map. Pointing out their position, and the flight-path up the west side of the mountains, and then their destination, the landing zone or 'LZ'. Andy looked for, and recognised, the lake – long, narrow for most of its length but widening at its eastern end, reaching from Chile right through the Andes and deep into the Argentine.

'That's about it, then.' The lieutenant's blue pencil-tip tapped the plastic over the LZ again. He shouted, 'After we deliver you, we'll be spending the day there, lying up. Come the dark, we take off again, and Bob's your uncle!'

30

No. Bob's my brother. Except he calls himself 'Roberto' now. Roberto MacEwan, pronounced as if it might be spelt MacJuan. Lieutenant-Commander MacEwan of the Comando de Aviación Naval. . . .

Hosegood had yelled, 'All the way back?' He looked as if he found it hard to believe. 'What'll you do for gas?'

A thumb jerked: 'Got it with us. Extra tanks, internal.' The navigator swung away, preparing to go through his spiel again with Jake West, who was sitting in solitary state halfway up the cabin. Geoff Hosegood winked at Andy, then folded himself back into his seat, shut his eyes and seemed to fall instantly asleep. As easily as *that*, Andy thought. They continued to impress him, these people – with their skills, their confidence, quiet acceptance of huge problems and extraordinary risks. He'd asked Cloudsley, for instance, on the subject of certain clothing – Patagonian-type, civilian clobber in which they were intending to disguise themselves for the journey across country – whether it wasn't a consideration that a man not wearing uniform when taken prisoner in enemy territory could under the internationally accepted rules of warfare be regarded as a spy and shot; and Cloudsley had said yes, sure, that was the case. He'd added, 'But we don't reckon on being caught. We plan it so we *won't* be, you see.'

'But if you were?'

He'd frowned. 'This operation's approved at a high level. And it can't be carried out in uniform, obviously. So we have to do it the only way it can be done, and accept the consequences of any balls-up.'

The consequences being a firing squad. And Geoff Hosegood sound asleep, breathing deeply and evenly, a suggestion of a smile curving his mouth under the floppy black moustache; maybe dreaming, Andy guessed, of that young wife and baby daughter.

31

3

West complained – several hours later, and in a deeply contrasting silence after that long stretch of continuous, deafening noise – 'I dig what SBS stands for now. Special Bloody Sherpas.' He asked Cloudsley, 'What else is in them packs? Bricks?'

Cloudsley had his back against a rock. He was wrapped in a *poncho* and wearing a cloth cap with earflaps dangling loose. *Bombachas* – baggy pants – stuffed into well-worn riding boots completed the external picture, but under the *poncho* he was also wearing a *campera* of reversed sheepskin, and the overall effect was to double his apparent bulk. The others were dressed similarly, having changed in the helo into this gear which had been rounded up in England from second-hand shops and other out-of-the-way places. Andy had specified the type of clothing, and approved the final selection.

Cloudsley said amiably, 'You'll be getting a free ride tonight, Jake. Count your blessings.'

The *ponchos*, made of alpaca wool, weren't only for disguise; they gave protection against the wind that funnelled up the valley. Higher ground and the peaks above it were already white, under autumn snow; northward, the great receding

33

march of the Andes was hazy-white over blueish lower slopes, while here on this north face of the ridge black shadows lay over them, daylight strengthening on the Argentine side. From the LZ about four miles away, where the Sea King was now pegged down and hidden under camouflage nets, the five men had trekked uphill under their heavy loads, through a neck of rain-forest and then out of it to the treeless ridge with the lake below them on its other side, silvering in the mountain dawn.

Geoff Hosegood grumbled, 'Sooner not talk about bloody riding. Five days since I was on one o' them things, I *still* got a sore arse.'

They'd arranged lessons for him. While Andy had been learning to parachute, practising unarmed combat (as well as close combat with a fighting knife) and in the intervals running – not jogging, *running* – incredible distances over hill country under a heavy pack, Geoff had been learning to sit on a horse and steer it. In fact horse-riding was not the kind of ride Harry Cloudsley had referred to a moment ago. Horses were for later – for tomorrow, *if* Tom Strobie had come up to scratch – and tonight's ride would be in the inflatable they'd brought with them, four metres long, designed to carry six men with full equipment or eight more lightly armed. Its fabric was a new product, ultra-strong and lightweight, and the boat's special value was in its strength/weight/capacity ratio, with a resulting high degree of buoyancy. The outboard motor was also new: lightweight, delivering eighteen horsepower, and sound-proofed, the engine itself enclosed in a glassfibre pod with a flexible 'drowned' exhaust. The noise reduction was said to be in the order of sixty per cent, and Beale and Hosegood, who'd tested it in sea conditions, confirmed this.

'Lightweight' was a comparative term, of course. 132 kilogrammes was a definite improvement on the 180 kilogrammes of a standard Gemini – a four-man lift on its own, without an outboard or any other gear such as weapons, clothing, rations, let alone more esoteric equipment such as that for castrating an AM39 missile.

They'd all slept during the long flight, and they had the whole span of daylight hours ahead now before it would be safe to move. Plenty of time for more sleep, and no hurry for it. Except for Hosegood, who was already yawning. Andy mentally pinched himself to make sure he really was awake, not dreaming this whole business. And aware of Cloudsley studying him – of wide-set eyes sombre, thoughtful, trying to see inside his skull maybe. You could hardly blame him, with these men's lives (and indirectly, out there at sea, many others) in his hands, and knowing that his guide into unknown territory had a brother there who was clearly their enemy.

Cloudsley did not, Andy thought, know anything about Francisca.

The two civilians, well, men in civilian clothes – one young and abrasive and the other middle-aged, mild-mannered – who'd spent most of one day interrogating him and had then presumably cleared him, had known about her but had not linked her with him. Only with Robert. They'd known as much as they had about her, of course, because her father, Alejandro Diaz, was a prominent man of obvious interest to any Intelligence service. The younger of the two had asked him, 'This man Diaz. . . . He's a neighbour – right?'

Andy had confirmed it.

'A big wheel politically?'

'Counter-insurgency. He was a commander in the Argentine fleet air arm before, then resigned and took on this state security job.'

'Meaning torture, disappearances. . . .' The younger one had added, 'One of his colleagues being Alfredo Astiz, for heaven's sake.'

'So one heard.'

Astiz was 'wanted' by several governments, to answer questions about the imprisonment, torture and disappearance of some of their nationals. (More recently, he'd been taken prisoner on South Georgia.)

The older of the two interviewers put in suddenly – as if he'd just woken up to what was being said, and found it shocking – 'This man's your *neighbour*?'

He'd nodded. 'Happens to have a sheep-station to the north of ours.'

'And an American wife, am I right?'

'Did have. She left him, some while ago. Took off with a rich Yank polo player. Her brother's a Congressman, incidentally.'

'Quite. But there's a daughter, isn't there? Married to *your* brother?'

'That's – correct.'

Both of them staring at him. As if expecting him to comment, or make excuses. He kept his mouth shut, because there was nothing he could have said that seemed to be any of their damn business. A minute later, they came back to Francisca's father.

'Alejandro Diaz. . . . D'you know him well? As a neighbour you must have seen a lot of him?'

'Not so much. I was over here at school, and so on, and in the early years he never spent much time at his *estancia*.'

'What sort of man would you say he is?'

'Very ambitious. Ruthless. Socially he's smart, sophisticated, moves in all the best circles, as they say. Dislikes Americans, one heard, because his wife ran out on him. But if you want the whole low-down on him, why not ask *her*? Or ask your opposite numbers over there to talk to her?'

He'd thought this suggestion was a good one to have made, as a way of distancing himself from the Diaz family. But they kept to the same subject, or near it, asking about his attitude to Roberto's marriage. The older man asked, 'Did you approve of your brother marrying the Diaz girl?'

He'd hesitated, thinking, *Christ, what a question. . . .*

'Not entirely. But you see – looking at it objectively – out there where it's been happening, what they call the "Dirty War", the activities of people like Diaz weren't by any means universally disapproved of. People who'd had friends or relatives murdered by the *Montoneros* or ERP for instance, or who were in danger from them themselves, would see it as a matter of beating terrorists at their own game. I know, a hell of a lot of completely innocent people were victimised – I'm not excusing it for a moment, but—'

'Quite.' A nod. 'Difficult to justify wholesale murder by the State. Eh?'

He'd held that stare, and nodded. 'Diaz is not a *nice* man. If that's the opinion you want.'

'But your brother wouldn't have had any compunction—'

'My brother isn't a particularly nice man either.'

Looking round the faces now: at Beale, Cloudsley, West, Hosegood. Not sure they were trusting him entirely, even though those two characters had cleared him at least to the extent that he'd been brought along. For instance, he was fairly sure they had their plans drawn up to the last detail, but he wasn't being let in on much of it, only on as much as he'd have to know for today, tomorrow. He'd no idea, for one thing, how they were intending to get away after the task was completed – only that there was supposed to be a submarine involved. Where or how they'd get to the coast hadn't even been discussed in his presence. OK, he understood it – the less anyone knew the less could be extracted from them. Interrogators, he'd been told, would be more likely to use drugs than torture in present circumstances, because they'd know (or in his own case, believe) they were dealing with men who'd been conditioned to withstand pressure, and because time would be vital to them; so they'd take the short cut. . . . But he'd still have liked to know something about the final exit route. *Not* knowing was beginning to feel like going into a tunnel that might not have an opening at the other end.

More immediately, he didn't know where Jake West and Monkey Start were going, tomorrow, after they made the rendezvous with Start. They had some separate objective of their own – the two operations apparently overlapping only in these early stages, Start making the essential arrangements with Tom Strobie, West helping meanwhile with the 'Sherpa' stuff, then away on their own business.

But these others knew, he thought.

Tony Beale met his eyes as he glanced round the circle of recumbent men again. The colour sergeant suggested, 'How's about a bed-time story, Andy? How the MacEwan family came to be farmers in the Argentine?'

West nodded. 'And like how you come to be on *our* side.'

The question had a sting in it, even if he hadn't meant it that way. But Beale answered for him. Tony Beale was about six-two, long-limbed and spare – like a greyhound compared to Cloudsley's bull-mastiff. He was a year or two older than the others; and married, with two toddlers at home in Hampshire. He said, 'He's British, Jake. That's how come.'

'Yeah, but – I mean, family *here*, an' all?'

'All the family I have is one brother.' Andy took over – appreciating Beale's defence of a member of his own team, even a civilian member, but also accepting that West had been perfectly justified in asking. Not *every* Anglo-Argentine, by a long chalk, was on 'our' side. He told them, 'I was born in Edinburgh, and my father was born near Inverness. He was brought out here when he was a baby, just before the first war. So Tony's dead right, I *am* British. Actually, there was an old great-uncle out here, been here since about eighteen-seventy when sheep-farming first started, and he'd died with no wife or children. My grandfather Robert MacEwan was a crofter, in Inverness, and he just upsticked with his wife and baby son.' He asked, thinking he might have told them enough to explain his origins, 'Want any more of this heart-warming saga?'

'Yeah. It's interesting.' Jake West had a foxy look. Unshaven, as they all were, purposefully stubbled as well as tanned and shaggy-headed. As he wasn't part of the main team, only Monkey Start's partner in whatever the other thing was, he hadn't been around as long as the others had, and Andy didn't know him as well. He did know he came from Nottingham and wasn't married, and that he was twenty-four, the youngest man in this circle of what could easily by the look of them have been Chilean *peóns*. He told them, 'Grandfather pegged out suddenly, food-poisoning or some such, in nineteen-thirty. My father was twenty then – name was Bruce – and he took over the running of the place. His mother, old Granny Fiona, was a very domineering woman and she was the driving force behind him, most of his life – long as he *had* any driving force. In fact he didn't lose it, she transferred it.'

Geoff Hosegood asked, 'Who to?'

'Well – my father didn't marry until he was in his middle

38

thirties. In nineteen-forty-five actually, year the war ended in Europe. My mother was then eighteen. She was half Welsh and half Italian. Small, very feminine – what in Scotland they call a "wee smasher". . . . Granny Fiona was against the marriage. She was a great horse of a woman herself, and she was contemptuous – I dare say jealous – of my mother for being pretty and petite. Also for being what she called a mongrel. The old bag told my father, "Och, she'll nae gi'e y bairns – an' they'd be weeds if she did!" '

He'd slipped naturally into his grandmother's Scottish accent, vividly remembering the tough old woman who'd treated his mother like a servant girl, called her 'Joannie' instead of by her real name, Juanita, and fought her on every detail of how the house and family should be run.

'My father should've put his foot down, of course. But anyway, the first child came in nineteen-fifty – that's my brother Robert. Big, ginger-headed like grandfather Robert. *Too* damn big, my mother nearly died having him. Granny Fiona was wild about him, though, spent all her time trying to take him over, same as she'd taken over everything else. And Robert made it easy for her. . . . Incidentally, I've had most of this family history from Tom Strobie, who watched it all happening.' Andy explained to Jake West, 'Strobie's the guy your Lieutenant Start's been visiting – we hope. Neighbour; land adjoins my family's. He arrived in Patagonia about the time Robert was born, and he and my father got to be close friends. Very different characters, but they got on. For one thing they both drank a lot; and my father used to get away from his own place whenever he could, avoiding having to face up to the old woman. Rough on my mother, of course. . . . But then when she got pregnant the second time, he took Tom Strobie's advice and whisked her away to Scotland, to make sure she was properly looked after – because, as I said, having Robert had nearly killed her. My father did love her, there's no doubt of that, he just didn't have the strength or the guts to handle his mother, so she browbeat him ninety per cent of the time. On that occasion he defied her – and we were doing well in those days, money wasn't any problem. That's how I came to be born in Edinburgh. Everything went fine, and we came home. Granny Fiona had made good use of her time alone with Robert – had him eating out of her hand, Strobie told me. And she used to sneer at me, called me "Joannie's runt". I happened to be smaller than my damn brother, that's all. But having brown hair instead of the MacEwan ginger didn't appeal to her either. Mongrel blood, you see.'

He nodded to Tony Beale. 'There you are. One bed-time story.'

Cloudsley said, fingering the stubble on his short, cleft chin, 'But you went to school in Scotland, too. How did that come about?'

'Another idea of Strobie's. I owe that old guy a lot, you see. They were having Robert schooled near BA, and Tom suggested to my father that it might be a good idea to give one of his sons an education back where we'd all come from. Who knows, he said, the boy might not want to spend all his life out here, specially as it doesn't look as if he and Robert are likely to find much in common. Which was smart, considering Robert was still a kid and I was a toddler. Anyway, my father must have trusted old Tom's judgement, and as he was doing very well financially – despite his drinking habit – that's what did happen. Granny Fiona didn't care much; she was glad to have me out of the way while she went on grooming Robert to take over. Shoving him along, really brainwashing him into becoming her idea of what a MacEwan ought to be – you might say, a fourteen-carat shit.'

'Happy families.' Beale's tone was ironic. From the expression on his strong-featured, bony face you'd guess he'd been there. Cloudsley was using a very small pair of binoculars, studying the lake shore below them. Andy told them, 'After my mother died – in BA, in the British hospital, having a still-born daughter – there was no stopping the old woman. I was four, then, so I don't remember much, not even much about my mother, except not being able to believe it when they told me she wasn't coming home. I do remember *that*. . . . But most of what I know of those days is what Tom Strobie's told me at various times. My mother's death just about finished my father, and the booze problem went from bad to worse. By the time I was away to school in Scotland I knew my father was a soak, my grandmother a tyrant and my brother had all the makings of a – I don't know, a storm-trooper. Just as the old bitch wanted him. But in one way he ran foul of her. She had this contempt for anyone who wasn't British and preferably Scottish, but her beloved Robert was steadily becoming more Argentine than Anglo. I dare say his school up at BA was an influence, or his school chums. They were pretty well all what my grandmother used to refer to as "dagoes". They used to have real battles about it.'

What Andy was *not* about to tell anyone was that when he came home in 1973 for a long pre-university break, he and Francisca Diaz fell in love. She'd spent her childhood in BA and around naval airbases where her father had been stationed, but at this time she was living at the family's Patagonian *estancia*, Santa María. This was because Alejandro Diaz had resigned his commission in order to take up a political appointment, and there was some delay – a back-wash, Strobie thought, from General Lanusse having not that long ago taken over as President from the equally useless General Levingston. But an influence in his making this change was his wife having left him, the year before. Elaine Diaz, who was American and a beauty, prominent in BA society, had skipped with a polo-playing Bostonian millionaire, run off back to the States with him and then got herself a divorce in Reno. Francisca hated her mother for this, sided completely with her father. She was seventeen that year, Andy eighteen; she was taller than him by an inch or so, *very* pretty, pale blue eyes, black hair, a long throat and a vital, athletic body. They rode together, played tennis, hunted, danced. She'd dance shoeless to make up for the difference in height, of which he was over-conscious. And they got to be lovers that summer.

Tony Beale yawned. He murmured, 'Our raconteur has dried up.'

He came back to earth. Or rather, rock, and full daylight now. He told them, 'My father died in nineteen-seventy-five. The old woman had already gone by then, she kicked the bucket during my last year at school. I didn't come home for that. But my father had been missing for two days, in mid-winter – deep snow, and blizzards. If you're lucky you won't see it, we won't be here long enough, but in a hard winter like that one Patagonia's a wilderness – hundreds of miles of bugger-all except snow and wind, wind never letting up for a minute. Robert had been out with the *peóns*, searching for him, but they gave up and went back home. Strobie heard that he'd said to the *mayordomo* – the manager – "He'll be holed-up some place, stoned. He'll show up when it settles. *Maybe*. . . ." And he did show up – his horse brought him home, semi-conscious, out of his mind. He died – hypothermia, the doctor said – within twelve hours, and I got a cable, flew home for the funeral.'

Most neighbours braved the weather for it. Including the Diaz family, father and daughter. Andy's sorrow at his father's death had been mitigated by the prospect of reunion with Francisca, but she was no more than friendly, and much less cool – he'd thought he was imagining this at first – with Robert, who was calling himself 'Roberto' and talking to Diaz about buying a small airplane and getting himself taught to fly it – which in practical terms was a good idea, seeing that it could take a week on horseback to get round outlying paddocks, inspecting the stock and checking that the *puesteros* were doing their jobs. The MacEwan *estancia*, La Madrugada, contained more than 250 square miles of paddocks. Diaz was of course an airman, although by this time retired, in the government's political service, with his own organisation in BA and growing influence everywhere else, and as an ex-flyer himself he was all for Robert's plan. He was in favour of 'Roberto' from other points of view as well, including the fact that he and Francisca were spending more and more time together. His approval would have had some influence on her, too; since her mother had deserted him she'd been her father's determinedly loyal daughter.

The day before he left finally for England, Andy asked her, 'Remember the *vizcacha* game?'

A *vizcacha* being a small, furry animal, an Argentine

marmot, and the 'game' one that the local Indians had indulged in, years earlier. Robert would have heard accounts of it in the *peóns'* reminiscences. They were all Criollos now, mixed blood, mainly Indian and Chilean. There probably wasn't a full-blooded Tehuelche in the whole of Patagonia by this time, while down south the Yaghans were certainly extinct; but the stories and traditions lived on, and they'd told Robert – probably in the hope they'd see him wince, so they could laugh at him – about the sport their forefathers had had with the inoffensive little *vizcachas*. The trick was to catch one and skin it alive: an acquired skill, to get the pelt off in one piece and leave the animal otherwise undamaged and mobile; then to release it among the thorn-scrub, to be slashed and impaled as it dashed around, frantic with pain and terror. They'd have rocked with laughter, describing it, as their fathers had laughed to see it; and Robert had decided to try his own hand at it, then to invite Andy and Francisca – who to him at this stage were just a pair of children – to come and watch. He'd had the *vizcacha* already skinned, in a sack, had only to shake it out and give it a shove with his boot to start it running. Francisca had screamed a protest; then mounted, ridden her horse straight at him, screaming – well, wild, hysterical – but Andy had snatched the rifle from his saddle and put a snap shot through the dying *vizcacha's* head. Robert had been busy dodging Francisca's charge, laughing at her tears and fury; then he was derisive of Andy, angry with him for having spoilt the fun.

Francisca had answered his question – typically, taking it head-on, with no attempt to avoid the implications.

'*Certainly* I remember. But that was *then*. Little boys pull wings off flies, don't they? He's not like that now, he's – look, he's grown up, like I have too. He's a grown man, right? You're still studying, Andy – you're a student, you're still a *boy*. . . . I can see how you feel, I really can – and I'm sorry – but this is how it *is*, that's all!'

West asked him, 'Did your brother get the farm? When your father snuffed it? Why you settled in the UK, an' all?'

'No, we inherited equally. That's how the law goes, in the

43

Argentine. But he and I never got along. We could have split it, taken half each, but there'd have been a lot of complications and you can't make a small farm pay, it wouldn't have worked at all. So I still own half – half the profits, when or if there are any – but he runs it and lives off it, and I work for a firm in London.'

Beale commented, 'Brother Robert's the farmer, you're the city slicker.'

'He's the farmer, but he's also a flyer now.'

'So I heard.' Beale nodded towards Cloudsley. 'In the Sea King.'

It would be why he'd wanted to hear the rest of it, the family background. Andy explained. 'He had a light aircraft, a Beagle, for getting out to the paddocks. It's a lot of ground to cover, you know, about thirty square leagues.'

'A square league being how much?'

'A league's five kilometres, so a square league's about three miles by three, nine square miles. But the flying thing – a neighbour is this man Diaz. He's a high-up now, a prominent Junta supporter, but he was a commander in their fleet air arm before he went political, and I'd guess he personally taught my brother to fly and then encouraged him to join the naval reserve.'

'Your brother could be flying against our ships, then?'

'Yes. He could.' Cloudsley was pulling the *poncho* close around his large frame; he'd said something to West, who was moving, going higher up the ridge to take the first watch as lookout. Andy told Beale, 'He's what they call *acriollado*. Means he's become one of them. It's complimentary or derogatory depending on who says it. If Alejandro Diaz says it, it's an expression of approval, but if *you* did you'd be saying the guy's gone native.'

Letting sleep come: inviting it, while memory crowded in and held it at bay. The others' fault, for having set the old reels

44

running. He knew it would be as well to get some sleep, because there mightn't be much chance of it tonight on the water, with five of them plus all the gear packed into the inflatable's twelve-foot length.

Still recalling the *vizcacha* episode; and the most impressive recollection was of Francisca's immediate quick and violent reaction. Initial shock, then the blaze of anger: the way she'd flung herself on to her horse and charged at Robert, spurring the horse into a gallop, clearly intending to run him down – no holds barred, no thought of consequences.

The key to Francisca? That shock in her face; most young girls would have turned away, covered their faces, wept. She must have felt the same impulses, he guessed – he'd seen them there, fast as a camera-flash, the stricken look, horror; then she's snapped out of it and *acted*.

As she had with Robert? Accepting her father's guidance – because it was her inclination to obey him, support him, make up for what her mother had *not* been to him; this reinforcing her admiration – one might assume – of 'Roberto's' own forcefulness, a quality of ruthlessness (which her father certainly had in abundance) matching her own?

In her case, Andy thought, 'decisiveness' might be a better word for it. Having decided what she wanted, or how she was going to achieve whatever aim she had in mind, that was the way she moved.

They'd arranged a secret rendezvous, in the summer of 1973/4, at the old Sandrini place, which was on a point of Tom Strobie's land but between Diaz and MacEwan territory. He'd ridden over from La Madrugada, and she'd come southwest, a much longer ride, from her father's *estancia* Santa María. The clandestine meeting in the wilds of nowhere, as far as he remembered his own feelings about it at the time, was a basically innocent conspiracy born of the strong attraction they had for each other, the fact they revelled in each other's company and preferred not to have anyone else around, but at the same time it wouldn't have been so far removed from much younger kids meeting in the branches of an apple tree or in a seashore cave – a place to themselves, away from adult

45

interference. The attraction between them was sexual, obviously, and compulsively exciting, but at no time had he consciously acknowledged to himself that sex was the purpose of the rendezvous.

There'd have been little shelter in the Sandrini place in winter. (He'd suggested to the SBS that they might use it, but that was something else entirely.) It was a ruin, none of it snow-proof or wind-proof, and even in summer the wind never stopped blowing; but the *peóns'* quarters – a bunkhouse with a cooking and eating area added – had survived better than the house, at least the stone walls were intact. Strobie could have fixed this part up, easily enough, if he'd wanted to, but its only use would have been as a *puestero's* shack and he had no need of one right out at this remote corner.

Sheep had spent time in here, and they'd used the main house as well. Francisca scraped the floor with a pane of window-glass, while Andy built a fire. She'd brought *chorizos*, a kind of spicy sausage, and *galletas* – small rolls of hard, unleavened bread, and his own contribution had been wine. He'd built the fire with scraps of wood and poplar branches from the withered trees which had been planted to screen this place but were either dead or dying; he'd got it started with the aid of a sprinkling of lighter-fuel, and it was taking hold at last. For ten minutes he'd been crouching at it, blowing a smoulder into flame.

'Andy, this is no time to bust a gut, you know.'

He'd finished the job.

'We're away now.' Getting to his feet; winded from acting as a bellows. Francisca, who'd been waiting close behind him, began to unbutton her shirt; she put her arms back for him to slide it off her shoulders. Wordless: as if this *was* what they'd come here for, both known it when they'd planned the rendezvous. His mouth on hers – wide mouth, drawing him in, his a little higher than hers because he still had his boots on and she'd kicked hers off. He felt her hands working at his belt buckle; turning her wet lips from his then, leaning back to give her hands room and for her bra to fall away; then *his* hands. He'd murmured something about her breasts and she asked,

46

'Just *noticed*, did you?' Wrenching his breeches open, starting on his shirt as he crouched to undress her: snakeskin belt, jodhpurs, uncovering her small, sleek waist, belly silky under his palms, nipples risen to his tongue; she'd asked him later, 'Would you have started if I hadn't?'

He would have, of course. He'd dreamed of her that way – night dreams and daydreams – and the excitement had been almost intolerable, he remembered, anticipating the rendezvous. He'd have made some kind of move, he'd have *tried*. . . . But without confidence in how she'd react. He'd have been cautious and therefore awkward, half expecting a rebuff and therefore easily rebuffed – might well have bungled it. Partly because she was *so* exquisite; he'd had the feeling he'd be reaching for the moon, for something like the ultimate even before he'd started living. Whereas she had known, had been absolutely sure – and had taken the initiative because she'd known there was a chance he might *not*.

Tom Strobie had said, a few weeks after that rendezvous in the back of beyond, 'Heard you were up at the Sandrini wreck, Andy. You and – h'm?'

'Heard?'

'One of my *peóns* – Anselmo, know the fellow? He saw we had visitors, so he rode up for a closer look and recognised both horses. He's one of the old brigade; see a nag once, he'll know it ten years later. He'd know it was your horse even if he didn't recognise *you*, boy.'

'I see . . .'

'He's a wise bird, though. You can rely upon it, I'm the only person he'll have told. But all the same –' the old man's hand had fastened on Andy's shoulder – 'more remote a place is, more conspicuous you are in it. Might be no one there in half a year, but—'

'We met for an *asado*, Tom.'

Asado meaning 'barbecue'.

'Surely. I'm telling you it's not a good spot even for that. Anyway, not with that particular young woman. For whom as you know I have a soft spot, a warm admiration – as well as respect, Andy, for your taste and good fortune. So' – he'd turned away – 'if you want some place to meet her, meet her here. I shan't play gooseberry. I'm out and about a lot, you know.'

He'd wondered then, right at the time, what might have been Strobie's motivation in making this offer, of which a lot of people would have been highly critical but of which he and Francisca had taken full advantage all through that summer. Strobie's paternal attitude to him, and the fact it had spread now to embrace Francisca as well, was hardly enough. Then a clue had emerged from one of Tom's rare personal revelations, the story of a young and adored wife who'd died of polio when Tom had been away at sea on the other side of the world, and of whom Francisca reminded the old man. Over the years since, he'd come to accept that this had been the heart of it.

Cloudsley stirred them at dusk, for a bite to eat before moving down to the lake shore. The first job was to unpack the boat, fit its deckboards and inflate it, and unpack and prepare the outboard. They'd done it before, of course, as a drill and in the dark, working to a stopwatch, and it took only a few minutes. The boat's fabric was black, the motor's pod and even its short shaft dull grey, gas-tank and spare jerrycan the same; there was no reflective surface anywhere.

West asked as they started loading – Tony Beale meanwhile checking wiring points and plugging in headsets for'ard and aft – 'We liable to meet patrols on this pond, Harry? At the border, maybe?'

'Yup.' Cloudsley hefted a pack, slung it down to Hosegood, who stowed it snugly against the inflatable's swollen port side. The next went end-on to it, balancing a similar stowage-plan on the other side. Down here at the water's edge it was already dark; the sun's last efforts still lit the heights above them but were cut off from the valley floor by the ridge they'd spent the day on. Cloudsley said, 'We'll tell 'em we've nothing to declare. Take the green channel. But – patrol or no patrol – no ruckus, remember. We lie doggo, or we run for it.' He added as if to himself, 'Circumstances permitting, of course.'

Policy, dictated from on high: no firefights or killings, except in self-defence, last resort. The enemy was to be avoided, not confronted, and the SBS motto *By Stealth, By Guile* was to be the keynote of the operation. Each man except for Andy was carrying an Ingram 9-mm Model 11 machine-pistol with suppressor, but the hope was to take them out of the country clean, unused, their 30-round magazines all full.

'Looks like the lot.' West straightened. 'What'll *we* do – swim?'

'We sit on top of the cargo, Jake. But you can swim behind if you like. Tony—' Beale was climbing into the bow: Cloudsley told him, 'Get set with your PNG.'

Passive Night Goggles: a smaller type than the helo pilots had used, but effective up to eight hundred metres, with the image in green and black. Cloudsley continued his distribution of body-weights: Hosegood already in his appointed place. 'Andy, you next. On the centreline.' Peering down. . . . 'Now you, Jake. Right. . . . Last, but very far from least' – easing himself over, sliding into the stern – 'the driver.'

'Nothing sophisticated like remote control, Harry?' Andy suggested. 'From up front so you'd see where you were going?'

'Waste of space. This is all we need.' Holding up a headset – small plugs to fit in his ears and a spring-loaded throat microphone. It plugged into wiring that was integral to the boat's starboard blister and connected him with Tony Beale who was at the sharp end with the goggles.

'Any more fares?'

Nobody offered. The boat lurched from the shift of Cloudsley's weight as he swung back on the lanyard. The outboard coughed, then roared, went a lot quieter as he shut down the soundproofing glassfibre lid over the starter mechanism. Shoving off then, Beale with a long leg out against rock.

Gathering way. Black lake water lifting, rolling away in a wide, smooth 'v', while under the boat's stern the water shivered, fragmenting, glassing over again before it was lost to sight. Ahead the mountainsides rose towering, forming a huge canyon which, from this beetle-like object creeping into it, was daunting, overpowering in its immensity. Cloudsley opened the throttle another notch: you felt the surge, and the engine-note rose but there was no significant increase in volume. Keeping one hand on the tiller Cloudsley removed his cap, pushed the headset on and settled the plugs in his ears, adjusted the position of the tiny mike against his throat. Cap on again, pulling it down all round, and its flaps down over the earplugs; he spoke quietly, the words indistinguishable even though he was only a few feet away. 'D'you hear me, Tony?'

No answer. Beale didn't have his set on yet, he was still getting the Litton's PNG in focus. Cloudsley waited, then winced when the colour sergeant said in a normal tone of voice, 'Testing comms. . . .'

'Keep it *down,* Christ's sake!'

'Sorry, Harry.'

'And don't suck your teeth, Tony, d'you mind?'

With a throat microphone you had to be careful how you salivated.

Bloody cold. And you couldn't swing your arms or stamp your feet, could hardly twitch a muscle. It would have been much worse without *ponchos* – and in Andy's case, thermal under-wear – but it was still tooth-rattling cold. They all had their caps on with earflaps down, muffling the steady swish of lake water, hum of the night wind and the steady grumble of the muffled motor, which was pushing the boat along at a fair rate of knots and hadn't – yet – faltered even once. It could happen at any moment, of course; the others had made gloomy prophecies, earlier on, all of them having had unpleasant experiences at other times with outboards, apparently. Moun-tainsides rose sheer to a starless, black infinity, and Andy thought about the coming day, the Argentine side. If they made it that far, they'd be landing thirty miles inside enemy territory, and then would come the moment of truth when you'd discover whether the HALO dropper's mission had been successful.

Strobie might well be dead. He was of an age when people died – quite apart from the fact that his survival of the last forty years had been fairly miraculous. There wasn't anyone who'd have written, sent the news if Tom had died or been removed to hospital, whatever. Francisca, he guessed, would have kept in touch with the old man. (Knowing she would have been seeing him from time to time had made that paragraph in his letter – the accusation of having given her up too easily – exciting, full of a sort of fustrated hope, when he'd read it. Guessing it might not have been only Tom speculating, that she might have said something to inspire it.) Strobie really loved her, and she'd enjoyed that rough, no-strings affection; but she wouldn't have written. She'd have done whatever might have been necessary for Tom – nursed him, or helped in any other way including burying him; but she wouldn't have brought him, Andy MacEwan, into it. She would *not*, in fact, have said anything to make Strobie write that in his letter. The hope had been wishful thinking, hadn't taken account of the kind of person she was – that she'd made her choice, picked her bed to lie in, would be loyal to that decision. Roberto's bed; and Roberto in close cahoots with Alejandro Diaz – who'd made *his* choice too, was playing for high stakes, for power, both of them – or you could say all three of them, because Francisca would be a part of it, wouldn't have allowed herself to be shut out – the Diaz-MacEwan alliance with its future riding on the outcome of this fight for the Falklands alias Malvinas.

The silence woke him. As startlingly as a gunshot might have.

Not *total* silence. The motor had cut out, that was all.

He loosened his earflaps. Wind's gusty thrum, water lapping, a soft thumping from under the inflatable's flat bottom; and the others stirring, questioning. Cloudsley growled,

'Quiet. Get down. *Right* down. . . .'

Trying to make himself smaller, between West's crouching, bony length and the awkward heap that was Geoff Hosegood doing his best to become invisible. Hearing Cloudsley ask 'Where is it now?' – using his intercom with Beale – and a very quiet reply whispered from that end. It wasn't engine failure, anyway: he guessed the PNG had picked up some hazard out there ahead. He was fully awake now, shedding the aftermath of a dream in which they'd been burying old Tom, Alejandro Diaz scattering a handful of dirt into the open grave and Francisca, old, wrinkled, a crone shrouded in a *mantilla*, clinging to her father's arm. Still enough reality about it so that he'd wondered, since waking in this tense silence, why Roberto hadn't been there too. . . .

Cloudsley informed them in a whisper, 'Patrol boat passing, right to left, four hundred yards ahead. Haven't seen us yet.'

Andy heard the chugging beat of a diesel engine.

Beale hissed, 'Turned towards us.'

Cloudsley shifted, squirming round without rising, groping for the lid of the outboard's glassfibre pod. He flipped it up, found the wooden toggle and took up the lanyard's slack against the spring. Ready to start up; then to open the throttle and run for it.

If this was the border, Andy thought – which it might be, to justify the presence of a patrol – you'd only have to retire a mile or so into Chilean waters, then try again later. The Argies surely wouldn't follow very far that way. Chileans and Argies had certain differences of opinion, some of them of long standing, and the Argies wouldn't want to create problems on a second front – unless they'd consider 'hot pursuit' worth the diplomatic consequences.

'Three hundred yards.'

No way on the boat now: just drifting, turning slowly. The diesel sound seemed very close – so close that he was straining his eyes into the dark and expecting to see the approaching boat at any second. Watching for it with his head down, watching under his eyebrows, knowing from wildfowling experience how a face, the whites of eyes, could show up.

Wondering how close Cloudsley was going to let them come before he made his break for it. Could be leaving it a bit late, Andy thought: for instance, if the outboard didn't fire on the first pull – which obviously they'd hear. . . .

'Stopped!'

The diesel was still audible, but idling, chuntering to itself in neutral. But the boat would still be closing in this way, because its momentum would be carrying it on. You could imagine them with their glasses up, trying to decide whether one of them had actually seen something or only imagined it. A minute ago – or however long ago it had been – a flicker of broken water might have caught an Argentine eye. Another question sprang to mind: how many of them? Few enough for this team to handle, if they came in close?

Probably. Andy thought the four men with him in the inflatable could probably deal with three times their own number, and think little of it.

But – if they shone a light this way, saw the huddle of crouched intruders, wouldn't they open fire, look for identification later?

Cloudsley might have had the same thought. He whispered, 'Geoff. Jake. Be ready to return fire.'

Shifting: Ingram automatics emerging from the heavy layers of *peóns'* clothing. The Ingrams' thirty-round magazines emptied themselves in one and a half seconds, Cloudsley had told him; it'd take that long to cut a man in half.

Quiet movement from Cloudsley now. Getting set to jerk the lanyard back, shatter the night's peace. . . . But the other sound thickened: there was a wrench into gear, then a stronger, deeper beat. Cloudsley's head lifted an inch as he listened to whatever Beale was whispering over the intercom. He'd grunted an acknowledgement; then he held the mike away from his neck for long enough to tell them, 'Moving on, leftward. Sit tight, keep quiet.'

Five or six minutes – or three or four – dragged like ten or twenty.

'Tony?'

'Yes. All clear.' Beale let out a breath as if he'd been holding it since yesterday. The diesel sound had faded some time ago. He added, 'Well out of sight, Harry.'

'Some guide, we have.' Holding the microphone clear again, and jossing, pulling Andy's leg. 'Leads us smack into an Argie patrol!'

'Balls.'

'Did *Mr* MacEwan make some remark then?'

Chuckles: humour not difficult to trigger in the sharp relief from tension. Andy said, falling into the trap and defending himself unnecessarily, 'I don't know a damn thing about this Chilean side, you know that.'

'We aren't *on* the Chilean side, chum.'

'How d'you know?'

'Distance run, for one thing. For another, half an hour ago there was a patrol boat showing lights – inshore, no threat, we let you layabouts sleep on. But a boat showing lights would've been Chilean, wouldn't it? The Argies are the ones playing silly buggers. . . . We'll push on, now. Keep your goggles peeled, Tony.'

The outboard wouldn't start.

Cloudsley swore, and Hosegood murmured, 'Have to get out and push.' West said, 'Many a true word. . . .'

'How far to go, Harry?'

Beale had asked it, but no one answered – except the motor, responding to about the sixth pull. Relief was enormous: it would have been a long, long paddle to shore, and then a very long trek indeed, carrying all the gear and missing by maybe two or three days the rendezvous which he *hoped* Start would have set up. But – say thirty miles to go, and there were roughly seven hours of darkness left. A lot to be said for long nights and short days, at that. If nothing else delayed them – and the outboard's reluctance to start did shake one's confidence in it, somewhat – they'd make it with time in hand.

'*If*. . . .

The boat was gathering way, and Cloudsley was turning it back on course. Beale using the PNG, searching for any sign of the patrol returning. But if it was far enough away to be out of range of those goggles its own engine noise would cover the distant sound of this one. Which sounded OK now, and the stink of petrol which had been strong a minute ago had gone.

No need for any guide. Navigation was a matter of keeping roughly in the middle, mountains equidistant right and left. . . . Cloudsley, however, knew more about it than he'd let on, and wasn't surprised when Tony Beale picked up an island with the PNG. He put the tiller over, slanting towards it on Beale's directions, and after about ten minutes rock loomed over them, a whaleback shape with stunted firs like bristles along its spine. He slowed the engine as they approached, then cut it and let the boat drift in.

'Hope the bloody thing'll start again. . . . Look, I'm landing here. Geoff, come with me. Bring those binos. You come too, Andy. Jake, fill up the tank, will you. Tony, you might break out some nutty and a thermos or two.'

'Nutty' meaning chocolate, a sailors' word for it. The thermos packs were disposable, and easy to dispose of too, when you had deep water all around.

The landing was on rock, and steep. Cloudsley led, then Hosegood, then Andy. A slightly dangerous scramble, then, aiming for the top, a tree all on its own. All the trees bent exactly the same way and looked as if they'd been chewed; there was hardly any soil, and he guessed they'd be rooted in crevices in which wind-borne dirt had settled; wind-borne seeds as well. Cloudsley explained, 'At this end the lake gets wider. And we want to land in its northwest corner, right, Andy? So I need a course to steer – that's to say, I know the compass course but I need a mark or marks to steer by.'

His compass would be useless in the boat, because of magnetic interference from the outboard and other metallic elements in the gear. Up here they were well away from such influences.

'OK.' He had his landmarks. 'That'll do it.'

Hosegood, meanwhile, had been using binoculars to examine that end of the lake, and found nothing except for some lights on the southern shore. Which figured: there was a settlement there, the map had shown it. Cloudsley pointed into the darkness. Resting the other hand on Andy's shoulder he said, 'We steer that way now, about six hours' run. *If*—' He moved that hand, rapped his forehead with its knuckles and muttered, 'Touch wood. . . . *If* our blessed motor keeps up its so-far impeccable performance. . . .'

4

Shropshire, rocking through a moderate northeasterly wind and sea, had the oil-tanker *Tidebreak* fine on her bow and about one cable's length ahead. Distance lessening fast. John Saddler was in the bridge wing but only watching, leaving the conning of the ship to David Vigne, his navigator. From this close, the 27,000-ton tanker's heaving stern, looming white-fringed through the dark, looked about the size of the Palace of Westminster.

About which the less said the better. BBC news bulletins had referred to members of Parliament objecting to the sinking of the enemy cruiser *Belgrano*. And the loss of life from that action was shocking, certainly, had shocked everyone here in the Task Force, let alone at Westminster; but for an explanation of it those people should address themselves to the Argentine naval command, not to Northwood or Downing Street. . . . Saddler heard Vigne's calm tones bringing the ship up into position, using the bridge-wing microphone, its lead plugged into a socket in the windbreak. *Shropshire*'s stem about to overlap the oiler's stern. . . . Distance apart had to be one hundred feet, which in the dark and a lively sea called for skill and concentration from the man handling her: the evolution being known as an RAS – replenishment at sea – and in this case an RAS(L) – 'L' for liquid: oil, and fresh water. They'd completed an RAS(S) for 'solids' earlier in the night, topping up magazines and shellrooms and other stores, but the fuel replenishment was a routine carried out every forty-eight hours or so as a matter of course. This time, perhaps, with an added sense of purpose: London had given the Admiral authority to go ahead with the San Carlos landing plan, at his own discretion – which meant, in effect, subject to weather conditions being suitable.

There'd be a decision, Saddler guessed, any minute now.

'Stop both engines. . . .'

This was the modern way of doing it. Instead of creeping up, gradually adjusting speed to match the tanker's, you came up fast, stopped engines and let the ship's momentum carry her on into position, and exactly as she got there you put the screws ahead again at the required twelve knots. It was a faster and neater way of doing it, and practice made perfect. . . . From the wheelhouse now, three decks down in the ship, a voice from the loudspeaker reported, 'Both engines stopped, sir,' and Vigne lifted his microphone again to order, 'revolutions one-zero-four.' Those revs would give her twelve knots when he ordered the engines to be put ahead again – which he'd do as the fuelling points arrived opposite each other. A single light glowed down there on the upper deck where a small party of seamen and engineers waited; there was a corresponding light on the tanker's deck. *Shropshire* arriving in the right spot about – *now.* . . .

'Half ahead both engines.'

Kingsmill leant over the windbreak and bellowed into the wind, '*Duck!*'

A Coston gun barked from the tanker's deck, and the weighted end of a line soared across the gap. A Coston shot could go wild, and the weight was heavy, which was why you ducked. In fact the line had fallen across the foc's'l: a sailor snatched it up, ran aft with it, bringing it to the fuelling point. The Coston cracked again and a second line came flying.

'Steer zero-four-zero.'

Yesterday the amphibious force – the assault ships *Fearless* and *Intrepid*, with LSL's – landing ships logistic – plus *Canberra* and a supporting train of STUFT ships – the letters stood for 'ships taken up from trade' – had joined the Task Force. The day before, the *Atlantic Conveyor* had come with a reinforcement of twelve Harriers, while another four had since flown in, direct flight from the UK via Ascension with mid-air refuelling; so there were now thirty-five Harriers here. Every one of which would be needed, Saddler thought. He leant over the windbreak, seeing them hauling in on the line, dragging the hawser across from the oiler. It would be secured to the jackstay fitting, an eyebolt on the superstructure, and at the tanker's end it would be triced up high so there'd be a slant downward to the destroyer and the fuelling hose, slung from a 'traveller', would come rushing down to be received and connected to the fuelling intake. The other line, up on the foc's'l, was for a check on the ships' distance apart, one end secured to the oiler's rail while on *Shropshire*'s bow an oilskinned sailor held it taut and watched the flags that marked it at twenty-foot intervals.

'Revolutions one-zero-zero.'

Freshwater hose on its way over now, running down the hawser just as the fuel line had. Saddler watched, as far as the dark allowed, thinking that every one of those jump-jets was going to be needed because if the landing was to go ahead – if the Admiral was satisfied that the weather outlook was favourable – then that small force of Harriers was about to take on the entire Argentine air force. The Argies hadn't been beaten in the air – hadn't even been scratched in the air – which right from the start had been seen as a prerequisite for troop landings, for the simple reason they'd stayed out of sight. You could bet they wouldn't stay away much longer, once the landing force moved in.

Fuelling was now in progress, and both ships having settled down to it had now recommenced zigzagging, a long-legged zigzag pattern with alterations of course made in ten-degree steps. A refinement of the art of RAS, necessitated by the submarine threat. Altering now – both ships, this one very small-feeling in such proximity to the other's bulk. . . . Dark sea leaping, thundering between them. John Saddler, looking down into that seething torrent, was thinking now that it was about time *Shropshire* had a mail delivered. The arrival of letters and newspapers was always a fillip to morale. Not that morale was bad – far from it, and their successful action against the blockade-runner had sent it soaring; but it tended to have its ups and downs, and boredom had to be kept at bay, after so long at sea and with so little, so far, to show for it.

'Captain, sir?'

The door into the wing had banged open; Saddler turned, identifying himself in the dark, 'Yes?'

'You're wanted on the Secure Net, sir!'

'Right. Thank you.' *Running.* . . . The Secure Net was the scrambled communication line which the Admiral used for conversations with his captains, and you could only take a call or initiate one in the MCO, main communications office, next door to the Ops Room. Lift gates slammed shut; in pitch darkness he pressed the 'down' button, and the floor seemed to drop away under his feet.

Like a hangman's platform. Except that when he hit the bottom he was still alive. Passing the Ops Room entrance, and into the MCO. 'Morning, Chief.' He took the telephone from Chief Yeoman of Signals Harriman. 'Saddler here.'

'John, this is Willy.'

Not the big white chief himself, after all. This was a senior member of the great man's staff. Telling Saddler crisply, 'Point one, John – Operation Sutton is *on*.'

'Sutton' being the code-name for the San Carlos landing.

'D-Day, subject to weather, twenty-first. Meaning we move in tonight. Your orders are on the way, but – point two – conference on board *Fearless* this forenoon at ten. Weather predictions'll be complete by then. Can do?'

'Can indeed. Thank you, Willy.'

He replaced the telephone. CPO Harriman asked, 'All right, sir?'

Several pairs of eyes were focused on him, waiting for an answer – a statement, a hint, a clue. . . . He told them,

'Depends how you look at it. It's all right for you, Chief. *I'm* required to attend another bloody conference.'

His caginess was less in the interests of security than of maintenance of morale. If he'd said *We're landing the commando brigade tomorrow morning,* and there was a postponement – for weather reasons or any other – it would be a let-down. Those signalmen, wno'd have passed on the red-hot 'buzz' as straight from the skipper's mouth, would have suffered a loss of face.

After this *Fearless* conference, if the intention was confirmed by then, he'd make an announcement in the proper way, over the ship's broadcast.

The RAS had been completed. *Shropshire* and *Tidebreak,* with the Type 22 frigate *Boreas* in company now, were steering northeast towards the battle group. Saddler, with half an hour to spare before he'd have to get dressed up for his helicopter trip to *Fearless,* was taking a walk around the ship, dropping in on this and that department at random, but mostly picking ones he'd missed out on his last solo 'walk-about'. He'd gone aft along 01 Deck, visiting the canteen, sickbay, galley and servery, dining hall, then over to the starboard side to the Seacat transmitting station. The port Seacat director had been fixed up and was fully operational now, Vaughan had reported – which was a relief, even if one didn't have such a hell of a lot of faith in the Seacat missile system. You had to make yourself trust it, because it was all you had – for close-range defence against anything like an Exocet. The petty officer in the TS, name of Hobbs, asked him, 'We *ever* going to put our lads ashore, sir?'

'Oh.' Saddler turned from the TV monitor. 'I'd say you can expect that pretty soon now. With the right weather conditions, of course.' He changed the subject. 'How's your family bearing up, Hobbs? Heard from your wife lately?'

Out – having had a run-down on the Hobbs family's house-moving problems – and down to 02 Deck for a call at the Seaslug missile test equipment room. As distinct from Seacat, which was a close-range system of air defence, Seaslug was the ship's surface-to-air long-range weapon, designed to cope with fast, high-flying aircraft. The Seaslug magazine occupied most of this deck, from the checkroom amidships right to the launchers on the stern. It was something like a car-deck in a ferry – except it was gleaming white and packed with the missiles ranged on their trolleys, which could be shifted around by remote control, hydraulics worked from a control panel in the MTER – to move them out to the launchers, withdraw them or shuffle them any other way, like a move to the checkroom for maintenance. They travelled at high speed and you wouldn't want to be in there when it was happening. The missiles themselves were sharp-nosed, predatory looking, with white bodies but a delicate shade of pink on wings and fins.

Carter, a fleet chief petty officer with red hair and deepset eyes, asked him, 'Reckon we'll get to poop some off, sir?'

'Bound to, Mr Carter.' Looking past him through plate glass into the checkroom. 'When the Argie air force shows up, eventually.' Thinking, *Not that Seaslug's likely to be much use to us.* . . . Forward of the checkroom was an extension of the magazine called Crated Stowage, where missiles still rested in their protective cases. The entire magazine deck took up a very large proportion of the ship's interior, and it was also a highly explosive space: if an Exocet struck here – or for that matter lower down, below it. . . .

He thought, briefly, of the SBS section who by now would be inside the Argentine. But even if they did their job to perfection, there would still – as Cloudsley had admitted – be the missiles already deployed on the airfields.

'What about the Bootnecks, sir? We going to let *them* loose, some time?'

Bootnecks – derived from the older term 'Leathernecks' – meant Royal Marines. Saddler assured him, 'Can't be long now. Probably *very* soon.'

Donald Sale arrived then. He was a lieutenant, one of Hank

Vaughan's bright sparks in the Weapons Electrical department. Sale was a BSc, his immediate superior Jimmy Lampard BSc and AMIEE, while Vaughan himself had so many letters after his name he could never remember half of them. Saddler spent a few more minutes in there, discussing the new British sea-skimming missile Sea Eagle, which when it emerged from development stages was likely to put Exocet in the shade. Sale then gave him some news: the 965 radar, the long-range air warning set, had 'thrown a wobbly'. Vaughan had men working on it, had been trying to contact Saddler to report it as out of action, meanwhile. . . . Leaving the MTER – more phlegmatic than depressed by that news – he went down one deck to visit the machinery control room; and considered then going aft to the Chinese laundry but decided against it because conversations with Mr Wu tended to be lengthy and difficult to cut short, and he didn't have all that much time left. Instead he paid a quick visit to the computer room – another area where you wouldn't want a missile impacting, since it would completely paralyse the ship – and then down to 04 Deck to the gunnery TS, where they deserved a visit and a pat on the back after the success of the previous night.

He was asked the same question, or some version of it, everywhere he stopped. *When do we put the booties in?*

Natural enough. It was what they'd all come out here for, what would have to be done before they could go home again. Saddler very much hoped that after this morning's conference he'd be able to give them the news they wanted. He was on his way up through the ship, with five levels to climb to reach the bridge, when he heard the broadcast 'Hands to flying stations. . . .' So he'd timed it well, because that pipe was in preparation for his transfer by helo to the assault ship *Fearless*. He could fit in a brief visit to the bridge now, a word with Kingsmill and Vigne – and with Vaughan about the defective radar – before climbing into his goon-suit for the flight.

5

Hosegood stared down the rocky, fissured landscape, muttered, 'Bloody moonscape, innit!'

They'd trekked uphill from where they'd landed, humping all the gear including the deflated and repacked boat. No petrol, only the empty tank and empty jerrycan. Andy didn't ask for reasons: there wasn't breath for chat, only a mass of equipment to be hauled up steep gradients and in a hurry. Nobody had said anything, but they'd all been conscious that minutes counted – daylight growing, a rendezvous to be kept, a long cross-country transit after that. By heading to the right from the lake shore they could have gone *down*hill, into a valley with a river that was fed from the lake: trees, green country. Whereas from here now, having made the long climb, the lie of the land eastward was only a gradual descent and not green at all. Grey dawn light increasing from the east stippled the broken, rock-strewn terrain with shadow, emphasising the moonscape look on which Geoff Hosegood had commented.

Cloudsley muttered, 'So what now. . .?'

They'd piled the gear, and were looking less at the scenery than for what they'd expected would be here in it. Primary requirement being horses. Cloudsley using binoculars, slowly pivoting; and Andy having to face the implications of that question – or rather, comment: that from this plateau the reception party should have been in sight.

Would have been – if they'd been here at all.

Cloudsley said it again, as a question: 'Andy – what now?'

He thought, *We'd be hearing them, too, if they were anywhere near*. Thinking of the sheep; never having known any that were mute. He asked, 'Borrow your glasses?'

'Won't help you any.' Passing them. 'Bugger-all, down there.' He and Beale exchanged glances, expressions of sharp disappointment matching each other. Hosegood frowning, sucking at his moustache. Andy, sweeping slowly with the glasses and finding nothing, heard Jake West mutter 'Looks like more slog for the Sherpas', and Cloudsley's growl of 'Unfortunately there isn't one kilo of gear in this lot we could do without'. Obviously his thoughts had been turning to alternatives – looking for any that might exist, thereby admitting that this did seem to be a dead end. Beale was talking to him now, quietly, making some kind of suggestion, but it was only noises-off while Andy wiped the lenses of the glasses clean and started his search again – despite a growing acceptance that Cloudsley was right, nothing here except themselves and league upon league of 'bloody moonscape'.

It amounted to being stranded. A hell of a long way from anywhere, and with about a ton of gear to shift.

A hand on his shoulder, and Tony Beale's voice. . . . 'May as well face it, Andy Mac. Doesn't have to be your fault, y'know. All we know, Lieutenant Start may've run into some fuck-up.'

But he was remembering something else: something vital. . . .

There was supposed to be a *mojón* hereabouts – down that slope, maybe a couple of miles down. A *mojón* was a stone cairn: you came across them now and then in these remote parts, old survey beacons from heaven knew how long ago. The Indians, when Indians had populated the territory, had used them as markers. And there should have been one *here*. One of a set of aerial photographs had shown it, and he'd mentioned it in the verbal message which Monkey Start had memorised for Strobie. If he hadn't been in a state of panic in the past few minutes – a desperate anxiety to find the horses, to be able to say casually to Cloudsley 'There they are. . .', it was the *mojón* he'd have been looking for, for a landmark. On that bare slope, nothing would have been easier to spot. So either they'd come to the wrong place – which was impossible because they'd followed a compass course after landing at exactly the right place on the lake shore. . . .

Coordinates wrong on the aerial survey?

But this light was still tricky, a contribution on its own to the 'moonscape' look. And the coordinates could *not* have been wrong, for God's sake, the whole thing had been checked out, had been checked and re-checked. Cloudsley had told him, 'We're belt-and-braces men, whenever we can be. That's how we get away with – well, whatever. . . .' The phrase in Cloudsley's voice echoed in his memory just as he began to realise – *saw*, in a way, but not exactly, it was a matter of applying imagination to the visual process, guesswork to what was actually discernible – that the expanse he was looking at might not be a simple continuation of the down-sloping scree, might be a lot farther away, beyond the edge of an escarpment, an escarpment they'd be standing on now. In which case there'd be a cliff-like drop, then more downward-sloping ground but at a much lower level – and a mile or more of dead ground intervening.

He turned, lowering the glasses. Simultaneously Cloudsley reached a decision.

'All right. We'll assume they've been delayed. In which case we'll meet up later, somewhere down that way. And since there's no time to waste, we'll start yomping.' He saw that Andy was waiting to interrupt. 'Well?'

'I think they're probably quite close.' He pointed. 'Just down there. Mind if I take a look?'

'Christ.' Cloudsley waved a hand downhill. 'We've been *looking*. I've looked, you've looked.' Glaring. 'Haven't we?'

They were all staring at him. He explained, 'I think a mile or so down there could be an edge to this escarpment. It looks like a slope running on for ever, but I don't think it can be. Mostly because there should be a *mojón* in plain sight from here.'

West asked – a mutter addressed to Geoff Hosegood – 'A what?'

'Remember, in the photograph?' Cloudsley nodded. Andy said, 'The fact it's not in sight is what woke me up to this. Could be a stretch of dead ground down there, at the foot of the escarpment – which surely is where they *would've* camped. . . .'

'Could be right.' Cloudsley had reached for the glasses and he was scowling into the small but powerful lenses. 'Doesn't show, but—'

'I'll go on ahead, Harry. OK? If they're there, and if there's a way up that's not too steep. . . .' The photographs, taken from above, hadn't shown any more than you could see now, and in both cases the apparent perspectives could be misleading. He was beginning to feel confident that his theory was right – that it was the only explanation that fitted. He suggested to Cloudsley, 'Quicker to bring some horses up, rather than try to move the gear ourselves at half the speed?'

Cloudsley's expression suggested that such decisions were for *him* to make, not his guest artist. But he nodded. 'All right.' Glancing round. 'One of you go with him. Geoff – '

'Better be me, Harry?' Jake West added, 'If Monkey's down there?'

Because Start, the HALO dropper, was his partner and might want him there. Cloudsley agreed. 'OK. While they're gone, the rest of us can start humping the stuff along. Say in five-hundred yard stages. Starting *now.*'

Beale moved toward the gear: 'Right. . . .' On the same wavelength, all of them, sharply aware they had to get to the missiles before the Argies deployed them. Or while there were still *some* there to be doctored. Andy understood and shared their impatience. Speed of transit depended on having horses; so did 'cover', a *safe* transit. And there was still no guarantee, you could be clutching at a non-existent straw. . . . Remembering another remark of Cloudsley's, something about there being mountains to climb between the start and finish of this operation, translating that figurative statement into reality, the prospect of what might still lie ahead was staggering. First to get there at all – even with the horses and with Strobie's help; then to get inside not only the base but the actual warehouse – hangar, store, whatever – and to do whatever they intended doing to the missiles, which from something Tony Beale had said to Cloudsley at one stage was apparently a dangerous operation in itself. Then to extract themselves – still undetected – and get away. Hundreds of miles of open country between them and the coast, so getting there would be a marathon on its own; and then there'd be the problem of getting *off* the coastline, which surely would be guarded. . . . The expression 'mind-boggling' didn't come near to doing it justice, and the nightmare aspect was suddenly more frightening because you were *here*, out on the limb which when you saw it at close quarters looked decidedly shaky.

Treat it – he thought – like you'd treat the Grand National course. One fence at a time. Like – now – finding the horses. . . .

He explained to West what a *mojón* was. Then answered another question, as they jogged downhill, about who owned the land below them. 'Family called O'Higgins. It's the northern end of their property, pretty useless except there's a small lake a bit to the southeast. Water's a problem, you know, it all falls in Chile, *that* side of the mountains.' You had to watch your footing as you ran. He added, 'It's not likely we'd meet anyone up here, though, this time of year. Most will have brought their sheep down into the valleys by now. We'll be all right – just – because luckily the weather's holding. Anyone seeing us might think we'd cut it pretty fine, but that's about all.' His words came in spasms as he trotted. 'Another couple of weeks, it'd be too late, you'd be getting blizzards. Then you lose animals, if they're still on the high ground.'

'Through what – the snow?'

'The cold, yes. Then foxes, when they're weakened. Pumas too, some areas.'

'Here?'

'Most likely. Not enough cover for them lower down. You'll see, it's just low scrub, *no* cover. But the pumas would make forays down there for food.'

'And you lose sheep to them?'

He grunted an affirmative. 'Used to hunt them – with rifles. They're worst when they've littered and the mother's teaching her cubs to kill. Instead of knocking off one animal for a meal she'll kill maybe a dozen – demonstrating the technique. Then you find the carcases just rotting.' He jumped a crack in the rock. 'They love sheep's tongues – that's another charming habit. You can find sheep wandering around blind with pain, dying from a gash in the throat where the tongue's been ripped out. . . . Hey, look *there*!'

No tongueless sheep. The edge of the escarpment.

Distantly, the land continued, but two or three hundred feet lower and buff-coloured instead of grey. From here it was obvious, but from fifty yards back it hadn't been. Slowing to a walk. . . . Fifty yards *ahead*, the rock ended and the land fell away abruptly – if you'd gone on running, you'd have needed a parachute. He was anxious again now – because there was no certainty of Strobie's people being down there. Tightness in the gut was fear of new disappointment: because *without* horses there'd be very little chance of getting there in time.

He'd let West pound on ahead of him. Heard him shout now, 'Andy, you're a bloody marvel!'

At the edge, he dropped on to all fours, beside the Marine. Seeing – like a dream come true – several hundred feet lower, a group of men round a fire, a wide scattering of greyish-white sheep like lice on a brown blanket, and – horses. . . .

Ten, at a quick count. Apparently wandering loose, but he knew they'd be hobbled. Getting his breath back, enjoying the sight of what amounted to salvation, thinking *Thank you, God* and telling Jake West in a voice aimed at sounding matter-of-fact, 'I knew old Tom wouldn't let us down.'

There'd be about a hundred sheep down there, he guessed. Hearing their voices now in the thin, cold air. They were almost as important as the horses. The one way, he'd realised, back in London, when they'd been struggling for a way of doing this – the *only* way for a group of men to cover a biggish distance here in Patagonia, openly and in daylight without attracting undue notice and suspicion, would be if they were

70

herding sheep. Especially at this time of year when flocks had to be brought down to lower pastures before the onslaught of winter. So he'd proposed it to the planners: to arrange to have horses to ride and sheep to drive – because otherwise you'd have been down to travelling on foot and by night only, and with so much gear it wouldn't have been practicable.

Now here it was – a wild thought translated into reality. He could see the *mojón* too. There were three men, one of whom would be Monkey Start. It seemed almost too good to be true: as if he'd waved a magic wand and seen his wish materialise.

Thanks to Tom Strobie, of course. To whom he had a few debts already.

'May as well find a way down, Jake.'

'There.' West pointed. 'OK?'

Forty yards to the left, the start of an old sheep trail, slanting down. Not that there'd be any logical reason for sheep to want to come up here, where they'd find nothing at all to eat; but sheep had never been great on logic. It was a track anyway, would have been used by pumas as well as sheep, by the long-legged Patagonian foxes and by an occasional human too, and it would be negotiable by horses, all right. He counted them again as he followed Jake down the track; he'd been right at the first count – ten. Two would be mounts for Strobie's *peóns*, the drovers who'd brought the sheep up here and would now be driving them back again, and Start and West would be taking another two. It left six for four men, so there'd be two that could be loaded with most of the gear.

The snag was still the lack of time. Sheep tended to move at their own pace, and you'd have to stay with them because you'd be conspicuous without them. There'd be no other reason for a gang of riders to be coming from nowhere, going *somewhere*, with a top-secret military installation not very far away.

They were halfway down when one of the three at the fire looked up and saw them. He jumped up, pointing. Then the others were on their feet too. Andy called, '*Buenas!*' and drew answering shouts – one clearly audible, '*Don Andrés!*' Then a gust of laughter and a kind of dance, a squat figure in a *poncho* hitting a taller one on the back . . . celebrating. Andy and Jake West trotting now, down on to the flat as the trio came to meet them; and that was Torres, Pepe Torres! 'Squat' was the word, all right: he was built like a tank but with a lower centre of gravity than most tanks; swarthy, four or five days' growth of beard – most of it grey, Andy noticed, realising that Tom Strobie's *mayordomo* couldn't be much less than fifty now.

'Don Andrés? Can it truly be Don Andrés?'

'Believe it or not, Don Pepe, it *is*. And very glad indeed to see you, after so long!'

He'd have the scruffy looks of some *puestero*, of course, and he was glad not be easily recognisable as Andrew MacEwan. Torres had seized both his hands: 'It has been a long time!'

A glistening of tears, for God's sake. . . . And now the other one – Andy didn't recognise him or remember his name, which was Félix – was bowing, while a smile twisted the craggy features: 'Don Andrés, your return brings us much joy.'

Older than Torres. A *Chino* – mixed Indian and Chilean blood; and he did remember him now. . . . Leaving one hand in the *mayordomo*'s grasp – mainly because it was trapped there – he gave the other to the old *peón*. Félix might not even be aware there was any fighting going on, but in any case he and Torres weren't welcoming a Brit, they were greeting a young friend of their *patrón*. He asked them both, 'How are things here? Your wives are well? Your children – how many now? And Don Tomás – his health is no worse?' 'Don Tomás' meaning Tom Strobie, of course. But in the interests of politeness there was a lot of ground to cover, while behind him he heard Jake West say, 'You made it then!' and Start's reply, 'You look like someone just dug you up, Jake.'

As if *he* looked so immaculate. . . .

Pepe Torres' family were all well. Don Tomás was – the thick hands spread – a little older, a little – hands waggling, suggesting uncertainty, disability. . . . 'Don Tomás is a father to us, Don Andrés, a true father! Do you know what he has done for us, did you perhaps have an account of it from him?'

What he did appreciate was that Tom had sent the one man he could most completely rely on – and whom he could least

72

spare – who could be trusted not only to carry out his instructions to the letter but also to keep his mouth shut and ensure Félix did the same. No *peón* would risk disobeying Pepe Torres. Andy got his hands back, finally. He said, 'I've heard nothing from him for a long time. What is it he's done?'

'Don Tomás has given me, my wife and our children, his own house.' Torres had pushed his face up close; the rank breath wasn't easy to stand up to. 'My own humble dwelling is now his residence. Because we are many and he is one man alone, he says, because he has no need of many rooms and no strength to climb stairs – as you will perhaps recall, Don Andrés, even before your own departure—'

'I remember.'

It had been a long time since Tom had used the stairs. He could get on a horse – but that was different, something he *had* to do. Andy remembered him asking Francisca – she'd sup-posedly been staying with friends somewhere else, for yet another weekend – 'How does it look up there? All dust and cobwebs?' The upper floor, under the red-painted tin roof, had been theirs, Andy's and Francisca's, that summer.

Torres was shouting, 'But imagine it, Don Andrés! What other *patrón*, other than Don Tomás, would display such generosity of the heart?'

'But this also' – Andy pointed at the horses and the sheep – 'and your own help to us, Don Pepe, to have come yourself when all the work is already on your shoulders – this too is generosity—'

'MacEwan' – Start's voice broke into the exchange of Spanish – 'how was the jump?'

He meant the para drop into the sea. When they'd last met Andy had been just starting his short, sharp period of training for it. He said, 'I managed to survive it, God knows how. . . . No problems your end?'

'None that lasted.' The SBS lieutenant did look a bit like a monkey. He was tanned, like the rest of them – pre-tanned – and bearded, with small, round eyes now red-rimmed by the wind. 'Some character, your old pal!'

'No beauty, is he?'

73

'Well.' Start shrugged, and told Jake West, 'Hadn't been in his shack two minutes, he'd read the note, then asked what exactly did I want. I told him: horses, and some sheep – please. He sat blinking at me, not much enthusiasm around, and I thought *Hell, he isn't going to play.* . . . But he read the letter again, and said, "All right. Meanwhile I take it you drink Scotch?" '

Andy said, 'Hasn't changed much, then.'

'No, he's the man you said he was. But' – Start checked the time – 'on the subject of horses, now. . . .'

Down to business: initially the question of how many horses to take up on the escarpment to bring down the loads. It was decided that Andy and Jake would go back up with four animals, and the whole party would then come down on foot, leading them. By that time, Torres said, he and Félix would have a meal ready. Two sheep had already been killed and butchered, and the fire was about right now. Two sheep seemed somewhat excessive, but Andy didn't argue. For one thing, they were already dead and dismembered. For another, Cloudsley had ordained that as soon as contact was made with the home team, nearly all their Service-issue rations would be either eaten or discarded – because they were civilians now, locals, would have to be able to pass close inspection if the worst came to the worst. Another factor was that in these low temperatures the meat wouldn't go off too quickly.

The *mayordomo* indicated Monkey Start with a jerk of one short, thick arm. 'This *señor* has told me he and another will be travelling by some other route, to some other place. So those horses we may not see again?'

'We have *pesos* in sufficiency, with which to pay Don Tomás.'

'Ah.' Torres beamed. 'I would have assumed as much, Don Andrés. No one could have doubted.' His relief was pretty obvious, all the same.

They could smell roasting mutton when they were coming

74

down the track an hour later, leading four burdened horses. Cloudsley said, 'That doesn't smell too bad.'

'It'll take some chewing. Those sheep have had a lot of exercise lately.'

Strobie wouldn't have been such a fool as to provide his best specimens, either.

'Forty miles, did you say, to the old guy's place?'

'Forty to his boundary fence. Another six, roughly, from there to the *estancia*.'

'Do we *have* to camp at night? Can't push on through?'

'Unfortunately we can't. Sheep'd scatter during the night – if they hadn't collapsed from exhaustion. We'll ride as long as it's light, then camp, start again at dawn. Cover a few miles today, then tomorrow dawn to dusk, then a second night and get there the day after.'

'Don't they use dogs in this country?' Tony Beale was looking down at the camp – at sheep and horses, men close round the fire, a pile of saddles and other gear near it. 'I mean sheepdogs?'

'You don't see many. Not around these parts anyway. It's cheaper to use Chileans. And the locals couldn't train a dog, they're bloody awful with animals.'

'D'you mean cruel?'

'Tony, you wouldn't believe it.'

Cloudsley said, 'Andy. Bear in mind, please, we don't want to hang around this camp any longer than we have to.'

'I'll tell Torres. I think he knows, anyway; Monkey was working on him. But we'll have to redistribute the gear, won't we? To only two horses – and our personal packs on the ones we're riding?'

'*One* pack-horse is all we'll have.'

'But there are ten in all, so—'

'Monkey and Jake will take three. One each, and one for the boat and the outboard.'

Silence, then, except for the plodding hooves, clattering sometimes on stone, the horses' hard breathing. Andy absorbing this new angle: having assumed until now they'd be keeping the inflatable with them, that it would be their transport out to the submarine when the time came. He looked back at Cloudsley. 'You certainly don't let cats out of their bags before you have to, Harry.'

'Come again?'

Knowing perfectly well what he'd said. . . . Andy explained it, though, and the big man looked surprised. 'Can't see it concerns you or me, old chum, if Monkey needs a boat for something or other. . .?'

'OK. . . .'

They weren't necessarily distrustful of him, he guessed. It was probably more a matter of not burdening him with information he didn't need to have. That was the easiest way to explain it to yourself, anyway.

At the camp, following a round of introductions and courteous Anglo-Hispanic exchanges, Cloudsley gave Start and West the job of unloading the four horses and getting their own ready. He mustered the others round the fire, where Félix was already cutting meat, and told Andy, 'Interpret this for me, please. First point – I want to move out as soon as we've eaten, if not sooner. Second – when we stop tomorrow evening, instead of spending that second night in camp I'd like to leave the sheep to these characters, and ride on, make it to Strobie's place before daylight. This feasible, and OK with him?'

'It's feasible. By tomorrow evening we should be within a few hours' ride of Tom's *estancia*, without sheep to slow us down.' He translated Cloudsley's proposal. Torres had no objection, but he pointed out that their route wouldn't be a straight line from here to Strobie, since they'd need to reach water on both evenings, for the sheep and horses' sake. Tonight he'd be aiming to reach Lago Perdido, the O'Higgins *puesto* there, and next evening another waterhole which had no shepherd's house near it but did have an enclosure for the stock.

Andy explained this. 'It'll add a few miles, that's all. Essential, anyway. And he agrees, he and Félix will bring the sheep along on the third day.'

Torres began to talk again, mostly with his mouth full,

76

grease running down his chin. They were sitting now, a rough half-circle, back a little from the fire's heat. He was suggesting that the six of them should split into two parties, each with roughly half the sheep, and put about a league between them. If they stayed in one group it wouldn't look right, nobody would waste so many herdsmen on such a small flock. As well as making this division, he'd send Félix off on his own to ride around as if he was searching for more strays.

'On O'Higgins land? He'd find Strobie sheep?'

The *mayordomo* smirked.

'There was a gate swinging open in the wind, Don Andrés. Some trespasser must have broken the lock. This would be how it happened that Strobie sheep ' – he pointed at them – 'these, had strayed through. We saw their ordure – Félix and I – and came to recover them before the snows.'

The sheep would all have Strobie ear-marks, of course. . . . Andy translated Torres' proposal to Cloudsley, who didn't much like it.

'More delay, damn it. Separating by five miles before we can make any progress where we *need* to go?'

'We'd only diverge a bit, then turn parallel. Me with one lot, Torres with the other – so each group has a Spanish speaker, everyone else keeps his mouth shut.'

'How many people are we likely to run into, for God's sake?' Cloudsley was looking exasperated, muttering that this wasn't bloody Oxford Street, while Andy asked Torres whether he thought there was any real risk of them being seen by anyone at all.

Torres pointed upward. 'Aeroplanes. Many here, these days.' Gesturing northeastward: 'They come from and to the new *aeródromo*.'

Cloudsley had caught the gist of that. He asked, 'Here? Might overfly us *here*?'

Tomorrow would be more probable, Torres said. Air activity was mainly in the north, and especially over Diaz territory, and chiefly by the kind of *avión* they called a Pucará. Cloudsley gave in: 'OK. We'll do it his way. Let's finish eating and get started – *soon*. Tell him that, will you?'

A minute or two later Tony Beale asked him some question about distances and directions, a point of detail in connection with the likelihood of air patrols coming near them on either the first or second days. The easiest way to answer it was to draw him a map, scratching outlines in the dirt with the end of a mutton bone. The long reach of O'Higgins land from the escarpment east to Tom Strobie's boundary fence; then Strobie territory, shaped like a lopsided kite, eight miles from west to east at its widest and fourteen from north to south, Tom's *estancia*, El Lucero – the name meant 'Morning Star' – was slightly below and to the right of centre; and about six miles northeast of it, in the top right corner, was the Sandrini ruin. At that point, the kite's northeast corner, you had MacEwan land to the east, Diaz land north and northeast. The missile dump and airbase was a lot farther north, northwest of the western Diaz paddocks. A sheep-station there, El Amanecér, had belonged to a family called Coetzee, who must now either have moved out altogether or sold that section to the government.

'It's poor land. I'd say they'd have been glad to offload it. 'Specially now when nobody's making any money out of sheep.'

'The Coetzees are not to be trusted, you said?'

'They're Afrikaners, by origin. Came around the start of the century from Cape Colony – getting away from *us*. . . . Quite a lot of Boers did, settled mainly around Sarmiento. They don't like anyone much, but mostly they hate the British.'

Beale nodded, studying the pavement artistry, refreshing his memory. 'I didn't think of it until now, but is Strobie's place that much smaller than yours or Diaz's?'

Andy nodded. 'He has about a hundred square miles. But what matters is how many sheep the land can carry. All the land south of Tom's *estancia* is low-lying, you see – with several good waterholes, and also a river of sorts on his southern border. He can keep more animals to the square league than you could anywhere on the Diaz land.'

Cloudsley began talking to Geoff Hosegood about ration packs. Meanwhile Monkey Start and Jake West had fixed up

78

their gear and horses, and they'd come over to the fire for some food. Cloudsley broke off his talk and warned them, 'Andy was right when he said this sheep-meat would be tough. It's like chewing old rope.'

Start had his mouth full of it. A map in one hand, a lump of dripping meat in the other. Chewing, folding the map one-handed then stuffing it away inside his *poncho*. . . . He mumbled, 'Not all that bad. For a guy who still has his own teeth.'

'Which way are you riding now, Monkey?'

Start looked surprised at the question. He looked from Andy to Cloudsley – who seemed not to have heard it. Start said, 'Doesn't matter, not all that much.' He asked West, 'Which way shall we go, Jake?'

West shook his head. 'Don't give a bugger.'

'You're right.' Cloudsley belched. 'Doesn't matter at all. Long as you finish up intact and in the right place. Wherever that might be.' He tossed away a bone. 'But now, Andy – can you persuade the *señors* to get off their bums and saddle up?'

6

The weather yesterday had been as prayed for; Saddler had recorded in his diary: 'TEZ transit. Weather northerly force 6, low cloud base, poor visibility, ideal.' But now in the early hours of 'D-Day' the sky was clear, stars like the sort on a Christmas card. There was a hope in one forecast of the 'clag' closing in again, but his own weather sense made him doubt it.

Since nightfall there'd been a number of air-attack warnings, mysterious and anonymous radio voice warnings. *Four Mirages taken off from Rio Gallegos* – time, course, speed. . . . Or *Six A4s closing you now*. . . . Saddler visualised SAS teams hidden in the mainland hills, camouflaged men in camouflaged holes, using high-powered binoculars and maybe with headphones linking them to electronic watchdogs of some kind; and nukes off the coast, out in the deep water between here and there, their periscopes and radar and radio antennae slicing the black surface – while here, now, holding its collective breath and with taut nerves, the assault force drove in towards its target, having linked up with the heavier troop-carrying units. Astern of *Shropshire*, now that the forces had joined up you could see (all too easily) the 'great white whale', *Canberra*, frighteningly easy to pick out through the darkness because of her size and the white paint which there hadn't been time to do anything about. But the whole force ploughing south, entering North Falkland Sound.

David Vigne murmured, 'Should come round to two-four-zero, sir.'

He was navigating visually, by shore bearings. Saddler agreed, 'Bring her round.'

'Starboard fifteen. . . .'

At eleven knots, the ships were pitching to the sea running up astern, *Shropshire* swinging away to starboard, turning her beam to it, and the 'great white whale' swimming on past, massive as an iceberg swimming grandly on into the Sound.

'Midships. Steer two-four-zero. . . . May I come up to fifteen knots, sir?'

Exactly as they'd planned it, as was now laid-off on the chart, in the chartroom at the back of this bridge. He heard Vigne order 'Revolutions one-two-eight' and the quartermaster's report of the course as now two-four-zero; it was the course for an attack on Pebble Island, a bombardment which would be timed to coincide with landing-craft ramps splashing down in San Carlos. Saddler heard distant gunfire from the east, and Jay Kingsmill's murmur of '*Glamorgan*'s at it again'. Their sister ship would be bombarding the north shore of Berkeley Sound, on the other side of East Falkland and not far from Stanley, where the Argies might well be expecting a landing to be made. Other diversions would be starting soon: there'd be a joint SBS and SAS raid on Fanning Head, which commanded the San Carlos approach, the attackers landing by helo from *Antrim* who'd then provide gunnery support, and an attack by SAS on the garrison at Darwin. During this period *Shropshire* would be lobbing shells onto the Pebble Island airstrip, where the SAS had done a fine job a week ago but which might well have more Pucarás on it by now. One way and another these sideshows should guarantee General Menendez getting enough conflicting reports to confuse him thoroughly while the beachhead was being secured.

Saddler told Jardine over the Open Line, 'I'll stay on the bridge for this shoot. Is the White system ready?'

'Closed up and cleared away, sir.'

The gunnery lot were very self-confident, following their success in destroying the blockade-runner. There'd been mention of it in a BBC news bulletin, which had delighted everyone.

By now the assault ships would be in the entrance to San Carlos Water, flooding their docks to float out the landing craft which would be waiting packed with heavily armed men. The beaches and their immediate surroundings would be secured before the big ships – *Fearless* and *Intrepid*, and *Norland* and *Canberra* with supporting vessels – entered the narrow gulf and anchored.

Shropshire was rolling a bit, on this course. The sea noisy, engines' thrum an accompanying and familiar background sound as she closed the dark land.

Five Mirages taken off from Gallegos on course zero-nine-five....

The fact that none of the reported take-offs had yet materialised as raids didn't mean they wouldn't be coming. Come daylight, you could count on it.

'Five minutes to go, sir.'

Landing craft would be moving in towards the beaches, which during recent nights had been checked out by SBS teams. The SBS men, who'd been living in holes on the hillsides around the landing areas for most of the last week, would be at the tide-line to meet the first commandos when they splashed ashore. 2 Para and 40 Commando.... 2 Para would be heading for Sussex Mountain which they'd hold against any interference from the direction of Goose Green, while light tanks of the Blues and Royals spearheaded a move inland through the settlement. 45 Commando would be going in at Ajax Bay, 3 Para landing at Port San Carlos.

'Ready to open bombardment fire, sir.'

He said informally, 'Go ahead.'

The island was part of a dark visual confusion to port. Saddler took off his headset, went out into the port wing of the bridge and focused his glasses on the area where the airstrip had to be. Vigne had brought her round to 270 degrees, due west: the target would be engaged for five minutes on this run, then the ship would be brought-about and there'd be another five minutes' shelling while she steamed back eastward.

Before he'd left the bridge he'd heard all the preliminaries, war cries, over the Open Line, but they still hadn't opened fire. Distantly, *Glamorgan* still banging away. . . . The wing door flew open, crashed shut, and Kingsmill told him, 'Some fault in the firing circuits. . . .'

Saddler thrust past him; then he was in the bridge, pulling on his headset: 'Are you going into independent?' Meaning local control, from the turret. . . . Vaughan, Commander (WE), came on the line: 'Vaughan here, sir. Guns won't fire. Some fault between the TS and—'

'How long?'

'Can't say, sir, until we've—'

'Wait.' Three seconds for thought, and no time to waste: this bombardment was as important as any other action on the periphery of the landings, there had to be some loud noises in this sector, *now*. He said over the Open Line, 'Stand down the White system. Load Seaslug launchers for CUSTARD shots. One missile every thirty seconds for ten minutes.' The bombardment was to have lasted ten minutes; over the same period there'd be fewer bangs, but bigger ones, and the Seaslug missiles could be expected to create large disturbances on the surface of the airstrip. CUSTARD was an acronym for constant angle of sight with terminal dive; he'd never used Seaslug in this role before.

'Should we come round, sir?' Vigne was sighting over the gyro repeater. 'To zero-three-zero?'

So that the launchers would be pointing towards the target area. Saddler concurred, and Vigne ordered starboard helm.

'Range one-eight-zero!'

'Fifteen of starboard wheel on, sir. . . .'

Seaslug was a beam-riding missile with a range of twenty-four miles. Within that distance you could put it down wherever you wanted it, although it was primarily a surface-to-air weapon. All the control data the Seaslug director needed now would be in the computer already, fed into it for the aborted gun action.

'Seaslug launchers are loaded, sir.'

'Course zero-three-zero.'

'Engage.'

Only yesterday, he remembered, Fleet Chief Petty Officer Carter had queried whether they'd ever fire one of his cherished missiles. He'd be losing twenty of them now. Saddler heard the first one leave; then the report, 'One Seaslug away. . . .' It wouldn't be a popular move, in some quarters. Seaslugs were in short supply, weren't being manufactured now that the system had been declared obsolete. But he'd had to do something, and by now there'd be commandos ashore at San Carlos.

At noon *Shropshire* was patrolling on a figure-of-eight track in the northern approaches to San Carlos Water. She would have been with *Antrim,* available for NGS on call from shore, if the gun circuits hadn't still been u/s. She was here now for AA defence, a fielder out in the middle where she might well become a target herself, Saddler guessed, when the Argie air force finally showed up.

Four thousand men had been put ashore unscratched. You could see some of them on the hillsides digging trenches, and the Union Flag was flying over the settlement. Sea King helicopters were ferrying Rapier missile-defence batteries ashore – personnel, launchers, missiles, generators and ancilliary equipment – the helos depositing their loads at pre-selected hilltop sites and racketing back to the ships for more. Guns, stores, vehicles and men were flowing in over the beaches, but the Rapier system was a priority because this peace wasn't likely to last much longer. The sky was clear, visibility excellent; the weather, hitherto pro-British, had changed sides.

He walked into the Ops Room; pausing, looking around, tasting the atmosphere, hearing (or maybe imagining) the edges of alarm in some voices, seeing awareness of the imminence of action in some young faces. And that was OK: it would have been unnatural if there had *not* been some signs of tension.

'Delta Eight Charlie reports hostiles two-eight-four, forty miles!'

Delta Eight Charlie was *Boreas*. She was down to the south: she and her Lynx helos had been searching the coves down there for patrol boats or other lurking dangers. So far they'd drawn blank. But from that report, the action might be starting soon. The most recent warning before that had been a cryptic call of *'Eyes open, west!'* and minutes before that, *'Six Mirages taken off from Rio Gallegos. . . .'* There'd also been chat on a different circuit – from Harrier pilots in the CAP – combat air patrol – which was operating a long way out, outside the circumference of the missile defence zone. But there'd been no actual sighting or radar contact until that shout from *Boreas*.

'EWD – anything around bearing two-seven-zero?'

Two-seven-zero would be roughly the bearing from here of *Boreas'* contact. EWD being the electronic warfare director – a PO at that console monitoring a radar system which auto-analysed and identified hostile radar transmissions.

'Only Blue Fox in that sector, sir.'

Blue Fox was the weapons radar in a Sea Harrier's nose. And the more of them, the better.

Warning voice again: four Skyhawks had now left Gallegos eastbound. Then news that two more Harriers had taken off from *Hermes* to reinforce the CAP. . . . A shout now – the fighter controller's voice: 'Blue Leader has two A4s visual, going buster!'

A ripple of excitement, a hand raised with fingers crossed. . . . Saddler checking radar monitors, then the big plot where radarmen with chinograph pencils were marking-up the picture as it thickened and the ranges closed. 'Blue Leader' was a Harrier pilot at this moment going in for a kill. Saddler considered returning to the bridge: the attackers would be here soon, and down here there wasn't a lot he could do except listen, preside – which he could do just as well up top, but also *see* it. . . .

'Blue Leader has splashed one Skyhawk, other's legged it!'
Cheers.
'Four Mirages taken off from Rio Gallegos!'
Another foursome. Take-off intervals seemed fairly regular.
Arrivals would be similarly regular – once the first lot arrived.
'Delta Eight Charlie, birds away!'
Boreas had launched missiles. She was a Type 22 and
therefore had Sea Wolf, which was a weapon for close defence
with either TV or radar tracking and one launcher for'ard, one
aft, each of them six-barrelled. Saddler would have given a lot
to have Sea Wolf right now, instead of Sea Cat.
'I'll be on the bridge, Ian.'
Prince, AAWO, nodded as he switched his radar monitor
from one set to another. 'Aye aye, sir.'
'Delta Eight Charlie, one Mirage splashed!'
Delight in that tone; clapping greeted it. Not a bad start, two
splashed in the same minute; if you could keep that up, the
Argies might run out of aircraft before long. . . . Joe Nicholson
looked across at Saddler and suggested, 'Threat warning red,
sir?'
Instinct, more than any evidence of an immediate threat
here in the Sound, told him *Yes.* . . .
'PWO.' Jardine looked round. He told him, 'Air warning
red.'
'Aye aye, sir.' Into the broadcast: 'Air Threat Warning Red.
On anti-flash. Oerlikons and Seacat Red and Green, on your
toes!'
Saddler paused at the GOP – general operations plot –
where Adamson, the navigator's yeoman, was rubbing out old
position lines on chart 558. Those were the pencilled tracks
and fixes from *Shropshire's* transit of the TEZ with the Special
Boat men on board. It felt now as if that might have been a
month ago; and there was a question-mark lingering in his
mind, about that Sea King. . . . He asked Adamson, 'In the
right place, are we?'
Pointless remark, of course: although the GOP was a
navigational plot, he'd only said it for the sake of saying
something to this quiet, rather introspective lad. But Adamson

smiled, and answered, 'I'd sooner be in the Dog and Duck, sir.'

Saddler's chuckle was drowned by the broadcast: 'Aircraft in the Sound!'

He ran for the lift. In, slamming the gate shut, whooshing up. Out – and round the corner; then into the bridge, hearing the crash of gunfire then a louder, impacting torrent of sound as the first attacker hurtled over at mast-head height. Two bombs away. He saw another Delta-shaped aircraft screaming in over Fanning Head. Sea spouting where those bombs smacked into it – closer to *Argonaut* than to *Shropshire*. *Shropshire*'s rudder hauling her around. . . . Oerlikons in action, and lighter machine-guns, Blowpipe missiles from launchers hand-held by soldiers on *Canberra*'s and *Norland*'s decks, the air a futuristic tracery of missile trails; a Skyhawk swooped up from the sea-skimming height and a Seacat missile rose with it, exploded under its tail – debris starring, pock-marking the water around the central splash.

Noise dying, smoke clearing. End of round one, and in *Shropshire* no damage or casualties. Three Seacat missiles had been fired. One of the Oerlikon gunners was sure he'd hit an A4, he'd seen his 20-mm shells impacting on its wing, then lost track of it as it swept over and he'd switched to a new target. There was no indication that the Seacat which had splashed the other Skyhawk had been *Shropshire*'s, neither the Red nor Green director would claim it. Radar, Nicholson reported from the Ops Room, had been confused by land clutter. *Argonaut* had three men wounded, one seriously, and a chunk of her 'bedstead' 965 aerial blown away. Harriers of the CAP has splashed two Mirages, bringing the CAP's score to three.

Kingsmill came back to the bridge. He'd been up top, visiting the Oerlikon gunners and organising what he called the 'for'ard battery' – sailors with rifles and one machine-gun to join in the close defence. Saddler thought, glancing at his executive officer, *Why not bows and arrows?* Thinking also about one very near squeak, a bomb that had passed about ten feet from the front of the bridge and exploded in the water thirty yards to port; HQ1 – damage control headquarters –

had reported only minor shock-damage. But as to the men up there with self-loading rifles and a GP machine-gun – well, you could say every little helped, that the more lead went up in the faces of Argie pilots, the tougher – slightly – their job would be. *Shropshire* was under helm again, heeling to the turn: Holt, who was OOW at action stations, conning her under the navigating officer's watchful eye, keeping her on the move but out where she'd help to block attacks coming into San Carlos Water at low level and on straight courses for the ships anchored farther in, off the beaches; and if this was where you had to be you might as well muster every pea-shooter you could find. Playing Aunt Sally was what it amounted to – particularly with radar so useless in here that visual sightings were the first warnings you could expect.

'Eyes open, west!'

That would be a pre-recorded, automatic transmission, he guessed, triggered by take-offs at the end of some runway, or ends of runways. More specific alerts could only come from live, human observation. Maybe they – observers – were alerted by that call and then stood ready to amplify it. Maybe. . . .

Vaughan reported that the White system, the gun, was now operational. Some defective piece of circuitry had been located and replaced. Saddler initiated a signal reporting this – to *Broadsword*, senior ship in this group, and to the Admiral. The 965 radar still wasn't functional though, Vaughan said. In fact it wouldn't have been a lot of use in any case; going by other ships' reports it seemed that attacking formations were dipping to sea-level when they were still a hundred or more miles short of the islands, and only an airborne warning system – aloft and looking downwards, the kind the Task Force didn't have – could have countered this tactic.

'Eight Mirages taken off from Rio Gallegos. . . .'

Hold muttered, 'Any advance on eight?'

Because it was the largest formation so far reported. And there were at least two attacks *en route* ahead of that one.

Saddler told Vigne, Holt and the PWO, Jardine, 'I'll be taking a walk round the upper deck now.'

'Aye aye, sir.' Vigne watched him remove his headset and put it on its hook on the command console. He suggested, 'Five minutes before the next lot, would you say, sir?'

It was a hint, of course. Tactful way of asking *Do you think you should?* He checked his watch. 'If the CAP don't intercept it. But I'd think more like ten minutes than five.' He was thinking of those intervals between take-offs. He met Kingsmill outside; the commander reported, 'I've set up an after battery, sir, on the flight deck. Flight deck party, plus some odds and sods.'

'I'll pay them a visit.' More riflemen, for God's sake. Even in World War Two they hadn't found it necessary to resort to rifle-fire for AA defence, he thought. But then they'd had a better profusion of close-range weapons, hadn't placed so much reliance on the high-tech stuff which didn't always work or suit all circumstances. . . . 'I'm going aft, Jay, for a chat with the Seacats.'

He went aft 'over the top' – from the bridge wing, up fixed rungs on to the bridge's roof, aft across it and along the starboard side to the signal deck and gunnery defence position. The riflemen were GDP crew and signalmen; they looked self-conscious, Saddler thought, clutching their SLRs, but glad to be visited. The Oerlikon gunners had some yarns to tell: one gun had jammed just at the moment he *would* have scored. Saddler told him, 'Better luck next time. It won't be long.' Thinking that it was fairly ludicrous to be defending a modern, missile-armed destroyer with SLRs in the hands of signalmen – then qualifying the thought, because it was twenty years since *Shropshire* had been 'modern' – but wondering how long it might be before the Marines ashore were issued with pikes and halberds.

He was talking to the port Seacat operator when the next assault came in. The operator was a seventeen year old named Pitts; he had bright yellow hair under his tin hat – which made him look rather like a mushroom – and a face scarred by acne, with dark, quick eyes. His job entailed sitting inside the director, which was a structure about the size of a telephone kiosk with a seat in it and a binocular sight mounted on top where his head protruded. The launcher, loaded and ready, was below him and to his left. The way the system worked was that the Seacat transmitting station on 01 Deck locked the director to its target, and when the missile was launched Pitts had to hold it in the centre of the binoculars, steering it by movements of his thumb on a joystick control not much bigger than a matchstick.

'It's this side we had a defect on recently, isn't it?'

'Yessir.' Pitts nodded. 'OK now.' He grinned. 'I 'ope.'

'Did you get any shots away, just now?'

'One, sir.' He added, 'But I lost it. Gets confused like when there's all the smoke an' that.'

'Easier at night.'

'Oh, yessir. See the tail-flame, then.'

'Is it impossible to see it in daylight, if you could concentrate on just that and nothing else?'

'Well, I dunno—'

'Aircraft! Aircraft!' The broadcast, booming excitedly. 'Red and Green systems, for'ard and after batteries, stand by!'

Saddler shouted to Pitts 'Good luck!' and ran – into a mounting blurr of noise, gunfire and already the screaming approach of aircraft. Vigne had been right – *five* minutes. . . . He saw *Antrim* hit. She'd launched a Seaslug, then two A4s swept over her in close succession. He had only an impression of it as he ran for'ard, but he thought they'd hit her with bombs and rockets too – or that might have been cannon. . . . A deafening blast of sound as a Mirage crashed over, drowning the snarl of Oerlikons and the random popping of SLRs; cannon-fire was part of the bedlam as he raced up a ladder, rushing for the bridge. Splinters flew from hits along the port side of the upper deck where he'd passed only seconds ago; he was in the bridge then, his eyes on smoke pouring from *Antrim*'s stern. Reaching for his headset and binoculars. *Shropshire*'s Seacat had fired; a report of 'Birds away!' from the Green system, the side he hadn't had time to visit. Then the explosive roar of the last of this particular bunch of attackers flashing over – bombs falling, whacking in and raising spouts close to the ships at anchor inside there – *Canberra* and

91

Norland – much *too* close. . . . The Argie pilots had flown right through that curtain of fire and now as they swooped away Seacat, Blowpipe, Seawolf, Seaslug and Rapier missiles streaked after them, curving their trails across the sky, cats' tails of flame and smoke that became static, hanging and then thinning, the wind wiping the sky clear again.

'*Eyes open, west!*'

More coming. Showing their hand *now*, all right.

Jay Kingsmill came to the bridge to report. Cannon shells had punctured the hangar on the starboard side, wounding three men inside it and one member of the 'after battery' on the flight deck. The after first aid party had taken care of them, and two men had been transferred to the wardroom where the doctor, Alec Claypoole, aided by a team of assistants which included Peter Ridpath the chaplain, had set up a dressing-station and temporary hospital. Apart from these casualties, damage was superficial and the Wessex helo hadn't been touched. Whereas *Antrim* – reports were coming in now – had lost the use of her Seaslug and Seacat systems, had virtually no defence left with which to resist the further attacks now on their way. One bomb had penetrated her Seaslug magazine, but, thank God, failed to explode, although it had done a lot of damage. It was fairly plain that the ships, not the beachhead, were today's prime targets.

The last attack of the day was the worst.

By that time *Broadsword* had been strafed and suffered casualties – and splashed two Mirages with her Seawolf – and *Argonaut* as well as *Antrim* had sustained major damage. *Brilliant* had been hit in her Ops Room, important cables had been cut and she'd lost all her weapons systems except the after Seawolf. The CAP Harriers had splashed several of the attackers, mostly on their way home.

But in the last assault of the day, they got *Ardent*. She was mobbed by a mixed force of Mirages, Skyhawks and Aermacchis; bombs plastered her stern, knocking out all her weapons systems. Helpless to defend herself, listing to starboard from flooding on that side, she was out of control and heading for the shore; Saddler saw men running for'ard over her foc's'l, then an anchor going down just before another wave of attackers hit her. This time it was the kill. *Yarmouth* closing in to help . . . . Smoke poured from *Ardent*'s stern, which looked as if it had been destroyed internally – gutted, and the glow of fire inside her plainly visible – oily black smoke oozing like blood and against it the day-glo orange of men in 'once-only' survival suits on her canted decks and in the water. *Yarmouth* ran in alongside the dying frigate and embarked survivors over the port side for'ard before she sank.

That night Saddler summarised the day's action in his diary. *Shropshire* was steaming south at fifteen knots, after a bombardment of the Goose Green area, to rendezvous with the oiler *Tidebreak* for a liquid RAS. He added on that page of the diary, having listed the ships sunk and damaged – and knowing he ought now to be starting a letter to Anne, who'd be getting fragmentary news of the fighting and would be trying to convince herself and Lisa that she wasn't worried sick – 'Tense and tiring day. Morale however still high. Landings successful, 17 enemy aircraft destroyed.'

'May I come in, sir?'

Jay Kingsmill, in the doorway. 'Of course, Jay.'

'Sir.' He shut the door; Saddler waved him to a chair. 'News flash on the BBC, sir, thought you'd want to hear it. I sincerely hope it's not as rotten as it *seems* to be, but – well, the Chileans have reported a Sea King crashed and burnt out. On Chilean territory, near Punta Arenas.'

The words in his own neat hand in the diary blurred, out of focus. Visualising the crash, the fireball on some lonely mountainside. Kingsmill's voice adding, 'Of course, doesn't have to be that one, I suppose—'

'No. It doesn't.'

Might have delivered its passengers to the LZ before the crash? Might have been on its way back?

If it had *had* a way of getting back. How this was to be accomplished was a question he'd raised when they'd given him his orders before the rendezvous for the para drop. Knowing a Sea King's fuel capacity, and the weight factor which if they'd fitted it with extra tanks would impose another limitation, and the distances involved; also wondering whether, if its crew did have some facility for refuelling – Chilean help, perhaps – it might become his task to move out to the western edge of the TEZ, or beyond that, to make the recovery. But the answer had been dismissive: 'All taken care of, John. Not your pigeon.'

In other words, *Mind your own business*. . . .

7

It was getting dark when Félix, who'd ridden on ahead to find the lake and the O'Higgins *puesto*, returned to meet them and guide them to it. For several hours, having left the plateau behind, they'd been crossing greenish, quite fertile country, land watered by overspill from the Andes rains. The lake, stream-fed and in a slight depression, wasn't visible until you were right up close; there was no track to follow to it, from this direction, no way a stranger would have found it except by stumbling into it. Besides which, the light had gone now. While Félix had been scouting ahead, the two groups – Torres and Beale with half the sheep, and Andy with Cloudsley and Hosegood driving the rest of them – had been converging; Torres had organised this, getting them integrated into one flock while it was still just light enough to see. But now from the right there was a drumming slither of hooves, then Félix calling in Spanish to Torres: he'd have them in silhouette against what brightness remained in the western sky.

On Andy's right, Cloudsley reined in. Torres kicked his nag into a trot, slanting to the right, towards the voice.

'*Qué tal,* Félix?'

'Not so far. This way, a little!'

Shouting across the cutting, constant wind.

'Did you speak with him?'

'*Sí*. All is well, and he has a pen we can use. But no entry to the *puesto*, not even for you, my friend! He has a new woman — eh?'

'Old Agustín, a new—'

'Believe it!'

Wheezy laughter. 'Not quite *new,* I'll bet. But she'll still break his spine!'

Andy was pushing his horse out to the left, to turn the flank of the milling crowd of sheep and edge them the other way. He told Hosegood as he crossed ahead of him, 'Félix says it's not far now. Want to get down and walk?' Hosegood had been pretending to have saddle-sores. Beale called over, 'Sleep on your face tonight, Geoff. . . .'

They'd seen no other human being, in all the hours of riding. No aircraft either. He'd noticed Cloudsley keeping a constant lookout for them, watching the sky more than the barren landscape. They'd chewed mutton on the march, and drunk from their water-bottles. A condor had dived on some small prey almost under the hooves of Andy's horse: swooping red-eyed, talons lowered and hooked, tail-feathers down for an air-brake. Hosegood had muttered, staring after it as it flew away, 'Now I *seen* it. "Nature red in tooth and claw". . . .'

'Plenty of that hereabouts, Geoff.'

'Yeah? What else besides eagles?'

'That was a condor, not an eagle.'

He'd told them about other predators. The *carancho*, for one — a carrion hawk that specialised in killing lambs and pecking out sheep's eyes. *El Carancho* had been a nickname — spoken invariably under a man's breath — for Alejandro Diaz, at the time Andy had left the Argentine for good. Or had thought he was leaving for good. The recollection had turned his thoughts back that way — via Diaz to his daughter — when the nature-study talk had died away.

The sheep were moving the right way now, and he and Torres had them between them. Félix, invisible from here, was leading. Tony Beale – he had the pack-horse on a rope behind him – called, 'Andy, what's a *puesto*?'

From the left, a fox screamed. He waited for the eerie sound to fade, then told Beale, 'Shepherd's house. Shepherd is a *puestero*. Each one is way out on his own, in these outlying paddocks, has to live on the job.'

'Must be bloody lonely.'

'It's a life they're used to.'

Lonely for their wives, or women, he thought. It would be lonely enough even for Francisca on a large, comparatively civilised *estancia* like La Madrugada, particularly if Robert was away. There'd be only the *mayordomo* and his family, and the *peóns* and theirs, sometimes a neighbour passing by. Francisca hadn't been brought up to the farming life. Despite her father having his own sheep-station, *Estancia* Santa María, her stays in the wilderness had never been protracted. She was a town girl at heart, a bright lights girl. Buenos Aires and these remote provinces of Patagonia were different worlds, and however much she'd enjoyed some aspects of the country life she'd always been a visitor in this one.

She might well be living in BA now, he guessed. In his mind he'd picured her as being at La Madrugada, he supposed, because he'd been coming to the neighbourhood himself and – facing it honestly – because there'd never been a time when she had not been in his thoughts. Since heaven knew how long ago; it felt like for ever – and thoughts of the future, despite all that had happened, had always had her in them, however vaguely. . . . But it was more likely she'd be in the capital now, he guessed, using her father's big, ritzy house. Very much a different world: not just comfort but luxury, and drenched now in the *Junta*'s propaganda, bombast and heroics – one of the heroes being her bloody husband, no doubt, while here the hero's brother, dressed as a *peón*, rode with his head down through a freezing, wind-swept night behind a bunch of stinking sheep. .

A shout from up front: '*Holá*!'

A light there; a lantern swinging, held aloft by a horseman spectrally illuminated under its pale glow. The *puestero* had ridden out to meet them; he and his 'new' woman would doubtless welcome a break in their isolation.

'Tastes bitter. What's it made of – or shouldn't I ask?'

Tony Beale passed the gourd of *maté* to Hosegood. Andy explained: it was tea made from the leaves of *Ilex Paraguayensis*, Brazilian holly. In fact the tea itself was called *yerba* and *maté* was the gourd in which they served it. You drank it through a straw; this one, belonging to Pepe Torres and before that his father, was silver tipped with ivory. There was a ritual involved: for instance the water, heated in a tin kettle, had never to be allowed to boil; and the first man drank, spat it out, refilled the gourd, drank this time without spitting and then passed it on.

The sheep were penned and so were the horses – rubbed-down, fed and watered, and one of them tethered nearby – the *nochero*, kept ready in case of some emergency in the night. Torres and Félix had been admitted to the *puestero*'s house – a shack made of adobe and plastered externally with lime and sand, roofed with tin – but only for long enough to pay their respects – so Torres had described it, to Andy – to Agustín's woman, who was a *Chinita* from the south and not at all bad to look at. Agustín evidently had more on the ball than you'd have guessed from the look of him, Torres and Félix agreed.

'*Qué va.* When you've been in the saddle all day—'

'You're right. You're right. . . .'

The others had kept their distance and had been careful not to speak in earshot of the *puestero*. He was in his house now and the six of them were lying around the fire which Félix had built. Packs – not Service-issue bergens but special packs, unattributable, made in Czechoslovakia – served as backrests.

Torres was proffering an unlabelled half-bottle that had once held whisky. The liquid in it was colourless, like gin.

'For the fire in the belly, Don Andrés!'

The suggestion was that he should put some in his *maté*. Torres assured him it was of the finest quality.

'I have no doubt it must be the finest *caña* ever made. But this time, Don Pepe, I'll have to pass it up.'

'Just a little! *Mínimo, mínimo!*'

'We have a long ride tomorrow. No camp — we'll be leaving you, remember, riding on through to the *estancia* El Lucero.'

Torres shrugged, tossed the bottle to Félix who caught it deftly and whipped the cork out. Andy advised the others, 'Safer to lay off. *Caña* — local firewater.' Félix was lacing his *maté* heavily with the raw spirit — then offering the bottle to the others, who declined. Cloudsley turned to Andy. 'Listen, now. A word or two about the programme from here on.'

He was more than ready to hear it. Having seen Monkey and Jake ride south this morning, and knowing he was the only one in the dark about where they were going. . . . OK, so he could see the point, but it still left him feeling more of an outsider than he'd have liked to be. Cloudsley said, 'Assuming we get to Strobie's place some time tomorrow night, we'll spend the following day getting some rest and then push on as soon as it's dark. I've been reckoning on two nights' yomp from Strobie's to the target, lying-up for one day *en route*, but having given it more thought, today mostly, seems to me we might have a shot at doing it in just *one* night. By having you come along, Andy Mac, as far as the ruin, the Sandrini house. We could take a pack-horse that far, then at the ruin we'd transfer the stuff to our backs and yomp on, and you ride the nag back to Strobie's. All right?'

'Well — as far as it goes—'

'Then you stay with Strobie, drink his Scotch — if Monkey left any, which I wouldn't count on — and keep your head down. *Right* down — adopt the profile of a pancake.'

It would be no hardship to spend a few days with old Tom. He asked, 'How long, roughly?'

'Depends. How many missiles we find there, how long it takes to fix each one, how many hours of each night we get to work in. And one or two other unpredictables. But from Strobie's place to that ruin is — what, six miles? With a horse for the gear, we'd get there in next to no time.'

'Why not take horses to ride, too? I can lead 'em all back.'

'Why not, indeed. . .?'

'And why bother with the Sandrini place? You'd get a much better start, and I'd still have plenty of time to get back before daylight, if we rode directly north, cut off that corner. You're going out of your way, otherwise.'

'I thought the ruin might be a good place for the change-over. Cover of sorts – which there can't be much of?'

'There's none. But cutting the corner, you'd be ten miles nearer your target before you have to start humping your own loads.'

Beale said, 'Make a big difference, Harry. Bloody marvellous.' His eyes with the firelight in them seemed to glow; and teeth gleaming too, in the dark, bony, bearded face. Cloudsley asked, 'Without that Sandrini ruin as a starting point, are you sure you'd be able to point us in the right direction?'

'Absolutely. I'd take you to Diaz's western boundary. All you'd have to do would be follow that fence up to the northwest corner of his land, then strike out on a pre-determined compass course.'

'So we'd make it *easily* in one night.'

Geoff licked mutton-fat off his fingers. 'And Andy'd have time enough to get the gee-gees back where they come from.'

'It sounds very good, Andy.' Cloudsley nodded. 'We can go over navigational detail when we're at Strobie's – compass course, etcetera. . . . But now before we all hit the sack, there are a couple of other points I want to run over with you. First, question of cover story – because once you've left us up there and you're on your own, it has to change, d'you see.'

The present cover story – for use in the event of capture and interrogation – was that they were on a search and rescue mission. A Sea King helicopter carrying an unarmed intelligence-gathering party had vanished, was thought to have crashed, nobody knew where. Andy, as guide and interpreter with this rescue team, was leading them to the *estancia* La Madrugada to set up a base from which enquiries and searches could be made. It didn't matter that this might have been a silly way of going about it, Cloudsley had pointed out; the place did half belong to him, it was natural he'd make use of it. He could give the questioners plenty of convincing detail: his own recruitment and crash-course of training could be described, for instance, with no loss of security that mattered in the least; the only omissions would be any mention of Exocet missiles or of the real names of SBS personnel.

Cloudsley said, 'As before, it's to be hoped you won't have any need for any cover story. But if you did – well, you've come to visit your brother and/or his wife and if possible find some way around the trade sanctions. You disapprove of this war, you think the Malvinas rightly belong to Argentina. You never heard of the SBS – you'd ask, "Don't you mean *SAS*?" Not that you know anything about them either, but you've heard of them, who hasn't. . .? The only way the war has affected you personally is it's shut down your firm's trade, so you took a working holiday to the States to see if you could stir up some business – Argentine business via New York, right?'

'How did I get here?'

'The obvious way. Pan Am flight New York to BA, ten days ago. For obvious reasons you booked under an assumed name. Carlos Henriques, you *think* you called yourself, but you wouldn't be bothered if they produced some passenger lists and couldn't find that name. It was a spur-of-the-moment move, you didn't make notes, just took a chance and showed your own passport when you landed. Your Argentine one, naturally.'

'It happens to be a year out of date.'

'I know. Here, you'd better have it with you.'

It came out of a pocket inside Cloudsley's *poncho*. Andy had last seen it when he'd slid it across a table to the two men who'd interrogated him in London. It had seemed to gratify them that after he'd taken up permanent UK residence he'd let it lapse and applied for a British one, to which of course he'd been entitled.

Cloudsley yawned, stretching.

'So. You showed that at Ezeiza airport. But the guy only just glanced at your photo in it, and flipped it back to you. Matter of fact there's one badly smudged stamp that he might have put in, but you can be vague, there's no reason you'd have been

101

watching every move. They aren't likely to disbelieve you or to bother checking; this is *you*, you have roots here, you own half that bloody great farm – right?'

Andy nodded.

'You see, it's a natural. And the great thing is that if you were nabbed on your own it wouldn't involve *us*. We're out in the clear, getting the job done, nothing's lost.'

'All right.'

'So far, so good.' Cloudsley went on, 'Here's a logical extension to it now. Suppose at any stage we had to split up – *were* split up, for any reason. Any foul-up of that sort, what you should do is take advantage of your local connections, go to ground and sit out the rest of the war under cover. OK?'

Watching Tony Beale cleaning his knife, scraping mutton residue from its blade, Cloudsley added, 'Should be easy for you – *chez* Strobie?'

Beale sheathed the knife inside his *poncho*. They all wore them – not commando fighting knives but the hunting kind, of similar weight and size to the ones they were used to, and serving all the same purposes, but in no way identifiable as Royal Marine equipment. They'd given Andy lessons in using his in close combat, but he fervently hoped that was one thing he wouldn't need it for.

'You're saying I may be stuck here.'

'Wouldn't it be easier to stay put? *If* the worst happened?'

'While the rest of you—'

'Andy, that's the whole point. You don't have to worry about the rest of us.'

He'd said 'you don't', not 'you wouldn't' – as if it was all planned, intended. . . . All right, so they had their special, extraordinary skills, and he could see that an amateur might cramp their style and slow them down; and the only really important thing was to get the job done. This would certainly be their view, and he happened to share it. He told himself, *So what the hell, it's only common sense. . . .*

He nodded. 'OK.'

Suppressing – partially – the feeling he'd been conned. . . . Tony Beale's gaze was on him thoughtfully, understandingly;

and Geoff Hosegood too, Geoff displayed a hint of amuse-
ment, but it was an amused *sympathy,* in that steady regard
and the absence of any comment. Cloudsley said, 'Good
man', and settled back; then he asked casually, an afterthought, 'Nothing in your pockets to connect you with us, is
there?'

For breakfast, before sunrise, the *puestero*'s woman provided
coffee and *tortas,* doughnut-like buns made of maize flour.
Andy saw her only as a shadow outlined by the glow of the
fire's embers; he'd heard a low exchange in Spanish as he
woke, her voice and either Torres' or Félix's, then she'd left the
urn and the basket of *tortas* and slipped away. Cloudsley was
returning from a visit to the bushes. Torres ribbing Félix: 'You
must have won her heart, you old devil! Slipped in there in the
night, did you?' Laughing his wheezy laugh, nudging Andy:
'They flock to him, you know, he keeps a stick to beat them off
with!' Félix, a haggard scarecrow, leant to the fire and spat.
Cloudsley mumbled, 'Wonder how it's going. Whether the
boys are ashore yet. Seems like a million miles from here,
somehow. . . . Don't tell me this is *coffee*?'

Tom Strobie would have a radio, Andy told him. They'd
catch up on the news when they reached his *estancia,* about
this time tomorrow.

The thought of being discarded and left here had given him a
bad night. He'd lain awake for several hours, hearing the night
sounds – the wind, the fire, foxes, and sometimes the sheep's
alarm, and the men's snores and mutterings. . . . Trying to
sleep, but thoughts incessant and repetitive, finally in half-
sleep the concept of hiding-out at his own *estancia*, La
Madrugada, with Francisca there, Robert away at the war,
Francisca as she had been so often – in his arms, the young,
warm, *lovely* Francisca. . . .

Ridiculous, in retrospect. She'd made her choice. He knew
it, had reminded himself of it hundreds of times. The dreams

103

still came, though, and not all of them in sleep. Even now, as they saddled-up in the dawn's grey light and Torres and Félix extracted the sheep from the O'Higgins pen, that one lingered.

They rode as they had the day before – Andy with Cloudsley and Hosegood, and Torres with Tony Beale a few miles off to the left, each team with about half the sheep. Félix, as before, had a roving commission, ostensibly quartering the ground for strays but also keeping in touch with both groups so he'd be able to steer them towards each other at the end of the day. The line of march was due east, aiming for a waterhole still on O'Higgins land which Torres had used on his drive west three days ago.

Cloudsley said, 'Knows his stuff, that guy.'

'He ought to. Done nothing else all his life. Tom gave us the best man he has.'

They were riding about fifteen yards apart. Andy in the centre, Cloudsley and Hosegood on the flock's right and left flanks, the sheep moving more slowly than Cloudsley would have liked but without any checks to their progress, no tendency to wander. The men rode long-legged, relaxed in their saddles. Each saddle had a sheepskin over it, fleece outward, for the rider's comfort, and a thick felt rug under it for the horse's.

The sheepskin softness made Geoff Hosegood's claim to saddle-soreness an obvious exaggeration. So the others had been telling him.

Andy asked Cloudsley, 'Have you three worked together before, operationally I mean?'

Cloudsley shook his head. 'Not Geoff.'

Hosegood told Andy, 'I'm like you, see. First time out.'

'Not *quite* my shade of green, I'd guess. . . .'

But he was surprised to have been given any answer at all. He tried for another – asking Cloudsley, 'What kind of operations before? I mean where?'

Plodding hooves, and sheep bleating. . . . Hosegood leaning down, muttering something to his horse. Andy ignored the silence, added, 'I suppose you get called to places we don't hear anything about. Nobody really *has* ever heard anything much about the SBS. . . .'

'Andy.' Cloudsley seemed to emerge suddenly from deep thought. 'What did you say this colour of horse is called?'

'All right.' He smiled. 'I'm just generally interested, that's all. In my fellow men, you know. . . .' He told him, 'It's a *malacara*.'

So called because it had a white star on its forehead. The Indians had had literally hundreds of colour descriptions for their horses, a different word for every variation and combination. The thought reminded him of Strobie's *peón*, Anselmo, and his instant recognition of his horse and Francisca's. Then from that to some slight regret that he'd talked them out of using the Sandrini place for a stopover. He'd have liked the excuse to see it again; he explained to himself, *For old times' sake*. . . .

'What's this bugger, then?'

Down to earth with a bang; to see Hosegood nodding at his horse's ears. . . . Andy told him, 'They'd call that *colorado*.'

Chestnut, of sorts. As distinct from Cloudsley's white-starred animal, which was buckskin-brown. His own mount was a black, an *oscuro*, and the pack-horse, a grey roan, would be called a *tordillo*. Cloudsley said sharply, 'Hey, there.' Pointing. 'Aircraft.'

In the west – over distant Strobie land, maybe – but it wasn't easy to guess how far off. . . . He'd reined in. So did Hosegood; a hand up to shield his eyes, squinting into the wind. Andy saw three 'planes, slightly north of due west, flying left to right and banking now, the turn starting as he focused on them, turning this way. . . . He called to the others to close in round the sheep, up on the flanks, and urged his own horse forward. To hold the flock together – otherwise the 'planes might well scatter them. Although if those pilots had spent any time at all flying over Patagonian sheep-stations they'd surely have learnt to keep clear.

Meanwhile this would look right to them. Any *puestero* would try to get tight control of his animals when he saw that noise coming. And they *did* know: they were banking again, in file now, falling into the new formation as they turned towards

105

the south. They'd have seen the other part of the flock a few miles on the other side, he guessed. Rising in his stirrups, waving – in case any of the pilots might be glancing down this way to recognise the natural reaction of a simple man a hundred miles from nowhere. . . . He heard Cloudsley identifying the 'planes as Pucarás. Their markings were clearly visible as they banked away, exposing their undersides: green and grey-brown camouflage design, yellow tactical bands between the twin turbo-prop engines and the wingtips, white anchors superimposed on the yellow. Navy aircraft, fleet air arm – as distinct, contrarily enough when it was interpreted into English, to FAA standing for *Fuerza Aerea Argentina*, the land-based air force. Levelling now, showing yellow rectangles on their high tails, and a small, light-coloured splodge above that, a badge of some kind but too far now to see. Cloudsley shouted to Hosegood, 'They're bombed-up, did you see?'

'Yeah.' Hosegood was edging his horse over towards the centre; the sheep had held together, all right, probably hadn't been able to make up their silly minds which way to run; they'd jostled around a bit but it hadn't come to anything. Andy had seen the bombs – at the last moment, because he'd been studying the markings: there'd been one central and one out under each wing, fat white eggs, shaped more like fuel drop-tanks than any bomb as he'd have envisaged it. The Pucarás were swinging east now after that jink to the south. Cloudsley talking to Hosegood: 'The Argie HE bombs have yellow snouts. God knows what those were. Could be practice bombs, I suppose – since it's a training base.' Andy thinking, Fleet air arm training base – which figured, since it was close to Diaz land. Not that Diaz – or for that matter Roberto MacJuan – had necessarily to be around; Diaz might only have had something to do with setting the place up. . . . Cloudsley was looking back over his shoulder, staring after the three ground-attack 'planes as they dwindled – flying northwest, engine-sound faded out. He muttered, still with his mind on those odd-looking bombs, 'Like outsize rugger balls with fins on. . . . Hey, they're splitting up.'

One black insect banking right, one left, one holding on straight.

'Can't be far from where we started yesterday. The escarpment?'

He could be right, Andy thought. They'd have been making less than three miles an hour with these sheep, and the Pucarás would have been flying at more like three hundred.

Hosegood pointed: 'There's Señor Whatsit.'

Félix: on a rise, static, horse and rider in profile as he stared back at the smoke-trails. Hosegood added, 'Him Big Chief Pissing Bull.' It did look a bit that way: posed for the long-shot, Noble Savage in silhouette on the skyline. . . . But in the sector where the Pucarás had now disappeared Andy's eye was caught by a spark like a match not quite igniting; then it did ignite, flared, turned into a fireball. He'd shouted, pointing at it, the first thought in his mind being that one of those aircraft had crashed, but now you could see the fire spreading, separate outbreaks starting and spreading to link up, merging into a solid band of flame low and day-glo bright on that far-off rockscape.

Not that from here you'd know it was rock, if you hadn't been there.

'Napalm?'

Cloudsley said grimly, 'Right. . . .'

Félix had gone on, out of sight. The horses were restive, dancing. The fire still bright and a black smoke cloud above it streaming diagonally on the wind. He asked Cloudsley, 'Monkey and Jake wouldn't have been in that area, would they?'

'No.'

Of course they wouldn't. Crazy thought anyway. Who'd drop napalm on horsemen in a wilderness, for God's sake?'

Well, Robert might. If he'd run out of vizcachas. . . . Cloudsley said, 'Could have a target marked out, on that escarpment.'

'But the rock'd be blackened. It'd stink too, wouldn't it?'

'*Now*, it will, but they might not have used it before. And I'd guess that's to the north of where we came over. Wouldn't have to be marked, anyway, they could be given a map reference and told to plaster it with that filthy muck.' He looked over at Hosegood. 'Something new, Geoff. Those were navy flyers. Training with napalm.'

'Could napalm be used against ships?'

'Those fat-looking bombs were finned.' The big man nodded. 'So I dare say they could.' Scowling, thinking about it. . . . 'Napalm bombs are only containers, dropped with very little aim, as an anti-personnel weapon. But if you could use it more precisely – well, yes. . . .'

The image in mind then was of a warship smothered in napalm: any hit on any part would be enough for the liquid to spray all over her. Then she'd be coated in fire. And aluminium, of which modern warships' upperworks tended to be made, did burn – as the Task Force had recently been learning. You might have a frigate or destroyer with her entire upper deck, superstructure and top hamper ablaze; the men inside cooking, unable to get out.

Or a troopship, for God's sake.

Riding on: glancing back to where the burning had now died to a glow like a fading sunset. The Pucarás were evidently taking a different route back to their base: northward, one might guess. Cloudsley said, 'Tony may have a view on this. He's our aviation expert.'

Beale told them – later, at dusk when they were resting briefly at the waterhole – that a Pucará's normal warload would be six 110-pound bombs all on a centreline rack, below the fuselage. But he hadn't heard of napalm in bombs with fins, either. From what he'd seen as they'd passed over, the two finned cannisters on the wing pylons had been smaller than the one in the centre; he estimated 500-kilogramme bombs under the wings and one twice that size in the rack.

'What makes you a Pucará expert, Tony?'

'Told to bone-up on 'em, wasn't I? Before we left.'

Hosegood said, 'Got his wings, an' all.' Pointing with his chin at the colour sergeant. 'Intrepid birdman, is our sarge.'

They were drinking coffee. Standing around the fire, as a rest from sitting all day in saddles, while Torres and Félix saw to the sheep. Half an hour's break, Cloudsley had ordered. Beale explained to Andy, 'Got a private pilot's licence, that's all. Not unusual, two or three pals of mine done the same. . . . Pucará means "village", right?'

'More or less. Sort of fortified settlement, antique Indian.' He asked Cloudsley, 'We might leave the pack-horse for Torres to bring along tomorrow?'

Cloudsley said no, he wasn't going to risk being separated from the gear. Without it they'd be hamstrung, and if Torres was delayed tomorrow they'd have to sit around and wait for him. It made sense, of course. Andy went to find Torres, down by the water marshalling sheep, and asked him whether there was a padlock on Strobie's number five gate now. Torres confirmed that there was. He'd put a new one on it on his way west; number five was the gate from which these sheep were supposed to have wandered.

'Better let me borrow the key, then.'

'You will leave the gate unlocked for us?'

'No. I'll lock it, and bury the key beside the hinge post.' Beale was saying as he rejoined them, 'The napalm thing could be very useful intelligence, Harry.'

'It could indeed.' You could see he didn't like it, either. Changing the subject, asking Andy, 'Are we going to find the way there now, straight line and no messing?'

He nodded. 'There's a track to the gate in Tom's fence, and it runs on from there to the *estancia*. I have a key to the padlock on the gate too.'

'Do they lock their gates?'

'Gates in boundary fences, sure. Not invariably, but—'

'As I've observed before, Tony, this is a useful guy to have along.' Cloudsley's hand gripped his shoulder. Lifting a mug of coffee in the other, tipping it back, Andy thinking, *But you'll be shedding me, soon as I've served your purpose. . . .* Cloudsley shook dregs out of his mug. 'Now we'd better hit the road.'

Andy led the cavalcade. After a warm farewell with Torres, who asked him to inform the *patrón* that he'd have the sheep back in the home paddock, God willing, by tomorrow's sundown. 'You will still be there when we arrive, Don Andrés?'

He nodded. 'If you do get there before dark.'

'Then you go where? *Estancia* La Madrugada?'

'No.' He shrugged. 'Well, I don't know. Maybe.'

'*Qué va....*' A shrug of the heavy shoulders, meaning in effect *What the hell....* And adding: 'You will remember the matter of the horses and their tack, Don Andrés, before you depart? In case we do *not* meet at the time?'

Three of Tom's horses, he meant, to be paid for. Plus their saddles and bridles. Andy had assured him, 'Don't worry, I'll remember.' He turned now in his saddle, looking back to the others who were riding in his tracks – four men now, five horses. They'd redistributed some of the loads, to give the pack-horse a break; each rider had some gear up behind him now. The fire was a tiger's eye glowing back there in the dark, throwing them into tall relief. 'OK to speed up, Harry?'

'Yeah.' A long arm lifted, from that dark, gigantic shape. 'Let's step on it.... Geoff, hold on now!'

Pulling his leg. After two days in the saddle Hosegood was quite competent to stay on.

The track was easy to see and follow. Andy put his weight back, pushed his horse into a slow canter, the sort of easy ambling gait that could be kept up across this kind of open country for hour after hour. Hunched against the wind, eyes slitted against the cold but still tending to weep, breathing adjusted to the rhythm of thudding hooves. An eye on the trail – knowing that if he lost it he could have the devil of a job to pick it up again – and looking back from time to time to check the others were still with him.

The first time he looked at his watch it showed a few minutes past two, and he felt he'd been riding for a week. In fact this was the fourth night since taking off in the Sea King from John Saddler's destroyer, and it was one week since they'd left England for Ascension Island. They'd spent only one hour on the air base, Wideawake, transferring from a VC10 to a Hercules; at the time he'd had a hollow feeling in his gut at the prospect of the para drop looming closer every minute. Now, it was the pleasure of reunion with old Tom that was approaching; and thinking beyond that – across Strobie territory to the MacEwan boundary, just a few hours' longer in the saddle – well, *if* she was there, and not in BA. . . .

It was only – oh, a daydream, an idea to toy with. Not to do anything about. But still, after so long, to be so close – maybe. . . .

Better, he told himself, not to know whether she was around or not. Not even to enquire. Then he saw the posts – Strobie's wire – and called back to the others to ease up: reining in, and the rest of them bunching up behind him. He told them, 'That's Tom's fence. Less than an hour from here to his *estancia*.' Pulling his horse to a stop, feeling for the key in a pocket, then finding the padlock by feel in the dark. Unstable on his feet, after the hours of riding.

'What's this fence made of, Andy?'

'Ever hear of wire?'

'Oh, *very* droll. . . .'

'It's high-tension wire, eight strands – maybe ten, if you want to count them. The posts are made of a wood called *quebracho,* comes from the north of the country and the word means 'axe-breaker'. In other words it's as hard as iron. The posts last sixty years without attention.'

Beale was at the fence, leaning from his saddle to examine it, what he could see of it. Andy fitted the key in the padlock and was relieved when it turned. Beale said, 'Post here doesn't reach the ground.'

'It's not a post, then, it's a dropper. There's a post every fifteen metres, you'll find, with a dropper between them – a spreader to keep the gaps between the wires regular. If you look closer you'll see that's only a two by one, something like that. But the fence is about as strong as you could make it, and still flexible.'

'Must cost a bit. Hundreds of bloody miles of it?'

'Well, nobody'd invented inflation when they put these up.' He swung the gate open. 'Come on. Straight up the track, Harry, I'll catch you up.' He had to lock the gate and bury the key, using his sheath knife to make a hole for it, for Torres to

111

use tomorrow. Then he swung himself up, trotted after the others, and forty minutes later saw the gleam of a light from the *estancia* El Lucero.

8

Walking into Tom's shack was like action in a dream. Unreal, timescale gone crazy. . . . Apart from which, his own perform-ance in getting here felt out of character, beyond his own known capabilities, so that he felt like a stranger to himself. Not to old Tom, though: the smile of welcome on the old man's face might have looked to the others like a fixed grimace of pain, but the warmth in the old man's eyes, above a tangle of grey beard, was intense, movingly real. He'd aged, of course. The surgeon's stitchings around his mouth, for instance, had ribbed the lips in vertical corrugations which hadn't been as prominent before. His lips, like other areas, had been reconstructed, forty years ago. Tom Strobie was a man of medium height but he was shortened by a stoop: wide at the shoulders, thick-bodied, but very little belly noticeable. He had a stick in his left hand and he was wearing his old reefer jacket with the black buttons instead of brass ones.

They'd unsaddled the horses and turned them out to graze, joining a lot of others on the flat, grass area called the *mallin*. First thing in the morning, the horseboy would ride the *nochero* out to round them up and put them in the horse corral.

'This is unbelievable, Tom.'

'Makes me happy too, boy. . . .'

He had one short eyelid. They'd done a poor job on that.
And he'd developed an old man's way of staring – peering,
with a big effort in it. He wouldn't have considered going to a
doctor, of course; he'd always said he'd had enough of doctors
to last a lifetime, if what they'd already done to him didn't
keep him going he was damned if he'd let them have another
go. . . . He was looking out into the dark as Andy moved
inside: 'Four of us, Tom. Bit of a crowd, I'm afraid, but only
until this evening. Torres said to tell you he'll be here by then,
incidentally. And Tom – thanks. Thanks a hell of a lot.' He
introduced the others as they crowded in: Harry, Tony,
Geoff. . . . Cloudsley had suggested during the approach to the
estancia that there'd be no need for any surnames.

'You're very welcome, boys.'

He wanted them inside quickly, Andy could see – and the
door shut. Partly to keep the cold out, but also because he
wouldn't want to advertise their arrival, not even to his own
employees. Cloudsley was saying as they shook hands, 'But
look, sir – rather than crowd you out' – his eyes had done a
quick recce of the shack's interior – 'an outhouse would do us
very well. As Andy said, we'll only be here for the daylight
hours. Just somewhere we can flop – and of course if you could
run to a meal—'

'Bloody oath. . . .' Strobie swung his stick-hand towards the
door; telling Beale, 'Shut it before we freeze, lad!' He asked
Andy, with a jerk of his beard towards Cloudsley, 'Who's this
midget, anyway, laying down the bloody law?' Glaring up at
the SBS man's towering bulk. . . . 'Cupboard under the bunk,
Andy – you'll find some Scotch. Glasses on the shelf. Food's
ready when you are – but sit down now. . . .'

It was about three a.m. by Andy's watch, but a ship's
chronometer in a wooden case showed nearly midnight.
Cloudsley saw it too, and nodded: 'We'd better change to local
time. Your clock's right, sir, I take it?'

'Don't call me "sir".' Tom let himself down into a sagging
armchair and dropped his stick beside it. 'Of course it's right.'

114

Peering at Andy: 'Go on, fill 'em up. And listen' – using his chin again as a pointer. 'There's one bed and spare mattresses in that room. Door off it leads to heads, wash place and shower. I sleep *there*.' A bunk, recessed and curtained, with drawers and the liquor cupboard under it. 'Carpentered that myself.' He swung round towards another door: 'Kitchen, and rear exit. And that's the lot. Not much of it, but you're better here than anywhere else. I'd have put you in the big house, but it's crawling with the Torres brood.' He was groping for his glass; Andy put it in his hand. . . . 'See if I've any memory working, now. I live here like an old fox in an earth, surprising I can still talk English. Talk it to myself, I suppose, that's all it can be. . . . But now – you're Geoff, right?'

'Dead right, Tom.'

The pointing right hand was blotched purple – from burns, or grafting, whatever. Eyes moving from face to face: 'You haven't changed much, Andy. . . . Now the *little* feller – you're Harry. And you – Tony. . . . *Right*.' He lifted his glass: 'Here's to you, boys, you and whatever you're here for. . . . Flew in by helicopter, did you? Type they call a Sea King?'

There wasn't a sound, while they all stared at him. He let it last a few seconds, then chuckled, took a swig of whisky. . . . Cloudsley asked him flatly, 'Why would you suppose—'

'*Suppose* fuck-all, old cock.' Wiping his mouth on the back of a hand. 'I listen to the BBC, that's all. Our Chilean neighbours have announced they've found a burnt-out Sea King down near Punta Arenas. Close to the border there, d'you see. Crashed, burnt out. I thought maybe you'd have been in it and I might *not* have the pleasure of your company.'

Tony Beale murmured, '*Could*'ve been. . . .'

'Take it as read.' Cloudsley pointed out. 'It takes the heat off us, doesn't it? That's to say, if there were any to start with, if anyone had reason to believe a helo had flown some of us in – could've seen or heard it from the Argie side when we flew in over the Strait. . . . They find the wreck right down there, they wouldn't guess it might have gone right up north and then back again, would they?'

Andy asked him, 'Throw away a Sea King? Just for that?'

'This job is not *small* beer, Andy.'

He looked at Beale. Hearing Geoff Hosegood murmur, 'Cheers then, Tom. . .' Andy began, 'I know, but—'

'If we pull this off' – Cloudsley was telling Strobie – 'we could be saving literally hundreds of lives. And ships. It's worth a hundred Sea Kings, on that basis. . . . But anyway' – looking across at Andy – 'that Sea King needed extra gas tanks just to get us to our LZ and then fly south. Couldn't have got any farther – unless the Chileans had refuelled it, which as neutrals obviously they couldn't. So having to ditch the helo anyway, they've done it where it points anywhere *but* in this direction. OK?'

Hosegood said, 'They'd reckon there'd been blokes going to Rio Gallegos. Just a stone's throw, innit?'

Strobie asked Cloudsley, 'What *is* your objective, Harry?'

'Well.' Cloudsley smiled. 'Mind if I ask a question first? We're all a bit thirsty for news – I mean we've been out of touch, the last few days. Have our lot landed, yet?'

'Lord, yes.' Strobie nodded. 'Must've been – oh, three days ago. . . . Were you with the Task Force?'

'Only briefly. Hello, goodbye. . . . A week ago we were in England.'

Andy noticed the slow blink of one working eye. To Strobie that statement would have been akin to saying, *We were on the moon.* The old man growled, 'You've moved fast, then.'

It hadn't felt like it, and didn't now. But maybe they hadn't done so badly, Andy thought. Cloudsley prompted, 'Tell us about the landing?'

'San Carlos Water.' The old man nodded. 'Early morning, the twenty-first. Royal Marines and Paras. No opposition, no casualties.' He went on, over their mutters of satisfaction, 'Then later in the day there were air attacks and a frigate was sunk. Quite a few Argentinian aircraft shot down, too.'

'Have they moved out of the beachhead yet?'

'No. They have not,' Strobie said. 'That frigate was the *Ardent.* Rotten news today was a second one's been hit. Might be my bad memory but I don't think they named her. . . . But I'll tell you, it's a lot better than listening to the BA radio, *they*

116

sink a ship a minute; if you believed them we'd have no bloody Navy left.'

'What sunk the frigates?' Cloudsley asked, 'Bombs, or missiles?'

'Both by bombing. *Sheffield*'s the destroyer that was done in by an Exocet. But that was earlier on, wasn't it. . .? Tell me what you're here for, Harry?'

'As much as my brief allows, I'll tell you.' Cloudsley paused. Handing out information weakened security, and it also made the recipient vulnerable. Strobie was vulnerable already, of course: having helped them this far, he was up to his ears in it. But the principle still held good, you didn't burden individuals with knowledge that couldn't do them or anyone else any good. He said, 'Our target's not far from here – which of course is why we've brought our problems to *you*, Tom. . . . A newish airbase – you'd know of its existence, I'm sure – used mostly if not entirely by their naval air arm. It could be, we think, for training some special squadron in napalm-bombing techniques. Up to the northwest of the Diaz spread?'

Strobie stared at the amber glow of whisky in his mottled hand. Eyes shifting then to glance at Andy.

'This is – closer to home than you realise.' Looking back at Cloudsley. 'The airfield's on land that used to belong to people called Coetzee.' Another glance at Andy. 'Remember that bloody-minded lot? They sold out to Diaz, and he's leased it – profitably, you can bet – to the government. . . . But I wouldn't have thought it was all that important, Harry. This much effort and risk of your lives?'

'The object' – Cloudsley told him again – 'is to *save* lives.'

Strobie still waited, watching him. Then gave up; accepting this was as much as they were telling him. And of course, he'd been at war, he'd understand. . . . He said, tossing back what was left in his glass, 'There's a stew on the stove in there. Beef. Reckoned you'd like a change from mutton. It's ready when you want it, but we'll finish this bottle first, huh?'

Holding his glass out. Andy topped it up for him, took some more himself and passed the bottle to Geoff Hosegood. He raised his glass to the old man. 'You've done us proud, Tom.

Incidentally, we owe you the price of three horses and the gear on them. Monkey – chap who came here with my note – had to go off on some other errand. I'm sorry. If I'd known in advance I'd have asked your permission, but – name your price, we've plenty of *pesos*.' Beale was screwing the top back on the whisky bottle; none of the SBS men had taken any more. 'I'll say it again, Tom; we're very, *very* grateful to you.'

Cloudsley nodded. 'Hear, hear.'

'What'd you expect? Think I'd tell that feller to bugger off?'

'No. I knew you'd help. I told Harry that if there was one man in Patagonia he could count on to the hilt, that man was Tom Strobie. All you've done is prove me right. The only worry I had was whether you'd be here at all. You might've been – well, locked up, or sick. . . .'

'Or pushing up the daisies.' The good eye blinked. 'I could, too. *And* wouldn't give a damn. Except I'm glad I'm here now – so you can forget the thanks, Andy. . . .' He looked at Cloudsley. 'That new base is only a training place for pilots, as far as I've heard. What makes it so interesting to you?'

'Well.' Cloudsley was sitting on the floor, his long legs stretched across the hearth in front of the wood fire. 'Not very easy to spell it out, Tom. If you'd forgive me skipping detail, I'd say there are things going on there – apparently – which call for a close inspection and maybe a spoke in some Argie wheel. . . . Although *you* think it's purely pilot-training?'

'All I know for sure is they have a squadron of bloody Pucarás racketing around the countryside. And a bombing range out in the west, I was told. . . . Pucarás were intended for anti-insurgency operations, as you probably know, long before this war. They called them Delfíns, originally – meaning Dolphin. . . . But anti-insurgency – that's Alejandro Diaz's great interest, you see; and he set it all up, of course. . . . Anyway – what I was going to say – couple of months ago, six weeks maybe, I sent him a very strongly worded note about his pilots scaring my sheep, creating bloody hell!'

'And?'

'As I said, he set it up, but it turns out he's not there now. They've promoted him to Rear-Admiral, and last I heard he was at Mar del Plata. Temporarily or permanently I don't know, but I'd guess more state security than straight navy. . . . Andy, I'm being a bit long-winded getting to the point, but are you ready for a shock?'

He nodded slowly. 'OK.'

'Well. The answer to my letter of complaint came from your brother. I must admit it was polite, even apologetic – *not* in character—'

'So he's on that base.'

'What d'you mean, *on* it?' Strobie scowled. 'He's *commanding* it.'

Staring at him: thinking about the machinations behind the scenes that would have brought this about; and what it might mean in terms of the SBS operation. . . . Aware of the others watching *him* as Strobie growled, 'He did stop those bloody fools creating havoc. Looking out for his own stock as well, of course. In fact I'm surprised bloody Huyez hadn't alerted him to what was happening. Scared to, maybe. . . . It was Francisca who told me about her father having become an Admiral.'

'Do you see her sometimes?'

'Well – not for a while, as it happens.'

'Francisca' – Cloudsley interrupted – 'being Robert MacEwan's wife, the Diaz daughter?'

Strobie nodded, and told Andy, 'She drops by, when she's down here. Or she *did*.'

He looked like a very old, tired bear, Andy thought. But – Robert commanding the establishment that was these people's target; and Francisca liable to 'drop by'. . . . He heard the bear's growl continuing, 'Could have been away. With him spending all his time on that airfield, or down at Comodoro Rivadavia. . . . All I can tell you that isn't plain depressing is she hasn't changed a bit. As pretty as ever – poor kid. . . .'

A silence followed. With no explanation of those last two words, and Andy wasn't asking for one, didn't want to stay on this subject, not here and now with the others listening and watching. Cloudsley murmured, 'Brother Robert in command. . . . Small world, eh?'

'It's a *sparse* world,' Strobie pointed out. 'Lot of square leagues per human being. And you see Diaz got that place going, Roberto his son-in-law is a navy-reserve flyer, and the base is right on both their doorsteps. Not really so extraordinary, is it? Certainly not to anyone who knows this fair land. Nobody'd dream of throwing a stick at nepotism, here.'

Beale asked, 'Would he be commanding the Pucará squadron, though? Or the base, like the ground command?'

'Well, he *is* a flyer, and still in his early thirties—'

'So he'd have the training squadron. Right, Andy?'

Tony Beale was being kind, he realised, telling him that Robert was unlikely to have any close connection with their target. The missile store was in one corner of the base, and the flying personnel wouldn't be likely to have anything to do with it. Andy nodded. 'Thanks, Tony. But – well, for anyone's future reference, I – I'm *not* my brother's keeper. That's to say—'

'We know what you're saying.' Cloudsley saved him from having to spell it out. 'And *you* know we aren't looking for trouble anyway.' He changed the subject: 'Tom, have you got any more to tell us – about personnel or anything else up there?'

The good eye did its slow blink. 'No way I could, is there?'

'Only that you knew about Andy's brother – and that was news to us. And his wife might have let something slip. . . . I suppose you wouldn't have seen Robert MacEwan since the war started, though.'

'Longer.' Tom's face could have been a Halloween mask. 'A year, at least.'

They knew quite a lot about the base already. For instance, by relating the length of shadows thrown by uprights in the guard-fence around the missile store to the date and time of day when the satellite pictures had been taken, they'd established that the fence was four metres high. It had barbed wire on the top, but no electrification, no power-leads connected to it, only to arc-lamps at each corner and to the guardhouse. Rubble still lay around, inside and outside the compound, which had been bulldozed flat before the erection of the hangar. Hangar, guardhouse, generator shed and fuel-tank, and the surrounding fence, had all been thrown up in a hurry in the early stages of Argentine preparations for war. The posts had been sunk in concrete – corner ones heavier than the others, three-legged to take the pull of the taut wire and support the weight of the lamps. The power for the lighting came directly from the generator, cables plainly visible, so you could be sure that whenever the compound was floodlit the generator would have to be running. The SBS had been pleased by this conclusion. And other photographs, taken at night, had provided other significant detail – so Andy had gathered, although he hadn't been at later conferences, after the outline plan had 'gone firm'.

Cloudsley raised his head and voice: 'Tom, if we're going to devour your beef, and then get some shuteye. . . .'

'Right.' Strobie pointed at one glass still half full, and the bottle still well up. 'Are you boys not whisky drinkers?'

'Not this morning, if you'd excuse us. When we've done the job, though – well, if you'd care to renew the offer?'

'Good.' Strobie groped for his stick. 'Delighted to know I'll be seeing you again. I mean it. Believe me, this is a treat, for me. . . . Tell me one thing, though: when you've done it, will there be a stink?'

'Not if we do it right.' Cloudsley reached to touch the edge of the table. It was a gesture Andy recalled having seen before, in Saddler's cabin in the destroyer, and it seemed at variance with the SBS man's hard-headed pragmatism. He was saying, 'Andy'll be back here before we are, Tom. If it's OK with you. He'll be with you a few days, could even be a week. . . . But no, with a bit of luck, nobody'll even know we've been there.'

'And when does Andy get back?'

'Before daylight. Incidentally, we'd like to borrow five horses again. He'll ride one home, leading the others. When it's finished and we come back, we'll be on foot.'

'Harry.' Andy broke into it. 'A point I was going to raise – having done some thinking, on the way here.' He felt almost as if he was *still* on the way: hoofbeats drumming in his head, the rhythmic motion, howl of the wind. . . . He thought, *It's the whisky*, and told Cloudsley, 'We were assuming I'd need to be back here before daylight. But as long as I'm on Tom's land by then, I'm home and dry. So you see, I could take you to within a few miles of your target, so you'd have horse transport all that way. . . . Right?'

Beale said, 'I've heard worse suggestions, Harry.'

Hosegood nodded approvingly. 'Lovely.'

'Saddle-sores and all?'

Cloudsley said to Strobie, 'I'm really quite glad we brought this bloke along.'

They ate the stew, then turned in and slept – under *quillangos*, quilts made of guanaco skins, distinctly moth-eaten. Andy's only private moment with Tom Strobie came just before they went to bed; he'd murmured, 'I'm mad to hear all about her, Tom. When I get back – good long talk?'

He'd expected to sleep for about twelve hours, but it was barely daylight when he woke, and within minutes the others were stirring too. Cloudsley's first words were, 'Better have the map out, Andy, check the bearing and distance of the airbase from wherever you're reckoning to drop us off.'

As if he'd been thinking about it all night. Maybe the planning went on in his sleep. Andy told him, 'OK, but breakfast first. Smell it?'

Ribs of mutton were being grilled – by Torres' wife, he guessed. Outside, the *estancia*'s generator was thumping away, pumping new energy into storage batteries. He went through to the kitchen and shook the *señora*'s hand, asked a few polite questions about her children; she was a brown-skinned, scrawny, hatchet-faced woman. There was a lot going on outside: horses were being saddled and the *peóns* detailed off for the day's work. The greybeard giving them their orders was old Anselmo, Strobie said.

'Remember Anselmo?'

'Certainly do.' He wouldn't have recognised him, though. 'Man with a keen eye for a horse.'

'And *that* seems like an age ago.' Strobie put a hand on his shoulder, neither of them thinking about the old *peón*, or horses. 'But I swear she hasn't changed a bit. . . . Except now she knows what a mistake she made.'

'You hinted as much, on a card the Christmas before last. Do you have any real reason for saying it?'

Strobie's shoulders moved: as if he thought it didn't matter, you could take it or leave it, just an idea he'd got. Thinking of it – Andy guessed – as something finished, a matter for regret but water under the bridge. Whereas the fact was it *did* matter, had never ceased to matter. There was a movement behind them, then – Cloudsley coming through from the other room, and Andy beckoned to him: 'Come and get educated, Harry.'

He pointed out the main features of the *estancia*. The 'big house' – iron-roofed and built originally of timbers taken from wrecks in the last century when there'd been no other wood obtainable. Every tree that was here now had been planted since then. The *bajo* – *peóns'* quarters, a bunkhouse and messroom for the single men; and the kitchen, the blacksmith's shop, barns. A blue pick-up in an open shed looked like the same old Ford that Strobie had been using about two decades ago. The meathouse, store, office, shearing sheds. . . .

'Your radio's in the big house still?'

'Reminds me.' Cloudsley turned from the window. 'Any news?'

'Not much.' Strobie told him, 'Lousy reception anyway. They could be jamming, from BA. But no move-out from the beachhead yet.' He added, '*That* radio is the one there, in the corner. The one Andy was asking about is the heap of old junk that connects us with the big wide world, our neighbours and so on. Transmitter-receiver – when it works.'

Anselmo had finished organising the workforce. He'd mounted, and was turning to follow others towards the gap in the sheltering belt of poplars. Wind-blown dirt swirling round the horses' legs. . . . Strobie said, 'Anselmo is my *capataz* now. Totally illiterate of course, but he's a good man with sheep and horses. Anything that has to be written down, Torres doe˙ it.'

Capataz meant 'foreman'. Andy said, 'I must say hello to him.'

'Well, I wouldn't recommend it.' Strobie qualified it – 'Unless you happen to bump into him. He's a good hand, I'd trust him all right, but – well, I wouldn't rub their noses in your being here. If you take my meaning?'

'That's good advice. I'd try to remain invisible, Andy, if I were you. Or at any rate *incognito*. . . .' Cloudsley turned from the window. 'Tom, it's like a whole villáge out there. I hadn't realised what an operation you have. . . . But – speaking of being invisible – won't they all know we're here, already?'

'Not to take much notice of. You came in the dark, you'll be leaving in the dark. They aren't likely to poke their noses in these windows – and if they did, what'd they see?'

'A bunch of tramps?'

Strobie nodded. 'Might wonder why I let you through the door. But that's about all.'

Andy said, looking at the lieutenant of the Royal Marines and remembering what he'd looked like in London, 'Can't see him at a Beating of the Retreat on Plymouth Hoe, can you?'

'Not – easily.' The old man thought about it. 'But I'd like to.' His eyes were wistful. With his face the way it was, the only signs of expression you could rely on were in the eyes: one of which had only half a lid to it and never shut completely. He'd sighed. 'By *God*, I'd like to. . . .'

Breakfast, then. Beale mumbled with his mouth full of it, 'Proper home from home, this is.'

Morning spilled over into afternoon. They'd had the map session, planned tonight's route. Strobie went out a few times, on *estancia* business. They all slept, some of the time. The BBC World Service said there'd been air activity over San Carlos, three Argentine aircraft had been destroyed, and a destroyer had been hit by a bomb that failed to explode. The frigate which had been bombed and sunk the day before was the *Antelope*. Some Informed Source was confident that an advance from the beachhead could be expected within hours. Shore targets including the airport runway at Stanley had been hit by Harrier strikes and by naval bombardment during the night.

Lunch was steak with fried potatoes. Strobie told them, 'They call it a "bife" in these benighted parts.' Hosegood said, '*I* call it bloody marvellous.'

Torres and Felix arrived late in the afternoon, and Strobie went out to meet them and inspect the condition of the sheep. He told Andy when he came back, 'He'll lay on the horses for your outing tonight. But he tells me I should demand some princely sum from you for the three your pals went off with.'

'I've been trying to get you to talk about that, Tom. Let's settle it right now. Three horses, three saddles, three bridles.' He saw reluctance in the old man's eyes, and insisted, 'Look, ask Torres to work it out and put it on paper. We'll pay whatever he reckons is a fair price.'

He knew that the *mayordomo,* conscious of his own responsibility for his *patrón*'s stock and gear, and on top of that deeply loyal to him anyway, would quote about double the going rate. Whereas Strobie would have halved it. Torres made his calculations, and brought them to Andy, Cloudsley got out the sheafs of *peso* notes, Strobie protestingly accepted them and locked them in an antique safe; it was fixed inside the cupboard where he also kept his liquor. He'd be needing every *peso* he could get, Andy guessed, to keep the place going in these hard times. He probably wouldn't have wanted to sell the horses anyway, which was a good enough reason to pay over the odds.

He said, to change the subject as the old man heaved himself up from the safe, 'Just as well the Cassidy gang aren't around now, Tom. They'd have had *that* old tin can opened double quick!'

'Dare say.' Strobie sat back in his chair. 'But I'd sooner have them at my throat than some of the charmers we have today, I can tell you.'

Hosegood queried, 'Cassidy gang?'

'They robbed banks, mostly. Trains too. Moved down here and lived respectably for a while, when things had got too hot

125

for them up north. Two men and a girl. What was the bird's name, Tom?'

'Was it Etta?' Strobie explained to the others, 'Before my time. Well, I'd've been a kid, back home. Start of the century. When their cash began to run out they started their old tricks again around these parts – Gallegos, Santa Cruz. . . . Etta used to hold the horses' heads outside the banks while her boyfriends went in and stuck 'em up.'

The Cassidy gang had departed the scene before grandfather Robert MacEwan had arrived in it, but the stories about them had been fresh then and old Fiona had absorbed them all, later frequently re-told them for the entertainment of her grandson Robert – while her other grandson, 'Joannie's runt', had also listened but from a distance.

Yarning, snoozing, clock-watching: a day in limbo, suspended in comfort but with nerves taut, between the penultimate and final stages. If there were to be later stages – like getting out of this country – he still wasn't sure he'd have any part to play in them. No certainty either way, and several conflicting indications. Beale and Hosegood were answering Tom's questions about their wives and babies, family life in England; listening intently to whatever they told him, Strobie was deeply absorbed. A lonely man, isolated, he'd been on the outside looking in – or looking back over his shoulder – for so long that he might have been a creature from some other planet asking about life on Earth.

He'd arranged for yet another meal to be ready before sunset – chicken stew with pasta, as proposed by Señora Torres. She was also providing them with local-origin rations to take with them: mutton, and a lot of hard bread rolls called *galletas*. Chocolate in plain wrapping was the only item from the Service-issue 'ratpacks' to be allowed; its origins wouldn't easily be identifiable. The same applied to 'hexie' blocks, fuel for the little Korean-made cooker that would heat their *maté*. The frugal menu, all they'd have for several days, accorded with the principle laid down by Cloudsley: 'If they caught us, we wouldn't be Marines. Wouldn't be anything. They'd shoot a bunch of God knows what.'

Geoff Hosegood suggested, 'Bunch of bloody wallies.' Strobie didn't know that word. He said, 'Diaz'd have you shot, all right. When he'd finished with you.'

US-made Ingram pistols – no bigger than the old colt .45s when their stocks were folded – were no give-away, Cloudsley pointed out. 'You could be an East German, or an Argentine, and carry one. Same as I might wear a Heckler and Koch, or a Makarov and it wouldn't make me German or Russian.'

Thoughts of capture, interrogation and firing-squads, Cloudsley's 'If they caught us', recalled to mind the phrase he'd used in an earlier explanation. *Consequences accepted*. . . . Reminding all of them, maybe; anyway there was a silence, Cloudsley staring into the fire, locked in his own thoughts; but he came out of them abruptly, glancing round at the others: 'Let's get the gear sorted.'

Watching from the doorway of the bedroom Andy had glimpses of various items as they vanished into the *ponchos'* numerous, specially made inner pockets. Some of the things were packaged and not identifiable, but he thought he saw, as well as such mundane articles as spare socks and rolls of toilet paper, a tube of rolled nylon mesh, a ball of brown string and a bundle of meat-skewers taped together. Field dressings, spare Ingram magazines. . .They were leaving a quantity of stuff here, which was encouraging, suggesting they really did intend returning this way. . . . Watching them open the big containers, divide the heavier stuff into three loads for the Czech-made backpacks. Each of which had externally, in nylon straps, a roll of rubberised material and what looked like a folding shovel. Beale explained, 'Sleeping-mat, civvie-type, and entrenching tool, campers for the use of. . . . Want to try this lot for weight?'

He could lift it – with some effort – but having got it on his shoulders he tried jogging with it.

'Christ. . . .'

'Yeah.' Beale took the weight off him. 'Thank God for the gee-gees.'

Back in the other room Andy told Strobie, 'We'll pay you for the food, of course.'

127

'No, damn it—'

'It's what we brought *pesos* for, Tom.'

Strobie drank whisky with his chicken. Outside, the light was fading. *Peóns* had been riding in, unsaddling and turning their horses out to graze on the *mallin*. The men's working hours were sunrise to sunset, Strobie said, with one Sunday off in every month. The meal was about finished when Pepe Torres knocked on the kitchen door and came clumping in, pulling his cap off and grinning as he bowed.

'*Señores.* . . .'

'How's it going, Don Pepe?' Strobie asked him, 'Are the horses ready?'

In five minutes, they would be. The same animals they'd ridden yesterday. Those five had had a good stand-off, and Félix was now preparing them, round at the back where there'd be nobody to witness the departure.

He didn't lead them due north as he'd proposed before. Working it out on the map this morning it had been decided to cut across Strobie's land to his number six gate, which was in the centre of the northwest section of his boundary fence. It meant starting out on the track by which they'd arrived last night, then taking a right fork. You had to use gates and therefore the tracks that led to them; these horses had never been asked to jump a fence in their lives. But even allowing for the fact that if they'd been yomping they'd have taken a much shorter, straight-line route, this way was still saving them about a whole night's slog – heavily burdened, at that.

Leaning down from the saddle, he identified the turn-off: he'd been scared of missing it but it was OK now, and they worked up to a canter. To the first fence, an internal one dividing paddocks. He opened the gate without dismounting, backing the *oscuro* so there was enough of a gap for the others to file through, then shutting it and spurring to catch up.

They rode with their chins down, eyes slitted against the

cold and the flying dirt. Cantering again, the easy, distance-covering gait to which the horses were accustomed; turning to look back from time to time like a riding-school instructor watching his pupils. At the boundary gate he dismounted to unlock it, and again waited for the others to pass through. Cantering up, then, between them and the fence that was Tom's northwestern boundary; it would be roughly three miles from here to the point where the fence met the public road and turned east along the road's south side. If you did turn that way along the road you'd have Strobie land on your right and Diaz on the left, all the way to the Sandrini ruin. The thought of this gave him an idea, and he pulled back to ride alongside Cloudsley.

'Harry – if you could set a night for it, I'd bring horses up to meet you. Using the Sandrini place as a rendezvous. Or I could be there several nights running. Even if I brought just one horse, for your gear?'

'Nice thought, and thanks, but' – Cloudsley shouted, over wind-howl and hoofbeats – 'could be anything from two nights to a week or so.' He had a hand up at the earflap of his cap. 'Any case we can yomp it, no problem – coming back. Won't have the grand piano, you see.'

Andy waved acknowledgement, and took the lead again. Cloudsley had his answers pretty well cut and dried, invariably. He wasn't dogmatic, but he had a knack of seeing straight through all the pros and cons and coming up with an immediate yea or nay, no hesitance at all. He'd said in the course of some debate this afternoon, beside Strobie's fire, 'This isn't some speculative adventure, old chum. You look at what's wanted, and if there's a way to do it you go ahead. If there isn't, you don't mess about, you leave it alone. We aren't either chancers or *kamikaze* warriors.'

Their confidence was one of the impressive things about them, and it would stem partly from that philosophy, he guessed. It was a quiet, unassuming confidence, with a complete absence of self-advertisement or self-satisfaction.

He shortened rein. 'Road's just here ahead!'

There was no fence to negotiate, both sides of the road now

being the former Coetzee property. The divide between the Coetzees and Diaz, even if Diaz did now own this territory as well, started on the other side of the road and ran due north. Andy walked his horse across, over two low banks with the road sunk between them, picked up the line of posts extending northward and waited for the others to join him. Straining his eyes into the dark, ears for sounds other than the wind's, as Cloudsley came up beside him. Cloudsley alert too, staring around, very upright in his saddle. There was a stretch of four miles to be covered now, to reach Diaz's northwest corner post; after which there'd be no more fences to follow, no markers, only the compass course they'd decided on this morning with the map spread on Tom's kitchen table. Hosegood and Beale pressed up from behind, their horses' hard breathing rasping against the wind, ears back at the sudden bunching. Andy dug his heels in, and led on.

On foot, as the SBS team *would* have done it, with all that weight on them this bit would have taken as much as two hours, he guessed. This way it took less than twenty minutes.

'Ready for the compass work, Andy?'

'Let's have it.'

The compass was Cloudsley's; he passed it over.

With no landmarks to sight on, and no stars visible, all you could do was hold the luminous compass down by your crotch as a backsight and use the horse's ears as foresight. He rode twenty yards ahead of the others, and they spread out – Cloudsley to the right, on his flank, Beale to the left; and Hosegood between them, astern of Andy, leading the packhorse. The target was still two leagues ahead, to the northwest. Cantering, maintaining that formation which they'd decided on first so the compass would be clear of the magnetic influence of gear in the packs, second because the nearer you came to the target the more likely it was you might run into a patrol. *If* the Argies had patrols out. There was no reason to believe they had, except for another dictum of Cloudsley's: 'You have to put yourself in the opposition's boots, ask yourself what *you'd* be doing. . . .'

In fact they rode into nothing except space — Patagonia's prime commodity.

He'd been concentrating on steering them as accurately as possible, while Cloudsley watched the passing minutes as a guide to how far they'd come. The yomp was to be started about one league, five kilometres, from the target. Unexpectedly soon Cloudsley came slanting over, shouting to Beale and Hosegood and closing up beside Andy in a sudden thunder of hooves.

'Far as you go, Andy Mac!'

The drop-off point, already. Time to dismount, unload the animals and load themselves. Time to say goodbye, good luck.

9

Saddler said into his microphone, 'Disregard. . . .'

The sonar contact was non-sub. They'd been tracking it for the last twenty minutes, and it might have been a whale: there'd been doubts right from the start, but doubts had to be solid before you relinquished a contact that *might* have been an Argie submarine stealing into San Carlos Water to sink ships. He saw disappointment cloud the young faces round the plot as one of the radarmen reached over to wipe out chinograph markings; he said into the Open Line, 'Officer of the Watch – increase to revolutions one-two-eight. Ask the navigating officer for a course.'

He pulled off the headset. The radarmen's faces showed strain as well as disappointment. He told Bernard Knight, 'PWO – I'll be on the bridge.' He was taking *Shropshire* northward out of North Falkland Sound – she'd been nosing up through it when sonar had picked up that contact – and thence east to join the carrier group's escort. Out there in the deep field they were to be allowed a quiet day in which to make temporary repairs to the bomb damage aft and to 30-mm cannon-fire wounds sustained this morning.

The ship was heeling to her rudder as he got into the lift.

133

Arriving in the bridge a few seconds later he heard the order, 'Midships, steer three-four-zero. . . .' Dark figures drew aside to let him through to his seat at the command console, in the starboard for'ard corner.

The bomb damage was two days old. Four A4s had swept over, in the Sound. An intensity of gun, missile and small-arms fire from *Shropshire* and from other ships nearby had discouraged three of the pilots, but the fourth had pushed his attack right home. The bomb had slammed into the port for'ard end of the flight deck near the hangar doors and slanted out through the crew's dining hall immediately below it, passing out through the ship's side without exploding or causing any casualties. The 'after battery' of riflemen on the flight deck had seen the bomb coming, thrown themselves flat and had difficulty believing, seconds later, they were still alive. But this morning's strafing attack, cannon-fire from a Mirage, had left five men wounded and one dead. The sailor who'd been killed had been the port Seacat operator, the yellow-headed Pitts. Three days ago in San Carlos Water – or four days ago – Saddler had stood beside the director and chatted with Pitts about various Seacat problems. He'd been talking to him when an attack came in and he'd had to run for it, but he could see the boy now like a snapshot in his memory, narrow acne-scarred face incongruously small-looking under the tin hat. He'd already started writing a letter to the parents.

On his high seat in the bridge now – wrenching his thoughts away from the problems involved in writing that letter – hearing Vigne propose a course of 343 instead of 340. . . . Saddler concurred. *Shropshire* would steer this course until she'd cleared the Eddystone Rock well enough to turn east and pass clear to the north of it. The carrier group would also be steering east, increasing their distance from the islands after a night of Harrier strikes against shore targets.

Yesterday the Argentines had celebrated their National Day by sinking *Coventry* by bombing and the *Atlantic Conveyor* by Exocet. *Coventry* had been in company with *Broadsword*, the pair of them forming a 'combo' to operate a missile trap to the north of West Falkland. The system had worked well on several previous occasions; the Type 42's long-range Sea Dart would engage attackers when they were visible only on radar, and then as surviving Argies closed in to take revenge *Broadsword*'s Sea Wolf would take them on at close range. *Coventry* had jollied up the celebrations by splashing three attackers before the fatal assault came in. It came in the form of four Skyhawks, two of them first at sea-skimming height; they'd swung away from *Coventry*'s shooting and headed for *Broadsword*, half a mile astern of her. In *Broadsword*, Sea Wolf was activated, but the two targets were so close together that the computer couldn't decide between them, suffered an electronic brainstorm and switched off the system. *Broadsword*'s gun and close-range defence were in furious action as the A4s flashed over, the roar of their passing punctuated by a ringing *clang* from somewhere aft as the bomb struck; some seconds elapsed before the realisation took root that this one wasn't going to explode either. The second pair of attackers came screaming in and this time the computer kept a clear head, Sea Wolf gained a solution and was about to fire when *Coventry* swung to starboard across the destroyer's bow, fouling the range. Two one-thousand-pound bombs exploded deep inside *Coventry*, tearing the ship's heart out.

Sickeningly familiar scenes, then. A stricken, burning ship, and the frantic efforts to save lives — efforts collective and individual and in some cases heroic. Afterwards, the reckoning, the heavy overhang of sadness and the permanence of loss; and awareness that the ship's name in the news bulletin could as easily have been *Shropshire* as any other, and that if the issue rested in human hands at all and not simply in blind chance, those hands were your own.

Shropshire was pitching harder as she ploughed out from the Sound's shelter, seas almost phosphorescent-white in contrast to the surrounding blackness, sheeting back from her rhythmically plunging stem. The glisten of seas exploding across her foc's'l, and a tentative greying in the eastern sector, reminded him that dawn wasn't far away. He had a hope that after securing from dawn action stations he might have the luck to get a couple of hours' uninterrupted sleep. Except that first he'd finish the letter to the Pitts parents. There hadn't been much chance of anything more than catnaps, just lately. In daylight there'd been the constant air threat, and nights had been spent 'on the gunline', lobbing shells into the dark, corrections to fall of shot coming by radio from forward observation officers who'd be crouched in scrapes on rain-swept hillsides to call down fire in support of operations by SAS and SBS. Special Force teams were all over East and West Falkland now, infiltrating enemy outposts and pinpointing their strongpoints.

The *Atlantic Conveyor* had been sunk by an AM39 missile from one of a pair of Etendards which had refuelled in the air north of the islands before turning south to attack the carrier group, the vital targets of *Hermes* and *Invincible* from which the Sea Harriers were operating. Thirty miles to the north the frigate *Ambuscade* gained radar contact, identified the nature of the threat and alerted the fleet. Warships fired chaff to deflect the missiles; the Etendards had launched them at a range of twenty-six miles and turned for home – safe, never in much danger. One of the missiles vanished, but the other swung aside from its intended targets, impacted on the *Atlantic Conveyor* two miles away. The *Conveyor* had on board ten Wessex helos and four of the giant troop-carrying Chinooks; they'd have been flown off that evening after preparation including the fitting of their rotor-blades, and they were important elements in the plans for an advance inland from the San Carlos beachhead. So those plans had been set back. Another point – in the back of Saddler's mind, and doubtless in others too – was that the Argies had been generally assumed to have had three AM39s left, and in this attack they'd used two of them. Leaving one: one deployed, probably already slung under the belly of an Etendard and ready for use. Saddler hoped to God that the SBS team, guided by Lisa's boyfriend, would by this time have reached their target and dealt with the reserve missiles before they were deployed as replacements.

David Vigne's voice rose over the exterior noise of wind and sea and the ship's straining hull, interior hum of machinery. . . . 'Time to come round – to zero-nine-zero, sir.'

About time for dawn action stations too. The new day was a distant flush of silver on otherwise black, heaving ocean. Saddler said, 'Yes, bring her round.' Wondering what he could say in his letter that would be anything but clichés, whether words existed that could even slightly mitigate the agony of Mr and Mrs Pitts.

The generator filled the night with its noise, supplying power to flood-lights which yellowed the missile compound and the hangar's walls 150 yards down the uneven slope. The near end of the perimeter fence was only about a hundred yards away, but there was a slip-road to cross before you'd reach it and the light spilled out on to the road too. The double gates – shut now – were in the longer, north side of the fence, with the guardhouse on this side of them. The sentry was there, at this moment, pacing up and down, probably as much as anything to keep warm – or less cold – and like the man he'd taken over from half an hour ago he worked to a set routine: every fifteen minutes he left his position at the gates and made one circuit of the outside of the fence – clockwise, each time, and never taking less than six or more than seven and a half minutes. Cloudsley had timed them both; the seven-and-a-half minute circuit had been when the previous one had stopped to pee.

This hide, the one nearest to the target and with a view of it, was finished. Cloudsley leant in to tie the loose end of a ball of string to a spike just inside the entrance, then squirmed around, keeping low to the ground because if the sentry or anyone else happened to look this way at the wrong moment he might otherwise have been visible against the skyline – would be soon, anyway, with dawn not far off – and crawled back to the other hide, laying out string as he crossed the fifty feet that separated them.

'OK?'

'About done.' Beale didn't pause in his work: minutes counted, now. He muttered, 'Roof in a mo'.' Hosegood said

137

from six feet away, 'Started, this end.' Cloudsley crouched, seeing dawn's left hand fingering the eastern sky – a warning, a steel-grey threat seeping over the low hump of the missile store and other less recent construction beyond it – an accommodation block, workshops, hangars, fuel-storage compound with its own safety fence around it. The napalm storage might be in that enclosure too: it was a point to check on later. Lights threw irregular pools and lanes of brightness among the other buildings, but the missile compound was the only area that was more or less comprehensively illuminated. Fortunately, not *quite* comprehensively.

The generator with its unceasing racket was a gift. It was going to help in another way too, in the nights ahead. He heard Beale mutter, 'OK, roof. . . .' It was a relief to hear it. Beale had been alone, working on this hide, until Cloudsley and Hosegood had finished the other. The actual breaking and digging had been completed some minutes ago, they'd only been clearing out the last of the loose soil. Excavated earth and stones had been disposed of at intervals, whenever the rubber sleeping mats had been piled with it they'd dragged them away from the hides and dispersed the stuff on the blind side from the target. In fact the set-up was ideal for soil disposal, because this area had had excavated debris, from the site of the missile compound, bulldozed across it.

Roofing the hide now; Beale on one side and Hosegood on the other, pushing in spikes vertically a few inches back from the top edges. Then nylon mesh, taut between the hooks and with its strips overlapping. On top of that, where in a grassed area (such as other SBS teams had had on the slopes above the San Carlos beaches) you'd lay turves which you'd have cut before the digging started, they used the next best thing, surface soil with fibrous roots in it. Finally a scattering of loose soil and stones, and at this end camouflage netting would hang over the entrance.

'String, Geoff.' He'd pulled a few extra yards off the ball; he cut it and passed the severed end to Hosegood. All part of the drill, you didn't need to talk much and you didn't need light. *Be light soon anyway.* . . . And one essential job not done yet.

He crawled back to the OP, slid in feet-first through the small entrance and went to the end where he'd dumped most of the gear he'd been carrying in his pockets. He came back to the entrance with what looked like a pointed metal bar, and worked it up through the roofing of net and earth. Muck scattering down through the nylon mesh. . . . Crouching in the entrance, with one hand inside to hold the thing in place, he reached with the other to locate its top on the outside and push a pierced rubber disc down over it, down to ground level. The rubber gripped the tube so it couldn't slip back. Now he unscrewed the pointed metal cover which had allowed the little periscope to be rammed through several inches of rough, stony soil. It stood about eight inches above ground, camouflage-painted, invisible even in broad daylight from more than a couple of feet away. Inside again, Cloudsley had his eye to the monofocal lens, adjusting focus, when Hosegood arrived in the entrance. Cloudsley edged back to give him room, but movement ceased and he heard a whisper: 'Hang about. . . .'

'What's up?'

Eye back at the periscope; seeing it for himself as Hosegood answered, '– looking right at us. . . .'

The sentry was motionless, facing this way and with his head up, light from the compound on his left side and profile and the greenish-coloured helmet, and throwing a long shadow across the service road which divided the long stretch of buildings from the open expanse of airfield.

'Still at it. Cheeky sod. . . .'

He'd whispered but he could have shouted, with the generator drowning any other sound. The generator was no more than twelve or fifteen yards from that sentry; you could have fired a gun here and he wouldn't have heard it. But he was turning away now, slowly pivoting like some kind of robot: Cloudsley was watching him still, through the periscope with its fourfold magnification. The sentry once again immobile, apparently surveying the dark runways instead of this western skyline. Hosegood said, 'Proper wally,' and slid down into the hide. Before, when the sentry had been looking this way, the movement might have been enough to catch his eye. Cloudsley, making way for Hosegood without taking his eye from the lens, saw the sentry patrolling eastward, his back this way and his face to the dawn, starting another circuit. Cloudsley said, 'He may have thought you were a *guanaco*.'

'Thanks a lot.' Hosegood suggested, 'Test comms, shall I?'

'Why not.'

Communications with the other hide, he meant. You could pass any message at all by Morse, using short and long pulls on the string, but there was also a quicker, special code of signals for alarms or routine messages such as 'join me' or 'I'm coming over'. Cloudsley had the 'scope focused on the sentry as he paced slowly along the wire – not looking around at all, apparently unconscious of any possible threat. He wasn't a septuagenarian or a peasant lad – as Intelligence had suggested local recruits for guard duty might be – but he still wasn't worth his rations.

Out of sight now, at the far end of the compound. In a few minutes he'd reappear on the southern boundary, but he'd have to be more than halfway down that stretch of fencing before you'd see him. Until then the dark bulk of the hangar, the missile store, was in the way. Cloudsley was taking a long, hard look at the compound, imprinting in his memory the precise extents of areas of light and shadow. The northwest corner, the nearest one, was of greatest interest. The generator shed was there, and its fuel-tank on breezeblock pillars. About five yards separating them. They were close enough to the corner light to give a wide spread of shadow which extended – thanks to the height of that diesel-oil tank – most of the way to the near corner of the hangar. In which, please God, there'd be some unspecified number of AM39 missiles awaiting treatment.

Vasectomy, some humorous boffin in British Aerospace had termed it.

Studying the layout, brighter and darker areas and the distances between them, thinking over the moves and their timing, for the four-hundredth time. . . . That shadowed area was the key to it. It was why he'd sited the hides here instead of at the rear, the south side, where in some ways they might have been more inconspicuous. Shadows reached not only to the missile store's corner – almost – but also to the back wall of the guardhouse on this side of the gates. There was no door or window in that wall. No reason there should have been: they'd placed the guardhouse to face the gates, at right-angles to them, not to look into its own securely fenced compound. . . . The sentry was in sight again now: Cloudsley moved the periscope fractionally to take a glance at him, then turned it back to where he'd had it. The shadowed part existed because of the way they'd set up the arc-lamps on the corner uprights. The lights were single directional floods, shining only one way, so they'd angled each one to shine along one side of the compound. The near one, northwest corner, shone south, the lamp on the southwest corner shone east – and so on, anti-clockwise. They should have had wide-angle lamps, or set them in pairs back to back. The fact was they hadn't, and this should make it possible to do the job without having to take out any sentries, which would have led to complications anyway, but you could say that the Argie shuffling along the line of that fence now might owe the continuance of his life to a design fault.

But his routine was silly, too. It was regular, predictable. Of course, if he'd spent all his time at the gates you'd have gone in on the south side, well out of his sight, and then moved around the end into the shadows. But the Argies could very easily have made this a lot more difficult than Cloudsley thought it was going to be. Touch wood. . . .

The concrete of the service road had been extended in an apron through the double gates and right up to the sliding doors in the north side of the hangar. There were two small access doors in those big ones. These details had been known and taken into account in the planning, but it was still a relief to see confirmed on the ground what had been deduced from photographs in an office overlooking the Thames Embankment. There could easily have been changes made, between then and now. He'd half expected the area of concrete, the size of a tennis court and sloping from the hangar towards the

141

road, to have been extended to cover the rest of the compound, for instance. It had looked as if that had been the intention, as if they might temporarily have run out of material. But there'd been no such change; it was still rough ground, unsurfaced.

The sentry was close to the southwest corner, the light from that corner post on him as he approached it; but less bright now, a softer yellow because of the slow growth overhead of the new day. As he advanced he had the guard fence, four metres high, on his right, and twenty feet on his left an ordinary anti-sheep fence – low, with eight strands of taut wire ringing the whole base, airfield runways included. You'd need it, of course, in sheep country. They'd be more alert, he guessed, to the potential hazard of sheep on their airstrip than to any human intrusion around the missile store. . . . He'd seen a flash of light: a reflection from the corner post as the sentry raised his head. He said, 'This guy wears glasses, Geoff.'

'They weren't far wrong, then.'

Hosegood was knocking accumulated dirt off the sleeping-mat he'd brought in with him. Two mats in the rear hide and one in this, although this was where two men would be spending their days. It wasn't as crazy as it might have seemed: in this OP only one man would ever be asleep, the other watching at the periscope, but in the other hide the occupant would be taking a day off, and they'd foregather there from time to time for a brew-up of *maté*. The cooker with its hexamine fuel tablets gave out very little smoke, and such fumes as it did emit would be filtered out through several inches of earth roof which in any case wasn't in sight from the airbase. The man in that hide could sleep all day, otherwise, with the end of the communication string tied to a finger.

Hosegood was blowing into his frozen hands. 'See much?'

'Not yet.' Except the sentry on his way up the near side of the compound. 'Be light soon though.' He looked round at the Marine's dark, hunched shape. 'We'll treat ourselves to a snack before you crash your swede. *Maté* to warm us up.'

'That muck.'

'By the time we're through, Geoff, you'll be hooked on it.'

Maté was a stimulant, of course. It was also local, part of the

142

act, the fancy dress. Whatever else, it would be *hot*. . . . He moved the periscope again to pick up the sentry, guessing he'd be at the gates by this time.

Two of them there.

Thinking about it – wondering how he'd handle it if they did double-up the sentry duty – he heard aircraft engines drowning the generator noise. Lights were moving out there on the field; and the blazing lights of a saloon car turning off the service road scythed over six or eight Pucarás swinging into line, wingtip to wingtip. . . . 'Hey. Roberto's boys must be *keen*. . . .'

A new day's light was strengthening when Andy slid down from the saddle to unlock Tom Strobie's number six gate and lead his five horses through. He'd brought them down gently enough, but they were steaming in the cold air. He'd taken it slowly partly to go easy on them after the hard ride northward, partly because there was no reason to hurry, and also because he'd wanted to have his eyes and ears open, avoiding any chance encounter. It wouldn't have been easy to explain leading a string of saddled horses through the deserted paddocks in the middle of the night.

Timing had been good, as it turned out – daylight now, and he was back on Tom's land. He swung himself up on to the *oscuro*'s back, pressed his heels in and jerked at the head-ropes to get them going. Taking a route via number five gate, riding southward along the wire: three miles to that other gate, then he'd turn east and nobody who saw him – Pucará pilots for instance – could guess he'd come from the direction of the airbase.

It had been Harry Cloudsley's suggestion. Harry the belt-and-braces man. . . . An owl, keeping late hours, whirred past his head, interrupting a mental picture of those three gone to ground by now, like foxes. He had his team moving at a brisk canter, the fence-posts of Tom's boundary rushing up and then

143

flicking away like telegraph-poles seen from a train window. . . . Relaxing in the saddle, munching chocolate. The metal water-bottle flopping against his knee. Cloudsley hadn't wanted to take metal bottles, which he'd said he'd known to split open when their contents froze. In Norway, above the Arctic Circle, he'd explained. He'd accepted them as necessary to the outfit, the disguise, but grumbled that plastic ones were better. Tony Beale had pointed out that it wasn't freezing yet, and Cloudsley had told him, 'Damn near to it. . . . If it takes us a week up there, who knows?' It was below freezing-point now, Andy thought. His and his horses' breaths jetted like steam and the ground was as hard as stone under their hooves. The winter blizzards wouldn't be long in coming.

Five gate; he swung his troop left, on to the track that led to Tom's *estancia*. Home and dry: nobody had seen him, no Pucará had defiled the wintry looking sky. In which there was definitely a threat of snow. He wondered how snow might affect Cloudsley's plans. The job they were doing now might not be affected much, but the withdrawal afterwards – the way snow held tracks. . . .

Last time he'd approached from this direction the first thing he'd seen had been a light, one in Tom's window. This time, in broad daylight now, he saw the poplars first and then the shearing sheds with the pens in front of them. His horse, scenting home, friends and water, had to be held in, restrained from breaking into a gallop. He waved to a group of riders passing at a distance: they'd turned to stare at him and his following of riderless animals, and he remembered Tom's advice about not advertising his presence here. That might have been Anselmo, too, who'd raised a hand acknowledging his greeting. . . . He rode through the gap in the trees, the open gateway; there was a gleam of water beyond them and more sheep-pens beyond that. He was heading for the horse-corral when he saw Torres talking with Félix – and Félix broke away from the *mayordomo*, came hurrying to meet him. . . . 'Don Andrés, if you please, I will take the horses!'

'Well, thanks.' He slid down, fondled the black's nose, wondering why Félix seemed so nervous. 'They're in good

144

shape, I think.' Torres waddled up, wearing his smile but also anxious-looking; glancing to his right where at a distance a young man in a *poncho*, wide-brimmed hat and shiny boots was leaning against the rail of the corral. In working hours, that kind of lounging wasn't usual. Torres said, 'Good day, Don Andrés.' Keeping his tone low. 'The *patrón* asks, would you please go to him directly, in the house?'

'Something wrong? Is he sick, or—'

'Nothing – of that nature. Thanks be to God. . . .' Torres was clearly apprehensive, though. 'Only – if you please, as the *patrón* desires—'

'All right. . . .' Crossing the yard, he was conscious of the young man's stare. He knocked on Strobie's door, then pushed it open. 'Tom—'

'That you, Andy?'

'Yeah. . . . Some problem?'

'Come on in, shut the door. . . .' Strobie craned round from his deep chair. 'I just told Torres to ride out and head you off. . . . Saw him, did you? More to the point, that young squirt see *you*?'

'Guy in shiny boots?'

'Damn. . . .'

'What is this, Tom?'

'Huyez. Paco Huyez. . . . Did he get a good look at you?'

'I wouldn't say so.' But he couldn't see that it mattered whether he had or hadn't. There wasn't a chance he'd have known him; any more than he, Andy, had known *him*. . . . Paco Huyez had been just a child, five years ago, when he'd pulled out. Paco's father Juan was *mayordomo* at La Madrugada. Robert's right-hand man, hired by old Fiona. Hired ostensibly by her son Bruce but actually by the old woman when Bruce began to drink really seriously, after Juanita died. The name Huyez derived from the Welsh name Hughes: Fiona had taunted her son, 'Ye've a fancy for mongrels, Brucie, now here's a *real* 'un!' Juan Huyez had reported to *her,* touching his hat occasionally to the drink-sodden man he called *patrón* and knowing damn well his own and his family's future, if they had any, would lie in the hands of grandson Robert. In retrospect it

145

was obvious that when the old woman had brought in Huyez she'd been hiring back-up to ensure the continuance of the MacEwan dynasty under Prince Robert – Bruce being a busted flush and Andy of no consequence.

Strobie was saying, 'If he did see you, and recognised you—'

'I know. His father'd hear of it and then Robert would. But it's a very big "if", Tom, isn't it?' We wouldn't have known each other if we'd been nose to nose. At thirty yards, as it was out there, I could've been a bar of soap.'

He added, cracking a smile at the old man's continuingly worried expression, 'Which incidentally, with some hot water, wouldn't do me any harm. . . . But really and truly, five years ago he'd have been – what, fourteen? You think he'd know me now – and with this beard and the fancy dress?'

'You might be surprised.' But he'd shrugged, turning away. . . . 'Took 'em to where they wanted, did you?'

'Yup. No bother.'

'Good blokes, those. Breath of fresh air.'

'Right. . . . Tom, what would Paco be doing here?'

'Chasing skirt. Daughter of one of my families. I don't like him hanging around, but it wouldn't be diplomatic to send him packing, seeing the girl's father doesn't object. Which he wouldn't – with Juan Huyez a bigshot now, in their eyes, running your place pretty well as if it was his own. . . . But you see' – coming back to the argument now – 'to you, Paco was just one of a lot of scruffy kids. To him, though – God's sake, you're a MacEwan, brother of his papa's *patrón* – he'd know your looks like you know Mrs Thatcher's!'

'But *five years*, Tom—'

'One way you haven't changed.' Strobie growled. 'You're just as bloody obstinate.'

'Did you say *I* am?'

Later, after a large breakfast, they sat by the fire, Strobie sucking at a pipe. He wagged a finger: 'You've got that wrong, boy. Diaz turned political because Elaine gave up on him, not the other way about. I'll grant you the process may have started before she actually took off, but it was all part and parcel of one progression – she'd had a fling or two, and from

146

what I heard—'

'From Francisca?'

'Possibly. . . . According to what I was told, she was only waiting for the right man – meaning some guy who could afford her. So Diaz had to show her what a big man she was running out on – show the rest of us too, to make up for it. That'd be the mainspring – how his neighbours and brother officers might see it. The Latin temperament, all the macho nonsense – not that you'd need to be a Latin, necessarily—'

'Right.'

'A lot of decent folk got locked up and God knows what else, you might say, to compensate for that lovely lady's departure.'

'Does Francisca see that angle?'

'Francisca sees what she wants to see. She's in total sympathy with her father. You can't talk politics with her – *I* can't, anyway. It's more than a month since she walked in that door, and *that's* political, of course.'

'How?'

'There's a war on, and she knows where I stand. I'm an ancient Brit, and I'll never be *acriollado*. OK, I'm so old, lame and ugly I can be tolerated, but while it's going on I very much doubt she'd come near me.'

'Yes. I thought you rather indicated that, yesterday.'

'She *might*, though.' Strobie shrugged his heavy shoulders. 'Fact is, since the war started she hasn't. Political caution, entirely due to her father's position, a feeling she mustn't let him down – and she'd know I'd understand this, you see. It's a passing phase, Andy, it doesn't affect what matters in the long run, the real issue as far as *you're* concerned, which is the fact her marriage is a bloody disaster. That'll still be a fact when this war's forgotten.' Strobie's eyes held Andy's: 'If it interests you?'

'Is it simply that they don't get on, or—'

'No idea. Women don't tell a man that kind of thing. Unless he's their lover. If I had a wife I'd hear all about it from her, no doubt.'

'But you're certain?'

147

'That she's unhappy with him, yes. And she's asked for news of you, more than once. Not directly, but—'

'What if she did come to see you while I'm here?'

'She's still her father's daughter.' Strobie nodded towards the bedroom. 'In there, sit tight till she's gone.'

He knew he'd have to stay out of her sight. Because of Cloudsley and the job in hand, and the fact that whatever shape her private life was in she'd always been a patriotic Argentine, more so since the desertion of her mother. And now she'd *have* to be.

'I might come back, Tom – from England, after it's all over. Maybe write her a letter first – care of you?'

'You'd need to be damn careful. Remember the dog in the manger, Andy. He wouldn't just sit and watch it happen.'

'Or she might come to London. Sort it out there, less strain. . . .' He shut his eyes. 'Crazy. It's just daydreaming, isn't it? She turned me down. The fact she doesn't hit it off with my wretched brother doesn't mean *that* situation's any different.'

'You're talking *wet*, boy!' Strobie had slammed a fist down on the arm of his chair. 'Can't you *learn*? Christ, you threw away one chance five bloody years ago, and now—'

'What else could I have done?'

'Oh, bloody oath, what d'you *think*?'

Stuck around, he meant, fought for her. . . .

Andy leant forward, forearms on his knees, thinking *You don't know, old man, you weren't in my skin, hearing her*. . . . Strobie was staring at him and looking his age, shaking his head in little jerks like a twitch, an old man's temper. . . . And it was all pie in the sky. A dream. Francisca had made up her mind five years ago and nothing Andy could have said or done would have changed anything then. The same applied now, despite his own five years of daydreaming and Tom's wishful thinking. . . .

They went on talking about her for another hour; talking about her, from Andy's point of view, being the next best thing to talking with her – and about as close as he was likely to come to it. He'd had to be here, almost in reach of her, to appreciate this hard reality. Also to understand the basis of the old man's hopes and motives past and present, as far as they showed through now or could be guessed at. Tom Strobie loved Francisca with a strong paternal affection which none the less might have had undertones of sexual longing in it, deriving from his own brief marriage half a century ago, a very young wife who'd died when he'd been on the other side of the world and who'd had a look of Francisca; and the same direct manner, he'd told them once – reminiscing· after a lot of whisky, talking to him and Francisca in front of the fire in the 'big house' where the Torres family now lived.

Andy had asked him, 'Got a photo of her, Tom?'

'No—'

Francisca, then: 'Why, that's dreadful! Not even a snapshot?'

Strobie had glared at her like some cornered animal; then muttered – softening only because it was *Francisca* bullying him – 'No, I never kept any snapshots. . . .'

He was heaving himself up now. He had farm business to attend to, he said.

'When this Falklands row's over and done with, Andy, come back here. As you say. You'd have reason enough, business reasons, wouldn't you? But as you said, write first – here – and I'll see she gets it. Enclose it in a note to me, huh?'

'Yes. I'll do that.'

Going along with it because arguing with the old man provoked this fierce irritation that seemed to exhaust him, left him shaky, *old*. . . . He was on his feet now, growling, 'You'd better catch up on some sleep now. Lock that door and pull the curtains. I shan't be back much before sundown, you can sleep all day.'

With only eight hours of daylight at this latitude, sundown came soon enough. But only Beale, in the rear hide on his own, had slept most of the hours away. Now, it was getting dark.

They'd locked the compound gates and a sentry had been posted, the generator was in full roar and the lights were burning. During the day one of the double gates had stood open some of the time, and there'd been comings and goings, but no movements of missiles either in or out. No sight of any civilians either. The implication, Cloudsley thought, was either that there were no French technicians working here or there were no missiles to be worked on.

But then they'd have no reason to guard the place.

In preparation for the night's excursion he'd taken the magazine out of his Ingram machine-pistol, emptied it of its thirty rounds, inspected it minutely and tested the spring for tension and smooth movement, then refilled it, wiping each 9-mm round before thumbing it in. Checking the pistol itself too. Hosegood had already been through the same maintenance routine with his. An oily rag gave it enough lubrication and protection before he pushed the magazine back into the gun, banging it home with the heel of his hand.

Hosegood had opened a pack of stun grenades and clipped three to his belt. He passed another three to Cloudsley, who was replacing the Ingram in its special holster inside his *poncho*. The suppressor fitted into a slot on the side of the holster, as did one spare magazine. Two others went into a pocket. Accepting the XFS grenades from Hosegood now. 'Thanks, Geoff. All mod cons.'

Cam grease now, black face-cream. Then black balaclavas and black gloves. They were skiers' gloves, made of very hard leather for some degree of protection against barbed wire.

All day, Pucarás had been taking off, circling the field and landing-on again. Most of it was obviously pilot-training, but two flights of three aircraft each had been bombed-up with the white napalm containers, taken off and returned half an hour later without them. Before take-off the Pucarás had been lined up just over the service road, this side of the control tower, which had a radar dome on it. The bombs had been brought out in tractor-drawn trailers from somewhere at the far end of the complex of buildings, not from the fuel compound.

Hosegood tested the sharpness of his knife on the ball of a

thumb, and re-sheathed it. He murmured conversationally, 'Feels like a hard freeze coming.'

'There was a hard one last night.'

'Not this hard, I'd say.'

This would be Geoff's first action, as distinct from exercise, with the squadron. He'd been a Marine for six years. You had to serve for about three years after the initial thirty-week training before you could go in for a specialist qualification like Special Boat, and then there was the SQ course itself plus a few other interludes. So he wasn't exactly wet behind the ears.

Dark enough now to bring Tony over, Cloudsley decided. He reached for the string – it was attached to Geoff – and passed the one-letter summons, felt the string jerk in his fingers as Beale acknowledged.

'Tony's on his way.'

He'd have been ready and waiting. Cloudsley put his eye to the periscope again.

No sentry in sight. OK, he'd be making his first tour around the compound. It meant you'd have to wait for the start of the next one before you could move. Say five minutes for the completion of this circuit, plus fifteen. He checked the time. But this was no problem, he'd have waited that long anyway for the darkness to thicken. Meanwhile there was no sentry in sight, nothing else stirring either. It was understandable: in these temperatures you wouldn't hang around outside if you didn't have to. . . . Beale came slithering in, bulky in the *poncho* and other padding, and Cloudsley muttered as he squeezed past, 'If I'm sent on any more larks like this one, I'm asking to have *little* guys with me.'

'Wouldn't help much with that fence, would it?'

'Oh, I don't know. . . . You fit, Tony?'

The fence loomed in their minds like Beecher's, at this stage. With the heavy packs to be taken over it. But at least they'd only have to contend with the worst of that on this first night.

The sentry came into sight now, advancing slowly along the southern perimeter. He walked like a duck, this one. . . .

Cloudsley swung the periscope to the left, where light spilled from the guardhouse doorway – light visible, door *in*visible, from this angle – making a yellowish stain on the concrete inside the gates. There was a little gate there as well, this side of the big double ones and right beside the guardhouse; you couldn't see it from here but there had to be one, because individuals had passed through the fence at that point when the main gates had been shut.

'Move in about eighteen minutes.' Checking the luminous face of his watch. 'Goon's on his travels now, we'll push off when he starts his next walkabout.'

He'd had the high-speed drill out and checked it over, given it a chamfer with the oily rag, and he'd stowed a number of the drilling bits in his pockets, the long kind in one and short ones in another. Vasectomy wasn't an easy operation to perform on a patient as sensitive as an AM39. They'd all three done it a few times on dummy missiles in a darkened workshop in the Bristol area, with scientists hovering round to instruct and advise, but even after several practice runs they'd still found it tricky. Not to mention the fact that at the British Aerospace establishment there'd been the comfort of knowing the missile wasn't likely to explode in your face while you were operating. In the hangar down there, there'd be no such certainty. The senior boffin at Bristol had only gone so far as to say there was no reason it should happen as long as they did it exactly right and were extremely cautious in handling the drill. The most important thing was to drill in precisely the right spot; then with the second, longer bit, stage two on each patient, to be very, *very* careful not to break through too roughly.

The drill was German made, ultra high speed and silent-running. The bits were knitting-needle thin, and made to a unique prescription by a small private company near Coventry. The drill, well wrapped and cushioned against shock – it was going to be thrown around, before it was put to use – was in the number one pack now, along with batteries and a few other bits and pieces. It was a heavy tool; that first pack was going to be the awkward one.

The sentry was back outside the gates; Cloudsley had been watching, saw him come to a shambling halt. He murmured, 'Fifteen minutes, gents.' He could smell the generator's diesel oil, and guessed the wind might have backed towards the east. The lights looked brighter than they had ten minutes ago, shadows deeper. He took his eye off the lens: 'Come and refresh your memory, Tony.'

Beale shifted along sideways. Cloudsley edging closer to the exit. *Bloody cold.* . . . During the early evening he'd done some thinking about the weather, decided it might be worth sending up a prayer for no snow until the job was finished. It was one contingency there'd been no way to prepare for. Beale murmured, 'Like Christmas in Oxford Street.'

'Check out the moves, Tony. See it happening.'

Once you slid out of this burrow and ran for the wire, there'd be no seconds to waste, no time for hesitation or looking to see what anyone else was doing. He wanted Beale to do what he himself had been doing – seeing himself and the others down there, superimposing their shadowy figures on that empty stage.

'OK.'

He'd been at the 'scope four minutes. Cloudsley said, 'Your turn, Geoff. If the sentry makes a move I want to know.' Hosegood and Beale began changing places. 'Tony, shove the packs along, will you?' The first one, which he'd be carrying himself, was easy to identify because of the extra items in it. He stacked it on top of the other two. 'Still at the gates, is he?'

'Yeah. Poncing up an' down.' Hosegood spent a few minutes studying the compound and the approach to it, then grunted, 'Right.'

'About six minutes to go.'

Actually more like seven. In six, the sentry should start his walkabout, but you'd have to let him get around the first corner before you moved. Taking over the periscope again he heard Hosegood mutter, 'Funny to think I joined this lot to paddle a fucking canoe.'

They were all qualified swimmer-canoeists. Cloudsley and Beale both SC1, Hosegood SC3: Hosegood would go in for the SC2 course when he'd done two years in the squadron and could be in line for promotion to corporal. The swimmer-canoeist qualifications included boat-handling, underwater swimming, diving in all the different types of gear, and other more esoteric arts. And Hosegood was right, they were a hell of a long way from salt-water now. Cloudsley said, 'We'll have some paddling to do before we're out of it, Geoff.'

He'd just seen the sentry raise his left arm and check the time. He thought, *Two minutes yet, señor.* . . . Beale muttered, 'Right – if that fancy outboard reverts to normal.' Meaning that outboard motors invariably let you down; although that special one had worked well enough on the lake. He added, 'Canoes might've been a better bet.'

'Not on that pond with all the gear.'

'No, right.'

The night was an arena of black and yellow drowned in the generator's noise. Counting out the seconds, Cloudsley was checking all around for any other sign of life. Not finding any. . . . Back on the sentry then; and catching his breath. . . .

'He's moving away.'

He made sure of it. Then crabbed to the exit, manoeuvred the first pack on to his shoulders before he poked his head out. Beale close behind, wriggling into his own straps. Hosegood would be at the 'scope. The sentry was approaching the corner: pacing so slowly he might have been following a hearse. But he was getting there – at last. . . . Rounding the concrete post. Then the light was on him from the next corner as he started south. Six paces; eight. . . . Cloudsley said, 'Come on', pushed himself out and began to race down the slope towards the lights.

10

He'd started within a second of the sentry going out of sight, actually launching himself out while he could still see him. Because you had two and a half minutes now—it was a realistic estimate, not a minimum. If the sentry paced faster than usual, you'd have less. But one hundred and fifty seconds, to get in there and out of sight. Cloudsley sprinted; crashing down the slight incline, the noise of it well drowned by the generator: seventy yards through darkness, then about twenty through semi-dark and finally in the glare of the arc-lamp from the left as he pounded across the road and over the rough verge between it and the wire. No shadow, no cover, and the light dazzling after the long wait in pitch dark. The other two behind him would have stopped short of the floodlit area and dropped flat. Seconds ticking by and that sentry pacing southward. . . . Cloudsley dropped his pack at the foot of the wire and flung himself upward, a scrabbling climb on yielding mesh before his gloved hands grasped the barbed strands at the top. Over it, then—and a lot to be said for the thickness of a *poncho* with a padding of leather and fleece inside it—into a vaulting action that carried him clear in a spectacular boots-first arc of movement, landing on his feet inside the compound. Still in the floodlighting, of course. Tony Beale was at the foot of the fence on the outside, two packs lying there now, Beale taking off like a giant spider-monkey and ending full-length along the spiky top; Hosegood arriving in a slithering rush, slinging the first pack up, Beale receiving it and passing it over his own body – so the pack's material wouldn't snag on the wire – all one swift continuous flow of movement (as practised on a specially erected fence, a copy of this one, on the range at Eastney) and the pack briefly in Cloudsley's embrace on its way earthward. It was on the ground and he was straightening to catch the second one, like a sackful of bricks thumping into his chest and in the back of his mind a snapshot image of the sentry encircled in that little telescope's lens as he rounded the southeast corner post and started westward. . . . Third pack. He'd at least broken its fall before it hit the ground, and in that stooped position he'd grabbed pack number one and slung it on to his shoulders as he trotted through the shadowed area towards the corner of the hangar. Beale crashed down on the inside, scooped up one of the other packs while Hosegood was doing his flying body-roll over the top, landing in a crouch a foot or two away from pack number three, hoisting it and following Beale who by this time was dumping his load in deep shadow between the generator shed and its fuel-tank, dropping beside it and beginning to dig, using his gloved hands first to clear surface rubble, then the pick end of the shovel and his hands alternately. Hosegood dropped the third pack beside Beale and ran on – at a crouch, the way a baboon runs – to join Cloudsley who was held up at the little half-size door inset in the nearer of the pair of huge sliding ones. The tool that would open this or any other lock had been looped to his wrist, was in his fingers – in the lock. . . . *Wouldn't bloody turn.* . . .

The sort of delay this carefully timed scheme of entry could not survive. Sweat bathing his skin under the layers of heavy clothes. Fingers sticky inside the glove; he'd torn his wrist on the wire. He twisted the tool the wrong way; and it turned. Lock had not been locked, for Christ's sake. . . . Unlocking it again, he pushed down on the metal handle, ice-cold even through a glove; the door stuck at first, metal-bound from the

156

frost, gave way inward when he put his weight on it. Several seconds had been lost and Hosegood was already right up behind him. Cloudsley had to double himself up to duck in, shoulder-first with the little door half open, Hosegood following and kicking the door shut against the flood of yellowish light, staying there while Cloudsley moved on into the hangar's depths with the thin beam of a flashlight probing. Outside, Tony Beale dropped flat, face down, head and shoulders in the hole he'd been scraping for the second pack. A little west of due south and about ninety feet away the sentry had appeared from behind the hangar's southwest corner, pacing westward, approaching that corner light. He'd pass out of sight again before he reached it, line of sight interrupted then by the diesel-tank on its breezeblock supports. Beale counted the sentry's paces, seeing them in his mind's eye and counting four – five – six . . . before he raised his head.

Gone. He'd be halfway up the western end of the compound before he was in sight again. Then he'd be just about literally within spitting distance. Meanwhile – digging, finishing this job. Gloved hands were more effective than the entrenching tool, which was awkward to use when you were lying full length. One pack was already buried, close to the concreted base of one of the pillars. Couple more inches of excavation and he'd have the other one in. Soaking wet from sweat; and with an eye on the section of fence where the sentry would reappear. It happened also to be the point where they'd come over. He couldn't *see* any signs of entry, any pieces of ripped cloth on the barbs, for instance. He reached for the second pack, to pull it into the hole, having good reason to want it in and covered before the Argie showed up and he'd have to pause again.

He'd got it in. Using both hands, then, to scoop dirt in around it. Burying the digging tool as well.

The sentry sloped into view. Round-shouldered, slouching, rifle slung. Green fatigues under an overcoat, field-boots, kepi-shaped cap; after one glimpse Beale was face-down again, flat on the shadowed ground, part of that shadow and as motionless as the ground itself. Counting the man's paces again,

157

knowing it would need six to take him to the corner and that the shed would then be between them.

Five. Six. . . .

And OK. One last arm-scrape of loose soil before he gathered himself to run like a big dog, fingers touching the ground, to the corner of the hangar. Not the front where the door was; there wouldn't have been time to reach it – *might* not have been time – and get inside and the door shut before the sentry's line of sight to it was clear from beyond the other side of the generator shed. One chance sight of movement – if he'd happened to glance this way and you'd taken a chance on it – would have been enough to blow the whole operation, costing three lives here and God knew how many more at sea. The sort of chance you therefore did *not* take, for want of a little extra care. . . . Beale was at the corner of the hangar, flat on his stomach at the foot of its end wall, on the west side of the corner, absolutely still again half a second before the sentry reappeared, taking his measured treads eastward along the front of the compound. A dozen or fifteen of those treads would put him out of sight behind the guardhouse; you didn't have to count or guess at it, you could watch him all the way, eyes over one forearm like a crocodile's just out of water, watching the distance shorten between him and that last stretch of cover. He wouldn't be behind it for long, and when he got to his position at the gates he'd turn for a routine glance inside, a look at the tall sliding doors. You'd have ten or at the most twelve seconds to be inside by then, to have vanished.

Starting *now*.

Doubled, and running. Noise didn't matter, thanks to the generator's. As he got to the little door it opened as if by electronic eye, actually by courtesy of Marine Geoff Hosegood, who pushed it shut again as Beale fell in. Cloudsley told him matter-of-factly, 'We've struck lucky, Tony. OK out there?'

'No problems.'

Except for the sweat that had become a coating of ice on his skin inside the padding of heavy clothes. He saw that Cloudsley had a silvery-blue AM39 in front of him on a wheeled trolley; there was another six feet away, also on wheels. Both of those were in position to be hauled out through the big doors at a moment's notice, whenever the boys in blue came for them. . . . Pencil-thin torch-beam swinging away and the big, silent-moving figure of Harry Cloudsley prowling deeper into the icy, echoey cavern, tin walls and domed roof strutted with angle-iron, new-looking concrete floor, the generator's roar reverberating through it like a booming inside a drum. . . . 'See here, Tony?' Six more missiles, but those were in racks. You could bet the pair on trolleys would be the first to be deployed, should therefore be the first for treatment. Cloudsley, having shown Beale the extent of the work ahead of them, wasn't wasting time on any more detailed viewing of the interior; his torch-beam had travelled across a work-bench with tools in racks and some bins, other odds and ends, but he'd turned back now and was bending over the number one pack, pulling out the stuff he was going to need. Beale joined him, lifted out the batteries, putting them to the side and clipping a pair of leads to the terminals of one of them. Cloudsley muttering as he worked, 'Jackpot. Worth the effort, after all.' Beale wasn't aware that anyone had doubted it would be; except for the gamble of whether or not they'd be here in time. Hosegood had come from the door to position himself in front of the first patient's gleaming snout, his hands flat on the smooth curve of its homing head, keeping out of the way for the moment but ready to help shift it when Cloudsley gave the word. It had to be right-way-up to start with, anyway, and when you turned it you'd do it from the tail. Cloudsley had set a torch down with its light shining away from the hangar's front wall. It wasn't going to be any problem, moving these things around, because this airborne version of the Exocet was the smallest of the family — fifteen feet long, with a wingspan of three feet. Cloudsley stooping over its middle section to push a multi-pin plug into a socket from which he'd unscrewed the cover: the socket was actually on top of the dividing space between the cruise motor and the booster motor, and when the missile was loaded in an Etendard's rack ready for launching this socket would take the plug from the firing-control in the aircraft, wrenching away when the launch was triggered. In the present set-up, however, it led to a black box which the boffins had referred to rather unscientifically as a 'liner-upper', and which was already connected to a battery. Cloudsley said, 'Switch on,' and put his ear to the missile's body like a doctor who's left his stethoscope at home; he heard a humming noise in short, pulsing jerks, the whole thing lasting about three seconds and then clicking off. So it did work; and that was all there was to *that* part of it. He pulled out the plug and refitted the screw cover, doing this while Hosegood and Beale, together now at the tail-end, lifted that end shoulder-high so that the wings were clear of the trolley, then turned the missile around to a belly-up position and eased its end down again. Cloudsley had now fitted one of the short steel bits into the drill, but he put it down on the concrete now and with one of the little Space-Age torches between his teeth crouched over the patient to measure – using a strip of metallic tape graduated in millimetres – an exact distance behind the lower wing, for his first incision. He scratched a cross there, over the guts of the booster motor compartment. It happened to be the largest compartment in the missile – unlike the ship-launched MM38s and MM40s or the submarine-launched SM39s, in which the cruise motor took up more space – and it was also, the experts had decided, the only place where this kind of rough-and-ready surgery could effectively be performed. You had the homing head – radar – up front, with the computer and radio-altimeter behind it and the vertical and directional gyroscopes crowded in there too, but none of this ultra-sensitive stuff, which might have been the easiest to screw up, could have been got at (with such limited expertise, time and facilities) without the interference being obvious at a glance. And next to that nose compartment came the warhead – which nobody had even considered messing with – then cruise motor, and booster motor. . . .

'Here we go.'

Proof of the pudding. Culmination of a lot of hard work and arm-chancing. Which might – if you weren't lucky now – finish in one super-colossal bang. Explosion of the booster motor detonating the warhead, of course. Cloudsley had looked round for some wood to touch before he started, but there wasn't any.

The drill had its own built-in light, a tiny spotlight shining straight down the bit. It came on as soon as he pressed the trigger and the silent-running power tool began to eat, very finely and gradually indeed, into the missile's outer casing. This was as much as it *would* penetrate in this stage of the drilling, the plain steel bit being of a length that would only reach into the paper-thin air gap between outer casing and motor casing. This was so you couldn't foul-up right at the beginning by breaking through so fast that the hot drill-tip would ignite interior gases. If you did this, you could be *certain* of an explosion, so they'd made sure it would be impossible to achieve. To continue into the next stage, the puncturing of the booster casing which was what would cause the missile to malfunction, you had to change to the other type of bit, longer and diamond-tipped and thus less heat-prone, and then still take it – as they'd said in Bristol – very, *very* carefully. Because the steel behind the diamond point wouldn't be exactly cool by the time it got in there: you'd be aiming to have the diamond through but only *just* through.

Hosegood had gone back to the door to keep an eye on movements outside. Beale was connecting the liner-upper rig to the missile on the other trolley, getting that one ready so that when Cloudsley was ready to move over he could do so without pause. He was bent awkwardly over the job, his height a disadvantage now; eyes slitted, peering myopically at the disc of silver brilliance around the spinning needle, his big hands holding the drill firmly enough to ensure it didn't slip or slant off-course but applying hardly any pressure. They'd said in Bristol, 'The weight of the drill's about enough on its own, all you need do really is guide it.' But when you knew you were working against time it took a lot of self-control not to try to hurry it along.

Hosegood joined Beale at the second missile's tail. They lifted it at that end and then turned it, twisting it round by using the tail-fins for leverage, then letting it down on its back.

Beale fetched the measure from Cloudsley's pocket and marked the drilling spot. Cloudsley hadn't noticed his pocket was being picked; he was concentrating hard on the physical job and also coping with mental arithmetic while the drill bit finely into the bright circle that was mesmeric to the point of being dangerous. You had to keep watching it, but he'd found it was important to blink, shift your point of focus from one side of the drill to the other – to counter the threat of an hypnotic trance. Mental figure-work served a similar purpose, initially: first stage drilling 60 minutes, cooling period 30, second stage 45, total 135 – 2 hours 15 minutes. . . . But you wouldn't waste the half-hour cooling time: it was the casing that had to cool, not the drill; the drill would have a new bit in it for each stage, each hole. During the cooling period you'd be working on another missile, making that first hole then returning to number one for the second stage. And so on. End result, allowing some time for changing over and for switching bits, ought to be two missiles doctored in about 240 minutes, four hours. So you might get four of the eight patients fixed up tonight; two nights' work to complete the whole job. Which would be a lot better than he'd dared hope.

The circle of light rose from the blueish steel: incandescent and expanding, growing towards him, a vortex of brilliance, blinding. . . . Just as it was about to burst in his face the drill seemed to shriek a warning, a whine that set his teeth on edge; but he'd been practically *over* the edge, took some moments to react while the drill still screamed. Jerking awake, pulling back – a moment ago he'd been swaying forward. . . . Tony Beale had a hand on his arm, having grabbed him to pull him back; the whining shriek had come from the nozzle of the drill hard up against the missile – because the bit had gone in as far as it could reach, its tip spinning in the air gap between inner and outer casings. Cloudsley said evenly as he withdrew the bit from the hole, 'Lucky it was a short one. Might've busted right through.'

Beale said, 'Let's have a go, Harry. You take a breather.'

'Why not.' Handing him the drill. 'The light gets to be hypnotic.'

162

'Yeah.' Fitting a new bit and tightening the grip on it: 'But I slept today.'

After this the three of them took it in thirty minute shifts. Hosegood completed the first incision in the second missile, then Cloudsley and Beale shared the second stage on number one. Hosegood took over again. Cloudsley had a tube of dental filling material which had been adulterated with colouring matter to match the missiles' bluey-silver surface shine; he pressed a small pellet of it into the drilled hole before they turned that first patient the right way up again. The plug was practically invisible, and it would blow out when the booster fired.

Outside, sentries relieved each other, paced around the wire every fifteen minutes. Generator rumbling on, hour after hour. Within a couple of hundred yards up to about a hundred Argies – base staff, aircrew and off-duty guards – dreaming the night away. Among them – maybe – Roberto MacEwan. . . .

It had taken nearer five hours than four, when the second missile was finished. Hard to know where the extra time had gone. In change-overs, replacing drilling bits and shifting from one patient to another, and maybe in some excessive caution in the handling of the drill. But by that time, with the pair on trolleys doctored and guaranteed to malfunction, another two had been prepared for surgery.

'Right. Two more. . . .'

Another five hours – or a little less. . . . Beale nodded; Hosegood tightened the drill's snout: 'Start this bugger, shall I?'

Taking it for granted they'd get the four done. For one thing, it would be unproductive to stop at three, because of the thirty-minute cooling period which could be spent working on the other missile of each pair. For another, although they'd got off to a good start, progress since then had been disappointing. You had to allow for hold-ups, get the best mileage you could out of each hour on the job. Because – third and most basic reason – the Argies might be about to start deploying these missiles. It was sheer luck they hadn't already.

Cloudsley murmured, 'Imagine us sitting up there, having

163

come all this way, watching 'em ship the bloody things out!'

'Sooner not.' Hosegood's pupils burned like a cat's, reflecting that spot of light with the bit spinning in its centre so fast you could detect no movement, only see the slow build-up of steel dust around it, fine as pepper. He repeated, to himself, 'Sooner *not*. . . .'

When it was finished they were bug-eyed, grey. The other two, Cloudsley noticed, looked as if they'd been crying. He was checking that everything looked exactly as it had when they'd got in here, and Hosegood was stowing the two nearly-spent batteries and the other gear in the pack. The batteries had performed as predicted by Aerospace technicians, each having powered the vasectomies on two missiles. If the same results were obtained tomorrow night – *tonight* – there'd be two batteries unused, and they'd be left buried. They were of Italian manufacture. Six had been brought along in order to allow for finding a dozen missiles here, the most one could have catered for or expected the Argies to have scrounged.

Beale was at the door. Withdrawal from the compound was going to be near enough the reverse of the entry routine, except there was only one pack to take out. Spots of fire behind the eyeballs weighed nothing; the sensation of a drill at work behind them, drilling into the brain, was something you couldn't do anything about. In any case – Cloudsley struggled to complete a thought he'd started a moment ago – re-entry tomorrow night – correction, re-entry *tonight* – would be really quite easy. There'd be a pack to bring in, but no weight in it, only the drill and the liner-upper.

Hosegood clipped the pack shut and carried it to the little door where Beale knelt with his eye to the crack in its hinged side. You had only to open it about an inch, to expose that gap. Cloudsley, inspection completed, joined them. He'd be the last out: he'd be bringing the pack as far as the wire.

'How long've you been watching the *señor*, Tony?'

'Three or four minutes.'

Could be at least twelve minutes to wait, then. He stooped beside Beale for a look at the outside world, the bone-chilling Patagonian night. It wasn't snowing, and that was a relief. If snow came before this job was finished he hadn't the least idea what could be done about it, about three men's tracks approaching a twelve-foot fence and continuing the other side, either inward or outward. The solution might be to send up a concerted prayer for more snow to fill the tracks as soon as they were made. He thought, *Anyway, play if off the cuff; and it may never happen.* . . . And meanwhile all was well – sentry outside the gates, generator pounding steadily, pale-yellow light reaching along the wire but leaving that blessed shadow. He'd glanced back at the sentry just as he began to shuffle off on his rounds.

'Goon's going walkabout.'

Beale took over as observer again. From here you wouldn't see the sentry as far as the corner post, you'd need to open the door an inch or two. Then when he went round the corner and you lost sight of him you'd do it by numbers, counting his next eight paces.

As long as nobody else emerged from the guardhouse, meanwhile. Relief sentry, whatever – like yesterday morning, when he'd seen a second one there suddenly. But that had been nearer dawn, the whole base had been stirring. . . . Barring the unforeseen, this should be simpler and quicker than it had been on the way in.

Beale said, 'I'm opening the door a bit.'

Left side of his whiskered and grease-blackened face close against the metal, left eye on the sentry's back.

'He's at the corner – almost. . . . Yeah, turning south.'

Breathing hard as he watched one-eyed. Breath might even be visible out there, Cloudsley realised – like puffs of steam through the crack. . . . Beale began his count-down: starting at eight but warning first, 'Stand by, Geoff. . . .' Muttering: '. . . seven – six – five – four – three – two – one and *go*!'

Hosegood burst out, sprinted for the fence. Beale gave him a start of five yards, then dived after him, running hard. Cloudsley ducked out, shut the door from the outside but didn't lock it, ran at a crouch with the pack on his shoulders into the cover of the generator shed. Pausing there for long enough to see Hosegood landing on the outside and Beale launching himself upward; then he broke cover, dashed for the wire. Beale was lying on its top; he caught the pack as Cloudsley slung it up to him, and tossed it over to Hosegood, who took off with it, across the road and away into the darkness, Beale rolling off the wire and following him with the style of an Olympic medallist, Cloudsley jumping for the top of the fence, pivoting on the top on his gloved hands and flying over, landing on all fours before he recovered and sprinted into the dark where the others had already vanished.

They'd gone straight to the rear hide. Cloudsley stopped at the OP, though, to check through the periscope that all was serene in and around the missile compound.

The sentry was plodding up this near side. Slouching past the point where within the last two minutes three men had charged out of the compound he was guarding, having neutralised half his country's reserves of their most potent weapon.

Other half tonight. After which – *Adios, señores.* . . .

Controlling the sudden glow of satisfaction; reminding himself, *Long way to go yet.* . . . He climbed out, paused to look back and see the sentry shambling on around the corner; then crawled across fifty feet of frozen earth to the other hide. Shivering inside his heavy clothing. Same thing every time you took a little exercise: you worked up a sweat and then it froze.

'Haven't you even wet the *maté*, yet?' He asked a second question although the answer wasn't hard to guess: 'Where's Geoff?'

'Give us a chance. . . .' Beale glanced round from the little burner. 'Only just got the bluey lit.'

'It's not a bluey, it's some Jap product.'

'Yeah, well.' A 'bluey' was a Service-issue cooker, the kind they usually had with them. Beale told him, 'Geoff's gone for a crap.'

Officially speaking, one of the others should have gone with him. That was the standard drill: one with his pants down, the other with sharp eyes and ears and an Armalite. Squatting, you couldn't do much to defend yourself. But there'd be no patrols out there, Cloudsley thought, these Argies didn't have the imagination to think of Bootnecks defecating around their airfields. He let himself down on one of the sleeping-mats. 'Not a bad night, Tony.'

'One more like it – home and dry.'

Wanting to touch wood, and not finding any. Shivering, instead. Beale had the cooker going now, steam rising. 'Might soak some of them little rocks in this stuff. Soften 'em up.' He meant the *galletas*, so-called bread rolls, which *were* as hard as rocks. Hosegood arrived, entering feet-first and looking happy: 'Where's this cuppa, then?'

Andy told Strobie over breakfast, answering a comment about Harry Cloudsley and others like him, 'They don't think of themselves as special. The SB squadron's just one of several things a Marine can go in for if he's up to it. They have their own helicopter pilots, for instance, and a landing craft company. And an outfit they call MAW – stands for Mountain and Arctic Warfare.'

'They seemed special enough to me.' Strobie poured coffee. 'How did you come to get mixed up with them?'

'Through a girlfriend.' Andy realised as he said it that he hadn't been thinking much about Lisa lately. 'Her father's in the Navy – captain of a ship in the Task Force, as it happens. I'd met him through his daughter, and he told someone he knew this guy who knew the country. Next thing was, I had this 'phone call. But you're right, they impress me too.'

'What's the difference between them and the SAS?'

'Plenty. For one thing, the SBS specialise in beaches and harbours and underwater action. Aquatic operations generally. They're parachutists too, of course. The SAS is a much bigger concern, isn't it? It has the whole Army to draw on, it's a regiment.' He put down his knife and fork. 'That was great. . . . Tom, what does Francisca do with herself all day, when she's on her own at the *estancia*?'

'Takes a hand running the place. Gets around a bit on

horseback, sees to this and that.' Strobie shrugged. 'When she's here.'

'And you don't know whether she is now?'

'No way I would, unless she came to see me.'

'You don't ever call there? Or call up on the radio?'

'What for? Cosy chat to your brother – or bloody Huyez?' The question had annoyed him. 'If she was there she'd either ride over or she wouldn't. If for her own reasons – as I explained – she's staying away, that's her own business, isn't it?'

'Wouldn't your people here – Torres, for instance – get to know when she comes or goes?'

'They may do.' Strobie gulped down the last of his coffee. 'But they'd have no reason to talk to *me* about it.' He pushed back his chair, reached for his stick. 'Listen, now. I'll be down in the south paddocks all day. I'm taking the pickup, and I could be late back. Help yourself to whatever you want – food, or Scotch. You may find something worth reading in those shelves. But stay out of sight, eh?'

Cloudsley was asleep, and Beale squatted at the periscope. After a burst of activity before and for maybe an hour after sunrise, the airfield had gone quiet again. Maybe the pilots went back to bed. . . . Hosegood was having *his* day of rest in the other hide, having first buried the two used batteries in the bottom of it. While he'd been doing that, Cloudsley had taken some water-bottles down to the stream and filled them, getting it done before the sky began to lighten and while the Pucarás were warming up across the road. You added things called puri-tablets to river water, to play safe. Also playing safe, they'd all used antiseptic ointment from their first-aid packs on cuts and scratches caused by that wire.

The floodlighting had gone out when they'd stopped the generator, and soon after that the compound gates had been opened to let in a truck, tanker, for topping up the diesel tank.

168

That had been some time ago, but the gates were still standing open. Some of the aircraft which had taken off before dawn had been gone a long time, but he thought he'd counted them all back now. Seven machines were drawn up in echelon on the far side of the service road, and ground staff with a tractor and trailer were working on them. Beale didn't know whether they were the same ones, refuelled, or another lot. He wanted to know, to have a count of how many aircraft there were on this base and whether they were permanently here or different lots flying in for short periods. He'd done some study of the Pucará – of the Aermacchi and Etendard as well, those two being types used by the Argie naval air arm, the ANA, and therefore aircraft that might be encountered on this trip – and he'd have liked a closer view. The periscope's magnification helped, but not all that much. He knew there were two kinds of Pucará in service, for instance, the IA 58A and the later 58B which had a deepened forward fuselage to take heavier armament, and from here it was impossible to see whether they were As or Bs. Leaning back, wiping the lens and resting his eyes a moment. . . . His interest in the matter wasn't academic: everything you saw here would have some Intelligence value, and having penetrated this deeply it would be a waste of unusual opportunity if you didn't memorise it all. Like the serial numbers – all starting with the letter 'A' – on the sides of the Pucarás' fuselages where they narrowed towards the tails. Intelligence already knew that the Pucarás of *IV Escuadron* were being reinforced by some from *III Brigada Aerea* at Reconquista, but whether or not the navy was getting them from that same source –

Those were armourers.

He'd realised it suddenly. Recollecting that a Pucará's twin 20-mm cannon were loaded from below the fuselage; which was what those overalled characters were doing. Browning machine-guns in the sides of the fuselage, and cannon – Hispanos – underneath. The ammo would have come out in that trailer.

He looked round at Cloudsley's *poncho*-covered, heavy-breathing body and decided against disturbing him. The only

169

importance of the information lay in the possibility that those aircraft were being readied for deployment operationally. But there was no way to get the information out, anyway. Radios having been banned, all you could do was *take* it out.

As Harry would have said – *Touch wood*. . . .

Helicopter arriving?

He loosened an ear-flap, heard the racket growing. Direction uncertain. Worrying things, helicopters; hovering overhead, maybe seeing the signs of excavation. . . . He glanced round at Cloudsley again. Snoring, now. Needing his sleep, at that, having had none in this past night or yesterday or the previous night; and in a team like this one each man's fitness was important to the others. Eye back at the periscope; tilting it to and fro as well as swivelling it, he spotted the source of the noise and recognised it instantly. A Chinook. No mistaking that very large and distinctive shape. It was coming from the north and obviously intending to land. Extremely loud, as it closed in and lost height, but the skull-thumping racket wasn't disturbing Harry Cloudsley. Turning to its left now across the front of the line of parked Pucarás. And transport coming, welcoming committee – one khaki-painted van, one pickup truck also khaki, and a camouflaged saloon car. . . . Men in overalls were dropping out of the back of the van, and a naval officer had got out of the staff car. The armourers working on the Pucarás had gathered in a bunch to watch the big helo setting itself down. It was huge, with twin rotors on twin engine-turrets and the word ARMADA in white capitals on its side. 'Armada' meaning 'fleet' or 'navy', even Sir Francis Drake had known *that* much.

Movement in the missile compound now. A tractor with three soldiers on it turning in through the gates. Beale guessed now what was happening or about to happen; he'd have captioned his report, *Deployment of AM39 missiles by helo*.

They weren't wasting time, either, weren't leaving the Chinook to hang around. Cloudsley, he decided, did need to witness this. It directly affected them, their half-completed operation. . . . He saw the tractor swing round, its driver reversing it as the other two men disappeared towards the front of the hangar. Beale knew he'd soon be treated to the sight of one or both trolleys being towed out to the Chinook, complete with doctored missile or missiles.

'Harry.' He reached, pulling at the *poncho*. The snoring stopped instantly and Cloudsley rolled up on to an elbow, asking, 'Yes, what's up?' Wide-awake: bearded face still streaked with the camouflage cream, whites of eyes and teeth gleaming in the half-light. Beale told him, 'Deploying our missiles. Chinook just landed.'

'Bloody hell. . . .'

Beale surrendered the periscope to him, but before he took his eye from it he'd seen crates being carried out of the helo and dumped in the pickup, and two of the helo's crew on the ground talking to the officer who'd got out of the staff car. The other thing he noticed – it sank in only after he'd stopped looking – was that the naval officer was wearing the gold-peaked cap of a commander or captain.

'Question is' – Cloudsley muttering, at the 'scope – 'how many they'll take?'

'Well,' Beale pursed his lips, pretending to consider it. 'Might see my way to letting 'em have four, today.'

'And the *right* four, please God. . . .' He was silent for a minute, watching avidly. Then: 'Looks like the Chinook's brought wines and spirits for the mess. And that fellow there' – he whistled – '*Shit, alors*, could be Roberto!'

'What I thought. Big sod, brass hat.'

'Right.' Shifting the 'scope again. 'Nothing much like Andy, is he. . .? They're bringing out both trolleys. One astern of t'other.'

Ground staff were doing something under the Chinook's fuselage. Preparing racks or cargo nets, Cloudsley guessed. They'd finished loading the pickup, it was leaving. . . . That commander and the two pilots were pacing up and down, the two in flying gear only shoulder-high to the man between them. 'Which direction did it come from, Tony?'

Beale told him, from the north. Which gave quite a number of options. El Palomar, the military airbase at BA, wasn't a bad bet, since it had brought stores down. But an even better bet

171

was that it would be taking the missiles down to Rio Gallegos. And when it took off, twenty minutes later, it certainly did continue southward. The trolleys were towed back into the hangar and the tractor parked itself inside the compound, on the concrete forecourt. Cloudsley said, 'Nick of time, Tony. *Bloody* lucky.' He looked pleased with himself as he lay down and wrapped the *poncho* around himself. Meaning, of course, that if they'd been one day later getting here, those would have been two *lethal* missiles that were being hurried south, instead of two that would take nosedives into deep water. He went back to sleep immediately. He had two hours' rest time left now, before he'd be due to take over as lookout, but in fact it would be time then for a *maté* break, first him and then Beale crawling back to the other hide for a hot drink and a snack, after dragging Geoff Hosegood out of dreamland by a sharp tug on the string.

During the next hour the Pucarás took off in groups and flew westward. Beale had memorised their serial numbers. The machine left after six had taken off had a pilot waiting beside it, kicking his heels until the staff car came back and 'Roberto' got out of it – a burly figure in flying gear topped by the gold-peaked cap. He handed the cap to the car's driver and received a white flying helmet in exchange, and as he walked over to the aircraft the co-pilot saluted him. They both climbed in; Roberto was fixing his helmet while the other man, in the seat behind him, pulled the hinged canopy down over them both.

Half an hour later all the 'planes came back, but only that one stopped at this end of the field. Roberto walked to the waiting car, and his co-pilot taxied the machine away. At the car, same routine with the cap. . . . Whether or not it was Roberto MacEwan, Beale thought, he certainly didn't like his rank to pass unnoticed.

From midday onward there were intermittent Pucará sorties, some with napalm bomb loads. Cloudsley was on watch then, fully rested by his forenoon's sleep and impatient to get going, get the night's work done and clear out. There couldn't be any move out until the night after, even then. . . . Time dragged, with nothing of interest happening. Individuals and transport moved around, there were repeated take-offs and landings — obviously by learner pilots — and the napalm flights returned, went to refuel. There were ground-staff in the missile store, had been since the Chinook's visit. They'd have two missiles to shift from racks to the trolleys, obviously, but that shouldn't have taken more than a few minutes. Boredom contributed to anxiety; he comforted himself with the thought that if they'd found anything wrong in there, the afternoon would hardly have remained this tranquil.

Early in the afternoon he began to notice visual signs of the wind's strength increasing. You didn't feel it in this burrow, but it was no less cold. He was keeping an eye at the periscope — thinking about the snow problem, how to cope with it if the blizzard weather started before this job was finished — and at the same time rubbing his hands together to encourage circulation, when he heard the Chinook coming back.

A helo, anyway; he assumed it would be the Chinook. Then realised the sound was different — the difference between two big engines and rotors and just one small one. He had it in the periscope's lens then; a helo about as big as a Chinook's chicks might be, if a Chinook ever got pregnant.

'Tony.' Reaching over to shake him. 'Wake up. Tell me what the hell this is.'

Beale crawled to the periscope, bleary-eyed. He mumbled, 'Helo's landing in the compound, by the looks of it. I mean it's about to.'

'What *kind* of helo, damn it?'

Sucking at his teeth. Foul taste, no doubt. Only to be expected, after *maté* and cold mutton. . . . He nodded. 'It's an Alouette. Made by Aerospatiale, our Exocet chums.'

Its arrival had obviously not been unexpected. Taking over the 'scope again, Cloudsley saw the staff car turning in at the gates of the compound, soldiers appearing from the guard-house and ground-staff from the hangar. The car stopped near the guardhouse, then moved again to make way for a tanker which then reversed in and parked. To refuel this Alouette, of course. The Alouette landing now, on the concrete. Roberto — back in naval uniform — was out of the car, posing with his

173

hands on his hips, feet wide apart, watching the pilot climb down and then come towards him.

Ground-staff were really bustling around. . . .

'Harry, what's going on?'

He told him; and added, 'Helo pilot seems to have flown here solo. He's saluting Roberto now.'

'Ah. Goes a bundle on that.'

'Huh?'

'Roberto. Likes the saluting bit.'

The deployment of missiles was evidently continuing. And in a rush: the refuelling was already in progress.

'What's an Alouette's range, Tony?'

'Roughly the same as a Lynx. Say three hundred miles.'

They were manhandling one trolley plus missile across the concrete. Half a dozen men maneoeuvring it towards the helo while others spread a cargo net on the ground beside it. Cloudsley saw a motorbike swerve into the compound from the service road. . . . He asked Beale, 'What sort of payload?'

'Considering it's supposed to be general purpose, bloody small. Half a Lynx's.'

'Couple of thousand kilos?'

'Not much more, yeah.'

You had to relate load to range: if that pilot was flying solo it indicated they were cutting weight to a minimum for the sake of the load/range factor. If for instance this Alouette had come all the way up from Rio Gallegos, a load of just one of those missiles would be stretching its capability to about the limit.

Supposition, no more. But you had to make guesses, to *try* to understand what might be happening. For instance – Chinook in transit from A to B, picks up two missiles en route, Chinook having other cargo on board already. Now the little fellow flies up from aforesaid point B to collect another. Short of helos, scraping the barrel, needing AM39s down there fast?

The motorcyclist had reported to Roberto, who'd now turned back to the pilot, was beckoning to the other naval men. Beyond them, the missile was being transferred from trolley to cargo net. Roberto acknowledging salutes as he went to his car and slid into it. Despatch rider leaving too, kicking life into his bike.

'Roberto's going home for his tea.' Cloudsley glanced round at Beale. 'OK, Tony, go back to sleep.'

Ten minutes later the Alouette took off, flying south with an AM39 under it liked a netted salmon. But the tanker – it was a massive one – was staying where it was, on the concrete area inside the compound; its driver strutting out through the gates, which were being left open.

This time yesterday, he'd watched them locking up. Well before sunset, which by local time would come at about four-fifteen. And no reason they shouldn't pack up quite early, considering they started their day's work well before dawn. . . . But from Cloudsley's point of view, by say an hour after sunset or 1800, say, at the latest, he needed to be in that hangar and starting another ten hours of drilling. Which with the hangar still open and Argies still hanging around – for some damn purpose. . . .

The purpose was clear enough. He cursed, under his breath.

'What's up, Harry?'

The colour sergeant's bearded face looked as if it might have been carved out of bone. Deepset eyes fixed on Cloudsley's profile at the periscope. . . . Cloudsley taking a long breath, like a swimmer about to duck under.

'Could be a shuttle operation. Another helo coming. Or helos, plural. Maybe your Alouette coming back. Whatever they're waiting for, they're leaving the place open for it. Leaving the refuelling truck inside there too.'

That was the clincher. You couldn't explain it any other way.

'Well, if we can't get in there tonight—'

'Christ's *sake*!' Cloudsley hissed it through gritted teeth. 'They're deploying the missiles, Tony – and four of 'em are still intact! We bloody well *have* to get in there tonight!'

11

Robert MacEwan got out of the staff car, walked heavily into the radio shack. He asked the NCO in charge of the watch, 'Personal call for me?'

The orderly who'd been sent to find him, arriving by motorbike in the missile compound, had reported, 'A call from your *estancia*, sir. A Señor Huyez, says it's a matter of utmost urgency. . . .'

'You could take it in here, sir, in privacy.' The petty officer pushed open the door of a small office. 'Unless you'd prefer it to be connected to your own extension. We were trying to locate you, but—'

'In here will do.'

He hadn't the slightest idea what Juan Huyez might have to talk about. There was no problem connected with the running of the sheep-station that he'd need to refer to his *patrón*. It was partly the fact of such a call being quite unprecedented that had persuaded him to leave the missile collection and come straight to take it. His fingers depressed the 'speak' bar in the handset: 'Roberto MacEwan. Is that you, Don Juan? What's your problem?'

'Not exactly a problem, *patrón*. I apologise most profoundly for such an intrusion, but I felt – well, that you would certainly wish to hear—'

'Come to the point, please.'

'You may find it hard to believe, Don Roberto. I myself could hardly—'

'Believe what?'

'The *patrón's* brother. He is staying at the *estancia* El Lucero. Incredible, but—'

'Don Andrés – at Strobie's, *now*?'

'It's the truth, *patrón*. My son Paco has seen him with his own eyes. He was convinced it was none other, but when he told me I thought, *Nonsense!* However—'

'It's a fact?'

'Si, *patrón*. This boy of mine has – a young female acquaintance, the daughter of a *peón* on that *estancia*. It is not at all a suitable – not a friendship I wish to encourage, but—'

'Stick to the point, for God's sake!'

'Through this person, further enquiries—'

'She confirmed he's there?'

'Si, *patrón*. He is disguised in clothing suitable for a *peón*, and he has grown a beard, but it is he, and he is residing in the small house that was formerly the home of the *mayordomo*. Eating *enormous* meals, it is said—'

'How long has he been there?'

'We cannot be sure, but several days, it seems.'

'And that's all you know about it?'

'Why yes, unfortunately. . . .'

'Hold on a minute. I want to consider this.'

He lowered the receiver. Slapping it in the palm of the other hand while he put his mind to this extraordinary development. Scowling out of the bare window. . . . Andy must have come into the country secretly; otherwise he wouldn't be lying low at the old man's place in some ridiculous disguise, he'd have come straight to their own home.

So what might he have come for?

Francisca saw Strobie sometimes. She wasn't aware that her husband knew of it, that Juan Huyez kept him informed of her movements and contacts when she was down there. Knowing

178

of the calls she'd made at Strobie's place, Robert had wondered – without bothering about it much – whether through Strobie she'd have news of, or even contact with, her former playmate.

Francisca. . . .

Even if what she swore was the truth, it was a truth that didn't apply to Andy's attitude towards *her*. In his juvenile fashion he'd always been demented about her. He might still be, might think – if she'd encouraged him, particularly – he still had some chance.

Francisca was the key to this. And *could be used* as such.

'Don Juan?'

'*Si, patrón.*'

'I'll arrange for Don Andrés to pay you a visit. He'll ride over from the Strobie place, in the belief he's visiting my wife. I can't say exactly when, but possibly in just a few hours. I want you to be prepared to – to *receive* him. That's to say, to keep him there, Don Juan. Lock him up. I can't possibly get down there myself – not for quite a time, possibly several weeks, this couldn't have come at a more awkward moment for me. So, I have to put it entirely on your shoulders. You'll handle it – as efficiently as you handle everything down there?'

'*Patrón* – of course, I am here to serve you. . . . But – you said *lock him up?*'

'Remember the one who went off his head? Until they could come for him we confined him in the *carnicería?*'

The meat house. It was a substantial building, and one of its rooms had no window and a good lock on the door. The *peón* who'd gone mad had been a powerfully built fellow and he'd flung himself around in there for more than a fortnight before the police were able to provide transport.

Huyez began cautiously, 'If this is your order, *patrón*—'

'Didn't you hear it?'

'Of course. Of course. . . . The only doubt in my mind – well, it would be far from – from comfortable, *patrón*. Even in summer it's very cold, Now we have snow coming—'

'Give him a blanket. Two blankets, if you want. But I want you to understand, Don Juan – it seems likely he's sneaked into

179

the country without anyone knowing he's here. Except the old man, of course — and *that* can be handled easily enough. But you see, in the circumstances, officially he does not exist. His disappearance would therefore pass unnoticed. You follow?'

'Perhaps not entirely—'

'I've said, you're to keep him there. Because I'd like to talk to him, discover what he came for. I have an idea, but I want to hear it from *him* — if possible. . . . But this is not of very great importance. What is of the utmost importance is that once you have him there he should not leave. In fact — listen, Don Juan. If keeping him alive should prove difficult, I would not — hold you responsible. For any — accident. . . . Is this clear, now?'

'*Si, patrón,* it is clear as you say it, but—'

'I *would* hold you responsible, however, if you allowed him to escape. If that occurred, neither you nor any of your family would have a future in my service. I think you know I am a man of my word?'

'Indeed, *patrón*—'

'You would naturally exercise every discretion. . . . The other way to look at this is that at present, you know, I'm only part owner of the *estancia*. And you would like some small share in it, a reward for years of hard work and loyalty, a future for your son. I have never forgotten that my grand-mother discussed this with you. And it would be simple to make the arrangements, you see, if I owned the place entirely. . . . Here again — remember — I *am* a man of my word.'

'This is well known, *patrón*. And I am overwhelmed—'

'You have your orders, and you understand them?'

'Clearly—'

'Good. Don't call me about it. I shan't be here much longer in any case. Final firework display tomorrow, then we move out — lock, stock and barrel, before we're snowed in. . . . Do what has to be done, Don Juan. I'll be with you — I don't know, *some* time. . . .'

He hung up. Lighting a cheroot; smoking it for several minutes, deep in thought. Then he went to the door.

'I want a number in Buenos Aires. You'll have it there — private residence of Rear-Admiral Alejandro Diaz.'

180

She'd thrown an angry glance at the telephone: 'Oh, *go away*!'

'Tell them to do that. *Please*.'

Ricardo spoke softly. He'd unhooked the strap, between her shoulder-blades. The bra still clung, its silk moulded to her breasts and pointed, swollen nipples. His fingers brushed it away now, gently cupped one breast as he stooped to kiss it. She was naked except for her pants; he, in contrast, was fully dressed, even had his riding boots on. The ringing telephone was on a white marble table with a French love-seat beside it, and his eyes followed her, resting hungrily on the motion of her hips as she walked over to it – telling him over her shoulder, scarlet-tipped fingers resting on the receiver, 'Get undressed, Rick, for God's sake. . . . Hello?'

Her eyes went back to him, as she sat down. Pale-blue eyes, charcoal-black hair, creamy skin. . . . Her left hand was raised in warning – a finger to her lips.

'Roberto! *What* a surprise!'

Ricardo's brown eyes stayed on her. He leant back against the bed, to pull off the highly polished boots. Eyes devouring her. Those fantastic breasts. . . . And her mouth, wide mouth with lips still wet from his kisses, lips parting now to ask her husband politely how he was, how his work was progressing. . . .

'All right, then.' Her shoulders – Ricardo had told her only a minute ago that they were the most kissable shoulders in Buenos Aires – lifted in a small shrug. 'Of course I'll listen. . . .'

He'd got rid of his uniform jacket, tie and shirt, and was loosening his breeches. Francisca watching with a light, anticipatory smile.

She'd frowned. 'But surely, that's not *possible*!'

Ricardo, pointing down at himself, eyebrows raised, whispered, '*This* isn't?'

She hadn't heard. Preoccupied. . . . He stood up. A tall, slim, brown-skinned man, chest and belly furred with tight black curls. Padding towards her across the deep-pile carpet, hearing from yards away her husband's voice rasping in the telephone. Whatever the slob was telling her, lecturing her about, it was

181

having a powerful effect. The interruption had become real, in fact.

And was not, he decided, to be tolerated.

'But how could he have come – at this time, with all—'

Ricardo knelt in front of her; hearing her try to get a few more words in edgeways: 'But even if he does still have a passport, surely—'

Interrupted again. Comments from this end seemed not to be wanted. But Ricardo had silently conveyed a proposal to her, and she was complying now while the voice from somewhere in the wilds of Patagonia droned on. She'd switched the receiver to her other hand, and putting the free one down on the cushions she pushed herself up a little, lifting her bottom so as to make it easier for Ricardo to remove her pants. He slid them lovingly down her thighs, over the beautifully rounded knees and finally from her bright-painted toes.

'But if he *is* here – what for? Unless to see you? On family business, since there's no trade now? Why should he have gone to Tom's place, though? I don't understand this at all, Roberto!'

Roberto's hectoring tone again. . . . The naked man on his knees didn't care what he was on about, for the time being. A touch of fingers on the insides of Francisca's knees caused her legs to part immediately. He moved in closer, his arms sliding round her long, supple waist, drawing her to him. She was protesting, 'You know perfectly well he means *nothing* to me! A childhood romance, a little summer flirtation before either of us was old enough to do more than hold hands! I married *you* Roberto. . . . If he has any such ambitions *I* certainly did nothing to encourage them!'

She gasped. Thighs spread. Rick's face burrowing, his arms tight round her hips and bottom, squeezing her towards him. Noisy, now, like a hungry man, Francisca tilting her pelvis, helping, fingers of her free hand combing his dark head. . . . She said abruptly into the telephone, 'Roberto – just one minute, please?'

Hand over the telephone, palm pressed across the mouthpiece. Moving her hips in a subtle, insistent rocking. Then

182

faster: thrusting to meet him, belly hollow, hips writhing. . . .
A huge intake of breath: her body arching in a long, convulsive
shudder. . . .

She'd pushed him away: a hand flat on his forehead, and
drawing herself back on the cushions. Out of breath.

'I'm so sorry, Roberto. A — domestic matter.' She added —
Ricardo stifling a laugh with his face against her thigh —
'Rosaura's getting old, you know, she insists on consulting me
over every little detail.'

Rosaura was her father's housekeeper. Francisca beckoned,
and Ricardo sat beside her on the love-seat. Her hand went to
him, fondling. . . . She said into the 'phone, 'I'd only just come
in when your call came. Yes — lunch at the Herreras. . . . Oh, a
very good lunch. As usual, yes. I envy her that cook of hers. . . .
Oh, yes, Ricardo was there for a short while, but he had to run
off — he's on some Staff or other, I don't know what, but they
keep him busy anyway.' She was examining him, at a range of
a few inches: his eyes, his lips, jawline. . . . 'Quite a pleasant
young man, I agree. . . . A little' — she glanced down, opening
her hand — 'a little full of himself, perhaps. . . .' She giggled.
Squeezing. . . . 'Anyway, Roberto — I suppose I must believe
what you've been telling me, but what exactly is it you want
me to do?'

The harsh voice began to grind again. Francisca covered the
mouthpiece; Rick was stooping, kissing her breasts, but now
he was coming up again and their mouths were wide open to
each other, the telephone two inches away. . . . The voice
stopped; Francisca pulled away, using the end of the receiver
to push Rick off. 'Suppose I did this, Roberto: what would you
— or *they*—'

A question, answering her question.

'Why shouldn't I be breathless? I'm *shocked*! You're asking
me to — *trap* him? So you can' — she shook her head at Ricardo
— 'tell me what for, what you intend to do?'

Listening intently now. And real shock in her expression.
Ricardo mustering the patience and sense to wait. . . .

'As I've told you a hundred times, he's nothing to me. I am
not in the least upset, not in the way you're implying. But he's

183

a human being, and an old, once close friend – and as a matter of fact an *innocent* if there ever was one – and for God's sake, Roberto, your own brother!'

Quite a long answer was coming through now, to that high-pitched protest. She was listening; her eyes re-focusing gradually on Ricardo. . . . 'No. Don't tell me. I don't want to know. I'll do what you ask, simply to prove—'

'All right. Yes. Yes, as soon as I can get a call through. Which as you know is not easy. . . . All right, the naval link – I'll give your name. . . . *Yes*, I just told you, I'll *do* it, but—'

'No. Of course I wouldn't. I told you, I'm only agreeing to this unpleasant suggestion so as to prove to you there's nothing, *nothing*— '

'Very well. . . . But now listen, Roberto – will I be seeing you, one of these days?'

Her blue eyes on Ricardo's brown ones. Seeking information of interest to them both. . . .

'I see. You're going – to the war? You'll be—'

Listening to the drone, her smile deepened: directed entirely at Ricardo.

'Then my heart and hopes go with you, Roberto. And my pride. . . .'

'Yes, I'll be waiting. . . . *Yes*, for heaven's sake, I *said* I would, I'll do it as soon as—'

'All right. Come back in one piece. Not too many heroics, please. Come home to me when we've won. *Vaya con Dios,* Roberto. . . .'

She kept the receiver at her ear until she'd heard him sign off. Then she leant sideways, dropped the receiver in its cradle.

'I could have *shrieked*. . . . *Then* how would he have believed I was talking to Rosaura. . .? You're a swine, Rick.'

'I know.'

He looked flattered. She laughed, kissing him. 'Want the same now?'

'On the bed.'

'Anywhere. . . . On the *roof,* my darling!'

'What was it all about?'

'Oh, hell, I have to make a call – at least book one—'

184

'Not now. Leave it till I go.'

'I only promised him for *our* sake. So we can be left alone. . . .' He was looking down, watching the blood-red fingernails, the slim hands' subtlety. She whispered, 'I don't think I'll let you go, Rick. Tell your damn Staff you're held up. Tell them I'm keeping you here for ever.'

'You'd get bored with me.' He picked her up. 'Wouldn't you?'

'Well.' Closing her eyes. 'Put it this way. At the moment I can't envisage it.' She asked him, on the bed, 'Want it with my mouth?'

'I could – *live* in your mouth. . . .'

'Be my guest—'

'Next time.' He'd stopped her, as she began to slide down. 'Now, I want to hear what's this thing you have to prove to your boorish husband.'

'Oh, I should've said, he's off to the war!'

'May he stay there for ever. . . . Why d'you have to do something you don't want?' He was on his back, pulling her over. Francisca straddled him, lifting herself. . . . Watching his face then, enjoying his eyes on her body. His hands held her slowly rotating hips; he murmured, 'Only one way this might be better. If you fetched the telephone, called him up to say goodbye again. . . . I really loved that, you know?'

'Me too.' Faster. Leaning to kiss him. . . . 'Why didn't we think of this before, Rick?'

'I've thought of nothing else every time I've set eyes on you.'

'I thought you were in love with your plump little wife.'

'Oh, I am. . . . Want me to call *her*?'

'Not' – she'd paused – 'right now. . . .'

'Tell me what it was about?'

'Later, Rick—'

'No – *now*.' His hands tightened: holding her almost still. 'Please?'

'All right. All right. . . .' His grasp relaxed. She began, phrases falling into the rhythm of new movement, 'Once upon a time – crazy little girl – loved this little boy. . . . Mind if I fall in love with *you*, Rick?'

'Might as well. . . . Tell me the rest now?'

Hair swirled as she shook her head: '*Lousy* story, Rick.'

'Come on. . . .'

'What d'you call *this*?'

'Come on with the lousy story.'

'*Thought* she was in love. But she was *not*. . . .' Francisca's voice was singsong now, matched to movement. . . . 'Sort of a spin-off, married the *other* one. For some *dumb* reason. . . . Because he's a *pig*, she can't stand him, only just for now she – needs to hang on. . . . Rick, you're *stupendous,* I'm going to be ahead of you again. . . . The puppy-love was *nothing*, you see? But to satisfy the pig she has to *prove* it, has to – oh, thing my Yank mother's people say' – shouting it, a shudder in her voice – 'sell him down the *river*—'

Getting towards sunset, the back end of a day that had moved along as sluggishly as treacle.

Andy opened Tom Strobie's liquor cupboard, took a bottle out and studied the label, put it back again. Sunset came early in this wilderness, and anyway drinking on one's own had never paid good dividends. Drinking another man's whisky – old man who probably couldn't afford it anyway – would be even less rewarding. Afternoon boozing would be different if you were in your eighties and semi-crippled, reclusive. . . .

He'd be back before long anyway. Then they'd have a few snorts together and it would have been worth waiting for. Also, there'd be something to take as an excuse for celebration: the BBC World News bulletin – at 10.00 a.m. GMT, 1.00 p.m. here – had reported Mrs Thatcher informing the House of Commons that 'British forces have begun to move forward from their San Carlos bridgehead'.

Advancing towards Goose Green, he imagined. Numerous 'experts' in recent radio commentaries had predicted a move that way. The Argies, one might guess, would have been tipped-off accordingly. He went to the bookshelves again and ran his eye along the titles; but he'd spent a lot of the day

186

reading and there wasn't much here that grabbed him. The other obvious way to pass time was sleeping, but he'd had a couple of hours of that after lunch. . . . What he wanted was exercise and fresh air, preferably on horseback, but he'd promised them all he'd keep his head down so in daylight that was another temptation – like whisky – to be resisted.

Maybe after dark. Except by then Tom would be home, wanting company and conversation; to which, heaven knew, the old guy was entitled. . . .

He was looking at the Scotch bottle again, when someone rapped on the door.

'Don Andrés?'

Señora Torres, for God's sake. . . .

He let her in – or rather, offered her entrance. She stayed on the threshold where a few seconds ago he'd had a flashing daydream of Francisca standing; just at the first tap on the door. . . .

'It's Señora MacEwan, Don Andrés—'

Impossible to believe this was what she'd said!

' – on the radio – asking to speak with you – very urgent, she told me. . . . I say, "But surely Don Andrés is in England?" She replies, "I do not question your veracity, it is plain to me you are not aware of the fact that Don Andrés is with Don Tomás in his residence. Please, bring him to speak with me. . . ." Don Andrés, what could I do?'

By the time she'd paused for breath he was less dazed. Her hatchet face back in focus; a hand on the door-jamb was a contact with reality, as distinct from what had seemed like illusion. He slung his *poncho* over his shoulders, and followed her, her voice continuing, 'No one is outside here at this time, Don Andrés. Don Tomás said he did not wish it to be known that you are here, but—'

'I know. I know. . . .'

He couldn't see it mattered much, if the news had got *that* far. Following her into the 'big house': it stank of mutton, damp, wool, unwashed bodies. But then – he remembered, following her through the house – even when Tom Strobie had lived in it it hadn't been exactly immaculate. Francisca had

187

laughed at the old man when he'd asked her if there were cobwebs upstairs; she'd told him that upstairs wasn't so bad at all, it was down *here* the house was like a stable. He'd growled at her, 'It's the way I like it – Miss. . . .'

The radio room was at the back, a lean-to extension. Señora Torres pointed at a hard chair near the bench on which lay earphones and an old-fashioned upright telephone fitted up as a microphone with a switch on its base for transmit-receive.

'*Gracias*. . . .'

He'd expected her to leave, but she hung around, pretending to adjust the ancient equipment. And it didn't matter: with Francisca he'd be speaking English anyway. He sat down, put on the tinny headset. His hands were shaking; he felt as nervous as he had before the jump from the Hercules.

'Francisca?'

He pushed the switch over, heard a squawk of 'Andy, my *dear*!' and pushed it back again. Despite the bad reception, that had clearly been her voice; his heart was racing as he pushed the switch back: 'Francisca, how did you know I was here? Why didn't you let Tom know *you* were here? God, I've been so *hoping*. . . . Francisca, darling, are you all right?'

'I'll tell you everything when I see you, Andy. That's why I'm calling – to beg you, *please*, come over?'

'To the *estancia*?'

'Oh, please. . . . I have to talk to you – must *see* you. . . . Andy, it's like a miracle that you're here!'

Now she'd added – as if on an afterthought: 'Over. . . .' She'd ignored the radio-telephone routine until this moment. And she sounded desperate; even with such rotten reception he could hear that edge to her voice. But he was thinking about Cloudsley and company too, the vital need for invisibility; and also of putting old Tom at risk – at worse risk than he'd brought to him already. But then – since she already knew he was here, and if he could get there and back in the dark – there'd be no *worse* harm done?

Put the clock back five years?

'Andy, are you there?'

Again she hadn't said 'over'. He waited for the click you

heard when the other end switched over, and there wasn't one.

'Francisca – if you're hearing this – of course I'll come. . . . But tell me this much, are you in trouble?'

Switching quickly to 'receive'. Her voice came through thinly, ' – tell you *everything*, my dear, when—'

Another break. Then she came on again – ' —now, d'you mean, *tonight*?'

It could be this switch that was defective. Distinctly possible, by the look of the equipment generally. He glanced round, but the Torres woman had gone.

'I can't think of anything I want more than to see you, Francisca. I'll be there in a few hours. All right? Over. . . .' He switched back to her, and her voice came in a surge, suddenly much louder but as if she hadn't heard him at all: '—if you could make it *tonight,* Andy?'

Hopeless.

But thrilling, too. Really, intensely thrilling. . . . Walking back to Strobie's shack, he decided not to wait for darkness. Better to be away from here before the *peóns* rode in at sunset. It would also avoid a meeting with Tom himself, inevitably an argument.

She hadn't asked him how or why he'd come, what he was doing here, why he was hiding-out at Strobie's. . . .

He stopped – halfway over to the shack – asked himself, *Am I crazy? Out of my bloody mind?*

Well – maybe. . . . But the possibility didn't change anything, or suggest alternatives. He walked on again – hurrying, with an inclination even to be running. Thinking that there were several horses in the corral, and that the tack room would be open. Build Tom's fire up for him first; scribble a note to say back soon, not to worry.

They were all in the OP hide. Cloudsley, on edge and uncommunicative, at the periscope. Sunset had passed and the land was darkening but in the foreground the missile compound, service road and control tower were lit up. Compound gates still standing open, fuel-tanker still parked inside, and there'd been no movement towards closing the hangar doors. Further deployment of AM39s was clearly imminent.

Should have got here a day sooner, he thought. Then we'd have had the job done just in time. . . .

Geoff Hosegood broke the silence. 'Might do it in eight hours, once we're in there. Did reckon four hours a pair, didn't they.'

Cloudsley grunted. The reality of the situation, as he was seeing it now all too clearly, was that the four missiles they'd doctored were the only four that *would* get the treatment. He made himself agree with Geoff: 'Maybe. If we push it.'

If we get in at all. . . .

No reason, though, to assume they'd pack up at all, tonight. If a helo came in the next few minutes there could just as easily be another two hours later. If they were using scant resources – like that Alouette – to cope with a sudden demand for missiles on the operational bases – at Rio Gallegos, most likely – they'd work right through. On the other hand, if it turned out better than he was now expecting, if you *did* get in – well, Geoff could have something, it might be possible to cut the time right down. Taking a risk or two, pressure on the drill, *literally* 'pushing it'. . . . You could slow up near the end of the second stage of drilling on each missile – the last twenty minutes, say.

Beale had been thinking about it too. 'If we could do 'em in eight hours, we could start as late as midnight.'

'Not really.' Cloudsley pointed out – his tone so calm that to himself it sounded false – 'These buggers are up and doing at least half an hour before sunrise. Playing safe, call that an hour. Means being out of it by 0730, you see. Very latest we could start would be 2300. Right?'

'Sure, to get four done. Starting later – if we had to – we could still fix one pair. Four or five hours' work – better than fuck-all.'

Cloudsley grunted agreement. Beale was obviously quite right; and they *might* not deploy the whole outfit tonight and tomorrow. But since you couldn't be anything like sure of it,

190

the aim had to be to finish the job completely – *if* the chance arose.

Beale concluded, 'So right up to 0300, we got a chance.'

He kept his mouth shut. It was all conjecture, hypothesis; and to him, the feel of the situation was all wrong.

The evening meal of meat, *maté*, and *maté*-soaked *galletas* had been consumed at sunset. They were ready – Ingrams cleaned, checked over and lubricated, stun grenades on their belts, equipment like drilling bits in pockets, and the pack containing the drill and the liner-upper lay near the exit. Once the Argies did decide to go to their beds, there'd be nothing to hang about for.

'Wonder how Andy Mac's getting on.' Hosegood, talking to pass the time. 'Soaking up the old guy's Scotch, eh?'

'Wouldn't blame him.' Beale's voice, from the end of the hide. 'Sitting there all day, can't show his face out. . . . Mind you, he's got a fire to sit by.'

'Think of *that*.'

'Not to mention chicken and pasta?'

'Tony – shut up.'

Beale added after a minute's silence, 'If we got it done tonight, mind – the lot – so we'd move out tomorrow sundown – big yomp south, not much gear on us – do it in one night, Harry?'

'Should do.'

The nights were long: the proportion, ignoring twilight periods, was about sixteen hours of dark to eight of daylight. Beale reached his conclusion: 'Day after tomorrow then, *we* could be shoving down fucking chicken and pasta.'

'And Scotch.' Hosegood recalled, 'Harry promised him, didn't he?'

The chatter was largely for *his* benefit, Cloudsley guessed. They sensed the pressure in him. It mattered just as much to each of them as it did to him but he happened to be the one who carried most of the responsibility. He glanced round: 'Anyone want to take a turn at this bloody tube?'

At eight, Hosegood crawled back to the other hide to brew up some warmth. When it was ready he signalled on the string and Cloudsley joined him. Then Hosegood relieved Beale in the OP and they were all back there, waiting and watching, by eight-thirty. The compound was still open, fuel still waiting, and there was occasional movement between the guardhouse and the hangar, no sign at all of anyone going to bed.

A few minutes before nine, Roberto MacEwan's telephone jangled, in the office adjoining his sleeping quarters.

'Your call to the residence of Admiral Diaz, sir. Señora MacEwan on the line.'

'Thank you. Francisca?'

'Again, Roberto?'

'To check whether you've done what I asked you.'

'I told you I would, and I have. I hate it, but—'

'He's – obliging you?'

'You're *so* amusing. . . . Yes.'

'Well done. But one other thing: tell me, please, what he's here for?'

'I have not the least idea.'

'Are you telling me you didn't ask?'

'I did what you wanted, and no more.'

'No feminine curiosity? Or – *no need* to ask?'

'Roberto, I *told* you, I have had no correspondence whatsoever—'

'Yes. You did tell me. . . . Anyway, you've done it. Thank you.' He checked the time. 'Let's not bother now with more farewells. I'll be back soon enough, don't worry.'

'I will – try not to.'

He put the receiver down. Looking at it as if he hated it. It rang again, under his hand, and he put it to his ear. 'Yes?'

'Signal just received sir. I'll send it round, but I thought you'd want to know immediately. From *XI Brigada Aerea: Weather deterioration in south necessitates cancellation of tonight's collections. All remaining AM39s are to be ready for loading in Chinook which will reach you approx 0700. The*

PO added, 'Time of origin, and message ends. Blizzards extending northwards, they say, sir. A light helo like the Alouette couldn't—'

'Quite.' Roberto cut him short. 'Connect me with Lieutenant Rodriguez. After that I'll be in a mess for an hour.' He waited, drumming his fingers on the desk. 'Lieutenant. Stand them down, in the Exocet compound. That helo won't be returning. We'll have a Chinook here instead about 0700 to clear the whole lot in one lift, so it makes no odds really. Stand-to had better be at' – he paused for a moment, working it out – 'well, make it 0630.'

Those lights up ahead were on the top floor of the house in which he'd spent his childhood, years from which only the most tenuous memories of his mother remained as anything to treasure. He'd been four when she died, and his image of her was of no more than a source of physical warmth, and fiercely reciprocated affection, and now – as remotely as if it was a piece of some old, old dream – a vision of dark eyes and a red mouth smiling.

As if the sight of the house had triggered a long-buried memory. . . .

Reining-in, easing the mare down from a canter to a walk, turning her off the track that had been hardened by nearly a century of MacEwan horses' hooves and rutted, since, by decades of MacEwan truck tyres. . . . At a walk now, soft thudding of the mare's plates along the softer, rough-grassed edge. That window with the light in it was the one in the end wall of the main bedroom. It had been Robert's and Fiona's room, then Fiona's alone – the old woman had refused to move out, make way for her son and his little 'mongrel' wife. As Bruce should have insisted she did, of course. . . . Now, Francisca would be in that room; and waiting for his knock. Incredible: he was conscious of this sense of unreality, of a need to convince himself that he was actually this close to her,

193

that within minutes she'd be in his arms. . . . Passing through the last gate – turning the mare while he hooked it shut again – he saw, fifty yards up the avenue of poplar and eucalyptus, that there were lights burning on the ground floor too.

Not much secrecy, he thought. But then, that would be in character, for Francisca. Would have been; evidently still was.

Riding slowly up the drive, he felt the first flurry of snow. He guessed that by the time he started back the blizzard would have taken over, would have obliterated tracks and roads. Presenting no problems at all when you could find your way around with your eyes shut anyway, but maybe a complication for the SBS team.

But they'd steer by compass, then follow the line of fence-posts.

Kicking his feet out of the irons, he swung his leg over and slid down. A dark figure appeared from nowhere at the mare's head: a man in a cap and a *poncho* with a hand on the bridle. His impression was of a *peón* who'd have been waiting – on her orders – to take care of his horse, and the strangeness was only the way he'd so suddenly appeared and hadn't spoken. Then he heard a cough *behind* him: felt a rifle-barrel jabbing him in the back: 'Not into the big house, *señor.*' Juan Huyez poked him again with the gun: 'This way – if you would be so kind. . . .'

Hosegood asked Beale, 'Any special reason they'd use Pucarás for napalm?'

'Yeah.' Beale was at the periscope. 'If they want to base 'em on the islands. And I mean, where else. . .? Only airstrip that's anything but grass is the one at Stanley – and that's too short for your Mirages or your Skyhawks. Any case, they'd want to use the grass strips, wouldn't they – on West Falkland, maybe? Pucará only need – well, less than a thousand feet, for take-off. Even your Aermacchi'd want three times as much.'

Hosegood said, 'Like having a mobile computer along, this is.'

'Did some homework, that's all. But they're highly manoeuvrable too – designed for counter-insurgency, knocking the shit out of blokes on the ground. Come to think of it, you wouldn't find better, would you?'

Cloudsley checked the luminous face of his watch. 'You should be in the BAS, Tony.'

'Did consider it, one time.' BAS stood for Brigade Air Squadron, Royal Marines who flew Scout and Gazelle helos. 'But flying's only a hobby, I don't know about helos, never touched one.' Beale moved suddenly: 'Harry. Don't like to speak too soon, but – *it's happening*. . . .'

Cloudsley took over at the 'scope. Beale told Hosegood, 'They're packing up, shutting the main gates! Panic over!'

'*What* panic. . .'

They were leaving the fuel-truck inside the compound, although they were shutting and locking the gates. A possible interpretation, Cloudsley thought, was they might have been waiting for a helo which now wasn't coming but would be coming later. In the morning, maybe. Otherwise they'd hardly be leaving the big tanker there.

Almost 2130 now. It would be a mistake to move in too soon: people forgot things, came back for them. On the other hand you couldn't wait too long either, having already lost several hours of drilling time. Give it, say, half an hour. Ten o'clock, for the start of eight hours' work; or more realistically allow for nine. Nine hours, or less; at any rate be finished and clear out by seven.

Having *done it*!

The surge of confidence was a reaction to several hours of depression. . . . Watching a group of men in overalls come into sight from the front of the hangar, and guessing they'd have shut the sliding doors. Might even have remembered to lock the little doors, tonight; he felt for the key, checking he had it strung to his wrist. Its secret was that it was pliable, adapted itself to any ordinary kind of lock. Those guys were walking towards the guardhouse – that small gate. He saw a van – same one – coming along the road, passing the front of the compound then stopping at this near corner to reverse into the slip road. Those three were outside now, talking to the sentry and lighting cigarettes. Could be Frenchmen, at that. . . . The van was returning, its lights sweeping along the wire; and stopping now to pick them up. Cloudsley told Beale and Hosegood, 'Fifteen minutes. After that, when the sentry moves – on your marks. . . .'

12

Shropshire pitched heavily, rolling too, wind and sea on her quarter. Her gun had thudded once, one dull *crack*'s vibration punctuating weather noise and ship noise, and now after a pause the distant flash of the shell's airburst explosion flickered in the dark circle of Saddler's binoculars. It wasn't snowing at the moment, but at any moment visibility would be down to zero again; there'd been showers on and off all through the early part of the night, snow and sleet driving horizontally over black, wind-whipped sea. . . . He lowered the glasses, hearing over the Tactical Line the echoey distant crackling of the FOO's voice – forward observation officer, somewhere on the eastern shoulder of Mount Kent – 'Bang on target. Twenty salvoes now, airburst, fire for effect!' A flow of gun-control patter followed, over the Command Open Line, the other ear-phone in his headset, before the 4.5″ turret's twin guns began a regular pulsing discharge of high-explosive shells. Unless the crew of that turret had cast-iron insides, Saddler guessed, they'd be puking all over its bright paintwork by this time – contending not only with the ship's violent motion but also with the constant to-and-fro jerking of the turret as the computer kept it lined up on target; and at that, in close confinement. . . .

'Airburst' meant shells fused to explode fifty feet above the ground – in this instance above an enemy artillery position overlooked from the FOO's perch and most likely pinpointed by SAS reconnaissance in recent days. That mountain top was crucial, and a force of Royal Marines was in the process of occupying it at this moment, knowing that whoever held it would dominate the approaches to Stanley .and the other hilltops and ridges, the battlefield of the coming days or weeks.

Days, please God. . . .

'Stop loading, stop loading, stop loading!'

'Rounds complete. . . .'

The patter included some interjections by the FOO's linkman, a warrant officer who was with the gun director down in *Shropshire*'s radar-glowing Ops Room. These bombardments were conducted according to pre-arranged fire plans, lists of coordinates as aiming points fed into the computer and then corrections to fall-of-shot coming by radio from the man ashore – who'd be exposed to all the worst of this weather, working in sub-zero temperature tonight and no doubt soaking wet. . . . Saddler heard the soldier's voice again, a muffled but astonishingly cheerful tone: 'We've malleted *that* lot, all right!' There'd be a fresh target selected in a minute. *Shropshire* was off Bluff Cove, 'on gunline' and tonight at the service of 'K' Company, 42 Commando RM, who'd have been deposited on Mount Kent by two PNG-equipped Sea Kings flying from San Carlos, their object being to seize and hold the summit.

David Vigne murmured, 'Come ten degrees to port, John,' and Holt, officer of the watch, passed the order via the wheelhouse microphone. The ship had to be close offshore for this gun-support job, but she had also to be kept clear of known or suspected concentrations of kelp. At this moment she was inside the range of Argie coastal howitzer batteries, but if any of them woke up to her presence the FOO on Mount Kent might be in a position to 'mallet' them as well.

Everything was on the move now. 2 Para had taken Darwin and won their battle at Goose Green – against odds of four to one, and at heavy cost. On the twenty-seventh, when 45 Commando and 3 Para had started out from San Carlos, yomping – because of the loss of the Chinooks in the *Atlantic Conveyor* – to Douglas and Teal Inlet, the SAS had already begun to invest the lower slopes of Mount Kent, preparing the way for tonight's capture of the summit. A Chinook would be going in behind the Sea Kings, lifting in some 105-mm guns and ammunition.

'Course two-four-five sir. . . .'

Shropshire's action damage had been patched or plugged, and all her systems were operational. Saddler was very conscious of the element of luck, supplementing reasonably good management, that had left his ship fighting fit and her crew's morale as high as ever. In contrast, the list of casualties in his diary now read: SUNK/*Sheffield, Ardent, Antelope, Coventry, Atlantic Conveyor*. DAMAGED/*Glasgow, Antrim, Brilliant, Argonaut, Broadsword, Shropshire*. AIRCRAFT LOST/*7 Harriers, 4 Sea Kings*.' Despite the fact the act was holding together pretty well, the Royal Navy of 1982 wasn't big enough to stand such a rate of loss and damage.

A new call for fire was coming through. Loading with HE; airburst; a multi-figure set of coordinates to be punched into the computer and pinpoint a new target. . . . Snow plastering the glass screen again as *Shropshire* pitched bow-down, ploughing her stem in deep.

'Salvoes – airburst – fire for effect. . . .'

He'd had a letter from his daughter, and begun to answer it earlier this evening while they'd been fuelling. Early tomorrow there was to be a RAS(S), a rendezvous with a fleet auxiliary mainly to replenish ammunition, and outgoing mail would be passed over then, mailbags being dragged over on the hawser to start their long, slow journey back to the UK. . . . Lisa had written, 'I'm really fed up with Andy. He's been gone ages and I haven't had even a postcard from him. He takes me so much for granted I don't suppose it would be anything but water off a duck's back if I were to tell him how sick of all this I am, but it adds considerably to one's frustration not to be able to. All I know is he's in America, but no address at all, he might as well be on the moon. His office people say they've no idea where he is or when he'll be back or anything. It's really too bad and *very* inconsiderate, and I suppose I've got to face it – better late than never – accept the fact he doesn't give a damn and there's no point going on trying, he'd better leave me to get on with my life instead of wasting time like this. Don't you agree? You don't give your opinions much in this kind of thing and I'd very much like to know what you really think. Sorry, I know I'm being terribly self-centred, burdening you with such petty problems when you're out there coping with heaven knows what awful—'

In the back of his mind he'd counted ten rounds as they'd left the gun; now in the lull he heard Vigne suggest, 'Might come about, sir, steer the reciprocal, before the next call?'

'Yes. Bring her round to port.'

He'd answered that part of Lisa's letter in stone-walling fashion: 'You have a good man there. You may not think so at the moment, and I can well understand how you feel – I sympathise, and appreciate you're going through a rotten time, but my advice – since you ask for it – is don't burn your bridges yet. Not if you really do care for him, I mean at heart, which I think you must do or you wouldn't have put up with it as long as you have. You're a very special girl and you have a great deal to offer any man, you don't have to tolerate casual treatment from anyone at all; all I'm suggesting is you might give him a chance to explain himself to you when he gets back – have a showdown, lay it on the line, etc, but I'd say don't commit yourself to paper before then. . . .'

Except, of course, Andy wouldn't be able to say a word about where he'd been or what he'd been doing. *If* he got back. . . . Saddler put a hand out to the console for support as his ship swung her beam to the direction of wind and sea, rolling practically on to her beam-ends, hanging there for some taut seconds before she began the slow swing back the other way. . . . There'd been no explanation of the Sea King that had been found in Chile, and no word at all of the SBS party from any source here either. For all anyone could know, they'd flown into the back of beyond and disappeared; Andy

200

MacEwan could be dead, might have the best excuse in the world for not writing postcards.

This time, when the moment had come to start running for the fence, Cloudsley had led but with Beale right on his heels, making a race of it. They got to the wire in a dead heat and far enough apart to swarm over it side by side but without getting in each other's way, landing just about simultaneously in the compound – Cloudsley facing the wire, staying there long enough to catch the pack with the drill and liner-upper in it which Hosegood slung over, lobbing it clear over the fence's barbed top and Cloudsley catching it like a rugger player taking the ball from a long, high kick, turning and running as his hands folded it against his stomach, and Hosegood on his way over the wire by then, Beale flat on the ground between the generator shed and its fuel-tank, unearthing one of the other packs. Beale and Hosegood made it to the little door in a photo-finish, the door being open for them to dive straight in and out of sight, Cloudsley having unlocked it with his burglar's tool and left it open for them. Hosegood pushed it shut – nearly shut – and stayed there long enough to be sure no alarm had been raised, while Beale took the batteries out of the pack and clipped the liner-upper's leads to the terminals of one of them and the drill's leads to the other. Cloudsley meanwhile on his back under first one trolley and then the other, with one of the little torches between his teeth and the millimetre measure in hand, checking the undersides of the missiles and finding the almost invisible scar on one of them. He was back at the first one now, unscrewing the cover of the plug socket, taking the multi-pin plug from Beale then and shoving it in. . . . 'Right.' Beale switched on, and Cloudsley heard the *whirr* and click of the booster motor moving into line: if you hadn't done this first, the second drilling would have gone into some area better not penetrated. Hosegood was tightening the drill's snout on one of the short drilling bits; he put the drill on the ground beside the first patient, and when the cover had been screwed back over the socket he and Beale were ready at the missile's tail-end to raise it and twist it around, belly up. Cloudsley did his measuring and marking then, handed the measure to Beale and picked up the drill. Checking the time: he was starting the first incision at four minutes past ten. It had been ten o'clock exactly when the sentry had been going out of sight and he'd pushed himself out of the hide. Urgency, after the hours of waiting and frustration, was like a clamp in his gut.

He put more weight on the drill than he thought he had last night. It wasn't easy to judge, and he was aware of the penalty for overdoing it, but it was plainly essential to get the job done faster this time. Hosegood and Beale were at the back of the hangar, at the racks, checking the other three missiles to make sure none of them had been one of last night's patients. If one had been, it would have meant the Alouette must have taken one that had not been doctored. This wasn't likely, the overalled men who'd brought the things out would have had to shuffle these racked ones around instead of taking them as they came; there could have been some reason for doing so, so you had to make sure. In fact all was well. Beale and Hosegood used the liner-upper on all three, then turned them and did the measuring and marking.

At ten thirty-five Hosegood took over the drill from Cloudsley. But at the end of this thirty-minute stint he wasn't through to the air space, and he stayed with it because it would have consumed some time changing over for just a minute or two. In fact that first stage took nearer seventy than sixty minutes, finishing at 2313. Then that missile had to be left to cool, and Beale started on the first of the three in the racks.

The first pair were finished at 0244. So it had taken four hours and forty minutes. It wasn't good enough. It was better than the first night's result, but they were going to have to do better still. Cloudsley had thought he was pushing it along as fast as he dared, and he was sure the others had been doing the same, but it was still unacceptable. He'd been doing the last half-hour's drilling himself – actually more than half an hour,

202

but roughly the last two-thirds of the second-stage drilling on missile number two – and while Hosegood now started the first stage on number three he went to the door to clear his head with some cold night air while he thought about it, got the situation in perspective.

Snow.

It took him by surprise. He'd envisaged it as a possibility, before this, but tonight he hadn't; he'd been looking at the problems they actually had already. So now here was a new one: snow swirling pale yellow in the beams of light and lying tinged yellow along the lines of the fence, but white in the shadows. It was settling as it fell on pre-frozen ground; and clinging to the sentry's overcoat, glistening on his cap as he paced at a hunched angle with his nose down in the coat's upturned collar; you could have walked up and poked a finger in his eye before he'd have known he had company. . . . But by the time they were ready to duck out of here – four and a half hours, say – if the snow kept on throughout those hours there'd be quite a lot of it lying around. The only hope – he'd thought of this before – was that it might be coming down fast enough to cover tracks very quickly.

Second hope, though: that with the sentries as half-baked as they seemed, more useless than ever in these conditions, they wouldn't see footprints if you rubbed their noses in them.

Back to the question of timing – the importance of getting the job done before the pre-dawn flying circus got going. . . . In the back of his mind – this was primarily what he'd needed to sort out – had been the possibility of the base coming to life even earlier than usual, if the postponed helo lift was also going to be resumed before dawn. But the snow might be a new factor too, might delay them even more, might induce them to cancel the early flying. . . .

Hope for that, then. Hope, but of course not count on it. Meanwhile, except for putting more muscle on the drill you didn't really have much choice. The job had to be completed even if it took longer than you'd have liked, even if finishing it meant you'd get trapped here. One AM39 left in working order might take a hell of a lot more than three lives. It could even – if it sank *Hermes* or *Invincible*, for instance, the Harrier platforms – lose the war.

But – four and a half hours, say. From 0244 – quarter to three, the time it had been five minutes ago when they'd finished the first pair – well, you'd complete at 0715.

His nerves were on edge. He wasn't used to it, and disliked it. It was unproductive and – he told himself – unwarranted. Things were a lot better than they might have been. At least you were in here, getting on with it – and you could have been still sitting in the OP watching helos fly in – missiles fly out. . . .

He went back to the others. Hosegood was drilling, Beale standing by for the next shift. Cloudsley put a hand on Beale's shoulder: 'Listen, we have to get this moving faster. The last pair took four hours forty minutes, these we've got to do in four hours *no* minutes. Lean a bit harder on the drill, Geoff. Let up right at the end, just the last few minutes of stage two.'

Hosegood shifted his feet, adjusting his posture and then bearing down on the drill. Eyes narrowed, fixed on the dazzling spot of light which most of the time was the only point of illumination in the hangar's icy darkness. Cloudsley told Beale, 'I'd like to be out of here by seven, Tony. But we're here until we finish, no matter what.' He added as he turned away, 'It's snowing, out there.'

They'd brought him to the meathouse and pushed him inside. Three sheep's carcases hung in the main working area, the big outer room with its blood-stained concrete floor. Huyez nudged him forward, through that part and into the storeroom at the back that had no window. Juan Huyez was standing in the doorway now with his Winchester levelled, Paco Huyez behind his father with the flashlight shining past him into Andy's face.

When they'd jumped him he'd been so completely taken by surprise that he'd forgotten he had a knife on his belt and had been taught how to use it. By the time he'd begun to think coherently Paco Huyez had switched on that torch, a probe of light blinding him through the dense curtain of falling snow while the rifle barrel prodded from behind. If the barrel had been pressed against him steadily he'd have known for sure where it was, might have been able to duck round and tackle the man holding it, but he'd guessed the *mayordomo* was standing back, reaching forward with it now and then to let him know how things were.

But also, in the first seconds he'd assumed it must be a mistake, that when they saw who he was they'd apologise. . . .

'Take the horse, Paco. Turn to your right, Don Andrés. To the *carnicería,* if you please.'

'What the hell is this?'

'We speak when we are inside. Your hands high, now!'

A jab with the gun; and Huyez had only just thought of the 'hands up' bit. All parties concerned in this were amateurs, Andy realised. But his brain was beginning to tick over and he was remembering that the Royal Marine instructors *had* taught him a few tricks.

'Are you under some impression you're protecting the *señora?*'

'I am doing what has to be done. *In.* . . .'

Facing him now, in the square, windowless store, with the torchlight outlining the *mayordomo*'s wiry, slightly stooped figure. . . . 'Don Andrés. I am authorised to kill you, if necessary. If you make no sound and no trouble, it should *not* be necessary. If others do not get to know you are here, you will have a better chance to stay alive than if you were so misguided as to shout for help or try to escape. . . . Do you follow me?'

'I'd better warn you, before you go any farther—'

'I warn *you.* . . . I will take the key of this door, so nobody can enter. You may hear some person try to open it, not knowing it has been locked, or why. If you call out to them' – the rifle moved – 'you get *this*, and a hole in the ground. Understand, Don Andrés?'

'I'll freeze, in here.'

Paco laughed. Paco's father nodded. 'You'll be cold, sure.'

'I'll die of cold. You know it.'

205

'I may provide a blanket. I'll think about it.'

'Why?' Paco spoke close to his father's ear. 'What does it matter if he's so cold he dies?'

'Why are you doing this, Don Juan?'

His guess was they must have overheard Francisca's radio call to him. They'd either be acting on their own initiative, guessing what Robert would have wanted them to do, or they'd reported to him and this was being done on his orders. That was the likely scenario: Huyez had said, *I am authorised. . . .*

'I have a question to ask *you*, Don Andrés.'

'Ask it, then.' Might dive under the gun's barrel. Pulling out knife *en route*. Drawing the knife would be a clumsy business, though, since it was under the heavy *poncho*. And there'd have been a better chance if Paco hadn't been so close up behind his father. On the other hand, Juan Huyez's reactions weren't likely to be very quick. He put his question now – the obvious one – 'What have you come here for?'

'To see the *señora*, of course. You must know that. You were waiting for me , obviously you heard her call me on the radio.'

'The *señora* called him.' Glancing back at his son. 'From Buenos Aires she calls, to invite him *here*!'

They both laughed: Huyez senior in a low, rough chuckle, Paco rather hysterically.

'Summon him here, calling from the residence in Buenos Aires of Alejandro Diaz! And he comes running like a little dog to a bitch on heat!'

Or a little vizcacha?

'Don Andrés – can it be that you have come all the way from England to visit the *señora*?'

That other bit, about BA, her being at her father's house, was beginning to sink in. It felt as if the world was in the process of turning upside-down. If she'd called from BA, pretending to be here, *she*'d set him up for this. Or helped in it. Presumably at Robert's insistence. Or 'instigation' might be a better word, maybe Robert hadn't needed to insist. She'd certainly made it *sound* good.

Christ. Of all the bloody fools. . . .

'From England, by *avion* – so far, to visit her?'

Paco sniggered: 'Or lie with her.'

'*Señor*, this is the truth?'

He nodded. Mind already beginning to firm up to this, to harden. 'She wrote imploring me to come.'

Paco giggling again. Huyez had his finger inside the trigger-guard of the Winchester and its barrel lined up on Andy's gut. Paco sneered, 'Implored him, so she could deliver him to her husband? Could it be the *patrón* instructed her to write such a letter to his brother?'

Huyez said, 'You have come a long way at huge expense to accomplish your own destruction, Don Andrés.'

'Destruction? I thought you said—'

'Papa.' Paco pawed at his father's shoulder. 'You have the information the *patrón* said he wanted, so why not finish it? It would be less simple to keep him here, and no risk at all, if *tonight* he can disappear?'

Huyez was thinking about it. Paco, encouraged, gabbling on, 'Better not with a bullet. A knock on the head – then into the river. A *peón* from nowhere, drowned. . . .'

Andy could see Juan Huyez liked it. He asked him, 'What do you stand to get out of this, Don Juan?'

'Can you not guess?'

'I suppose what you always wanted, what the old woman promised.'

Old family intrigue, to result in murder this long after? He had a sudden sense of total unreality; as if this couldn't possibly be happening. On the other hand it *was* happening, and it fitted the family background, a postscript perfectly dovetailed to everything that had gone before. . . . Paco had prompted, 'Papa?' and Huyez was shuffling backwards through the doorway, rifle still aimed and steady. 'Come. Out here.'

Intending, obviously, to kill him here. But in fact there'd be a better chance in that larger room, more room to manoeuvre.

'I'm to ride with you to the river, that it? So you can bash me on the head and throw me in?'

207

Paco said, 'Right here would be best.' He'd whispered it. Moving forward, watching the gun, Andy decided he disliked Paco profoundly. Despite the fact that hatred had never been an emotion he'd gone in for. He'd never hated even Robert, or his grandmother. Disliked, and feared; not hated. Perhaps it was Francisca he really hated, but right now it looked like Paco Huyez. Who'd turned, going to the outer door. He guessed they'd do it here, not risk him getting away from them in the open and with the cover of a snowstorm to help. Paco shut that door; Juan Huyez was backing round, with the gun on him, motioning with his head that he should pass him, approach the door. It would put him between them, of course. But also it would involve his passing between two of the slung carcasses, through a gap between them where there must have been another quite recently; an unoccupied meathook hung there, its S-shaped steel gleaming dully in the light of Paco's torch.

'Ride to the river? Moving me as it were on the hoof?' Moving the way Huyez had told him to move. 'Ever murder anyone before, Don Juan?'

Paco said, 'You present us with a wonderful future. We are grateful to you.' He smirked. 'And to the *señora*, of course.'

'Will you give her a message for me?'

He was sure this would hold them for a few moments. Whatever the message might be, for these two there'd be a joke in it. This was *vizcacha* country, all right. Moving with his hands up towards Paco, between the hollow, bloody carcasses of the sheep, his right hand was about to pass within inches of that hook. Double-ended, S-shaped, each end a curve of spike kept sharp to penetrate carcasses or hunks of meat.

'What should I say to the *señora*, your brother's wife?'

'First, that I was fool enough to love her—'

'*Si.*' They both smiled. 'It has not been entirely a secret. But surely, Don Andrés' – Juan Huyez put it to him – 'the foolishness was in believing the *señora* might love *you?*'

'That could be so; and I want you to tell her that now I've woken up to the truth, that she's a cold-blooded, murderous *bitch*—'

On the word 'murderous' he'd lifted the hook smoothly

208

from the bar on which it hung, ducked around the carcase on his right and swung the heavy steel implement into the *mayordomo's* face. Huyez reeled back, off-balance, dropping the Winchester as his hands went to his bloodied face. The hook was so light in Andy's hand it felt virtually weightless as he swung it again but this time with one of the spiked points leading, slashing downwards – as Paco rushed forward, going for the rifle, the hook's point embedding itself in the side of Juan Huyez's scrawny neck, blood spurting in a fountain as it skewered through into his throat. Andy unsheathed his knife as he went after Paco – who'd let out a high, womanish scream, having failed to reach the Winchester, met Andy's boot instead and turned to run, Juan Huyez convulsing in death throes and gushing blood, Andy close behind Paco slamming him against the door and pushing about an inch of knife-point through the boy's *poncho*, puncturing flesh in the region of his kidneys. Paco screamed again – twisting round, a vain attempt to see his father. . . .

'Be quiet!' Mouth close to an ear. . . . Then: 'Tell me all about it, Paco.'

'*Señor*, I beg you—'

'But a minute ago you were so happy.' He slammed his face against the door again. 'Get your hands right up, palms against the wall.' Paco obeyed, whimpering. 'I'll give you a start, then you go on. You saw me at Señor Strobie's, and you told your father about it. What then?'

'My father radio'd to the *patrón*—'

'Where was the *patrón*?'

'At the airbase, *señor*!'

'Go on.'

'He told him that you were here. He *had* to, it was his *duty*—'

'What did the *patrón* say?'

'That he would arrange for you to visit this *estancia*. He said you would come either tonight or tomorrow.'

'How was he intending to arrange this?'

'I think he did not say, *señor*.'

'I see.' It would have been difficult *not* to see. 'What were

209

you to do when I arrived?'

'We were to keep you until he could come. For weeks, he said it might be. But, if necessary, to kill you.'

'What kind of necessity?'

'He said if there was – an accident – my father would not be blamed for it. This was the *patrón's* order, *señor* – my father believed his true wish was that you should be killed.'

'Your father was most likely right, at that.'

He withdrew the knife and sheathed it, picked up the rifle, Seeing it all clearly enough now – except for Francisca's degree of involvement, degree of either willingness or compulsion. But she'd managed to act it out pretty well, managed to stifle any compunction she might have felt; so count her in, *right in.* . . .

It was still like the old world having gone, a new one forming round him.

'*Señor*, I personally had no wish at all to harm you or—'

'Shut up!'

Thinking it out. Putting his mind to an entirely new situation, trying to do it urgently but also logically, the way he'd seen certain others operate in recent weeks. But feeling, also, like a stranger to himself. . . . 'Who else knows what you were doing, Paco?'

'Nobody. My father wished it to remain secret.'

'So no one would ever know I'd been here.' It made sense and he thought he might build on it. . . . 'Where does your mother think you are at this minute?'

A sigh. . . . 'At the *estancia* El Lucero – there is a young lady—'

'Check. Where would your mother think your father might be?'

'Maybe in the office, or the big house. He works sometimes on accounts at night. . . .'

He had one dead Huyez and one live one. His own presence known only to this snivelling boy and to Robert and Francisca. They wouldn't admit having conspired to murder, so could hardly admit knowing he'd been in the country. In fact his having been here was a secret that would have to be kept both for his own sake in the long term and right now for the sake of Cloudsley and the others and their operation, including their safe withdrawal. But if he killed this boy – who did undoubtedly have to be silenced – then no one could doubt there'd been a third party here tonight. There'd be a country-wide hunt despite the fact they wouldn't know it was Andrés MacEwan they were hunting; it would be a disturbance of a major and – for the SBS team – highly unwelcome kind.

Patrols on the roads, for instance. Roadblocks. . . .

He saw the beginnings of an answer.

'*Señor,* please—'

'Shut up.'

Paco standing with his face against the door, arms straight up with their palms against the timber above his head, no meathook within ten yards. One *vizcacha* was as good as another, Andy thought. In fact this one was quite deserving. Roberto wouldn't have baulked at it; and Francisca, if she'd seen it as contributing to her own interests, wouldn't have hesitated to connive at it. Come to think of it, what Francisca had demonstrated tonight from a distance of about a thousand miles was a quality that had always been visible in her. Until now, he'd mistaken it for strength of character, a kind of directness and *élan* which he himself, he'd felt, sadly lacked. But he could see now that what he'd admired in her had been only a working combination of self-interest and amorality.

And – *when in Rome.* . . .

'Paco. Grab hold of the legs, drag the body in there.'

Into the small storeroom where they'd intended keeping *him* – until Paco had come up with a better idea. He was weeping now, crossing himself. . . .

'Get on with it!' Lifting the rifle. . . . 'No – by the *feet.* . . .' Watching him do it; with head averted, eyes streaming. . . . 'Now clean up, with the hose.'

It was a convenient place for murder, with a drain in the floor and a hose for sluicing the blood down it. Juan Huyez had bled profusely, the hook having ripped through his jugular. Watching the boy carry out his orders, sick-looking and shaking violently all over, Andy deliberately recalled to mind his laugh and the question, *What does it matter if he dies?* Even then, you had to suppress what might have been described as 'finer feelings'. Euphemism, he told himself, for the streak of softness, the soft core he'd always been scared Francisca might see and sneer at; which perhaps she *had* seen, and in consequence preferred Roberto. . . . He'd need to suppress it now, all right, because there was a long, long way to go yet.

While Paco was using the hose, Andy locked the storeroom door and pocketed the key.

'All right, that'll do.' Even to start with the floor hadn't been exactly immaculate. 'Where's my horse?'

A nod towards the door. Paco in tears still, shuddering with the sobs. Andy kept the rifle aimed at him, opened the door and saw Strobie's bay mare tethered close to it, already plastered in snow although this was the sheltered side. He turned back to Paco. 'We'll need a horse for you too. Is the *nochero* in or out?'

'Stabled, *señor*, but—'

'We'll go get it.' They'd have known the snow was coming, of course. . . . The *nochero*'s tack had been left handy in the outer part of its stable, but he told Paco not to bother with a saddle. These people often didn't; and a lad who'd just murdered his father and was so crazed as to be about to take his own life in an utterly bizarre manner wouldn't have given it a thought. Paco was fastening the throat-strap of the bridle, his hands shaking so much it wasn't easy for him. . . . 'All right. We return now to the *carnicería*. Bring the horse.'

Inside again, in the sweetish reek of blood, having tethered the other horse beside his own, he told Paco, 'Now strip. Take all your clothes off.'

'My – clothes?'

'Do it. Take all your clothes off, then roll everything up in the *poncho*.'

The boy hadn't moved. Andy pointed the Winchester at his lower abdomen: 'I don't care if you live or die. As you didn't care if I froze in there or drowned in the river. I'll count to three. One. . . .'

212

Paco stripped. He was crying, and he stopped twice as if he couldn't believe this was for real.

'Bundle it now. Boots too. Tie it with the belt.'

Francisca's voice in his memory: *Little boys pull wings off flies, don't they?*

He motioned with the rifle in his gloved hands: 'Out.'

A step forward, pleading: 'Don Andrés – *señor* – out there I'll *die*!'

Out of the mouths of babes and sucklings. . . . Andy reached, pulled the bundle of clothes out of the boy's arms, gestured again: 'Outside.' He pushed the door open, saw the two horses snow-covered and miserable; he felt sorry for the horses. . . . '*Out*, damn you!' Using the rifle as if it had a bayonet on it, slamming the door shut behind them both and unhitching his own horse. 'Mount!' He grabbed the *nochero*'s reins. When the naked, mewling boy was up, he turned the mare and urged her into a trot, leading the other.

'Don Andrés – in the name of Christ and the Holy Virgin—'

'*Ride!*' He threw him the reins. 'Stay in front now. If you want a chance of staying alive, do exactly what I say!' Paco had no chance whatsoever of staying alive but if he'd guessed it he might have made a break, risked a bullet. Not that he'd have got far. The snow was thick, blinding, driven on an icy, gusting wind, the cold would be eating into the marrow of his bones. Andy handled both gates, making Paco ride through and then following, shutting them; even though a madman might have left them open. Conceivably – he thought, herding the boy along – *he* was the madman in this party. But he'd never thought more clearly or acted more resolutely in his life; this was what he had to do, he knew it and he was doing it, having no alternatives and his mind as it were anaesthetised. . . . It occurred to him that *she* might have admired this if she could have seen it, seen the absolutely new Andrew MacEwan?

A mile from the *estancia* he called, 'Stop, Paco!'

He'd thought the boy might not have lasted this far, might have slipped off sooner, might have died by now of the cold or of his own terror. He rode at him, cannoning his horse into the other, reaching to grab one long white leg and yank it upward,

213

tipping the boy off then snatching the *nochero*'s reins and trotting clear. . . . 'Run! *Run*, Paco!'

On his hands and knees in the thorn scrub. His scream was thin, a cat could have made more noise. Andy rode at him again, swinging the rifle as a threat but careful not to touch him with it. 'Run!'

He'd got up: fallen. . . . Scrambling up again, stumbling a few steps then collapsing, up again as he heard the thudding hooves approaching. Stumbling forward. . . . The thorns ripping at his feet and legs would be nothing, numbed by the cold he might not even be feeling them. He'd covered a few hundred yards, part of that distance crawling, before he went flat again and this time stayed there. Andy put the reins back over the MacEwan horse's neck and gave it a whack across the rump; it trotted away into the whirling snow and he forgot it. He threw the rifle down, then opened the bundle of clothing and began dropping it item by item in a circle round the body, pausing only to take the storeroom key out of his own pocket and push it into one in the boy's *bombachas*. Why would a kid who'd slaughtered his own father ride out in a blizzard – with a loaded Winchester – and divest himself of his clothes? Remorse, a madman's torment? Only God himself, the *peóns* would say, crossing themselves, could answer such a question. . . . Andy leant from the saddle for a final look at what was already only a hummock in the snow; then he turned his horse towards Strobie's.

You couldn't lean on the drill all that hard, they'd found. A little weight on it was OK, caused the heap of metal dust in first-stage drillings to pile slightly faster, but overdoing it was counter-productive. You could only experiment in this way in the first-stage drills of course, because when you were cutting into the inner casings you didn't see it happening. But either the boffins had rounded off their stopwatch figures to provide those sixty-minute and forty-five-minute timings – which surely wouldn't have been very scientific — or the missile casings on which the experimental drillings had been carried out had been of a different tensile strength. Presumably inner and outer casings were made of the same steel alloy, but Cloudsley had no recollection of this being mentioned.

With a hundred per cent concentration, no hold-ups and lightning changeovers between operators and from one missile to the next, plus nobody allowing themselves to get hypnotised, he reckoned as the hours passed that they had a reasonable chance of just about making his 0700 deadline.

Tony Beale finished stage one on missile three at 0355. Ten minutes outside the schedule. Cloudsley's turn then, starting on number four and handing over after half an hour to Hosegood, who drilled into the air gap at 0504. About twenty minutes over, then. At 0540 Beale handed over on stage two of missile three to Cloudsley; and this was the part where you had to ease up as you came near the end. The diamond tip of his drill broke into the booster motor's guts at 0602: he knew it was through because of the feel of it and the faint hiss of escaping gas; he pulled back quickly to get the hot probe out of it and to let it vent, also so as to move without delay to missile four for the first part of stage two. By this time they'd broken all the boffins' laws on caution but it was still taking longer than it should.

'Snow's stopped.' Beale added, 'That's not all, Harry. There's Pucarás being moved out.'

He'd been at the door, and made his announcement quietly, breaking foul news so gently it was — in the circumstances — ludicrous. . . . Cloudsley stooped over the missile, sliding the bit in through the stage one hole, aiming for the geometric centre as he set the diamond tip against the inner casing. Hearing Beale mutter, 'Lying real thick now. Suppose they can still get off the ground.' He shut his mind to it — tried to, while Beale was packing the hole in missile three with the dental filling. In fact an early start to the pre-dawn flying was less of a menace — touch wood — than the snow was, snow thick enough to be imprinted with boot-marks but the snow*fall* finished, leaving the marks clear and the sky clear too for helos to come

215

shuttling in. *But forget it; forget everything on the outside, concentrate on* this, *just get on with it.* . . . He heard the other two checking over their Ingram pistols. It was two and a half minutes past six when he triggered the drill for the start of the last stage, last missile, the tiny spotlight focusing along the invisibly-spinning drill as he applied what experience suggested was about optimum pressure. Hosegood would have the tricky part on this one, when he took over in half an hour.

At 0633, in fact. The change-over didn't take more than a couple of seconds because the bit didn't even have to be removed from the hole for it. Beale murmured, checking his watch, 'Near done it, Harry.' Cloudsley nodded. He'd taken the magazine out of his Ingram and checked it; now he slid it back in again. 'Let's have the rest of the gear packed up.'

One battery was already finished with. They'd take these two out, but the spares buried out there in their Czech-made pack would have to be left. Might lie there for years. Cloudsley went to the door and opened it an inch. Crouching with his eye to the crack, seeing aircraft moving on the field but needing to get the foreground picture into focus first. Snow lying deep and unmarked under the flood of light; and a dark streak around the outside of the wire where sentries' boots had transformed snow into mush. A double-take on this; and a spark of hope. You'd land in that beaten track – OK, there'd be tracks on the inside of the fence, you'd have to trust to luck on that – land in the sentries' pathway, and then numbers two and three would follow in father's footsteps across the slip-road and into the dark. One smudged lot of boot-prints might pass for the spoor of a sentry who'd been taken short, retired into the dark to relieve himself. These characters weren't expecting trouble; they'd think at least twice before annoying their NCOs by raising a false alarm.

He felt better. In good heart anyway for knowing the object of the operation had practically been achieved.

The fuel-truck, almost end-on from this viewpoint, was a dome of white under its heavy thatch of snow. Beyond it – a long way beyond it – he saw moving lights.

Headlights, blinding. . . . He took his eyes off them. Lights

216

out on the airfield were tractor headlights, tractors parked to provide light for ground staff working around the Pucarás. One trailer to each group of aircraft. Bombing-up, he guessed, to herald the new day with napalm. Allowing himself to look back at the other lights. . . . Hosegood must have seven or eight minutes' work still to do on that last missile, he thought. The thought linked directly to what he almost *knew* he was about to see – and did see now, with sweat ice-cold on his tense, crouched body. It was the van, the one in which the Argies moved personnel to and from this compound, coming at slow speed along the snow-packed road.

13

Beale had screwed the suppressor on to the barrel of his
Ingram. He'd also readied Hosegood's for him and put it on
the concrete floor beside him. Geoff was still drilling, having to
take it carefully now, this final stage. Beale squatted near the
missile's head while Cloudsley, up front, watched through the
gap between the hinges of the little door.

He pushed it shut.

'They're coming. Geoff, we'll hold them off while you
finish. Just keep at it.'

The drill's pinpoint of light and its reflection radiating from
the missile's shiny casing was the only break in the hangar's
darkness; with Geoff's dark features, glittering slits of eyes
spectrally illuminated in it.

Cloudsley's last sight through the slit in the door had been of
four men with parkas over their overalls coming from the gates
towards the front of the hangar. They'd arrived in the van,
which had been moving off again along the service road as the
four entered via the small side gate; a soldier had been taking
his time over unlocking the big ones.

Cloudsley hoped he wasn't going to have to kill them. It
wouldn't be necessary if they put their hands up and stayed

quiet and docile while the job was finished. If they were civilian technicians – Frenchmen, maybe – you might hope for that. But now he was hearing Spanish, not French, voices raised above the diesel's racket. Right outside the hangar doors. And the sound of Pucará engines warming up. Earlier than ever: so *that* surmise had been correct. A crash – a boot, against the doors? – boomed through the hangar. Then rattling of the padlocked chains, a Spanish shout, other voices sounding angry. Cloudsley backed away – to give himself a clearer field of fire and to be less immediately visible when they slid the first door back. He heard Beale cock his pistol, and he did the same, drawing back the bolt-handle on top until the sear clicked in, engaging. As he did it, one of the men outside tried the right-hand small door and found it was locked. Another burst of explosive Spanish – as Cloudsley went forward quickly to the nearer one and locked that too; he was still there with his hand on the key when an Argie tried it then yelled something and hit the steel with his fist. Beale muttered, 'Silly cunts left their keys at home. . . .' Nothing was audible from close range, after that: only the steady pounding of the generator and the more distant but increasing noise of aircraft engines. Cloudsley moved back to his covering position, back from the doors, thinking *Bloody lucky*. . . . Then his brain switched on again and he went to the right-hand door, the one they'd wrenched at first; because you were *completely* helpless if you couldn't see out, see whatever might be coming, and a door they'd already found to be locked was a door they wouldn't be trying again, surely. He waited a few feet from it, listening. This respite might not last long – if the keys were in the guardhouse, for instance – but the delay had already guaranteed the job *would* be finished.

'All right, Geoff?'

'Yeah. Coming along. . . .'

Outside, a car door slammed. Close: he guessed, the fuel-truck. Fitting the suppressor; until now he hadn't had time for it. The point of using a suppressor was that the less noise and flash you made the less attention you might attract from elsewhere. Touch wood. . . .

He unlocked the little door. When they had their keys it would be the big sliding ones they'd be going for, anyway. Crouching, he turned the handle very cautiously, eased the door open about an inch.

Three men – three of the four he'd seen coming in – were walking away towards the gates, swinging their arms and stamping their feet in the snow. Three soldiers were acting similarly in front of the guardhouse. The gates were standing wide open. Blinding flash of light – from the control tower, fifty yards right, other side of the road. . . . Circling on, that lightbeam swept over the parked Pucarás – one on its own just near the road, then two separate groups deployed as if for take-off in two flights. He'd first seen them, and a tractor plus trailer with each group, when the van had come crawling up to the front of the compound and its headlights had washed over that area of the field, but now the revolving beacon lit it all brilliantly several times a minute, splashing over the front of this hangar too, lighting the compound and a wide radius of flat airfield. . . . Those three men had stopped near the gates and turned to walk back again, still doing physical jerks to keep warm, hunching like gorillas against the wind. He was watching them, wondering how the keys could be so long arriving, when he heard the helo.

Immediately, two conclusions: it was very close, or you wouldn't be hearing it over the generator's closer noise, and it was a Chinook – yesterday's sound again.

Another pair of headlights now – approaching from the right, low to the carpet of snow. He thought it looked like the staff car coming. Therefore, Roberto. . . .

Or the missing keys. Or both.

Hosegood said sharply, 'OK, that's it.'

'Quick as you like, gents.'

Plugging that last hole, then turning the missile right side up. Even now there was no point letting the Argies know they'd be deploying a load of duds. But there was also the last of the gear to be packed. . . . He changed his mind on that. There were tools and other items at the back of the hangar, and the drill, liner-upper and two batteries distributed amongst that lot

221

might not be noticed, at least for quite a while, and later it wouldn't matter.

'We'll leave the gear. Pull all wires out and mix it with that other junk.'

He couldn't help them, had to stay where he was and *try* to see some way out. Not that at this moment there looked like being one. The helo noise had faded: flown over, or something, and he hadn't had any sight of it, his view from here being restricted. Those three were in a close group halfway between the hangar and the gateway; turning now to see the staff car arrive, and moving out of its way. And to the right he could just see the fuel-truck's driver, using a broom to knock snow off his vehicle. Shoving with the broom's head, starting avalanches that thudded down so he had to jump back as they fell. The staff car turned into the compound, cutting deep tracks in the virgin snow, and stopped in front of the guardhouse, one soldier saluting and the other moving across to open a rear door. A naval officer got out of the front passenger seat, and then Roberto emerged from the back in flying kit plus brass hat. Closest view Cloudsley had had of the elder MacEwan. Big, with a wide, meaty face and a thick neck. . . . The way the car had parked its headlights tunnelled across the compound's northwest corner, lighting the area that was usually in shadow and shining directly on the other small door, the one which until now had been their private entrance and exit.

In fact it wasn't getting any better.

A roar of Pucará engines from the field. Their departure was unlikely to be delayed much longer, he guessed, or Roberto wouldn't have been togged up as he was. The machine on its own, parked so conveniently near the road, would almost certainly be Roberto's. A minute ago its co-pilot or observer had left it and come strolling over to the compound; he was near the gate, chatting to other aircrew. Helo racket suddenly loud again. . . . There seemed to be several different things happening at once, and trying to see a way through it, some way *out*, hadn't as yet revealed even the beginnings of one. . . . He saw the Chinook now, slanting down; he'd looked in the right place for it because that crowd of airmen had been

222

looking up – as were the three technicians and others, including Roberto in the foreground, and another group of flyers drifting this way from the parked machines – the control tower's beam flashing over them and circling on – and the tanker driver, who'd moved away from the front of his truck to get a view of it. . . . Cloudsley's own view was cut off as the helo lowered itself into a blaze of light at the compound's western end.

Beale and Hosegood were behind him in the dark. He told them, 'Chinook just landing, but these blokes are still waiting for the keys. Roberto's swaggering around out there.'

Gesticulating, facing the missile-handlers and waving an arm towards the front of the hangar, obviously wanting to know why the first missiles weren't out there ready to be embarked. The other naval officer was hurrying towards the guardhouse, maybe to telephone. Abrupt cut-off of helo noise indicated that it was down. It was obviously nearer the rear fence of the compound than the front, and in combination with the blaze of light covering the whole area this meant there was no part of the perimeter wire they'd have a hope of getting to – let alone getting over – without dozens of Argies seeing it happen. This left only the front gateway as an exit: which wouldn't exactly escape notice either. Cloudsley hadn't envisaged having to cut things quite this fine. Effectively, it was more that you were starting from scratch now with a new objective. Until a few minutes ago the whole singleminded drive in all three of them had been to get the missiles fixed: everything had been subordinated to this. Having achieved it, you were abruptly facing an entirely different problem, and solutions seemed – to put it mildly – elusive. There were only three options immediately visible, looking at it logically and objectively: you could hang on here and in due course – when the doors opened – surrender, or you could march out there *now* and surrender, or you could make a fight of it. The three of them could undoubtedly wipe out every Argie in sight within about ninety seconds, but this would not only be massacre and the kind of action that had been ruled out right from the start, it would also be unproductive except in the very

223

short term. Daylight wasn't so far off: how could three men on foot hope to get away across hundreds of miles of snow-covered *nothing* with a squadron of cannon-firing, napalm-dropping ground-attack aircraft right on top of them?

The Pucará boys would love it. From what Andy had said about his brother, Roberto would be right in his element.

You couldn't crouch here for ever. You had to spell it out. . . .

'Frankly, gents, we don't seem to have such a hell of a lot going for us. . . .'

His words faded into the surrounding darkness. He'd seen the fuel-truck driver climb up into his cab and pull its door shut. The truck's lights sprang up, then faded to mere glimmers barely visible on the snow's crystals when the driver pressed his starter. Repeatedly – and no joy. . . . Cloudsley went on – picking the last words up where they'd tailed off and talking fast because this chance wouldn't sit and stare him in the face for ever: 'Except this monster tanker. Rest of the compound's lit up and crowded. We'll be lit up here too, but – look, this is *it*, now. You know where the truck is – thirty feet to our right. Guys outside are all looking at the Chinook, far end. So – out this door, round the back of the truck to its blind side. . . . Come on!'

Should have warned them about the revolving beacon so they'd avoid looking at it and getting blinded. Too late now. He had the door open and was out – doubled, loping through yellow light, the others close behind. The tanker driver was preoccupied with the problem of starting his big old diesel. Blinding flash sweeping over as they dived behind it, Ingrams ready for use as they came round the corner of the hangar, but no opposition on that side. Cloudsley ran to the front, the cab's right-hand door, jerked it open and pulled himself in, landing virtually on top of the driver over on the left with space behind him for the others to crowd in before the Argie could know anything hostile was within a hundred miles of him. The cold end of the suppressor on Cloudsley's pistol poked hard against the man's cheekbone: a good place for it because he could see it in close-up and it was a fearsome-looking weapon viewed from that end. Pulling the driver's hands off the wheel and pushing them behind his head, using his left hand for it while the man collapsed backward against the other door – flabby with shock, probably wetting himself or worse – Cloudsley grabbed the front of his parka, yanked him over to Hosegood and Beale who eased him down into the well at their feet. Cloudsley was in under the wheel with his thumb stabbing at the starter button, that light dazzling again as it swept across. He'd put the Ingram on his lap, and Hosegood had his resting against the bridge of the driver's nose.

Battery about flat. . . .

The heavy engine was hardly feeling the attempts to start it. Motorbike with a sidecar – seen dimly through steamed-up windscreen: it swept into the compound, braking, skidding, its passenger jumping out and those other three men converging on him. Cloudsley said, 'Battery's fucked. Have to start her on the gears.'

'Enough slope?'

He nodded. *Hoping.* . . . 'And he's had the heater on, look, she *ought* to go.' The heater light was glowing. If it had been on for long, that wouldn't have helped the dying battery, but on the other hand it would mean starting on the gears ought not to be too difficult.

Hosegood's gun moved suddenly: 'Easy, *señor.* . . .'

Brake off: and – rolling. . . . In gear, with the clutch down on the boards. Two guards at the gate watching – looking this way, anyhow. He had an impression – a glimpse out of the side of his left eye – of the hangar doors sliding open, but he couldn't afford to turn his head. Whole crowd of airmen there: presumably they'd left their machines in the mechanics' hands. The centre of their interest was the Chinook, for some reason. The lumbering truck was picking up some speed now. Might prove harder to stop than start, once the vast weight of it was really moving. He gritted, 'Get her to the gates before I try it. If it doesn't work, get the hell out, run like buggery. East, then south. First rendezvous the Sandrini ruin, then Strobie's.'

'What if it does start?'

If the engine declined to fire he'd stop her in the gateway to

225

block it, delay pursuit in the staff car. The only Argies seeing the huge truck rolling with increasing momentum across the snow-covered concrete were the two at the gates, and they didn't look particularly animated. Fogged windows were a blessing. Guardhouse looming up. . . . Cloudsley muttered, 'Say your prayers' and let the clutch in, toed the accelerator. The gears locked, wheels locked, skidding through snow. And that was that. . . . Then the old engine barked, exploded, rumbled into life. Cloudsley shoved his foot down, waited for a good loud roar then eased off and shifted gear, shouting as the truck picked up speed through the gateway, 'Tony – you *know* about Pucarás, could you fly one?'

'Not on your bloody life!'

Straight over the road, bumping up on to the field. The dazzling beam swept over, circling to light the whole airstrip and the assembly of sleek-looking aircraft squatting on it in their neat formations – a tractor hauling two empty trailers clear, the other with ground-staff riding on it. Beale muttering to Hosegood, '*Fly* one! Out of his fucking mind!' The Argies in the compound would be expecting this tanker to turn and come back, but giving it a bit of a warm-up might not arouse suspicions yet. . . . 'You flew a twin-engined fixed-wing once, you told me?'

'Not *taking off*, Harry! You don't understand – I mean *Jesus*—'

'Always a first time. . . .' He heard Hosegood laughing. The Pucará that was on its own – Roberto's probably – was too near the compound, they'd be on top of you before you'd fastened your lap-strap. Besides, one of the echelons of Pucarás was almost right ahead, a rank of six drawn up slantwise, glittering as the circling beam swung over them. Tails would be more vulnerable than the rest, he guessed, and to wreck some would be a worthwhile effort on its own as well as thinning out the forces available for pursuit. Not that there was such a lot of hope of getting far anyway, you just had to avoid giving up before you had to; a matter of adapting to circumstances, doing whatever could be done, taking chances if there were any – when you saw them. For instance, the

226

hangar was now standing open and missiles were being wheeled out, and you weren't in there with your hands up as had seemed inevitable two minutes ago. Aiming for that bunch of aircraft – he saw aircrew scattering. Not brave, but wise. . . . The heavy truck smashed into the first tail, crushing it and spinning the aircraft round, then a second – lighter impact but tail-plane ripped away; third, a grinding collision that jarred through the truck and slowed it, Cloudsley changing gear and side-swiping a fourth tail then skidding on, revving in high gear between the last two of this lot, crumpling both wings. He shouted, 'Tony – no other way we'll get clear. If you can't get one off the ground you'd still put distance behind us, right?' The staff car was manoeuvring, turning, inside the compound. But that was a hundred and fifty yards away and the rest of the Pucarás were a lot closer. Having dragged the truck round in a skidding half-circle. . . . Hearing Beale yell, 'Wouldn't get three in! Two seats and—' And something inaudible, Cloudsley thinking *We can bloody well try*. . . . Pilots who'd been lounging around the Chinook were pouring over on to the field – maybe having heard that a tanker driver had gone nuts, run amok – meeting others who were going the other way. Soldiers too: if you can call them soldiers, he thought, our friendly neighbourhood sentrics, grey-heads with old Lee-Enfields, fix bayonets and charge at a slow trot and risk of heart failure? Two men running from the control tower, though, firing bursts from automatic weapons as they came, did constitute a threat. Beale turned his window down and pushed the stubby Ingram barrel out – he'd removed the suppressor from it. Snow beginning again now. Cloudsley shouted that he was going to ram the truck into the middle of the other formation of Pucarás, jump out and put an incendiary burst into its load of aviation spirit. . . . 'When we stop, Tony, take the machine at the end of the line, get it clear!' Beale sighted over his gun, hearing this and thinking *Won't get three of us in one Pucará. Three midgets maybe but not us*. No point telling him again though. He pushed the fire-selector switch to the right and gave the running figures several single shots aimed right at the toes of their boots, and it stopped them. You weren't aiming to kill, you were trying not to, the intention was to deter any who sought to stop you getting the hell out. If to achieve this it became necessary to shoot at them rather than near them you'd aim low, just slightly less low than he'd just done. The Argie cramped down by his knees was intoning what sounded like a prayer: Hosegood patted the man's head and shouted, 'Take it easy, Pedro. . . .' Cloudsley yelled, 'When we crash, shove him out and boot him away. Hold tight!' Beale worrying about that other Pucará, that the staff car would get Roberto to it any moment now and if its Brownings or cannon were loaded he might be able to use them on the ground. Then thought was erased as the truck smashed into one aircraft, ploughed on carrying it into the next, a third's wing tilting vertically as it went over in a continuing though slowing grind of impact and compression with a surrounding montage of wings, fuselages, tails, the truck sliding to a halt in it and Cloudsley roaring 'Out!' The word acted like a detonator – explosion, sheet of flame, savage heat. Napalm: no need to stop to ignite anything else, for God's sake; Beale was yelling, in case no one else had realised what it was, 'Napalm, Harry, *napalm*!' Pushing the screaming Argie out between himself and Hosegood, into tangled wreckage and against a wall of flame, heat reaching to your bones, into your brain too with the probability there'd be new explosions any second, a personal drenching in napalm. Cloudsley had dived clear via the other door; Beale left him to handle the problem of the staff car and ran to the Pucará at the end of the line, one of two that didn't seem to have been bent and weren't burning yet. Behind him there was another *whooshing* explosion, the last hours of the night as bright as daylight now, inferno of dancing light and blazing heat with the snow melting as it fell into it and the napalm's nauseous reek. He had to get into that aircraft and get it moving – somehow – get it clear before napalm showered it, or the blaze spread there along the line. The first batch hadn't been loaded with napalm, he guessed. A gun was firing from the control tower but he didn't have time to deal with it himself: reaching the aircraft, flinging himself up, finding the moulded plastic canopy standing open. He thought Hosegood was close behind him, for some reason, shouted all in one breath 'Stop that bloody gun Geoff where's Harry?' Dreading that Cloudsley might have been caught in that last fountain of napalm. In feet-first, hearing the suppressed blare of an Ingram somewhere near the aircraft's tail. Which in fact was Hosegood. He'd got rid of the tanker driver, sent him stumbling towards the crowd of Argies milling out of the compound gates, then seen Cloudsley huge and static with the blaze behind him, facing the staff car, Ingram up for a head-on shot. It flamed – *un*suppressed; the car's lights and windscreen shattered and it was spinning on slush towards the mass of burning aircraft and exploding napalm containers. Hosegood hadn't been able to continue in the spectator's role: some kind of machine-gun had opened up from the roof of the control tower, and two figures, quite likely the same ones who'd been deterred earlier by Beale, were zigzagging forward under its cover. Behind him at that moment came the biggest explosion of the night, about the loudest he'd ever heard, a powerful blast and an enormously brilliant incandescence: it could only have been the aviation spirit finally cooking-off. The Pucará with Beale in it had begun to move – none too soon, since its neighbour was already burning. Hosegood had lobbed an XFS grenade – and another – long throws, but accurate, he was good at it – at the two encroaching Argies, and now he gave the machine gun up there one whole magazine, by way of positive deterrence. He heard and saw the stun grenades burst – blinding flashes accompanying thunderclap detonations, both within the prescribed two metres of their targets – both Argies duly knocked out, and the GPMG on the tower had given up too. The Pucará was well clear and at rest again. Looking around for Cloudsley, hearing grenades in that direction – Harry discouraging initiative from the compound personnel – but then catching sight of a more alarming development, Roberto's Pucará rolling forward, turning its twin turbo-props into the snow-laden wind and beginning to move and gather speed. This would be Cloudsley's mark again: he was on his knees, from this angle in silhouette against the wide area

229

of flame but almost in the Pucará's upwind path; he'd banged in a new magazine and he was waiting, holding his fire. To the pilot, Hosegood guessed, he wouldn't be so visible, from that angle the flames would be blinding. He'd changed his own magazine and also unscrewed and pocketed the suppressor: he ran towards Cloudsley, to get close enough so both of them could open fire – simultaneously, one from right ahead and himself from this side as the 'plane's tail began to lift. The gun roared in his hands, then the napalm exploded under the Pucará's starboard wing and it was a fireball, somersaulting in a great Catherine-wheel of showering napalm as the other bombs erupted too. Cloudsley sprinting from it, this way, Hosegood reloading and staying to cover his retreat. He'd skidded to a halt, then – turning with one long arm back then whirling over, a grenade in that fist – soaring, lobbing well over and beyond the blaze of the Pucará before he began to run again, yelling 'Come *on*, Geoff!' Tony Beale had seen some of this, but he'd had his own preoccupations, first just getting the engines started, then locating the controls he needed just to taxi the machine away from the fire, and more recently turning it with the idea of using its guns – if he could find their triggers – on that last surviving Pucará; he'd expected this to be Roberto's intention, hadn't expected the attempt to take off. His own problem now was getting two large men into a space intended for one ordinary-sized one. The observer's seat was raised about ten inches higher than this front one, and it would be less suitable for Cloudsley than for Hosegood, as there was a two- or three-inch difference in their heights and Cloudsley might have had difficulty shutting the canopy over his head. Beale yelled as they appeared – one on each side – 'Geoff in the seat, Harry squeeze in after – OK?' Cloudsley shouted, 'Bloody cheek!' and let Hosegood in first while he looked around for any more trouble and changed his magazine without looking to see what his hands were doing, squinting round with his eyes slitted against the glare and heat. All the snow on the ground had melted and new stuff driving in just vanished in mid-air. Beale was concentrating on his own problems again: he'd allowed the engines to stop, somehow, and was having to start everything from scratch. The cockpit layout was totally unfamiliar and he was having to identify each item by guesswork, common sense or trial-and-error. No helmets, so no intercom, nothing fancy – and no backseat driving either. Muttering to himself: 'Trimmer – set. . . . Well, *should* be OK. . . . Throttle tension: maybe. . . . Mixture: could be why they cut out, but – oh, trust to luck. . . .' Thinking suddenly in protest, *What the hell am I doing, monkeying with this fucking thing?* Controlling the flare of anger, then, frustration born of the fact he was a man who liked to know what he was doing, know how things worked as well as how to work them. . . . 'Fine pitch – well. . . . Gas is on, must be – unless *that* was why. . . .' But it was on, all right. Concentrating: knowing seconds counted, but so did getting this right, and the other two could look out for whatever was happening out there. 'Flaps. . . . OK. Lock's off – couldn't not be. Check it, all the same.' The hell with temperature or pressure, he didn't have a clue to what the reading *ought* to be. *And bugger the undercart, bastard can stay down, reckon I'll need it more than I'll need bloody wings.* . . . He shouted, 'You both in?' Then: 'Shut the canopy!' Twisting round: 'Yeah, *that*!' Incredibly they *were* in; he clicked the canopy shut over the cabin that was less than ten feet long, about two and a half wide and four feet high, a lot of that space taken up by the two Martin-Baker Mk APO 6A Zero-Zero ejector seats. He'd forgotten to warn Geoff about the danger of ejecting himself – which if you were *really* careless you could do clear through the canopy. Too late now. He part thought, part mumbled to himself, *Start port engine. . . . Start starboard. . . .* Thank God, they did both start. *Throttle back now, Tony. . . . OK, brakes – brakes off. . . . Holy smoke, we're rolling. . . .* Then by chance he saw what he'd looked for earlier and failed to find and then forgotten, the switches of the bomb-release gear. Hesitating for about two seconds, thinking of referring this to Cloudsley, but then making his mind up and mentally crossing his fingers for luck as he released all three bombs: only a few feet to drop and not much speed on yet, but you couldn't be sure, had no idea how sensitive that muck might be: you

231

needed to lose any weight that could be shed, though, even without a bomb-load it was going to be a toss-up whether this machine got off the ground. Snow plastering the screen; but at least it showed him where the wind was. Bombs – gone. . . . Now the wiper: he found the switch, and the bullet-proof screen was cleared immediately. Snow streaming by all around and a flat white sea of it ahead. Picking up speed: control column forward, and opening the throttles, really moving now, feeling as if the tail might be trying to lift; needing left rudder – just a touch – to hold her straight. Tail *had* lifted. . . . So much damn weight, though – and no idea at all what take-off speed should be.

More throttle. Both of them wide open.

OK. *Now*. Or never. . . . He swallowed. *Pull back, slow.* . . .

Lifting?

Age of miracles is not—

Crash. . . . They'd hit the ground very hard indeed, then bounced back into the air. Waiting for the next great thump the thought flashed through his mind that it was as well he'd got rid of the napalm: they could have been a fireball now. Straining his muscles as if his own strength might hold her up: if he'd had wings instead of arms he'd have been flapping them. But she was climbing. Bloody *flying*! He murmured, truly surprised and absolutely delighted, 'Well, what d'ya know. . .' And immediately, a double-take – having decided he could afford to look at his gauges now. . . .

Focusing on the fuel gauge. Needle on zero. Tanks empty. Too little in there, anyway, to be registering on the gauge.

'You're a genius, Tony!' Cloudsley, head over the corner of the seat, screaming ecstatically in Beale's ear. The altimeter showed 200 feet: 210. . . . Cloudsley bellowed, 'Steer southeast – *southeast*! Got a compass?'

He gritted his teeth. They were flying southeast already, the direction the wind was howling from. He muttered, '*Of course I've got a bloody compass, what d'you think this is, a bicycle?*' Working at it, trying to keep the machine climbing – while its fuel lasted – but not stall it. Stalling speed with a normal load would be about 90 mph, he guessed. Just over 110 now; if it dropped below that mark he'd level her at once. Looking at the fuel state again. They must have left the refuelling for after the servicing of the Chinook. . . . Sea of white nothing down there. . . . Then, looking again but not sure he'd seen anything at all, he made out a ruler-straight line of black dots running due north and south: a fence between sheep-paddocks, and they were flying over it now, crossing it at a slanting angle from northwest to southeast. Two hundred and fifty feet on the altimeter; levelling her, and terrific relief in doing so, the climb and the danger of stalling had had him sweating. He was thinking of trying to get Cloudsley's attention, to point to the fuel-gauge, when it became unnecessary: the starboard engine spluttered and died just before the same thing happened to the port one. Then the starboard one coughed, picked up again for a few seconds, died. . . . Only the wind-howl now; nose down, gliding. . . . He shouted – Cloudsley's face thrusting over near his shoulder again – 'Out of gas! Going down! Hold tight!' The wind was a rushing scream enclosing the Pucará as it dropped, tilting and shuddering to the gusts, Beale fighting to hold the angle of descent and keep the wings level, hoping to God there'd be no fence ahead when they got down there. If it was just open sheep-paddock it might be OK; he'd brought aircraft down without power before, had been required to do so when he was working for his PPL, and the differences between this twin-engined job and the single-engined machines he'd flown before were now eliminated. Against that, he hadn't had time even to start getting used to the feel of this aircraft, and none of his landings had been made in blizzards or on ground covered in thorn bushes. . . . Fighting it, forcing its nose and the starboard wing down, telling himself that ninety-five per cent of the land around here was billiard-table flat. . . . One hundred feet. That thorn scrub wouldn't be any problem. Seventy feet: without the altimeter you couldn't have known, you could have been at five thousand; everything out there was a white blank, you'd know you were landing, he guessed, when you hit the ground. Fifty feet. Then suddenly, unexpectedly, a glimpse of terra

233

firma – greyish patches on the white, the thorn the sheep were daft enought to eat. Forty. . . . Thirty feet. Easy now, nose up a little just a *little*. . . . Twenty-five. Twenty. Ten feet, and stand by for the almighty smash-up. . . .

Thumping down. Snow flying in sheets like surf. All you could do was brake, fight to hold her straight and pray, *Please, no fence*. . . . Bouncing, shaking, his own bones feeling as if they were rattling too; then the violence was lessening, the snow flying by in flakes instead of solid. . . .

Cloudsley agreed, 'Which would mean we're now on Diaz land, and if we yomp south we'll hit a fence which could be either the Strobie or the MacEwan boundary wire. Where the road runs – right?'

Beale nodded. 'I was scared we might put down on that one.'

The first remark from anyone after the machine had come to rest at the end of its deep-ploughed snow track had come from Hosegood. He'd said, 'Beats canoeing, don't it.'

The fence that Beale had seen and which Cloudsley agreed must have been the north-to-south divide between Diaz and Coetzee land was the only clue they had to their position now. They'd ridden up that fence, on the Coetzee side of it, with Andy guiding them, on the way north to the target area. The fence's southern end was on the public road which ran along Strobie's northern boundary and then ran on east dividing Diaz land from the MacEwans'.

'How far would you say we flew, Tony?'

'Ten miles?' Beale shrugged. 'Fifteen?'

Hosegood nodded. Cloudsley said, 'Call it twelve, then. I'd guess – well, we're certainly on Diaz territory, and I'd guess fairly close to where the three farms meet.'

'Where the Sandrini place is, then.'

'Exactly. And our best bet is to go south until we find the fence, then look for that corner. May have to try first one way and then the other, or we may be lucky and guess right. But

234

once we find that corner we can't help finding the Sandrini ruin, which might be a good place to hole-up in for the day. Then push on to Strobie's after dark. Any better suggestions?'

'They're going to find this Pucará pretty quick, aren't they?'

'I don't know.' Cloudsley looked up at the weather. It was still dark and the snow was still heavy on the southeast wind. You'd have sunrise in about three-quarters of an hour, but you wouldn't have guessed it from the look of things right now. He said, 'If this keeps up – give it an hour, the Pucará'll be under snow. But if we were in the open and search 'planes came over – as they will, don't doubt it – we'd stand out like spare pricks at a wedding. So, gents – let's get moving, get under cover.'

Beale nodded. 'Right. But – Harry, it'll be a while before those engines cool enough for snow to settle anywhere near 'em, let alone *on* them. So if the Argies are quick off the mark—'

'All right.' Cloudsley nodded. 'Good point. And they may have had us on radar anyway. But finding it here on Diaz land doesn't have to point at Strobie's. As long as we don't leave tracks – and we won't, given an hour or two for the snow to cover them. This Pucará got as far as it could on the small amount of fuel that was in it – they'll know that, they can't *all* be stupid. . . . And anyway – damn-all we can do about it, except get to the Sandrini place and out of sight.'

Yomping south, then, Cloudsley leading, with an eye on his magnetic compass. . . .

'If we'd had enough gas to get to the coast, Harry, would you've carried on?'

The southeasterly course they'd been flying would have taken them where they needed to be. Cloudsley said, 'Hypothetical question. Why ask?'

'Just wondered. Quickest way to get there. Andy'd have been OK – like you told him, didn't you, keep out of sight till it's over?'

'We've spare kit and ammo at Strobie's, haven't we?'

'Ah. . . .' Beale added, 'Except getting there that fast we mightn't 've needed it.'

Hosegood put in, 'I got half a magazine. And we wouldn't

be walking straight off the coast, would we. . . . Harry, think they'll find the hides?'

'If they look, they will. May not occur to them. Only things of value we've lost are the periscope and my binos.'

'And some nutty and stuff.'

Today and tonight would be foodless, except for the chocolate in their pockets. Water-bottles had been left behind, but there was snow to drink. . . . They were moving south in file, one line of tracks being less noticeable than three. You couldn't count on the snow covering your tracks; it had stopped once or twice already and it could do the same again. . . . Beale broke a long silence: 'Wondering how long we'll have to hide out at Strobie's. They'll get an air search going soon enough, won't they? Even though we didn't leave 'em anything that'll fly. Fucked 'em up good and proper, didn't we? What I'm getting at – won't just sit and wonder, will they?'

'The weather may be on our side. Apart from that you're right, Tony, in fact you may not appreciate *how* right.'

He'd been doing some thinking, too.

Hosegood said, 'They'll get some helos up from Comodoro Rivadavia, won't they?' He was treading exactly in Cloudsley's snow-holes. 'Andy's big brother'll be shitting himself – if he's alive.'

'Doubt he can be.' Cloudsley ploughing on. Without packs you could cover a lot of ground very quickly. 'I'd guess he was either in the car we wrecked or in the Pucará. Nobody walked away from either.'

Hosegood was glancing eastward; there was a brightening, just a hint of it, although the snow wasn't easing off at all. 'Making Andy rich, eh, sole owner of the family estate?'

'No. Roberto was married. His widow'd inherit his share, wouldn't she.'

'Andy'd better jump in there smartish, then.'

'You're a callous sod, Geoff. But hardly – seeing she's the daughter of Alejandro Diaz. And look – even if Big Brother's snuffed it, they'll still be wanting our blood. OK, they don't know who we are – we could be the local revolutionaries, any damn thing. But one man who's going to jump to some logical conclusions is Diaz. He's a counter-insurgency expert – meaning anyone who gives him a funny look gets skinned alive. This is his land we're on, that airbase is on his land, it was his son-in-law in command and we knocked him off.' Shaking his head, trudging through the driving snow like some great white-shouldered *yeti*. . . . 'My guess is there'll be a manhunt now and Alejandro Diaz running it.'

14

Francisca: her face contorted, bloodless, eyes wide and blank, flesh the colour of dirty snow and her dark hair encrusted with it; she looked as if she'd died in a fit of rage. Paco flung aside the shovel he'd used to uncover her naked, frozen body, and reached for the meathook. The old woman, Fiona, pointing to where he was to hang her in a line of them – two sheep, then the space the old woman was indicating, then Paco's father with a hook's point protruding from the black wound in his throat. Paco shifting his grip on the hook then swinging it back, stooping over Francisca – Andy trying to reach him, to stop it, prevent the final horror, but he couldn't move his limbs or shout either, he'd screamed Paco no, don't do it, Paco NO *but a hand had clamped on his mouth – Paco's father's hand, the arm swinging from that—*

'All right, lad, all right. Wakey wakey. . . .'

Tom Strobie took his hand off Andy's mouth, having seen his eyes open. Andy blinking up at him: realising who it was and that he was in the bedroom, not a slaughterhouse. But behind Tom's shoulders, a new apparition which at first sight was just as unreal – Cloudsley, Hosegood, Beale. Like savages – as wild-looking and dirty, black-faced as if *they*'d been buried and dug up. . . . Strobie growled as he turned away, 'Had to wake you, you'd have had half the world coming to see where the pigs were being killed.'

'Fine time to have nightmares, Andy. Sleep all day, do you?' Cloudsley sat down on the bed; the way he let himself down you could tell it was a long time since he'd sat anywhere. Tony Beale said, 'Out tomcatting, I'd guess. Leave these young fellows five minutes, they're at it.' Pulling off a snow-covered *poncho*. Hosegood gathered all three of them: 'I'll give 'em a shake out. . . .' Pausing in the doorway: 'Could've been DTs, not nightmare. Been on the booze, Andy?'

'Yeah. All night.' Checking the time. 'Or most of it.' He was still half-asleep and still half in the nightmare. 'Hey – you've been a lot quicker than—'

'We've made good time, you're right.' Cloudsley explained, 'I'd intended sheltering in the Sandrini place until dark, but with the snow belting down so hard it seemed wiser to keep going. The fact is, we've got to – I mean we've got to move on from here too, sooner the better. . . . Maybe just a few hours' rest now, Tom – and would you be your usual kind self and feed us? Hot baths possible, d'you think? Then we'll shove off as soon as the light goes. Fact is, we really do have to put a few miles behind us bloody quick. I'd yomp on *now*, except—'

'Yeah.' Tony Beale nodded. Gaunt, scarecrow-like. . . . 'Except.'

Cloudsley turned his head, glaring at him. Like an outsize Rasputin who'd come through one week-long roughhouse and might be thinking of starting another. Beale explained, 'Only saying, Harry, we'd do best in the long run—'

'Pit-stop, like.' Hosegood, rejoining them, backed him up. Cloudsley told them with something like anger in his tone, 'We'll rest until it's dark. That's what I said.' Turning away: 'OK with you, Tom?'

'Of course.' Strobie said, 'Water's hot, and there's a stew made that only has to be hotted up. . . . Did you *do* it?'

'We did indeed. And that's the main thing.' Cloudsley told him, 'But our withdrawal wasn't exactly stealthy. Very loud, and lit up by one of the biggest bonfires you ever saw. Had no

240

option, really. . . .'

Andy could see and hear the tension in all of them: getting here, to a place where they could draw breath, would have released the suppressed store of it, he guessed. Not that he himself was exactly relaxed. . . . Cloudsley was saying to old Tom, 'You asked me whether there'd be a stink, and I said I hoped not. The fact is there will be – probably is already, and what's more I'd guess your neighbour Diaz will be in charge of things. So the sooner we can shove off, Tom, the better for your sake as well as ours.'

'Never mind *my* sake. . . .' Strobie, leaning on his stick, had the manner of a father among sons. 'Why not one of you take a bath right away?' He paused in the doorway, on his way to put the stew on to heat. 'Andy. While you were kipping, I had a radio shout from your *estancia*. From Huyez's wife.'

He'd been pulling on his boots; he sat tensely, waiting for the rest of it. Back to the nightmare which had become if anything more unpleasant in the act of waking, finding that waking was no escape from it. . . . He heard Cloudsley query, 'Huyez?' Strobie didn't bother to enlighten him; he said, 'Panic stations over there. She told me her husband and their boy vanished during the night, still weren't home – about an hour ago. She thought the lad might be visiting his sheila here, and Papa might've come to fetch him home or something. . . . But nobody here's seen either of 'em, and the girl's been with her mum all the time.' Strobie turned away. 'Anyway, Robert's short of a *mayordomo* and Señora Huyez is in a flat spin. . . . Go on in by the fire, lads.'

Drifting into the other room, the talk was about the Falklands news – mostly the capture of Goose Green and the Royal Marines' fantastic yomp the other way. But a dump of napalm had been found on the Pucará airstrip at Goose Green, and this and one other item of news – the arrival in San Carlos of Major-General Jeremy Moore – seemed to interest the SB men more than anything else. Comment from Beale was, 'Be all go now, then,' and the others agreed. Hosegood won a toss and went to make first use of the bathroom; Andy asked Cloudsley, 'Did you come here in a straight line from the

241

Sandrini ruin?'

'No, we were a bit cagier than that.' Cloudsley crouched low to the fire's warmth. 'Kept to the line of the fence, close up to it, in the hope our tracks won't show up – wouldn't if the snow had stopped. Walked about five miles south from that corner, crossed two internal fences and came to a boundary gate and a track passing through it that's fairly well buried now. By my recollection of the map it'd be the road to your MacEwan place?'

'That's right. And way out eastward beyond it.'

'We came west from that gate. Couldn't help leaving tracks, not being fairies, but by now they'd be hard to see. . . . It's air search I'm thinking of mostly – once the blizzard slacks off. They'll have to bring helos over from some other base, but it shouldn't take long.'

'You boys manage a little Scotch?'

They all looked at Strobie. Cloudsley began, 'Well, Tom—'

'Small ones wouldn't hurt. You'll be sleeping it off anyway.'

'Small ones then. You're very kind.'

Andy said, 'Amazing there's any left, after last night.'

'In return, you can entertain me with an account of what you've been up to. What did you blow up, or set fire to?'

'Didn't exactly set fire to anything.' Cloudsley was relaxing slightly, now. 'Things seemed to *catch* fire. . . . Didn't it seem like that to you, Tony?'

Beale agreed. ''Specially things with wings on. You should've seen it. I didn't get much chance to, not really, Harry had me stuck in this bloody Pucará trying to figure out how to make the fucking thing work, I couldn't look around much. Ought to've made us a video, Harry.'

Strobie handed out glasses of Scotch. Cloudsley raised his. 'To you, Tom, with a sincere vote of thanks. . . . Well, I'll tell you. We were living in holes in the ground, nipping into the base at night to do this job. Rather boring work, actually.' Beale groaned at the pun: he explained, 'Boring *holes*, Tom,' and Strobie asked, 'In bombs, by any chance?'

'Why would you think that?'

'According to the BBC, a lot of 'em have been hitting ships

242

and not exploding. Occurred to me this might be your line of work.'

'No.' Cloudsley shook his head. 'Some other bugger's, maybe. You wouldn't need to drill holes, you could change the settings on a hell of a lot of bombs in a few hours' work if you could get at 'em. . . . Anyway, Tom – we did our job, in two nights and just the nick of time – bloody lucky. But the second night, instead of a nice, orderly withdrawal before dawn, the Argies started work exceptionally early, and there we were – stuck. . . .'

Strobie was absorbed in it. But Andy, listening to Cloudsley and Beale recalling the highlights of their withdrawal action, was thinking at least as much about the local crisis. It seemed distinctly possible that the SBS firefight up north might be linked – by Diaz – whose hawk eyes and predatory habits had earned him that nickname of *El Carancho* – with the Huyez disappearances. Which could be extremely unfortunate. He agreed with Cloudsley: the sooner they could get out of here, the better.

He'd got back in the small hours of the morning and found Strobie waiting up for him, already half full of whisky and primed by Señora Torres with the information that Francisca had called through on the radio and spoken to him just before he'd taken off on horseback. Strobie had been twitching with anxiety, and the first part of their talk had been acrimonious; then he'd quietened down, and they'd sat on discussing it over a steady flow of whisky until well after dawn. To start with he hadn't intended telling the whole thing, but it had come out all the same. In fact there'd been some relief in talking about it. He'd described the conversation with Francisca and his reasons for agreeing to ride over to the *estancia*, and how Juan and Paco Huyez had been getting set to kill him. He described also, factually and as unemotionally as he could make it, killing Huyez with the meathook.

Strobie's mask of a face expressionless as ever, only the eyes reacting. . . .

'That was self-defence, wasn't murder. Need to be able to prove it, of course. . . . But what about Paco?'

243

'I pressured him into telling me what had happened. He was in a mess — scared to a jelly. So it wasn't difficult. He saw me here that day — you were right, Tom — and told his father. Juan radio'd the information to Robert at the airbase, and Robert told him he'd fix for me to visit the *estancia*. He didn't say how he'd do it, just that I'd definitely be coming. I was to be locked in a store in the meathouse until Robert could get home in a few weeks' time. Incidentally, I'd have frozen to death long before that. Juan said he might allow me a blanket, and Paco asked why bother, why not let him freeze? Oh — they both took it absolutely for granted I'd come to see Francisca, there was no thought in their heads that I might have been in the Argentine for any other purpose. They gave me the impression they knew she and I once — you know, had something going.'

'It wouldn't be any secret.' Strobie nodded. 'It's had plenty of time to hatch out. We're objects of interest to them, you know, we *gringos*.'

'Robert had also told Juan Huyez he wouldn't mind if they killed me. If I had an accident, Paco said. In fact his father had thought this was what Robert really wanted. In return for the favour of knocking me off Huyez would get a piece of my share of the farm — as promised years back by the old bitch? So it was an attractive proposition for them — and as I'm here clandestinely, who'd know? Obviously Robert told or asked Francisca to issue the invitation — whether she did it voluntarily, or if he had some way he could make her do it — well, to be frank, Tom, I wasted some time wondering about that, but now it doesn't seem to make a hell of a lot of difference.'

Francisca's involvement wouldn't be easy for Tom to take, and Andy had foreseen this, it had been part of the reason he hadn't wanted to spell it all out.

'So what did you do then, with Paco?'

He looked down at his whisky. 'Does it matter?'

'Of course it bloody matters!'

He nodded. 'What I meant was, is it necessary for me to tell you — making you an accessory after the fact?'

'I've been an accessory after more facts than you've had hot dinners, boy. And I have to live here now, with the effects of whatever it is you've done. When you skid out of here with your chums I'm left with the remains and the stink – right?'

'I – suppose. . . .' Of course he hadn't meant 'the remains and the stink' quite literally. He'd meant he didn't want to have to guess this way or that when splinters of truth began emerging from the wound; which in the long run was inevitable.

'I couldn't leave him walking around, Tom. He'd already done enough harm. Including trying to murder me. Now he'd seen me kill his father.'

'Go on.'

'You won't want detail. All I need tell you is – well, when they find him they'll conclude he went off his head and murdered his father, then did away with himself.' Andy met the old man's stare – one wide-open eye, the other hooded. . . . 'From the way Paco did it, Tom, nobody'll ever doubt he died mad.'

The working eye closed now: a slow blink. . . . 'My bloody oath.' He'd whispered it. Raising his glass, swigging whisky: a gesture like a toast. . . . He muttered, 'There've been times, boy, I thought you might be – well, a wee bit soft-centred. For your own good. I thought it was what she saw when she went over to bloody Robert. Wouldn't want to offend you, Andy—'

'You won't, don't worry.'

He'd felt the same. After she'd thrown him over he'd become more than ever conscious of it. Thinking now, ironically, *It's an ill wind.* . . . Strobie said, half to himself, 'And there wasn't a damn thing else you could've done. Except get knocked off yourself, or caught – *and* leave me and your chums in the soup. . . .'

'Thanks, Tom.'

'Thanking *me*?'

'For seeing straight. I suppose you always did.'

'Bloody *hope* so. . . . But let's see what we've got here. . . .'

Practicalities. What evidence existed or did not exist, who else might know or suspect he'd been over there. How Francisca might react when she heard what had happened; what Robert might do when *he* heard. . . . If he was tied up in his naval duties he might either send her down, or hand the problems over to Diaz. That was quite a large question on its own, whether either of them would want her father to know about it: whether the fact they'd conspired to murder – private, family murder – would be something to be withheld from a specialist in State-sponsored murder. But the Diaz/ MacEwan guidelines would surely – they agreed – hang on politics and self-interest, not ethics.

It had been broad daylight when Andy had finally gone to get some sleep. He'd stopped at the bedroom door: 'I'll have to decide what to do for the rest of this waiting period, Tom, won't I? I mean, wait here, or what. . . ? Now she knows I'm here, and that I know about *her*. . . .' Another thought seemed to clarify itself: 'I think she *will* spill it all to her father.'

'Not sure I agree.' Strobie was thinking clearly, unaffected by having drunk at least one whole bottle on his own. 'But what we'll do, Andy, is we'll move you out to one of the *puestos* down south. You can stay out of sight there until your chums show up.'

Cloudsley finished, 'So Tony put the thing down on Diaz land. About six miles northeast of the Sandrini corner, it turned out.' He glanced at Beale. 'Having done a fantastic job, I may say. They'll find it, but with luck not for a while, conditions being as they are, and in any case it won't lead them this way, Tom. The line of flight was nearer eastward, and also it's where it got to before it ran out of gas – which they'll know. . . . But Andy, look – I don't know if you caught on – about your brother?'

'Would have been him trying to take off?'

'Most likely. Almost certainly. I'd guess that 'plane's guns weren't armed, so he'd have reckoned on the napalm as his only effective weapon, and to use it on us he had to get airborne.' Cloudsley frowned. 'As I explained before, we weren't there to kill anyone – let alone him. For what it's worth' – his glance took in Beale again – 'we're sorry.'

They weren't to know that Robert had tried to have *him*

killed. He wondered whether Francisca, when she heard, would see the joke.

Beale muttered, 'Geoff gone to sleep in the tub, d'you reckon?'

A more important consideration than Francisca's appreciation of black humour was that other one – whether she'd tell her father that Andrés MacEwan had been holed-up at Strobie's. Because if she did, here at Tom Strobie's was where the hunt would start. He could imagine it happening: helos landing out there in the yard, Diaz-type troops running from them, battering on doors. . . .

'Tom – when we pull out tonight – what about you?'

'I'll be on my own again. Take an extra glass or two.'

'If Diaz's thugs arrive and put the screws on your people – Torres and his wife, and Félix, and plenty of others must have seen us?'

The Halloween mask showed nothing. Even the eyes in it were calm. Strobie said, 'None of 'em'd tell the bastards anything. They're idiotic enough to be fond of me. . . . Be a good chap, see how the stew's doing?'

Anyone could give way under torture: most people would find the threat of it enough. He gave the stew a stir: it smelt good and it seemed to be hot all the way through. He thought some of Strobie's quiet confidence might arise from his devotion to Francisca. Even now, after last night. Knowing she'd been ready to cut Andy MacEwan's throat but not believing she'd do the same to old Tom? Maybe not daring to believe it. You had to have something, and he didn't have much else. Didn't, for instance, have any other place to go, any other way he'd want to live or reason to want to go on living if he couldn't continue exactly as he was now.

He went back to the others. Cloudsley's quick glance round revealing the man's anxiety, impatience to be on the move. . . .

'I'd say it's about ready, Tom.'

They'd eaten it all, Cloudsley was in the bath and the other two

247

had turned in, when Señora Torres came to summon Strobie to the radio. A call from BA – from Señora MacEwan. . . .

It rocked the old man, for a moment. Behind him, Andy felt his hackles rise.

'I'll be right along. Thank you.' He pushed the door shut, looked round at Andy. '*Now* what. . . .' That headshake, like a twitch. . . . 'Come over with me. You can listen in.'

There was a spare set of headphones. He leant against the wall with a hand up to hold them in place – the spring had gone, probably about forty years ago – while Tom sat at the desk and used the speaker and its two-way switch.

'Hello? Francisca?'

'Tom, my dear, how *are* you?'

Her voice was surprisingly clear. And warm, affectionate. It made his skin crawl. The same voice; and behind it – *Christ*. . . . Strobie, however, had his head in the noose, he was talking to the Francisca he'd known and loved for years now like a favourite daughter and maybe a little more than that, too. . . . ' – got through to me from BA? How long did it take you, a week?'

That soft laugh. . . . 'They let me use an official line, the naval link. Quite quick, I'm pampered, you see. . . . Tom, have you heard about all this trouble?'

'I heard your *mayordomo* and his kid have left home. *She* called me, this morning, thought the boy might be here, which he is not.'

'She called me too, they had it transferred from the base so she came on navlink too. She'd been trying to get through to Roberto, and there's some upset there; they wouldn't let her speak to him. She was in a panic, doesn't know which way to turn; so I said I'd get on to Roberto and have him contact her, but it was the same for *me*, Tom! No outside calls; I shouldn't have been connected, I was told. I said I was connected because I'm privileged to use navlink, perhaps you didn't understand me, I am Señora MacEwan and I wish to speak to my husband, your commanding officer! I regret, *señora*, this person says, it is not possible, we have – I think he said a "war situation" here, an emergency, blah, blah. . . . I told him, don't bullshit

248

me, if you won't connect me with my husband I'll telephone my father, Rear-Admiral Diaz, you can explain yourself to *him*. . . . You hearing this, Tom?'

Strobie grunted. 'Sounds rum. . . .'

'So then this man – an NCO, I believe – says please *señora*, I only carry out my orders, but I will see if Lieutenant Rodriguez is available, he may be able to assist. . . . So I wait, and finally I hear this Rodriguez person stuttering and stammering. I tell him, I don't want apologies or excuses, I want to speak to my husband, what the hell's going on anyway? He tells me first that Roberto is "not available", then that he is not on the base at all and he can't tell me where he is, then – in strict confidence, he says – that Admiral Diaz is on his way there, flying from Mar del Plata via Comodoro Rivadavia, coming to "take charge", he says. Take charge of what, I ask, what's happening, for God's sake? He says then, "It is a matter of grave emergency, *señora*, and I am not at liberty to say more"! So – finally – I tell him, kindly inform Admiral Diaz on his arrival that his daughter is waiting at his own residence in Buenos Aires and would like to hear from him at his earliest convenience. . . . And that's all I know, Tom, I'm just waiting. . . . Have *you* heard anything?'

'Nothing at all. But then, I wouldn't. As you know, I live in this little hole—'

'Might there be some connection with the Huyez affair? Whatever *that*'s about?'

'I can't imagine *what* connection—'

'The way this Rodriguez spoke – I mean just guessing, from his manner – well, Roberto might be – I don't know, sick, or—'

'He may have been sent off on some special duty. . . . But guessing's no use, girl, just wait and—'

'You see, I spoke to him only yesterday. He called to tell me he was leaving in two days. Going to the war zone. He had one final day in which he was expecting to be very busy, some kind of *finale* for his pilots, he was calling me while he had the time to spare. So you see, whatever this is it was unexpected, he didn't know about it *then*!'

'Like his move being brought forward? If they'd decided to rush his squadron to the Malvinas?'

'You're trying to comfort me, Tom, I know. But – honest truth, it sounded more like – disaster. . . .'

They heard her sigh. Andy wondering whether she'd regard it as a disaster if her darling Roberto had broken his neck, or been fried in napalm. Because if Robert *was* dead, and she was the woman he now knew her to be, and through Robert's death now half-owner of the *estancia* – his own partner, for God's sake. . . .

'Please God I'll soon hear from my father. I'll let you know, Tom. . . . But meanwhile – Tom, a favour? Could you help Señora Huyez? She's alone, in a bad state of panic, without her husband and unable to contact her *patrón* – she sounds desperate. . . . So – could you look in there, Tom?'

The pleading tone was the same one she'd turned on last evening. And Strobie was reacting as she'd have known he would – despite his aversion to showing his face in public.

'Yes. I'll take a run over there. Snowing a bit, I'll use the pickup. . . . But in the longer term, wouldn't it be best for you to come yourself?'

'I may have to, I know. Depending on what my father tells me. For the time being I have to stay here, of course, until I do hear from him. . . . Tom, if *you* hear any news—'

'That's not likely. But I'm sure it can't be as bad as—'

'Then what's this "matter of grave emergency"?'

She'd snapped that at him.

Strobie said, 'I wouldn't try to explain it. Except – grave emergency in the Malvinas, maybe. . . . Francisca, did you call through to us here last night?'

Silence. Strobie glanced at Andy. Then her voice came guardedly, 'Why on earth, Tom, should I have—'

'Apparently Señora Torres took a call from someone who claimed to be Señora MacEwan and wanted to talk to Andrés MacEwan.'

'To – *Andy?*'

Another pause. . . . Then: 'But that's crazy. Surely he's in England?'

250

'But if you'd had some reason to think he might be here — and surely you'd be the first to know, any time he did contemplate—'

'I think someone was playing a stupid joke. A hoax, Tom. Someone who knows about — you know, the old days?'

'Apparently the caller sounded like you, but she was pretending to be speaking from *Estancia* La Madrugada. Señora Torres was sure you couldn't be there without us knowing it, so she — had her doubts. Rightly — it *couldn't* have been you — which is why I didn't mention it before.'

'So what happened?'

'Nothing that I know of. I think they just rang off.' He'd glanced at Andy again. 'I don't know, some silly hoax or—'

'I was going to say — someone trying to make trouble, Tom. It would be best if nobody heard about it, don't you agree? You know how fond I am of Andy, and you can't be the only one who knows it, we do have enemies and — it's Roberto I have in mind, Tom. If it was rumoured I'd had reason to think Andy might be there. . . . D'you see?'

'Roberto mightn't be very pleased, you mean.'

'So let's not mention it, to *anyone*? Would you ask the same of Señora Torres, too?'

Finishing the call, Strobie looked at Andy. 'What did you make of *that*?'

He put the antique headphones down. 'What counts is she's going to keep her mouth shut about me being here. Counting on you to give her the benefit of whatever doubts. . . . Anyway, she may *not* tell Daddy.'

Strobie had lurched over to the window. Leaning there, staring out at the driving snow. He swung round.

'But he's still coming. Not *here*, necessarily, but. . . . Andy, look. In this weather he can't do much. So you lot ought to get on the move while you can. And, she's given me a good reason to be on the road — visiting the Huyez woman. I'll pack you four in the pickup behind a load of fodder — and drop that off at my southeast *puesto* on the way back. That's real too, they'll be needing it. All right?'

'Leave right away?'

'There won't be any better time.'

'But if you were caught with us, Tom—'

'Doing Admiral Diaz's daughter a favour?'

'Well—'

'Anyway' – Strobie pointed the stick at him – 'I'm an old man, Andy. A *very* old man, and what there is of me is – well, you've got eyes. . . . But for the first time in years I have a chance to do something really useful – d'you see?'

He nodded. 'Yes.'

'Wake 'em up, tell 'em to get ready. They can go back to sleep when they're in the truck. I'll get it loaded, and snow-chains on.'

15

The Ford rumbled southeastward, the slapping of snow-chains on its worn tyres replacing other road-noise which the snow was muffling. It wasn't snowing now, and there were several hours of daylight left: this stretched the nerves and raised a question mark against the decision to start right away instead of waiting for the night. Except the old man did have good reason to be out in his pickup; and short of being stopped and searched there was no way anyone could know four men were hidden in the back of it.

An hour ago they'd left the Hermansens' *estancia*, Buena Ventura, their second stop. Strobie was navigating by the fence-lines; roads and tracks were hidden under snow but the *quebracho* posts were all you needed as long as you kept the right distance from them; which, having spent nearly thirty winters here, he knew all about. . . . Alone in the cab, hunched behind the thin, vibrating wheel, his thick body wrapped in sheepskin under a poncho and with a balaclava under his cap so that only his eyes were exposed. He'd told them, 'My standard rig for visiting. So the girls don't scream.'

They'd been about ready to start, then, having loaded the pickup with their own gear plus the guanaco-skin rugs for extra warmth, and at the last minute Cloudsley had surprised Strobie with a request to be allowed to take along four bedsheets. Andy had thought it was a joke until he'd added, 'For camouflage, in the snow.'

The back of the pickup looked solid with bales of fodder, but behind the cab there was a space for passengers. In the front passenger seat Strobie had stowed a jerrycan of petrol and two of the big LPG cylinders that fuelled his cooking and water-heating. This would give him an excuse for being out on the road after visiting the MacEwan *estancia*, he'd explained – changing them for full ones.

'Better than nothing. Little bull goes a long way, don't it.' Then he'd asked Cloudsley – having spread a road map on the kitchen table – 'Want to show me where you're heading? Not that I'm curious – only a matter of where I'd best drop you off.'

Cloudsley didn't touch the map. He told him, 'We just need to get to the coast, Tom.'

Strobie mimicked him: *'The coast, Tom. . . .'* Pointing. . . . 'See how much of it there is, along the edge of this bloody country?'

'Say the nearer part of it. Roughly southeast from here would be fine. But you'll need to get back here within a few hours, wouldn't you?'

'You're talking about a two-hundred mile hike, realise that?'

'Tom, we're certainly not asking you to—'

'Two hundred miles on foot in this weather – with half the security forces on your tails?'

'Well, you see, we're trained for it. And we won't be carrying much, nothing like the weight we're used to.'

His tone was patient. Everyone being patient with everyone else, because they were all tired enough to bite heads off, if they let go. Strobie, the octogenarian and physically handicapped, was the only member of the party who didn't seem dog-tired. Andy wished he'd slept a lot longer than he had, and the SBS men, who'd spent several days living on their nerves and in holes in the ground, and had just been woken out of the beginnings of deep sleep, looked like bearded spooks, grouped round Strobie as he ran a stubby forefinger across the map.

'I could cover myself by buying gas cylinders in – well, here at FitzRoy, say. Or Jaramillo, or—'

'But by the time we were that far, Tom, it'd be early morning!'

'So I'll knock 'em up. If the buggers want my custom, let 'em work for it. . . . Or, we could fork down this way. Any of those benighted little holes'd do me. And you'd be a hell of a lot closer, wouldn't you? Don't tell me, I don't want to know – but how'd it suit you if I let you off about *here*?'

'Why would you go that far for gas, Tom? If they stopped and questioned you – when you could get it a lot nearer home?'

Strobie glared at him. 'Simple answer. Anywhere around here, my credit's shot.' Hosegood chuckled, and the old man told him, 'No joke, Geoff. They could check up, if they wanted.'

'And' – Cloudsley asked, looking at the map – 'What speed would you think you'd average?'

'Not more than twenty, I should guess.' He folded the map. 'Come on, we're wasting time!'

He'd declined Andy's offer to share the driving. In the back of the pick-up, ploughing through snow towards the MacEwan *estancia*, Cloudsley had muttered, 'This old guy's eighty? And every movement hurts him, but he reckons to drive a hundred miles and back, in *this*?'

Andy said, 'He told me yesterday that driving's no effort to him. On a horse he's limited, in agony after more than three or four hours, but – anyway, don't bother to argue, you won't put him off.'

Francisca was the only one who'd ever been able to change his mind for him. She'd had a way of laughing him out of his own strong-headedness. . . . But it was peculiar, now, thinking about that girl: it was as if there were two Franciscas, the one he'd known and the one who was now in BA. . . .

'OK, Tom?'

Talking through the rectangular hole that had once had glass in it, in the back of the cab. It had a canvas flap on it now. Strobie answered gruffly that of course he was OK. Tobacco-

255

smoke seeped through: he'd pushed the pipe's stem through the wool of his balaclava. 'We were thinking, Tom. Hell of a long stretch to the FitzRoy area. Harry reckons even a quarter of that distance would be a better start than any of them would have hoped for. How about we settle for that?'

'Gate coming up, Andy. Your job – right?'

At the *estancia* La Madrugada the passengers had kept still and quiet while dogs barked and *peóns* crowded round. Andy heard one of them telling Strobie, 'His body was in the *carnicería*, Don Tomás. Butchered like a sheep. . . . Before you go to see her, I'll tell you this – the *mayordomo* didn't like for Paco to be courting that young lady, he wanted a better match for him, a rich one. They had many arguments. Even then, it seems small cause for such a catastrophe, such—'

'I'll go and see her.'

'She may not admit you, Don Tomás. You must excuse her, she's half out of her mind. . . .'

'Have the police been notified?'

'*Sí, señor*, and they are coming here. But not the *patrón*, as yet it has not been possible—'

'I know. Señora MacEwan told me.'

They were there about half an hour. Andy had to wake Hosegood because his snoring became a danger. Strobie told them after they'd started driving south, '*Peóns* found a storeroom locked, key missing, blood running under the door. They smashed it open, and there was Huyez with a meathook through his gullet. Seems pretty obvious the boy did it and then scarpered. His mother's in shock, of course. I promised I'd call in at the Hermansens' and tip them off, in case he shows up there. Their radio's out of action; and there can't be so many places he'd have run to. . . . Anyway, from there we can carry on down to the river road and turn east. Waste of time, making another stop, but it'll look good. . . . Snow's easing, notice?'

On this track they were driving straight into it, but it was definitely thinning. Strobie called again: 'Forgot to say, Andy – Paco took the *nochero*, last night, and it was back first light this morning, trailing a bust rein. He can't have gone far.'

And if the snow wasn't really setting in yet, it mightn't be long before they found him. . . .

The Hermansen call took only a few minutes. Strobie stayed in his seat, sent a child to fetch Piet Hermansen. Paco Huyez certainly hadn't been there, the Dane said. If he did show up, he'd try to hold him. . . . 'But how are *you* now, Tom?'

'Never better.' He jerked a thumb towards the load of fodder. 'Have to get along, though. Need to buy some gas, and dump this lot on my way home. Your south gate open?'

By the time he'd swung the pickup on to the south road between the Hermansen boundary fence and the river, stopping to wait while Andy shut the gate and climbed back in, the snow had stopped falling. Heading east now, noses towards the South Atlantic. Compressed between the side of the truck and the heap of slumbering SBS men, Andy remembered that until quite a short time ago he'd doubted whether they'd be taking him out with them; and here he was, heading for home.

London was home now. No more ambivalence.

What the hell was he going to tell her — where he'd been, why he hadn't written?

No answers came to mind. Except maybe take advice from her father. It was more than just the Official Secrets Act — although that was prohibition enough — it was the importance the SBS attached to secrecy. Which was absolutely reasonable, and binding. He shut his eyes, trying to relax in his tight corner, having failed to enlarge the small space they'd left him. Lisa wouldn't put up with total silence, he knew that much. She'd had to put up with quite a lot already. In fact she might not even *care* where he'd been. . . .

He slept. Maybe for ten minutes, maybe half an hour. Struggling out of what felt like a strait-jacket, he swivelled to get his face to the opening behind Strobie's head. The truck's motion was the same: lurching, rumbling over snow. Surprisingly, it was still daylight: he was looking out at a black-and-white moving picture divided by the old man's bulk. Fenceposts on the left, river on the right. Over Tom's shoulder he saw the old man's gloved hands vibrating on the wheel as if it was a pneumatic drill.

'All right, Tom?'

Pipe still leaking fumes; Strobie removed it from the balaclava. '*I'm* all right. How are the nightmares?'

'No more. That was – just a reflex.' He hoped. . . . 'Tom – while I have the chance to say it, you've been bloody fantastic.'

'Enjoying meself, lad. I don't want thanks.'

'You're getting them, anyway. You've done a hell of a lot for us.'

'Do some more, if this old crash-wagon keeps going. Tyres aren't up to much and the chains'll be knocking hell out of 'em. . . . Tell me this, now. How'll you handle it – Francisca being your partner, if Robert *is* kaput?'

'I haven't really thought it out. But as it looks to me now, I can't see I could do anything except get shot of it all. Put it in lawyers' hands – in due course. . . . Even if Robert's alive I'd want out – even more so, in fact.'

Strobie didn't comment, for a while. The pickup rumbling on, chains beating the snow with a sound like muffled drums. . . . Then he growled, 'Clean sweep, then. No MacEwans, and pretty damn soon no Strobie.'

'Oh, you'll have a few years yet, Tom. A man who can drink whisky all night and then drive miles through a blizzard—'

'Blizzard's finished, and I had enough sleep. And I'm not so sure I'd want your "few years", either. Give me one good reason I should?'

'Well, as long as a man's reasonably fit and in his right mind—'

'Balls. . . . Andy, you and I know each other pretty well. Better than we did before, even. So we can skip the bull-shit. . . . No, I'll peg out soon enough, and my place'll revert to the old trollops. . . .'

They were spinsters, distant cousins, younger than Tom although he'd always referred to them as 'old'. Old trollops, old lesbians. . . . They'd either given or sold him a life interest in the sheep-station, after he'd been beached with his George Medal and precious little else. He'd made a living out of it, in an environment that suited his requirements, although when there'd been profits the cousins had had most of them.

'When I kick the bucket they'll most likely sell out, too.

They'd never get a manager worth his salt for the pittance I've taken out of it. Alejandro Diaz might pick it up, shouldn't be surprised. For peanuts. . . . Mind you, if they lose this little war of theirs – which they will – Diaz could be out of a job. Could end up behind bars. If they lose, the *Junta*'ll go under, bet your boots.'

'Have you considered how it might be if they won?'

'Sure, I have. No stopping 'em. Military dictatorship till kingdom come. Detention camps springing up like mushrooms, and no one'd dare shake a stick at 'em. The buggers'd have a go at Chile next, over the Beagle Channel.' Tom puffed smoke faster and thicker as he thought about it. 'Chile, then Brazil. They have big ideas, always did have. The military, I mean. No accomplishments, just ideas. The rest of 'em should be bloody grateful to us – specially to Mrs T – for saving 'em from all that. Mind you I don't suppose they will be, they'll still be hankering after the bloody Malvinas. . . .'

He'd muttered something else. Snatching at his pipe, leaning forward to peer up through the windscreen. . . .

'Hear what I said?' The pipe-stem stabbed upward. 'Helicopter?'

Andy heard it, at that moment. Right over them.

'Harry! Helo, hovering overhead!'

Sudden stirring of large bodies, awkward in the confined space. . . . Hosegood muttering, 'Bloody hell, where are we, what's—' Andy was back at the hole behind Tom, thinking that this manner of withdrawal had seemed a bit too easy, quick and comfortable. . . . The truck was slowing, he realised. 'Stopping, Tom?'

Cloudsley woke up to it too. 'Tom, God's sake keep—'

'Village here.' Strobie gestured towards the right. 'If you can flatter it by calling it a village. Over the bridge. I'll buy my gas, then start back. Be dark in about half an hour; then we'll turn round again. All right with you, Harry?'

'I'd say you're a genius.'

'Bit late to have *that* recognised.' Strobie swung the pickup into the right fork that led over a stone bridge. There was rising ground on the other side, then from the crest they were rattling

259

downhill towards a cluster of adobe buildings. A sick-looking dog lay in the middle of the road: it bared its teeth at the oncoming truck. Strobie hooted, swerved round it, braked to stop outside a primitive-looking general store.

'Sit tight.' He banged his palm on the horn. The helo noise was loud, vertically overhead where you couldn't see it. Loud enough to be coming down; and there'd be plenty of room for it to land, Andy guessed, in this dirt square. Cloudsley warned, 'We don't want trouble if we can avoid it, Tom. If the helo lands, for Christ's sake *smile* at it.'

'The pilot'd faint.' Strobie watched a boy in a tattered *poncho* come shuffling out of the store, not looking where he was going, staring up at the helicopter. He wound down the window: '*Buenas*! D'you have gas cylinders, the big ones? I have two empties here, want to change them.'

'*Si*. We have them. . . .'

Still open-mouthed, gazing up. Nearly falling over the dog, then aiming a kick at it. . . . Strobie murmured, 'Not quite Harrods, is it?' Then he shouted over the helo noise, 'Round the other side, take 'em out, will you?' He pushed his head out of the left-side window for a look up at the helo; he was right to do it, it would have seemed unnatural if he'd shown no interest. Andy said, 'Tom – here. . . .' Pushing a roll of *pesos* through the aperture. 'It's your money. Meant to give it to you before, we owe you at least that much.' The wad of notes fell beside him; Strobie sang in a surprisingly tuneful voice '*Pesos* from heaven. . . .' and leant over, pushing the passenger door open so the boy could lift out the first cylinder.

Five minutes later the pickup was on the road again, passing over the bridge and then swinging left, back the way they'd come. Strobie pushed his pipe-stem in through the hole in the balaclava, mumbled, 'Stroke of luck, being the right side of that crabby little dump. Wouldn't have been another in forty miles.'

'Smart thinking, besides luck.'

Hosegood agreed, yawning. 'Been up the creek, wouldn't we?'

'And we'll learn our lesson from it. Won't push our luck any farther, Tom.' Andy was looking out under a raised flap of the tarpaulin, watching the helo – which looked like a giant wasp, and Beale had just said was a Lynx – still close, Argie eyes still checking on them, so that the argument starting now between Cloudsley and the old man seemed premature. Strobie had observed that the light was already fading, adding that as soon as it was dark he'd turn and head east again; Cloudsley, crouching at the aperture in the back of the cab, rejecting this, telling him, 'Soon as either it's dark or that helo's out of sight, we'll drop off and start yomping. Thanks for bringing us this far, and I can't thank you even half enough for everything else you've done for us. But truly, Tom, this is *it*.'

'Want to walk when you could ride?'

'Not from preference, no. In fact you might slow down a bit – no need to take us farther back than you have to. . . . Tom, there are sound reasons for us to drop off now. D'you want to hear them?'

Strobie grunted. Starting the wipers as another snow-shower came down. He pointed, 'Bugger's pushing off, see?'

The helo did seem to be departing. Either it had seen enough, or snow didn't suit it. Cloudsley explained to Strobie, 'First look at your own situation, Tom. You've made your courtesy calls, you've got your gas cylinders, you're in the clear and all you have to do is drive on home, dropping the feed off as you planned. . . . Then our angle; and first, yomping's no hardship to us. The trip ought to take four nights – we're travelling light, and the nights are long, and you've saved us a good bit already. Lying up by day in scrape-holes is also something we're used to. OK, Andy, something you'll soon *get* used to. . . . But no problems, you see, if there's a trouble spot we skirt round it, we aren't restricted to using roads, and – above all – *we get there*. . . . In the long run that's the only thing that counts. If we took advantage of your kindness, though, we could very well run into a lot of trouble. Helos, road patrols, whatever. One single incident, Tom, and this truck would be identified; you'd have had it!'

'It's a risk I'd take.'

He didn't want to lose their company, Andy realised. Or end

his own involvement in the operation. . . . Cloudsley was saying, '—but from our point of view it's not on, anyway. We've already thrown our weight around more than we were supposed to do – got away with it, luckily, but – well, suppose we had to shoot our way through a roadblock, for instance. OK, we'd do it, leave some dead Argies and push on. But (a) we're not supposed to be killing people and we'd really sooner not, (b) what would it lead to? We need peace and quiet, Tom, if we're to get away.'

'Surely they'll have guessed you'll be heading for the coast?'

'They'll have guessed we *might* be. But we could be going back into Chile – if we're Brits, but they don't know that either, we could be home-grown guerrillas, for all they know. Once we had a bust-up on the open road, though, our goose'd be cooked good and proper. They'd have our position, course and speed and we'd never get *to* the bloody beach, let alone off it!'

Strobie growled. 'Talks a lot, this feller.'

'So we'll drop off, Tom. Thanks all the same.'

'Ten minutes, it'll be dark enough.' Strobie wiped fogging off the windscreen. The snow was coming down steadily again, now. 'I'll run you back as far as the bridge, that turn-off to the village. . . .'

Cloudsley said an hour later, yomping across the shoulder of a flattish hill with the shine of a big river curling around it in a deep, wide valley on their left, 'Couldn't have taken him with us, you see. And if we'd run into a firefight – Tom and his pickup identified beyond doubt – well, what else could we have done for him, then? Hopeless even to think of taking him along; might be some rock-climbing, certainly small-boat work, and after we get to the coast we'll have a day or two to wait in hides – well, think of all that, with his disabilities. He couldn't have made it, Andy.'

'I know. But what's even more to the point, he wouldn't

have wanted to. Patagonia is Tom's idea of a hide.'

Hosegood muttered, 'Wonderful old guy.'

Beale's voice, from the rear: 'Wouldn't 've got far without him, would we?'

'Reckon he'll be OK now, Andy?' Hosegood again. 'Won't get on to him, will they?'

'I can't see *how* they would. . . .'

As long as Francisca didn't shop him. Which didn't seem likely; at least as long as it suited her book not to. The danger would be Robert – if Robert had survived. Which, please God—

Well. God, if he existed, might not be receptive to that kind of prayer. Unless he'd taken in the *vizcacha* games. . . .

Saying goodbye to old Tom had been a miserable experience. Andy had felt grateful to Cloudsley, when the SBS lieutenant had broken into the farewells with a briskly practical suggestion. 'Tom. In a day or so – say the day after tomorrow – you might report you've had three horses stolen? You could describe them accurately, the three we bought from you?'

Strobie's right hand had still been clasped in Andy's.

'Stolen when?'

'Well, during the night before you report it. Get Torres to inform you that they've vanished. If they had the time and inclination, and snow conditions seem right, you could even lay some tracks – three horses – heading southwest, ending at the river bank? The real horses could ride back east along the river, come back to your *estancia* separately, via one of your out-stations, whatever you call 'em? But that's for you to decide. The three horses might have been nicked by the desperados who beat up the airbase, mightn't they? So they could be heading for the Chilean border?'

'If there's snow on the ground there'll be tracks all over the shop anyway. They could take their pick.'

'Right. But red herrings apart, reporting the loss will cover *you*. If Diaz investigators noticed a shortfall in the stock. Or if the animals have been turned loose at the other end of this fair land, and they'd be wearing your brand – right?'

The old man turned back to Andy. 'He'll go a long way, this feller. I'd hang on to his coat-tails for a while, if I were you.'

'I'm planning to.' He tightened his grip on Strobie's hand. 'Believe me, Tom, I'd sooner stick around with you, if it was possible. But I may be able to come back – after a while. . . .'

Cloudsley had intervened again: 'Know what he said about you, Tom, first time your name was mentioned, when we'd asked him was there anyone in this part of the world who might help us?'

'He'd've said, "Ugly old sod called Strobie—" '

'He said, "Tom Strobie's a rock of a man." And I'll tell you for nothing – he was damn right.'

Then more practical advice: 'Before you tell them the horses have been pinched, Tom, make sure of two things. One, no trace of our temporary residence in your house, and two, that all your people have their mouths zipped shut. Can do?'

Strobie glared up at him. 'I was born eighty years ago, young man '

Hosegood interrupted: 'Our lucky day, that was.'

Andy put his arms round the old man's shoulders, and hugged him. 'It was certainly mine. See you, Tom.'

Cloudsley had said, *Something you'll soon get used to,* and in the next few days and nights he certainly did. He also learnt about skirting around trouble-spots. The long nights of fast yomping, never on roads but often close to them or on the hills overlooking them – overlooking the river valleys, which got wider as they neared the coast – were punctuated several times by views of roadblocks, usually at crossroads, military transport parked to block the roadway and armed men and machine-gun posts all around. Truckloads of soldiers patrolled the roads, approaches to villages were picketed by police, and by day there was frequent sighting of helicopters while they lay in shallow scrapes roofed with turf supported on nylon mesh.

264

He'd expressed his surprise at the ease with which men could travel such a distance across hostile territory, and Cloudsley's answer had come in the form of a question: 'Ever try to locate a flea on a dog's back?'

It was also surprising that men could stay fit and strong on a diet of biscuit and chocolate – cold mutton from Strobie's kitchen having lasted only the first twenty-four hours. Water was taken from rivers, with pills added to kill the bugs. And in a hastily excavated hole in the earth, its floor lined with one of Strobie's moth-eaten *quillangos*, he found he could sleep as soundly as he ever had on a mattress.

He thought the mainspring of it might have been the sense of satisfaction he was getting from it. Sense of getting away with it.

'Make a Bootneck of you yet, Andy Mac!'

He'd glanced at Geoff Hosegood's dark silhouette, trudging beside him.

'Might consider becoming one, at that.'

'Yeah?'

'Being already the proud possessor of a special short short-service commission – that's a start, isn't it?'

Cloudsley called back, 'Give up the fleshpots of the City, Andy?'

'Think they'd have me?'

'Don't know. You're over age, for entry. But as you say, with a foot in the door already. . . . Except I heard there was only one officer entry accepted in the last twelve months.'

'*One*?'

Beale said, 'Small force, see? Exclusive.' He raised his voice: 'Reckon he'd have a chance, Harry? If you put in a word for him?'

'After that party on the airbase, who's going to take any notice of *my* word. . .'

Cloudsley navigated by a parachute-silk map that came out of the lining of a boot. By night they followed compass courses, correcting as necessary after deviations around danger areas. When they dug in for the third day, with three full nights of yomping behind them, he announced that they were within a few miles of the coast.

'Right bit of coast?'

It was a silly question, but he was ferreting for information. Nobody had let anything out yet about their withdrawal plans, and he thought it was time he was told what lay ahead.

Cloudsley pointed. 'See those twin hills? And the taller one by itself to the right?'

He'd nodded. Daylight coming, and they were working fast to finish their scrapes. He'd become quite adept at building his own now. Cloudsley told him, 'That's our line of march tonight. Three or four hours' yomp, then the moment of truth.'

'What truth?'

'Oh, you'll see. . . .'

He saw helicopters during the day, patrolling what he guessed would be the invisible coastline, cliffs or beaches. No way of knowing whether it might be routine patrolling or a special effort in honour of the SBS. One helo woke him later, early in the afternoon, right overhead and low, very loud. . . . He lay like a corpse, face-down, while the noise went on as if the machine was hovering – which would mean its crew thought they might have spotted something. Like an ineffectively camouflaged hide. At a time like this you began to think that to have got away with it this long and this far was nothing but a fluke: you thought, *OK, so here it comes*. . . .

It didn't. It went.

He was thinking off and on about old Tom – who by now would have reported the horses as having been stolen. Alone in his shack with only whisky for any kind of company. . . .

'Moving out, Andy. Wakey wakey. . . .'

Opening his eyes to darkness. He'd been asleep for several hours, since that helo had made its slow pass over. Time now for a snack, and attending to other personal needs; and for packing any loose gear and collapsing the hide under its turf roof, leaving only a small depression complete with its realistic quota of snow.

Three or four hours, Cloudsley had said. Trudging on, with the twin hills on the left and the taller pimple on the right. . . . There was a minor road to cross – and a routine drill for doing

266

it. Tony Beale had advised him, *Never get to thinking it's easy, Andy. That's when you fuck it up. You need to be at full stretch every minute, no let up ever. . . .* Beale was behind him now, Hosegood's stocky shape ahead, Cloudsley as usual leading. To the left in front, the ground rose into vague silhouette against black, cloud-covered sky. He thought he could smell the sea, but that might have been imagination; the ground was hummocky, scrub-covered, patched with snow but not solid with it as it had been inland.

Cloudsley stopped, and they closed up around him.

'Tony – stay here with Andy. Might be patrols around, so watch it. You come with me, Geoff.' He put a hand on Beale's shoulder, turning him and pointing: 'See that hillock, in line with the right-hand edge of the promontory? Bears north seventy east, and that's the line I'm taking. Should be back here in about quarter of an hour.'

'Check.'

Cloudsley and Hosegood melted into the darkness. The bedsheets being earth-stained now, as patchy as the terrain, made perfect camouflage. Beale squatted with his machine-pistol in his hands. 'Lie flat, Andy.'

'Where are they going?'

'You'll see when they get back. Keep quiet now.'

The wind, and an owl or two, and more distantly a sound which suddenly he recognised as the sea, a much deeper, more powerful background to the constant humming and battering of the wind. It conjured images of white water surging across a beach, black water turning into foam, pluming against rock.

Fifteen minutes stretched into twenty, then stretched farther. When it came he didn't recognise it until Beale reacted. There'd been a whistle that might have been some night bird's call; the colour sergeant, crouching with his Ingram levelled, whistled back on the same note.

'Tony.' Cloudsley's voice sounded close. 'Four of us joining you, OK?'

'Come on then, Harry.'

A stirring in the snow-patched scrub. Names had served as

267

passwords. Beale asked without turning his head, 'See 'em yet?'

Not a damn thing. . . . But as they moved in really close, he smelt them. Then the vision matching that feral odour was of bearded faces smeared with black cam-cream, eyes furtive like the eyes of nocturnal animals. 'Hi, Andy Mac. Hi, Tony, you old sod. . . .' Jake West, and Monkey Start. Cloudsley's immensity loomed behind them: 'Save the endearments. Get the signal out, Monkey. . . .'

16

Start had got his signal away within a few minutes of his and West's surprise appearance out of the night. The transmitter was the size and shape of the kind of tape-recorder that fits in a briefcase, its aerial three hundred yards of thin wire which Jake unreeled from a spool as he crawled away into the dark, laying it out in a straight line over the rough, snow-patched ground. Wet string would have done just as well, Beale told Andy afterwards. It was a low-power HF transmission and the signal itself was on a cassette, a pre-recorded, pre-condensed burst transmission that went out in one flash at a touch on a button and would be received, stretched and decoded and placed before the Chief of Naval Staff or one of his deputies at Northwood, Middlesex, the subterranean Royal Navy HQ near London, within the hour. Northwood would then call through on a secure voice line to the Task Force Admiral in his carrier flagship. To the uninitiated, it was mind-boggling. . . . But while West had been laying out the wire, Start had muttered to Cloudsley, 'We have a sod of a problem here, Harry.'

West had come back then, and they'd been busy. Andy very much the uninitiated, the outsider conscious of his own uselessness. Crouching among them, trying to keep out of the way and understand from occasional cryptic exchanges what was happening or about to happen. While Start's 'sod of a problem' hung in the air, all the worse for being as yet unspecified; and for having been mentioned in those terms at all, since these people tended, he'd noticed, to minimise difficulties, not exaggerate them. Nobody was doing any unnecessary talking. Cloudsley, Beale and Hosegood were prone, facing outward like spokes of a wheel in a defensive, watchful circle with their machine-pistols ready while the signal was fired off to London and the gear then packed away.

'OK, Harry.'

'You lead.'

About ten minutes' cautious progress, then, in extended file over undulating grass and scrub. Finally they'd all crammed into one hide, Start's and West's. Others had been dug nearby, apparently. Jake West got busy with the bluey, and Cloudsley demanded almost explosively after his long, patient wait, 'So what's your problem?'

'Missile installation on the headland. They've just set it up, brand new. One MM38 plus radar and a small garrison. They're patrolling around this area, time to time, which is why I didn't much want to hang around.'

Cloudsley glanced at Beale and Hosegood.

'Well, well.'

Start went into detail. The missile was mounted on a flatbed truck, on the headland near the lighthouse, with what might be a converted furniture van, now a mobile radar station, set up in combo with it.

'Not nice, is it? They moved in after we got here, we watched 'em setting up house. But something'll have to be done about it, eh?'

Otherwise the submarine that was coming for them would be surfacing into a deathtrap.

'Since we've sent that signal—'

'Well, surely, what alternative—'

'Certainly. But as you say. . . .'

No question, the missile would have to be neutralised,

270

somehow. The essence of the problem, as Cloudsley had explained to Tom Strobie a few days ago, was that safe withdrawal from an enemy coast depended on stealth, silence, invisibility, and in the circumstances this might be difficult to achieve.

'How many Argies in residence?'

'About two dozen. Between twenty and twenty-five, say. Most of them live and doss in the hut near that lighthouse. Remember there was mention of a hut?'

Cloudsley nodded. 'Survival equipment in it. For ship-wrecked mariners withal.'

Tony Beale quoted, ' "... Promontory two miles wide projecting four miles from the general line of the coast, high with many sand dunes within which is grassland with clumps of scrub. . . . The lighthouse is a square concrete framework tower painted white and black bands, twelve metres in height, with a white hut containing survival equipment at its base, situated eight cables southwest of the eastern extremity of the point. . . ." How's that?'

Cloudsley said to Hosegood, 'Some people might call it showing off.'

'Yeah. Missed a piece out in the middle, though, didn't he?'

'Anyway' – Start confirmed – 'that's now the local barracks.'

'How many on watch, at night?'

'Two guys on sentry duty. Same by day. Another four spend their nights in the van. They might be all four radarmen, or maybe only two are and the others are duty watch for operating the missile. They'd need to be under cover, you see. It's bloody cold on that point, I can tell you, and ninety per cent of the time all except the sentries are inside the hut – which is very small for that number of men, must have bunk beds in it, I'd guess. And an oil-stove – downwind there's a pong of kerosene.'

'What about patrols?'

'Mostly in daylight and in pairs. Might just be going walkies, of course. But we've seen 'em out at night in fours too. They don't look as if they'd be much of a problem to anyone, it's just a fact that they're around, and we don't want 'em seeing us, do we. One thing is they don't seem to stray off the beaten tracks – haven't yet, that we've seen. There again, there's always a first time, isn't there?'

'What beaten tracks are we talking about?'

'Path around the clifftop, and a track on the north side – ' Start pointed – 'thataway, linking with the coast road. That's the way they come and go. They've had visitors, by the way – a carload of brass once, and a helo landed yesterday, took off again after about half an hour.'

'As you say' – Cloudsley nodded – 'we'll have to do something about it. And to start with I want to have a close look at it, Monkey.'

'Why not? We've got hours and hours of dark left.' Start had looked at his watch; he offered, 'Show you the beach as well, while we're at it.'

'Yes. We might split into two parties, then join up and put it all together. But look here – question of time.' He explained – glancing at Andy – 'Zero hour for the extraction is the second midnight after they get our signal. And they've got it now – please God. But we're keeping local time at the moment – 0100 – whereas it's Zulu time, meaning GMT, Andy, that counts. So in fact it's now 2200.' He told them all, 'Shift to Zulu now, gents, and nobody'll get confused. Time right now is 2204 – and a half – and thirty-*five*. . . . OK?'

Beale explained to Andy – everyone suddenly taking pity on his state of ignorance: 'Like Harry said, the R/V's to be at midnight – tomorrow midnight, that is – nine miles out. We motor out there in our rubber boat, and the sub sends in a Gemini to meet us. Then we carry on out together to where the sub surfaces again and takes us on board.'

Jake West interrupted: 'Steak and onions then, Andy. And chips – and—'

'What I'm saying' – Beale cut across it – 'is we have to shove off from the beach an hour or more *before* midnight, Andy.'

Cloudsley added, 'Hoping to God the outboard works as well as it did on the lake. That's no millpond out there. . . . Next question, Monkey. The boat, outboard, gas – oh, Christ, you did get petrol?'

'Siphoned it out of an army jeep.' Start grimaced. 'We're not just pretty faces, are we, Jake?'

'You can say *that* again. . . . But the boat, outboard, fuel, PNG – all that gear?'

'Buried at the top of the beach. As close as it could be to where we need it. Have to allow a bit of time, of course – digging it out, lugging it down to the surf-line, inflating it, loading up – and as you say, making sure the motor works. . . .'

After days and nights with nothing to drink except cold water, the tea was like nectar. Warmth burning down, radiating. . . . Jake had put more water on to boil, preparing for second helpings, by popular demand. Cloudsley put another question: 'Fixing up the boat and launching it – if the night happens to be a clear one, or the Argies on the headland have PNG or anything like it – any chance they'd spot us?'

Start shook his head. 'You saw the high ground out there, ahead of us as we were coming? That's the headland – we're on the promontory, as described in Tony's recitation, here and now. There's cliff all round, and a beach to the left – north – which *is* overlooked from the headland. That side there's an almighty great barrier of kelp too, so the choice of beach was obvious, one way and another. . . . Anyway, the cliff extends around like this, in a curve – it's irregular, little coves in it, but effectively it's a curve facing east then southeast, and a short south-facing bit where it falls suddenly to low-lying coast again. . . . That's your general layout, and no, they couldn't see us taking off because from where they are it's dead ground.'

'Any possibility of observation from anywhere else?'

'There's no manned O/P – other than this bastard – for three miles or so either up coast or down. We've checked both ways. By day you have random helo patrols, but that's all. Except for these local Argies, of course, when they send patrols out – and they'd certainly have a view from the cliff path on that side if they happened to be on it.'

'We'll need to make sure they aren't. Somehow. . . .' He

273

held his mug out for a refill. 'Thanks, Geoff. Bloody marvellous, I must say. . . . Monkey – the route from here to where the boat is – d'you go along the edge of the cliff?'

'Uh-huh. You'd get there, of course, but the direct route is straight across, southwestward, cutting off all that corner. Roughly one point six miles.'

'But you still reckoned this was the place to dig in?'

A nod. . . . 'The cover's good here, and non-existent lower down.' Start sucked up tea noisily. 'Also, although I admit we'd made the hides before the missile crowd showed up, as it's turned out we couldn't be much better placed – that is, if you decide to kill two birds with one stone.'

'It's what we'll have to do, isn't it.' Cloudsley agreed. 'So to kick off with, here's the immediate programme. Monkey will take me for a crawl around the headland, while Jake will guide you, Tony, and Geoff, over the route to the beach. See where the gear's stashed, take a gander around the area then come back over the same route.' He looked at Andy. 'You'll be on your own for a few hours, all right?'

'I might not wait up for you.'

'No reason you should. Long as you don't snore too loud. . . . But that's it, gents. We'll finish this char, then piss off.'

Andy asked him, 'This kind of missile's different from the airborne kind, is it?'

'Right. It's for mounting on ships. Each missile's inside a big steel container, not unlike the things they move cargoes around in. When you press the firing tit the front end gets blown off and the missile whizzes out. No need to aim, you launch it in roughly the right direction and the missile-head radar does the rest. It'd be particularly simple to use from a coastal site like this, with only one target offshore that it could choose to aim itself at. But if the point of your question was couldn't we fix it like we fixed those others, the answer is no we couldn't because apart from anything else it's inside this sealed, gas-filled tank and you can't get at it.'

'I see.' He had a question for Monkey Start too, though – since he was being allowed access to information hitherto withheld from him. . . . 'Monkey – did you ride here, straight from where you left us, up by the escarpment?'

'Uh-huh. Had another beach job first. Nursemaiding another crowd. Then we moved up here, suss'd the place out and dug the hides, and since then we've had two nights and a day for a surveillance job on the new arrivals.' He looked at Cloudsley. 'You did your thing all right, did you?'

Cloudsley nodded, grunting an affirmative as he swallowed the last of his tea. Start said, 'Congratulations,' and Jake West nodded: 'Yeah.'

The fact he hadn't enquired before this, Andy guessed, meant he'd simply assumed the operation would have been completed successfully. They were a fairly remarkable bunch, he thought. He asked Start, 'What did you do with Tom's horses?'

'Turned 'em loose among others, in three different places. Wouldn't expect the new owners to cut up rough, would you?'

'We paid Tom for them, anyway.'

'Yeah. Good. . . . How was the old gaffer when you left him?'

'In great form.' Cloudsley said it. 'Fantastic.'

'He's a one-off,' Start told Andy. 'You gave us the right man there, all right.' He turned his mug over, and shook out the dregs. 'I'm not house-proud. . . . Get moving, shall we?'

After they'd gone, Andy slept for a while – in the hide allocated to him and Tony Beale. Departing virtually wordlessly they'd left him with an impression of high-speed movement and cryptic utterances bridged by something like thought-transference; as if they understood each other so well that verbal communication was only a luxury.

The three hides were quite far apart, but linked by string for signalling purposes, and not only in sight of each other but so placed that if an Argie patrol stumbled on to one of them there'd be uninterrupted fields of fire from the other two. Awake now – they'd been gone for about three hours – he was wishing he'd stayed in the hide where Start and West had their tea-making equipment; Cloudsley's having been abandoned up at the airbase when they'd had to evacuate in a hurry.

He'd also been thinking, on and off, about the phenomenon of having become a murderer.

Killing Juan Huyez had been straightforward self-defence. He felt sure this view of it was sound; and Tom Strobie had reacted similarly. Paco Huyez though – Paco was something else; or might become so. He could see it as he guessed an outsider might; judging that the man who'd driven Paco to his death had acted in cold blood – methodically, even sadistically. It had *not* been so, but to an outsider basing judgement on a plain account of the sequence of events and actions it might well seem to have been. And to oneself it might in time come to seem that way. This was the point: whether in years ahead he'd begin to feel he had a particularly vicious murderer hiding inside his own skin.

It was all clear at this moment: the two killings had comprised one act of self-preservation – their lives or his own. But he needed to have it fixed and permanent, not take it for granted now and at some later stage wake screaming and shaking in the night – like he'd woken that morning at Strobie's. Unable to explain the horror to a wife in the bed beside him – or discuss it, ever, with any living soul. . . .

It would have helped to have been able to talk about it. The urge was all the stronger, he supposed, from having dwelt on it through these hours alone in the dark, half-awake and half asleep. Natural enough, he thought, to want the reassurance of an outsider's objective view. Tony Beale's, for instance; Beale would have been ideal to talk with about it. Intelligent, intensely pragmatic but also very much an ordinary human being – loving husband and doting father. . . . It would have been an enormous relief to have been able to blurt it all out to him, when he slid into the hide some time around 0230.

'That you, Tony?'

'It's not Galtieri. . . . Thought I'd have to wake you.'

276

'I did sleep. How'd it go?'

'OK. *My* end of it. And Harry wants us, over the road again. Brew-up and briefing – right away, OK?'

17

Saddler ordered, 'Stand by State Three.'

Getting dark. *Shropshire* at dusk action stations, rolling hard to the southwesterly blow. She was leaving the northwest rim of the Exclusion Zone on a heading of 302 degrees, preparing for fast transit to the mainland coast. Darkness was arriving here about ten minutes before it would spread itself across that coast, and in his mind's eye he could visualise the SBS team stirring after a day in hiding, making their own preparations for the rendezvous.

Expecting a submarine, not a County-class destroyer.

They'd done their job, all right. He'd seen the proof of it – yesterday and last night. At which time he'd had no idea he was about to be given *this* job. . . .

Radar had had a contact: closing, on bearing three-four-eight.

Like tonight, last night had been pitch dark. But the sea had been moderate and sleet-showers temporarily in abeyance. *Shropshire* had spent the preceding hours on gunline, and at this point – when she'd picked up the radar contact – had been in transit to join the carrier group southeast of the islands.

'*Action stations. Air warning red.* . . .'

'Range three-six miles!'

Ops Room patter gathering shape and density over the Command Open Line as men had hurried to their action stations, pulling on anti-flash gear as they ran. . . .

'Echo Nine Tango has hostile three-three-zero, forty!'

'That's *Boreas*.'

'Same hostile. Track 2801.'

'Seacat red and green, sharp lookout for low-level missile attack!'

Under helm: turning stern-on to the threat. . . .

'Missile-head radar on three-four-nine!'

Then EW had it identified: an AM39. Closing, therefore, at a speed of Mach 1.2. . . . Saddler ordered into the Command Open Line, 'Window Charlie two-seven-zero, fire!'

Firing chaff, the Charlie – 'C' for confusion – type meaning shells stuffed with metal foil, fired from the gun to explode way out on the beam, confuse the missile's radar by offering it a new point of aim. He heard Knight's broadcast warning: *Impact imminent – brace, brace, brace . . . Shropshire* plunging to the quartering sea – a fine, live ship and within seconds she could become a mass of flame, gutted and foundering, a funeral pyre in the wind-torn night. . . . The thud of the 4.5″ gun had followed so closely on his order that he knew the AAWO, Ian Prince, must have anticipated it. He ordered now, 'Fire four barrels chaff Delta, bows and quarters!' The 'D' of Delta stood for 'distraction' and again the Ops Room was on the ball, the EW director must have had the control box already set and his thumb close to the firing button. The warning hooters blared almost before Saddler had uttered the last word, and precisely two seconds after that klaxon roar the chaff-launchers, situated just abaft the bridge, blasted a protective screen all around the ship. It was only a momentary protection, in this wind, Saddler suppressing in that same moment a chilling vision of the AM39 impacting in or under the main Seaslug missile magazine, explosions ripping his ship apart; and the re-play then, the horror of flame, gushing smoke, the struggle to save life. . . .

'Green system fired!'

Starboard Seacat. The Seacat transmitting station would have locked the director sight to it: one anti-missile missile with an effective range of three miles had scorched away astern and the operator – one of the late Able Seaman Pitts' chums – would be holding the Seacat missile's tail-flame in the centre of his binocular sight. He had only to keep it there, steering it by means of his thumb-operated joystick, to achieve an interception. *If* two and two equalled four, tonight. Sometimes they seemed to make five. Twenty seconds had elapsed since the call to action stations.

'Radar lost target! EW reports missile-head radar faded!'

Seacat hadn't done it. Either Seacat had missed, or the AM39 had made its dive into the sea before they'd got together. Otherwise, there'd have been an explosion out there. Saddler had looked round at his white-hooded, white-gauntleted bridge staff – cautious about speaking too soon, tempting the Fates which time after time in recent weeks had kept his ship afloat and most of her men alive. Man proposed, but they'd all seen enough just lately to know that *dis*posal was quite another matter. . . . Anyway, Bernard Knight the PWO had been less hesitant: his voice had come over the broadcast right away, telling *Shropshire*'s crew at their various stations around the ship, 'An Exocet missile was launched at us from a range of about thirty miles, but it must've gone in the drink. Third dud today.' Then he was on the Open Line to Saddler: 'Relax the air warning to yellow, sir?'

'Yes please. And thank God.'

'Amen to that, sir.'

He told the OOW, 'Bring her back on course. One-four-seven, was it? Pilot, adjusted course?'

He'd discovered as he spoke that he was short of breath. In a period of tension, of course, your lungs worked harder without your knowing it, to supply oxygen for a faster heart beat. He'd begun taking deliberately long, slow breaths, to slow it all down; and thinking that Knight had spoken nothing but the truth when he'd said 'third dud today'. Two other missiles which had been launched at the Task Force's ships earlier – one in the afternoon, and the other after dark which

281

seemed to have been aimed at *Broadsword* – hadn't stayed in the air even as long as this last one had, had vanished from the screens right after they'd been fired. This, incidentally, had been the first appearances of Etendards in action for quite a while. The daylight attack had been a joint effort by a single Etendard and some Skyhawks, the Etendard's target being the carrier *Invincible* while the Skyhawks had picked on *Avenger* as a target for their bombs – all of which had missed. *Exeter* had splashed one Skyhawk with Sea Dart. The postscript to the abortive attack had come as a news bulletin from Buenos Aires claiming that *Invincible* had been hit and disabled. This was the third time they'd claimed to have hit her; on a previous occasion she was supposed to have been sunk.

A shrug was more appropriate than a laugh. A fourth time, it could be true.

Except – Saddler had reasoned – that so far all attacks on the carriers had been by Exocet-armed Etendards, and if all the Argies' remaining AM39s had been so to speak rendered sterile – three failures in one day did seem a bit much to be coincidental, he thought – well, a minute earlier he'd said 'Thank God,' and he had no intention of retracting that, but he'd wondered whether it might also be in order to thank the SBS. . . .

'Course should be one-four-five, sir.'

'Steer that.'

When he'd drafted a signal about the attack and the dud missile, he'd checked his Night Order Book to make sure he'd put down as much as needed to be there, then paid a short visit to the softly lit, electronic-humming Ops Room before retiring to his little hole of a sea-cabin in the hope of getting a few hours' sleep. In about one hour *Shropshire* was to have been taking station in the defensive screen around the carrier force as it withdrew from its own night's engagements off East Falkland, but he'd seen no reason to be on his feet for that. With luck, he'd thought, he might get to sleep right through to 0600, the time he'd put down to be called.

Everyone was getting a bit tired. Not least, the ships – weapons, sensors and machinery. The weeks were wearing on, they'd been a hell of a long time at sea and the weather wasn't getting any better. But it might not be much longer now, he thought. In the last two days 5 Brigade – including Scots and Welsh Guards, and Gurkhas – had been disembarking at San Carlos, were probably all ashore by now, and there could only be the logistical build-up to complete before the big advance began. Once it started, repossession of the island should be quick, with the ground already so well prepared. Like 45 Commando on Mount Kent, 3 Para on Mounts Vernet and Estancia, SAS on the Murrell Heights north of Stanley harbour. There were SAS and SBS teams in other places too: *Shropshire* had put some of them in.

A week or two – then home?

Well, hardly. Everyone couldn't buzz off at once. The ships in worst shape, presumably, would be the first to go, and *Shropshire* was in better nick than some.

Anne had written, 'Lisa has a new boyfriend. A young merchant banker. She says he's not a boyfriend, only someone she happens to have seen a few times, but I think it's a bit more than that. I may be wishful-thinking, of course, because I should really be delighted if she showed Andy MacEwan the door, after the way he's treated her. This disappearing trick of his really is the last straw!'

He'd drifted into sleep. Missiles – strangely shaped ones with deadpan MacEwan-type expressions on their faces – were fizzing into the ocean all round. Someone was quite unnecessarily trying to draw his attention to them: a voice repeating over and over, 'Captain, sir. . . .'

'I've seen the damn things!'

'Captain, sir. . . . You're wanted in the flagship, sir.' A faraway voice was booming 'Flying stations. Flying stations. . . .' Then the nearer one with its nagging tone again: 'Captain, sir. . . .'

'All right.' Up on one elbow, blinking at the messenger and the orange glow like disco lighting seeping from the Ops Room outside this cubicle. The boy said, 'The Admiral requests your presence in *Hermes,* sir.'

'Yes. Yes.' Saddler nodded. 'Tell the commander and the flight commander.'

'Aye aye, sir. Helo's been piped, sir.'

Checking the time. Awake now, swinging his legs down from the bunk. 'All right. Thank you, Hayes.'

He'd guessed, on his way over in the Wessex, that the Admiral might be wanting more detail about that Etendard attack. It was of vital interest, of course, directly affecting the security of the Task Force, the Navy's ability to last out and continue support of the land campaign. But if this was it, it was a waste of good sleeping time, he'd said it all in his signal. . . . Then abruptly the fast cross-decking was over, and within minutes, still in his goon-suit, he was in an office full of chart displays and his old shipmate Willy was telling him, 'It's about the SBS team you had with you a while ago, John. The group you flew-off by Sea King.'

'News of them, is there?'

'They're ready to come out, and you're the man who's going to perform the extraction. Your orders are here – Operation Sandbag, we're calling it. I'll run over the main points – OK?'

'But – surely they'll be brought off by submarine?'

'Would have been.' The balding head nodded. 'But they've warmed the bell somewhat. Several days ahead of the projected schedule. Incidentally, there are indications of a job well done – eh?'

He'd nodded. 'Certainly today's attacks. . . .'

'Right. But you see, we have only one SSK on station. *Onyx* – arrived a few days ago. The fact is, she's not available for this one. Couldn't get there in time even if she was. It's come up so much sooner—'

'Have they signalled?'

A nod. 'Catching us rather with our pants down.'

'So I'm to – Christ, take *Shropshire* right up to the bloody mainland?'

A five-thousand-ton destroyer and her crew of five hundred, to be risked within a stone's throw of that coast?

'It would have been done by SSK, John, as you say. For the simple reason we don't have one available, it can't be. And we have no way of contacting them to delay things, so – this is what we're stuck with. . . . Here, take a look.' He'd pointed at the appropriate chart. 'The submarine was to have surfaced about here, launched a Gemini, then dived and waited. The Gemini's task is to rendezvous with the SBS team in their own inflatable at this point here – Islote Negro. Risks of outboard motor failure are halved – either could take the other in tow, if necessary.'

'What coastal defences or patrols might we run into?'

'No patrols. Where they exist at all they're sporadic, and in bad weather – which the forecast suggests you'll have – you won't see one. . . . Look, the R/V at the islet is for midnight, Zulu time, twenty-three hours from now, so—'

'Shore defences, Willy?'

'Well.' A hand rose to stroke the pink skin of his scalp. 'As far as anyone knows, none at all. . . .'

John Saddler prayed – *Shropshire* leaving the TEZ behind her now, beginning her transit in towards the mainland – *Please God. . . .*

But there were other worries too, now that the moment had come. Such as the weather, which wasn't in the least bit suitable for excursions in small boats. Willy had been dead right about *that*, last night.

'Ready for State Three, sir!'

The gas boost: four gas turbines ready to add their power to that of the ship's main engines which were also turbines but steam-driven. He told Holt, the Aussie, 'Revolutions two-eight-two.'

The extra revs would push her along at thirty knots: and she'd need every knot of it, at that. He only hoped she'd stand up to the strain of prolonged high revs – after six weeks at sea, bits and pieces falling off with greater frequency than they'd been doing even a week ago.

'Secure from action stations, sir?'

'Yes. . . . And pass the word to the flight commander I'd like a word with him, would you?'

Shropshire would be in position – if all her machinery kept going – at 2330: the position in which the orders laid down that she should launch her Gemini. In a sea that might be even worse by that time, he guessed. Fifteen miles offshore, and the inflatable with its not-always-reliable outboard motor would have five miles to cover, to reach the R/V position where it was supposed to join up with the SBS boat. You could hardly launch a rubber boat over any greater distance, he thought, in such conditions, and even fifteen miles offshore would put *Shropshire* well inside the twenty-six mile range of any shore-mounted Exocet. Studying the chart, Saddler had decided that if he'd been in the Argies' shoes and had a missile to spare he'd have sited it on the headland slightly to the north of the beach, where it would cover the widest possible arc of sea approaches. His ship would be lying at about the same distance from the headland as from the beach.

So he wasn't planning on hanging around in there any longer than he had to.

'Two-eight-two revolutions set, sir.'

He'd felt it: the surge of power, and the sea's fiercer resistance to *Shropshire*'s bomb-scarred hull. . . . A voice asked from behind him, 'Wanted to see me, sir?'

Robin Padmore, the helo flight commander. Stocky, bearded, a lieutenant-commander with one year's seniority in that rank and thirty-two years of age. He was an observer, not a pilot. Short legs braced apart, his body jammed against the side of the bridge close to Saddler's console.

'Yes, Robin. I did. . . . How long would it take to remove the sonar gear from the Wessex?'

A moment's hesitation suggested surprise at the question. Then the flight commander answered with another, in his West Country burr: 'Whole works, sir? Body, drum and winch?'

'No.' He knew the answer to *that*. It would have been a good twenty-four hours' work. 'No, leaving the winch.'

'Well, maybe three hours, sir. Allow three and a half, when we're banging around like this.'

'And how much weight would it save?'

'Four hundred pounds, sir. With the winch as well we'd save more than twice as much.'

Four hundred would compensate for the weight of two additional, large passengers. Saddler had been told there'd been six in the SBS party – although he was only aware of five having flown in – but if he needed to use the Wessex at all it would be in some kind of emergency and he'd have his own two-man Gemini crew to take care of as well. *Might* have. *Shropshire*'s helo was a Wessex Mark III, an anti-submarine helo as distinct from a Wessex V which was a commando carrier, and with two pilots and one observer on board – none of them could be dispensed with – winching up another eight bodies might come close to overloading. He wasn't prepared to reduce the two-thousand-pound fuel load, either – for several sound, precautionary reasons.

'All right. Have the body and drum removed. This is only an emergency back-up, Robin, I may not use you at all. . . . Look, I'll brief you at 2300, up here. Better bring Anstice and Lincoln with you.'

George Anstice and Sam Lincoln being respectively the first and second pilots. Behind Saddler in the darkened bridge watchkeepers were changing over as the ship relaxed to the second degree of readiness. Jay Kingsmill busy organising special lookouts in the bridge wings and up on the GDP to make up for the fact that electronic silence was now being observed: no beams or pulses would be emitted that might be picked up on the mainland, and this included radar.

Geoff Hosegood was in the hide's entrance keeping lookout: all the rest of them crammed into the dark, cold hole. In the hours since last night's planning session they'd been in their separate hides, but now with new darkness to cloak movement in the open, string signals had brought them together again.

Tea was being brewed. And there was plenty of time in hand. The beach party consisting of Start, West and Andy would be moving out at 2045, and the other three an hour later so as to be in position on the headland by 2200. Three dry-suits, one abseil rope and two body harnesses had been brought up here last night from the gear stashed on the beach;

Cloudsley had had his plan pretty well firmed-up in his mind when he'd returned from the night's recce, and he'd brought this stuff back with him.

There'd been several alarms during the day, one particularly tense moment when a four-man patrol had passed right between the hides. Four Argies in file, carrying rifles and looking more alert than in fact they could have been. Enfilading fire from machine-pistols would have cut them to pieces if they'd had the bad luck to notice anything, but luckily the snow on the ground last night had been only patchy, and since noon more of it had been driving in from the southwest, so there'd been no tracks to see. One other foot patrol had passed, but at a safer distance, and there'd been several helicopter transits. In each hide one man had slept while the other kept watch, and there'd been enough alerts to keep the watchkeepers awake and edgy. Andy had done his share of guard duty.

'You'll be pulling your weight tonight, too,' Cloudsley told him. 'It'll be hard work while it lasts.'

He nodded, feeling the tea's heat permeate through his body, and munching biscuits and chocolate. 'OK.'

'And be warned – it won't be comfortable. We wouldn't be going out in a little boat in this weather if we didn't have to. Quite likely, Andy, we'll have to improvise, when things don't go exactly as they should. Like the outboard, for instance. . . . Just take your cues from the rest of us – and bear in mind this is our element, the kind of action we're trained for – OK?'

'Sure. I'll do what I'm told.'

Hosegood said from the entrance, 'Couldn't've done it without him, could we?'

Cloudsley agreed: 'We could not.' He shrugged, a movement under the tent-like *poncho*. 'At least, we might've busted in there somehow. Or someone else might've. But I doubt whoever did it could've got out again.' His hand moved, to touch the wooden haft of his knife. Because they weren't out again yet anyway. . . .

'I suppose the submarine may be out there already, lying doggo, waiting for the time to surface and send its boat in?'

'Very likely.' Monkey added, 'Warm, dry and on an even keel. They don't rock about, you know, once they're under the rough stuff near the surface. So around 0100, Andy, with any luck we'll be sitting down to a good meal in the greatest luxury – including a tot or two, bet your boots!'

The bluey's glow lit Beale's bony, bearded face. Deepset eyes gleaming. . . . 'Drink old Tom's health, shall we?'

At eight-forty-five the beach party crawled out into driving sleet and moved off southwestward. Start leading, Andy between him and West. They'd timed this trip carefully and Monkey knew every bush along the way. Scheduled ETA at the cache above the beach was 2115, but they got there a few minutes early; he'd allowed extra time in case the 'guest artist' slowed them down. The wind was gusting strongly with sleet in it, a wind straight from the Antarctic, and down at this level there was salt spray in it as well. First job was to dig out the inflatable and other gear, unpack three dry-suits and pull them on over the top of all other clothing except *ponchos*. In such bulky clothes, getting the thin rubber suits on was a performance like that of fat women struggling into girdles – in pitch darkness, hopping around on a wind-swept, spray-lashed beach. . . . Ingram pistols were strapped on outside the dry-suits. Then the boat was inflated and fitted-up, and its paddles and other gear – PNG equipment, tow-rope, balers, strobe beacon, lifejackets – stowed inside it. The outboard, stripped of its sand-proof bag, was carried with its separate fuel-tank down to the launching point, and a second trip had to be made to bring down the boat. A minute or so after ten o'clock they were ready, sitting or kneeling on the boat's blisters with a white wilderness of icy, leaping sea in front, blackness of the empty land behind, Monkey's voice shouting over the roar of surf, 'Ten minutes' breather! Nice going, Andy!'

A pat on the head for the civilian. . . .

They had to be off the beach, afloat and on the way, by a

quarter past the hour. Time in hand had certain advantages over a shortage of it, but it wouldn't have been wise to start too early. Hanging around close off the rocks below the promontory might not be too easy; you wouldn't want to try it for longer than you had to. Outboard motors did break down, and paddles, Monkey had pointed out, weren't going to be a lot of use in a sea like this one. Exactly how long they'd have to wait off the headland would depend on the headland party's being able to keep to the planned timing. They'd be in position by now – ought to be – ready to start their action at 2205. In two minutes, in fact. . . . Monkey was taking the lifejackets out of the boat: he pushed one at Andy and yelled at him to put it on. Spray or sleet or both made for a solid, continuous icy rain, and the sea's noise was deafening. Monkey and Jake, who'd been wearing their riding-boots until now, rather incongruously over the dry-suits, discarded them and put on swimming fins instead.

Cloudsley had dumped the coil of abseil rope where he wanted it. The other two were already wearing their body-harness over dry-suits. *Ponchos* over the top of everything else were already whitened by the wet, clinging sleet. There'd been only one abseil rope with two sets of harness and Holk pieces, because Monkey had had to leave some gear with the party he and Jake had looked after down in the south, and one rope had been wanted in the inflatable. But Cloudsley had decided this was OK, all they needed.

The sentry was to his right now, pacing towards the rear of the hut. The other one was on the far side of the radar van: Tony would be taking care of him. The Exocet MM38 container on its flatbed truck was a rectangular mass about ten yards on Cloudsley's left, and there was a tractor parked close to its rear end. The tractor would have been used to tow the truck here from the road, and its use now would be to drag the flatbed around to point in any desired direction. From this headland there was an arc of open sea of about 135 degrees, NNE to SSE, which might call for some rudimentary aiming, certainly if there happened to be any choice of targets.

The wind, with sleet and snow in it, was gusting across the headland strongly enough to rock the radar van on its springs, loudly enough to drown out any smaller sounds. More good luck, he thought: up at the airbase they'd had the generator to cover whatever noise they made, and here they had the beginnings of a storm. Although the luck in that might be somewhat less obvious once they were out there in the inflatable.

No 'might be' about it, actually. It was going to be bloody awful. He'd tried to warn Andy but he hadn't told him the half of it.

Four minutes past the hour. The sentry was pacing back this way. Cloudsley waited for him, watching meanwhile for other movement in the darkness. But in present conditions it wasn't likely that anyone who was entitled to remain indoors would think of shoving his nose out. Monkey had been right – there *was* a smell of paraffin around the hut. Most likely paraffin lamps in there too, going by the weak light that showed under the door.

The hut's door wasn't visible from here, it was on the sheltered, inland side. Beyond the hut, to the west of it, the bulkier shape of the lighthouse rose, black and unlit.

The sentry came into the open, halted and faced right. His back was this way now, face toward the radar van. His pacings and turns were exactly as his (or another's) movements had been last night – when Cloudsley had lain in this same spot, working it all out. He thought – moving forward at a crouch, swiftly and quietly, with the sleet a solid whiteness driving from his left: *Silly sods. . . .* Geoff Hosegood, also moving forward, saw the tall, wide shadow rise, two shadows then merging into one, and knew from the sudden, convulsive jerk that Harry's left forearm had clamped itself across the Argie's throat, the man's helmet then knocked forward; he heard the thud and then saw the shadow separate into its component parts, one part slumping to the ground and the other moving

291

left to join up with Tony who'd have dealt similarly and simultaneously with sentry number two. As he crossed over Cloudsley tossed a rifle over the cliff to his left, slid the weighted blackjack into his *poncho* and drew and cocked his Ingram. The two sentries wouldn't be left lying around loose for long, but in the meantime Geoff would be keeping an eye out for any movement from either of them as well as standing guard on the door of the hut.

Cloudsley opened the back of the radar van and slid in with Beale close behind him. One man on a mattress on the floor and two in wall-mounted bunks stirred, muttering to themselves as they woke slowly. The fourth, on a stool set in front of a flickering green radar screen, sat with his mouth open and his head twisted almost completely round; his eyes were fixed on the levelled machine-pistol. Cloudsley asked, 'Any of you speak English?' Even without the gun in his hands he would have been an awe-inspiring sight. Beale was pulling the other two off their bunks, putting them down with the one on the mattress. They were all dressed, in the usual green fatigues, had shed only their boots and overcoats. The one who'd come off the starboard bunk said, 'I speak. . . .' and the radarman on the stool – a scrawny man with greying hair and a pleasant expression now he'd mastered his initial fright, said surprisingly, 'I am as fluent in English as I am in my own tongue, *señor*.'

'You'll do nicely, then,' Cloudsley told him. 'We don't want to harm any of you. We'll be here about one hour, and if you do what I say you'll be OK. You'll be joining your friends in the hut now. Tell them this, please – if they sit quiet they'll be safe, but anyone who tries to get out, tries *anything*, is likely to be shot. After one hour, you'll be on your own. Got it?'

The radarman nodded, almost a bow. . . . 'I will tell them, *señor*.'

Beale had taken a knife from one man. He said, 'That's all, Harry.'

'So now move!'

Hosegood was ready at the hut's door; he pulled it open, glanced inside, stepped back to allow the four men to be pushed in, the radarman already yelling in Spanish, answering a flood of questions, protests. Door shut – but Beale and Cloudsley had each retrieved his own sentry, and Geoff opened up again while they slung them in. By the time the door slammed shut Beale was back inside the radar van, smashing the screen and circuitry and wrenching wires out. It took only a few seconds; then he'd jumped out, shut the rear door and run to the front, climbed into the driving seat. The engine fired immediately, gears grated into reverse and he backed it up against the hut, slamming hard up against the wall that had the door in it. It was an outward-opening door and so was the one at the back of the van, so to get out they'd have to smash through the door and the van too. By this time Hosegood was on the tractor, having a tougher job than Tony had had, but after a struggle the engine started. Cloudsley had meanwhile fixed its towing chains to the flatbed truck and unplugged a power cable that led to it from the direction of the lighthouse. Hosegood pushed the tractor into gear and eased it forward to take the strain. . . .

No good. Revving harder: the truck still wouldn't move.

Concrete blocks were serving as chocks under the flatbed's double tyres. Beale's flashlight found them; he ducked under, dragged the blocks clear. . . . Cloudsley's original idea had been to put the truck with the missile on it over the cliff, but he'd decided against this because he wasn't sure it wouldn't explode, which might attract attention from far and wide. Instead, Geoff got the whole assembly rolling the other way – inland – over uneven ground into the dunes. A slight downward slope now, the container jolting and swaying, Geoff having to accelerate to stay ahead of the lumbering mass behind him. Then he was angling round behind the lighthouse, round in a half-circle until the assembly was pointing the wrong way entirely. If the missile could be fired now, it would fly inland; and they wouldn't be able to move it without this tractor, so the tractor was now to be immobilised. Geoff left its engine running, jumped down, used one of the tiny flashlights to locate a water-trap on the fuel line, and smashed its glass bowl with the butt of his pistol. The diesel would run for a minute or two, but after it stopped it wouldn't be starting again.

Beale had secured an end of the abseil rope to the front axle of the radar van: the rope was the standard number 4, 11-mm nylon with a breaking-strain of 4200 pounds, and there was plenty of it to spare. The cliff here was about 130 feet high and almost but not quite sheer. Cloudsley yelled into the howl of wind, 'Away you go, then!' He thought he'd done it – this part of it – couldn't be much more except convince the occupants of the hut they weren't being deserted yet. He went back there, hit the side of the van a few times, shouted some orders like shoot to kill if you have to, Tony. He thought they'd have heard, all right, although from outside with the noise of the wind and the deeper, more distant roar of the sea you couldn't hear voices from inside. Anyway, the SSK could surface in safety now – instead of being blown out of the water almost before its hatch was open. He went to the rope, waited until he felt it go slack when the second man got off it, then grasped it in both hands, facing inland. He was edging backwards over the cliff edge when he saw the car's lights coming.

Up the track from the road, the track skirting the north side of this promontory. It was a rough track and the lights were bouncing as they approached, but the car – transport of some kind, anyway – was coming quite fast, the skeletal lower structure of the lighthouse already starkly black in silhouette against the glare.

A moment for thought. He could stay here, ambush them, cut them down. . . . Then leave. Or – just slip away. And he had to decide immediately.

Not much to be gained by killing them. Whoever they were, they couldn't do much harm. And killing had never been on the agenda for this trip. So – OK. . . . He flattened himself on the wet, scrubby cliff edge, slid backwards over it with his legs dangling into the noisy darkness until he was right over and could swing his feet up against the rock-face. Then down – weight on the rope, and walking down the face. Cautiously, not fast and swooping as the others would have done it, obviously; they'd be on the fringing reef now, locating the inflatable – please God – and giving Monkey a torch-flash to show him where they were and let him know it was running to time. By the time Cloudsley joined them they should be all set and ready to go. The wind howled in his ears, buffeted and clawed at him, sleet plastering him, the rope wet and slippery and tending to swing like a pendulum as he shifted weight from one foot to the other. Below him the South Atlantic was a white maelstrom thundering as it fought to tear rock from rock – as it had been doing, successfully, for centuries, millennia. . . . Of course if Monkey hadn't made it, if the outboard had refused to start or the boat had come to grief in the surf, you'd be stuck down there on the rocks with a whole crowd of ill-disposed Argies loose on the clifftop; you'd have pretty well had it. It made him think *Should have taken out that carload or whatever,* then hands grasped his shoulders, Geoff taking some weight while he got himself to rights, Geoff shouting in his ear, 'They're here, Harry, twenty yards out, maybe thirty!' He saw them as he left the rope and turned – a flash of light and the torch's glittery-wet reflection on one gleaming blister of the inflatable as it tilted almost to the vertical. He shrugged off his *poncho*: the others had left theirs on the clifftop or maybe thrown them over. The inflatable couldn't be allowed in any closer than it was now, one reason being the array of sharp-edged rock and the enormous strength of wind and sea that would fling the comparatively flimsy craft on to it, another the kelp which even if it hadn't been here before would be now with the southwesterly driving it in to fringe the reef. The thing was to get out there, quickly, while the outboard was still doing its stuff, get the boat out to sea where breaking down would be bad enough but not as bad as it would be here, particularly with Argies up above. He yelled, 'Go on, Tony!' and saw Beale lunge forward and flop in like an outsize seal: they were all ludicrously swollen by the clothes inside their dry-suits. He gave him a couple of lengths' lead then banged Geoff on one rubber shoulder, shouted, 'Go!' Into their natural element – rougher than usual, *too* rough for a long haul in a rubber boat, but he'd swum in worse, and colder than most; but they'd all swum in and under ice, before this, and for a lot longer than this little dip was going to take. The kelp was like nets trying to hold you, and the turbulence did its best to wrap it round your arms and legs. . . . Tony was in the boat, Geoff now launching himself up and into it, the boat half on its side and white water seething over. The others were baling – there'd be a lot of baling to do before they made it to Islote Negro. Cloudsley was up, half out of water, forcing his rubber-enclosed bulk over the port-side blister while Tony kept his own weight on the other side. Others baling furiously as the inflatable turned its bow seaward, motor's note rising as one thin, foreign element in a deafening roar of wind and sea. Looking up at the headland, Cloudsley saw the loom of the car's headlights: he was edging into the stern, squeezing between Jake and Andy who were doing the baling – hanging on with one hand and working with the other, crouching as low as possible as the boat pitched and swung; Cloudsley shouted close to Monkey's ear, 'Transport of some kind arrived when I was leaving. Lights – see?' Monkey glanced round and up just as a small searchlight – something like an Aldis, a spot, maybe part of that vehicle's equipment – flared out, silver beam lancing the snow-filled dark then dipping to finger the wilderness of sea. Monkey having seen it was ignoring it, concentrating on his job as coxswain. The plan was that having got a few miles out they'd use PNG to locate the islet, but this weather hadn't been in the reckoning, this amount of wet. . . . The light found them after less than a minute's search. It had passed over them, one dazzling flash in Cloudsley's eyes then travelling on, apparently not having seen them, but then it had paused, swung back. Cloudsley had been getting ready for it, he had his Ingram out, its stock extended, and he'd switched to single-shot action; now he was sighting on the light. *Trying* to. . . . The Ingram was reputedly accurate up to fifty metres, which he guessed was about the slant-range now. A rifle bullet cracked past his head, the light holding the boat as if it was a spear in a fish, and there were several rifles in action up there now – men shooting from solid ground – probably prone on the edge – instead of a roller-coaster. . . . Two single shots banged away not far from his right ear – from

Beale or Hosegood, West was still shovelling out the water, getting it out about as fast as it was coming in – before Cloudsley squeezed two off without observable result and decided to switch to automatic, spray the clifftop with the rest of the magazine. They didn't seem to have automatic weapons up there, thank God. He had one spare magazine in its slot on his holster and he'd have no other use for it, and with lengthening range chances were lessening fast – but not so for those riflemen, who'd have plenty in hand yet: A rifle-shot hit the outboard's fibreglass pod, a sharp *thwack* of impact – and that was all, the plastic must simply have absorbed the bullet. He'd had visions of the outboard being hit, also of the boat's blisters being punctured: the blisters were subdivided, of course, but it wouldn't have helped, exactly, and it could still happen, in fact the odds on getting away didn't look so hot unless someone could hit that light, and quickly. . . . The shooting from the headland was slow and steady, apparently unhurried – which was the best way to do it if you could afford the luxury; even if they were cross-eyed the laws of chance had to pay off for them soon. On target suddenly, he squeezed his trigger, sent twenty-eight rounds in a swathe across the light, but he'd only been on target *before* his finger had tightened, the boat had tilted bow-down and dropped like a stone, noticeably flexing itself as it toppled over the crest of a shoreward-bound roller. This sea, he'd already begun to appreciate, might turn out to be a bit *too* much for them. They'd taken in a lot more water and the balers were working frantically as he began reloading, feeling the sluggish motion that came from having so much weight in her; he was banging in the only accessible magazine he had, the light still blinding him and the riflemen still taking regularly-timed pot-shots; then a single shot cracked out close to his already singing right ear, and the light went out, smashed. Beale whooped, 'Nice one, Geoff!'

Immediately you knew that your real enemy was the sea. As it had been before the searchlight had come up as a more immediate threat.

He could see the headlights again now. The beams were

swinging, a swathe of yellow in distant, slanting sleet. He guessed they might be trying to use whatever kind of vehicle it was to tow the flatbed truck and its missile back into a firing position. Might make it, too. It could be a four-wheel drive, and they'd have that whole hutful of soldiers to add muscle power. Might *well* set the bloody thing up again. . . .

Should've killed them. Should also have punctured the flatbed's tyres.

But – this hit him suddenly, relief as the inflatable crashed down into a trough, water-walls towering all round – it wouldn't help them to get it back in place, because they still wouldn't have radar. OK, so they might fire blind, assuming there had to be a target out there somewhere, but it was highly unlikely they'd happen to catch the submarine in one of its two five-minutes appearances on the surface. So forget it. There were two hazards that *were* worth worrying about – one, the sea, and two, danger of the outboard failing.

They'd been fighting their plunging, jolting way out to sea for half an hour before the motor began to stutter.

As if they'd all been expecting it as well as dreading it, all heads turned, faces staring aft. Hanging on two-handed – except for the balers, who were having to take their chances: baling had to be continuous because shipping water was continuous. But the outboard had suddenly picked up again – was back on its high scream of full power, Monkey straightening from its controls and turning to check the course. Then it faltered again, the boat lifting vertically as a wave ran under its flat, flexing bottom, tilting it end-up and slamming it down again with the starboard blister almost under water; in that position all you'd need would be one really solid, swamping sea, and even as it was the balers had been put back on the wrong side of square one now. Cloudsley and Beale were using their own body-weights as balances, throwing themselves this way and that to counter the sea's efforts, and Monkey was working the throttle, cutting to half power and pausing there, then revving up again, varying the speed because it might have been too long a period at constantly high revs that had started the motor oiling-up. It had been OK on the lake for hours on

298

end, but conditions here weren't comparable with that. Full revs again now, and for the moment smooth-sounding. Slewing back on course. Cloudsley grabbed the baler from Andy, and Tony Beale followed his example, taking over from Jake.

It was a relief for Andy to be able to use both arms now for holding on, despite having no feeling in his hands. He was sitting in swirling, icy water, keeping low, centre of gravity as low as he could make it, to reduce chances of being flung out. There'd been several times already when ejection had seemed both imminent and inevitable. It had also seemed likely that the boat would be hit by rifle-fire from the headland, and it was surely only a matter of time now before the outboard would start backfiring again and this time *not* recover. So that the end of this whole extraordinary episode might be six rubber-suited bodies washed up on an Argentinian beach. He recognised – without enjoyment – that such an end would be justified by the accomplishment, by much larger numbers of other lives having been spared. That phrase – *consequences accepted* – still applied. And in his own case, although obviously he'd do anything he could to stay alive he had to admit objectively that there'd be no huge loss involved for anyone else. He couldn't think of anyone who'd weep for long, if at all. Probably *not* at all – because Lisa Saddler, who in any case hadn't been exactly exuding affection the last time he'd seen her, wasn't likely ever to hear anything about this. Andrew MacEwan would remain her most unpleasant memory, the rat who'd run out on her. As for Francisca – well, until a week ago, up to which time you could say she'd been the secret mainspring of his life, he'd have reckoned on some tears from her. Not too many, at no time would he have mistaken her for what might be termed a *serious* mourner; but some little show of grief.

In fact she wouldn't know about it either. Wouldn't even get the chance to laugh.

Unless she heard of it through her father? If the body was identified as his? It was a possibility. . . . But new images succeeded that one now: Paco's body naked and frozen in snow, his murderer's frozen on a beach. Poetic justice: an entire family wiped out, its hirelings too. . . . Both arms wrapped round the starboard blister, his forehead pressed against its cold, wet rubber: still here, not drowned yet, with thoughts very much like fragments of a dream, entirely visual while breaking into them now was Cloudsley yelling at Beale to let Geoff take over baling while he, Beale, got cracking with the PNG. It was like waking up, as if he'd been a long time hidden in his own imaginings. Monkey had the PNG beside him in its waterproof container, and he passed it forward now via Andy to Beale, Cloudsley shouting, 'God's sake try to keep it dry!' Cloudsley had to be out of *his* mind too, Andy thought, to imagine any such thing was possible; he was also surprised that it could be time to start looking for the islet. Cloudsley's voice again: 'Sixty feet high and smothered in birdshit, Tony — should be easy to pick up!' Rocking over — sliding down edgeways, more sea slopping in. . . . But the submarine's inflatable, Andy thought, *that* wouldn't be easy to pick up. Another boat like this one, more inside the sea than on it, hardly visible from more than a few yards away, he guessed — except when it was thrown up on a crest — hanging there for seconds before it was sucked down again — like *now*. . . .

Both boats would have to be on wave-crests simultaneously, at that. Otherwise they could be within a short distance of each other and still not know it. In the troughs, you saw nothing. You were deafened by the noise, the incredibly loud roar of it, and you were buried. You could pray, if you hadn't run out of prayers. . . . Climbing: the outboard driving them up a sheer incline of black ocean towards a whitish, towering, curling ridge. Hanging on tight and praying for the noise of the outboard, a harsh scream piercing the sea's thunder, to continue without faltering. . . . He was looking astern when the inflatable again rushed upward to its zenith and began to swing over, toppling in preparation for the next roaring *schlüss*. He glimpsed, miles astern now, as small as an image seen through a telescope the wrong way, faint light flickering on the headland. And from Cloudsley another bellow suddenly — 'Sea's getting easier, Monkey! More regular, d'you notice?'

*

'*Some* damn thing going on. . . .'

John Saddler had shouted it over the howl of wind and the racket of the sea, his ship's groans and rattles as it tore and battered at her. He was in the open wing of the bridge, starboard side, binoculars at his eyes, having come out into the freezing dark for a clearer view of the lights and activity on that headland fifteen miles away. *Shropshire* was lying stopped – stopped in the navigational sense, her screws turning at slow speed to hold her in position stemming the weather while her stabilisers fought a losing battle to hold her still. He'd sent the Gemini away half an hour ago and half a mile nearer inshore: they'd been too close in there, though, too close to possible drifts of kelp – on which the inflatables were going to have to take their chances. David Vigne was beside him now, Jay Kingsmill also out here, all three with glasses up and braced against the ship's violent motion while they studied the shoreline and in particular that headland.

It wasn't comfortable, to have to sit still and wonder what was going on ashore there. Particularly when you had an idea what the answer to it might be. But there wan't a damn thing *else* to do but wait.

Well, there *was*, actually. But—

He shook it out of his mind. Necessarily, but unwillingly. He had to resist the temptation although it seemed to him the only alternative to leaving his ship exposed to danger: the ship, and the five hundred lives which through six long, hard weeks now it had been his primary concern to safeguard.

At least no hostile radar was illuminating them – yet. Electronic silence applied only to emissions, and the passive systems were still operative. If there'd been radar on them the EW department would have known it, and if there'd been a Guppy around passive sonar would have heard it. Theoretically the absence of radar transmissions from shore should have been reassuring, but those lights were still keeping him on edge. The lighthouse itself was unlit, but the headland had light and movement on it, shifting patterns of light indicative of work in progress. It wouldn't take very long, he guessed, to haul an MM38 or MM40 on to a headland site, set up a

301

portable radar – a small, short-range set would do – switch it on, find a target, press the firing button. . . .

Damage control parties were closed up and alert to the danger. Saddler had briefed his engineer commander on that basic fear of his, and Chamberlain was now at his usual action station, HQ1, the damage control headquarters just across the gangway from the Ops Room. From there he had open lines of communication to his teams in all parts of the ship; and pumps, hoses, emergency leads all in place. You couldn't specify action to be taken until the emergency actually arose, but at least they were alert to the fact this wasn't any sort of routine situation, that missile attack from shore was an immediate threat. The damage control slogan displayed in the Ops Room was FLOAT – MOVE – FIGHT – the aims in order of priority. If *Shropshire* should be hit by an Exocet here off the mainland coast you'd have to settle for the first and second – keep her afloat, get her away. . . . And be damn lucky if you managed *that* much.

The Gemini should by this time be getting close to the R/V position. Saddler had added a third volunteer to its crew, an MEM1 – marine engineering mechanic 1st class – who was said to be a genius with outboard motors. He was also a strong swimmer, which was an essential qualification. It meant there'd be nine men instead of eight to be lifted if the worst came to the worst and he had to send in the helo, but having removed that much of its sonar gear – the job had been completed in less than Padmore's estimated three and a half hours – and with more than ample wind-speed for hovering under something like maximum load, the flight commander had agreed that he and his pilots would be able to handle it. There were two main problems in using the Wessex: one, the SBS team were expecting to be picked up by submarine and their reaction to a helo's appearance would be to assume it was hostile and shoot at it, and two, in this weather and total darkness, without PNG or other equipment such as a thermal imager, searching for two very small, dark-coloured rubber boats in several square miles of rough sea would make looking for needles in haystacks seem like child's play.

The lights on the headland were making him sweat. Radar or no radar. This close to the mainland and this far from any chance of support of any kind, and with certain recent scenes still only too vivid in memory. . . . It brought him back to the temptation which he'd been resisting and had to go on resisting. A quick and easy way to remove that source of anxiety would be to use the gun, plaster the headland with high explosive, douse the lights and break up whatever it was they were preparing. But to bombard the mainland of Argentina was unthinkable, would alienate the entire world – most of which at this stage of events was still well disposed.

Islote Negro was about two hundred yards on their right. Monkey had throttled down, to cope with a new outburst of stuttering, and with reduced power the wind had gained the upper hand and pushed them back, farther away from the little island with its peak of guano-whitened rock than they'd been ten minutes ago. It was something like half an hour since Cloudsley had made that surprising observation about improving sea conditions; Andy was sure he'd said it only for *his* benefit, by way of morale-building, and that it had been totally unfounded. But since then he'd kept his head up, and Cloudsley had later come out with another one, a shout to Start to the effect that this prototype inflatable had certainly proved its capabilities: even the fucking outboard—

He'd lost the end of it, in the howl of icy wind as the boat had risen into the lashing sleet.

Engine-note rising again; Monkey cautiously re-opening the throttle. Gas might soon be running low, Andy thought. They had only the one tankful, having left the jerrycan on the beach to save space and weight. And the PNG was useless, could *not* be kept dry. Beale had abandoned attempts to use it, now. It had been Cloudsley who'd sighted Islote Negro with his naked eyes, but how anyone could hope now to spot another inflatable, about as prominent as a floating log. . . .

303

'*Light!*'

A scream from Jake West. But they were submerging again; crests all around rising higher, enclosing, drowning. . . . Andy wasn't sure now that the word had been 'light': it could have been 'right' or 'Christ' or—

'Starboard beam, Harry! Saw a flash, I'd guess the loom of a strobe, just as we—'

Words lost on the wind again. Lifting: starboard blister down, climbing on a steep slant and with the stern being pushed around as she rose; they'd be near-enough bow-on to the rock now. . . . Then he saw it, they all did, blinding bright and flashing in three short bursts, then one long flash before it was gone again, the inflatable still up high for another few seconds but the light had vanished. Then they were blind again as they swept downward, thump and swirl of sea crashing in over the port side, the SBS men agreeing that the SSK's Gemini was roughly a hundred yards away, midway between themselves and the rock and almost certainly flashing SOS, therefore in trouble and most likely outboard trouble, but they'd be drifting this way, downwind. Cloudsley yelled, 'Steer straight towards them, full throttle if she'll take it!'

'OK!'

'Where's our strobe? Someone gimme the bloody. . . .'

Lifting. . . .

Even on a crest you wouldn't always see them. The other boat had to be on a crest too. Every third or fourth surfacing, but sometimes two consecutively. . . . He was used to the stomach-churning motion now. Or numbed to it. Hosegood passed the strobe light aft to Cloudsley. Andy thinking it would be *this* outboard giving up the ghost next. The only real hope would be if the submarine came in and picked them up. Which presumably it would not do, or the arrangements wouldn't have been made the way they had been: no doubt for good reasons, but—

'Read that?'

'K – E – L – P –'

'Stuck in *kelp* there!'

He heard Cloudsley shout against the gale as they shot up again — white sea swamping in over the port blister, Beale and Hosegood baling — Cloudsley had yelled, 'Monkey, I'll need your fins!' And Start was groping one-handed in deepish water, then he'd found the fins and he passed them over. For the job on the headland of course they hadn't had any with them, and their short swim from the reef had been made without them, but Monkey and Jake had worn fins when they'd swum out from the beach, swimming alongside the boat to get it out through the surf without impinging on rock; then Monkey had slid in over the blister and got the outboard started before Jake had come in over the bow where he'd been steadying her. Cloudsley was putting the fins on now; then knotting an end of the tow-rope round his waist. Thick waist, massive body, all the clothes inside the dry-suit bulging it out, and in all that clobber swimming surely wouldn't be too easy. Shouting something about a signal to look out for and not to let this boat get any closer to the kelp. Which was why he was taking to the water, Andy realised: splashing over, now. . . . He'd disappeared. Hosegood was letting the nylon rope run out steadily through his hands, Andy having taken over the baling chore from him. Of course there *would* be kelp this side of the islet, the stuff would be growing all around it and the wind and sea would be trailing it out this way; on the weather side it would be packed in densely against the rocks. Beale was waiting with the strobe as the inflatable rose again; he began flashing fast morse, SWIMMER — and then they were down in a trough, Jake West shouting something, words indistinguishable, Beale waiting again with the light ready for the next upward rush. Then, on the crest again — just catching a flash from the other boat's strobe — he was winking out the second word so fast that only an expert could have a hope of reading it, the word, COMING. So if they *had* read it the submariners would be looking out for Harry, ready to get him inboard. . . . Monkey had his boat back on a seaward course, outboard at about half-speed. Climbing — hanging on one-armed, baling furiously, having some catching up to do, Jake working at it just as hard — climbing into bright light, the glare of the other

305

boat's strobe at a range of maybe sixty yards, a beacon for the swimmer they'd been told was on his way.

Cloudsley got his arms over the Gemini's blister, lashed out with his fins and at the same time felt hands grasping his shoulders and hauling him in. The dry-suit hadn't stayed dry, maybe because it was under such strain from the padding of gear inside it, and all that padding was now soaking wet, adding to the enormous weight being dragged into the boat. He sat up, asking 'Kelp? Round the screw, or—' Choking then, coughing up pints of the South Atlantic, and with a feeling he was enclosed in frozen lead; he heard the answer in a scream against the wind, 'Screw's gone! Hit kelp, got clear, tried her again and she raced. . . . No bloody screw – pin sheared, see?'

He could breathe again. In the centre of the boat as it hurtled down a wave, dug its snout in and scooped in a lot more sea. . . . 'No spare screw, I suppose?'

They did have one. The sailor shouting answers in staccato bursts against the wind and between inrushes of ocean was an MEM. He'd brought various bits with him in his pockets, including a spare prop and boss and a pin for it, but he hadn't wanted to lose this one as well so they'd been paddling to get clear of the kelp before he fitted it. Listening to the explanation Cloudsley had unhitched the rope from his waist and passed the end to the crewman in the bow; he hung on to the bight until he knew for certain it had been made fast. He yelled, 'OK. . . . Signal – one word – T-O-W!'

'Aye aye—'

'How far out is your submarine?'

He'd shouted his question to the boat's coxswain as a sea crashed and flooded aft; the man yelled back, 'Submarine? We're from *Shropshire*! Destroyer, not submarine!' Then the strobe flared into brilliance: Cloudsley had his back to it, turning to look for the headland, see if the lights were still visible. The Gemini tilting, rushing downward stern-first and swinging fast: with no motive-power there was nothing to

306

hold her against the wind. He *could* still see light on that clifftop: he groaned, 'Oh, Jesus Christ. . . .' Thinking of the Exocet back in place and *Shropshire* lying out there, awaiting the Argies' convenience. . . . The boat soared up an incline of toppling wave and the strobe's brightness broke out again, snowflakes whipping through the brilliant aura spreading round it as it flashed, T – O – W. . . . Do that two or three times, he thought; they'll see it at least once. Please God. They'd be waiting for it, anyway, they'd have been ready for it from the moment when the rope stopped running out. . . . Down again, steeply and abruptly into the abyss. Saddler could have no idea what was on that headland, and he might find out the hard way, any moment; and it would be one's own fault, for not having made a proper job of it. *Shropshire,* though, for God's sake, what a risk to run for just six guys! The wind hit the Gemini's up-raised forepart as they shot up into its full force, flung up and then that huge thrust of gale-force wind threatening to turn her over end-over-end; Cloudsley launched himself forward, sprawling beside the crewman as a counterweight just in time. Behind him as he edged back again the strobe was repeating its urgent message, T – O – W. . . .

After a quarter-hour of effort which in the first few minutes had seemed likely to pay off, Monkey realised they weren't going to make it. Every time he opened the throttle to anything like full power the motor threatened to choke off and he had to cut back again to such low revs that with the weight of the tow dragging on them he doubted if they could be making as much as one knot. He knew that on this coast, this close in, there was a half-knot tidal stream setting southward, a set they'd known about before they'd left England but which they'd discounted because in a flat-bottomed boat with no keel it was the wind you had to reckon with mostly, and when you could make eight or ten knots such a small drift wouldn't count for much anyway, over a short transit. It counted now, though. If he eliminated the lateral effect of the wind by steering right into it, he'd drift back into the kelp, tow and all; and if he didn't steer into the wind in this handicapped condition he'd be blown back towards the headland.

Beale was in the stern with him now, keeping the nylon rope clear of the motor and its screw. Monkey shouted, 'I'll steer into the wind while you haul in on the tow! When we're round, get Jake on it with you, haul 'em in close – over the beam, OK?'

Beale yelled back, 'But they're under way!'

Monkey felt it too, in that moment. What Tony had already felt because he'd had his hands on the rope. The strain had come off it. . . . Andy, baling, heard Beale's voice high and thin across the wind and the roar of sound that was part of the icy oblivion surrounding him, ' – no weight there at all!' He wondered almost detachedly, *Rope parted? All that for nothing?* Working at the baling process like a machine. It was all he could do. He wasn't even a passenger, he was cargo. Cloudsley had spoken nothing but the truth when he'd said this, the sea, was their element: a boatload of Andrew MacEwans wouldn't have survived the first ten minutes, they'd have been swamped, the boat turned over a hundred times, the beach obscenely littered in the dawn. Beale's voice again, Beale handling the nylon rope like an angler playing a big fish, his tone exultant as the inflatable tipped forward and plunged over a rising crest, ' —still *there*!'

The outboard faltered – picked up – stammered, died. . . .

The MEM had accepted Cloudsley's urgings to take a chance on having got clear of the kelp. He'd leant out over the Gemini's stern with the coxswain hanging on to his legs, and fitted the spare screw and the boss and cotter-pin by feel, with his head and shoulders intermittently under water. Now they were overhauling the SBS inflatable, guiding themselves to it by the nylon rope, the leading hand gathering it in yard by yard as they closed up. Monkey was obviously driving at half-speed or less, Cloudsley realised. And there was still a five-mile stretch of ocean to cover, which was going to take a dangerously long time, with *Shropshire* wallowing out there — a sitting duck waiting for the Argies to let her have it, right on their doorstep. . . . He shouted in the coxswain's ear, 'There's an Exocet missile on that headland! We fucked it up but they've been working on the bloody thing for hours!' The Gemini stood on its tail, climbing a dark mountain that broke back over them in a torrent before they'd reached its summit. It was a minute before anyone could speak again or think about anything much else; then the coxswain told Cloudsley, 'Skipper has the helo standing by. Might see the strobe, if—'

Sea sweeping over, interrupting. . . .

'—hold it up high, flask 'em an SOS?'

Saddler had waited too long already. Whatever was happening on that headland, it wasn't a welcome-to-Argentina party. The threat seemed to him to have become both intense and imminent: he could feel it in his bones, his gut. The order burst out of him like something under pressure: 'Action helo!'

Then to Holt, the Aussie OOW, 'Stand by State Three, revolutions two-eight-two.' He'd told Padmore in his briefing that as soon as he'd got the helo off the deck *Shropshire* would start moving east, to wait thirty miles offshore.

In less than one minute the Wessex was clattering up into the night, banking away towards the land. *Shropshire* under helm and gathering way, Saddler telling his PWO over the Command Open Line, 'Warn Seacat port and starboard that the threat sector will now be astern.' This hadn't been an easy decision to take: the urge to ensure the safety of his ship was one thing, the knowledge that the inflatables and their human cargo might be well on their way out from the R/V and that the Wessex might fail to locate them was quite another. You had to balance one set of risks against another. He'd told the helo crew, 'If I have to order you away, it'll be in your hands from there on. Has to be.'

Padmore, in the lurching helo's main cabin — entirely separate from the cockpit where the two pilots sat — had a gull's-eye view of the ship turning, thrashing round, curve of broad white wake disappearing only yards under her stern in that boil of sea — his view of it receding, turning on end and withdrawing as the Wessex lifted, swung away. . . . Landing-on wouldn't be any problem: once *Shropshire* was out of range of any shore-mounted missile her flight-deck lights would be switched on when they were needed. The only tricky thing about landing-on would be the load, and that was going to be OK too, thanks to having shed some other weight. Padmore only hoped to God he'd *have* a load — nine live men. Finding two small boats somewhere on or near a line five miles long between the take-off point and Islote Negro was going to take some doing.

So he'd reckoned. But they'd only been in the air about four minutes when George Anstice's voice came explosively over the intercom: 'See what I see, Robin?'

Lights. . . .

He'd seen them at about the same moment, and hardly dared believe in them. Fixed, blazing, right *in* the sea, as if the lights themselves were floating, the waves rising close to them actually throwing shadows. The one to the left went out while he was looking at it. Sam Lincoln muttered into his helmet mike, 'Oh, shit, what's—' and then the strobe came on again, flashing: s – o – s. . . . A pause, that one extinguished again while the other burnt on steadily, and the morse letters were repeated. Anstice had been angling the Wessex out to starboard but now he was turning in, upwind, the helo juddering to strong gusts as it banked and began a gradual descent. Padmore was on the point of moving from his seat — with work to do now, safety-harness to put on before he could open the cabin door — but as he turned his eye was caught by a blueish flash — from that headland, a tiny fizzing streak instantly disappearing seaward. His heart raced and he couldn't breathe for seven, eight, nine seconds — until the explosion, vivid double flash splitting the darkness maybe three-quarters of the distance out to where the ship would be now: scorching the sea's surface, flaring upward and then dying, leaving the scene pitch-black again. He whispered in a sort of gasp – forgetting his throat microphone – 'Oh, *lovely* Seacat!' then heard Sam Lincoln ask, *'What* say?' George Anstice told him, 'Something about a Seacat. . . . We'll take the boat with the five guys in it first, right?' Neither of the pilots could have seen it, Padmore knew; didn't need to have their concentration interrupted with the news now either. Anstice had begun muttering to himself, 'OK, you guys, now keep your peckers up and hold your water, here come the Queen's Navee. . . .' Murmuring gibberish to himself at such times, all of it coming over the intercom of course, was an antisocial habit about which the flight commander had remonstrated with him on previous occasions, but he didn't now because he'd just transgressed similarly himself and also because it was all beginning to turn out rather marvellously and he knew George was simply happy – as they all were, at having found the boats so quickly, being about to lift nine lives out of the sea. Padmore was standing by to open the cabin door as soon as the helo was in position over the first boat and hovering; the lever for operating the winch was above the door, and there was no need to go down on the wire because those were all trained men, quite able to hitch themselves on. George Anstice was actually singing as he went into the hover – singing for joy, although from the dirge-like sound no one who didn't know him could have guessed it.

18

Shropshire making heavy weather of it, in position 51 degrees 31 south, 55 degrees 10 west, in transit to R/V at first light with a royal fleet auxiliary for transfer of personnel and mail. The SBS team had been crossdecked to *Invincible* twenty-four hours ago, might by this time be on shore again, on East Falkland. . . . John Saddler, at his desk in the day cabin, unfolded a letter he'd been writing earlier to his daughter, and added a postscript to it. 'This won't be going by fleet mail, as I have a courier who'll deliver it to you personally. Don't ask him for explanations, because he won't be able to give you any. Just take this at its face value, I mean accept it, and give him – give yourself, my darling – a break, as our US cousins say. Bless you.'

He folded the flimsy sheets, pushed the wad of them back into their envelope. Glancing across the cabin at Andy MacEwan, who in about an hour's time was to be transferred to the storeship for passage to Ascension and thence onward by Hercules to RAF Lyneham in Wiltshire. Saddler said, 'It'll be some while before you can expect to hear anything about your brother, I dare say.'

'I suppose so.'

313

Not that it mattered. Either way, he'd sell out when he could. When the dust settled and lines re-opened, he'd instruct lawyers to negotiate with – well, Robert's or Francisca's, the MacEwan family lawyers. No doubt with Alejandro Diaz calling the shots from the background, if Robert wasn't there to do it. But it truly didn't matter, it was all mere triviality in comparison with one's recent experience, the huge, extra-ordinary achievement.

Tom Strobie, of course – he mattered. How old Tom came out of it would remain a source of sharp anxiety, until some word came.

He got out of his chair, and accepted the letter from Lisa's father. 'I'm very grateful, sir.' Shifting his feet quickly: with the weather on her bow, *Shropshire* was demonstrating her tricky corkscrew roll. Saddler said, 'Don't tell her any more than she can guess – which'll be more than enough, so make sure she keeps *her* big mouth shut. I'm breaking all the rules by letting her know this is where you've been. Can't help it – since I want what I think might be best for both of you, no other way to do it. . . . Best thing, Andy, might be to convince yourself it really didn't happen, you *dreamt* it. Right?'

Harry Cloudsley had suggested something rather similar. Cloudsley who might at this very moment be crawling up some dark, wet beach. With Tony Beale in company, maybe – and those other dimly-perceived shadows would surely be Geoff – Monkey – Jake West. . . . Could be others too, others like them – if you could stretch the imagination to the possibility of there being others even remotely like that bunch. . . . Saddler's quizzical stare and outstretched hand pulled him back into the present; the dreamlike images faded as he shook the hand. 'Right. . . .'

The aftermath of a war game that
went terribly wrong . . .

THE FIFTH ANGEL
A ONE MAN KILLING MACHINE

DAVID WILTSE

Sergeant Stitzer, said the officer who'd trained
him, was a hero. He was also one of the most
dangerous men ever to wear a uniform.

These days, they kept Stitzer in the cell at the end
of the corridor. TV cameras watched him night
and day. A broken yellow line on the floor marked
the point of no return.

Five years on, Stitzer had still not surrendered. In
his crazed mind he still had a mission to fulfil. And
the major knew that while Stitzer had breath in his
body he'd find a way to carry out those orders.
And not even the most secure military hospital in
the world would hold him back . . .

'Pacy, original and very readable' THE TIMES

0 7221 9107 3   ADVENTURE THRILLER   £2.95

A selection of bestsellers from Sphere

FICTION

LADY OF HAY	Barbara Erskine	£3.95 ☐
BIRTHRIGHT	Joseph Amiel	£3.50 ☐
THE SECRETS OF HARRY BRIGHT	Joseph Wambaugh	£2.95 ☐
CYCLOPS	Clive Cussler	£3.50 ☐
THE SEVENTH SECRET	Irving Wallace	£2.95 ☐

FILM AND TV TIE-IN

INTIMATE CONTACT	Jacqueline Osborne	£2.50 ☐
BEST OF BRITISH	Maurice Sellar	£8.95 ☐
SEX WITH PAULA YATES	Paula Yates	£2.95 ☐
RAW DEAL	Walter Wager	£2.50 ☐

NON-FICTION

BOTHAM	Don Mosey	£3.50 ☐
SOLDIERS	John Keegan & Richard Holmes	£5.95 ☐
URI GELLER'S FORTUNE SECRETS	Uri Geller	£2.50 ☐
A TASTE OF LIFE	Julie Stafford	£3.50 ☐
HOLLYWOOD A' GO-GO	Andrew Yule	£3.50 ☐

All Sphere books are available at your local bookshop or newsagent, or can be ordered direct from the publisher. Just tick the titles you want and fill in the form below.

Name _____

Address _____

_____

Write to Sphere Books, Cash Sales Department, P.O. Box 11, Falmouth, Cornwall TR10 9EN

Please enclose a cheque or postal order to the value of the cover price plus:

UK: 60p for the first book, 25p for the second book and 15p for each additional book ordered to a maximum charge of £1.90.

OVERSEAS & EIRE: £1.25 for the first book, 75p for the second book and 28p for each subsequent title ordered.

BFPO: 60p for the first book, 25p for the second book plus 15p per copy for the next 7 books, thereafter 9p per book.

Sphere Books reserve the right to show new retail prices on covers which may differ from those previously advertised in the text elsewhere, and to increase postal rates in accordance with the P.O.